LOOKING TO SCORE

ALLEY CIZ

LOOKING TO SCORE

ALSO BY ALLEY CIZ

.

.

.

.

.

.

Stay Connected With Alley

Amazon

FB Reader Group

Website

BLURB

@UofJ411: Who's the girl? # CasanovaWatch # CasanovasMysteryGirl

They call me Casanova.
Football God. Ladies Man. Campus Celebrity.
Guys want to be me and girls want to bed me.
Commitment? What's that?
Then I saw *her*—tiny, gorgeous and oh so…**MINE.**

Mason Nova is an egotistical jerk.
Player. Persistent. Pain in the Pom-Pom.
I don't care if he's the star of the gridiron or how tight his end is.
I know his stats both on and off the field. My answer will always
be **NO.**
The last thing I need in my life is another charmer who's looking
to score.

LOOKING TO SCORE is book 1 in the U of J Series and is an enemies-to-lovers, new adult, college sports romance. If you like pint-sized sass queens for heroines, and too-charming-for-their-own-good playboy heroes you'll love these two. There's banter for days…so much so that these two characters are the stars of books 1, 2, and 3. All books out now.

Looking To Score (#UofJ1) Paperback

Alley Ciz

Paperback ISBN: 978-1-950884-11-7

Cover Designer: Julia Cabrera at Jersey Girl Designs

Cover Photographer: Wander Book Club Photography

Cover Models: Megan Napolitan & Wayne Skivington

Editing: Jessica Snyder Edits, C. Marie

Proofreading: Gem's Precise Proofreads; Dawn Black

 Created with Vellum

DEDICATION

*To my MINS and Taco girls. If it weren't for you the U of J would only
exist on my computer.*
#BookFriendsAreTheBestFriends

AUTHOR NOTE

Dear Reader,

The U of J is a brand new world. If I'm new to you and you haven't read my BTU Alumni books you're fine.

If you have met my other crazy squad of friends and Covenettes there are a few cameos in here you might enjoy, with a tiny time gap between the two series.

XOXO
Alley

<u>BTU Alumni Cameos</u>

BTU1- Power Play (Jake and Jordan) *U of J Jordan Cameo Mention*

BTU1.5- Musical Mayhem (Sammy and Jamie) *U of J Cameo Mention of Jamie's band Birds of Prey*

IG HANDLES

CasaNova87: Mason 'Casanova' Nova (TE)
QB1McQueen7: Travis McQueen (QB)
CantCatchAnderson22: Alex Anderson (RB)
SackMasterSanders91: Kevin Sanders (DE)
LacesOutMitchell5: Noah Mitchell (K)
CheerGodJT: JT (James) Taylor
TheGreatestGrayson37: G (Grant) Grayson
ThirdBaseAdam16: Adam
CheerNinja: Rei
TheBarracksAtNJA: The Barracks
NJA_Admirals: The Admirals

PLAYLIST

- "Whip My Hair"- Willow Smith
- "Sing"- Ed Sheeran
- "BLOW"- Ed Sheehan with Chris Stapleton
- "Guys Don't Like Me"- It Boys!
- "Girls Just Want To Have Fun"- Cyndi Lauper
- "Stack It Up"- Liam Payne feat. A Boogie Wit da Hoodie
- "Better Now"- Post Malone
- "Runaway Baby"- Bruno Mars
- "Teeth"- 5 Seconds of Summer
- "Good As Hell"- Lizzo feat Ariana Grande
- "Good Thing"- Zedd with Kehlani
- "Shape Of You"- Ed Sheeran
- "Frustrated"- R.LUM.R
- "Lips On You"- Maroon 5
- "Rumors"- Lindsay Lohan
- "Burn It to the Ground"- Nickelback
- "I Warned Myself"- Charlie Puth
- "Thunderstruck"- AC/DC
- "Blow Your Mind (Mwah)"- Gua Lipa
- "Say Amen (To Saturday Night)"-Panic! At The Disco
- "Papercut"- Linkin Park
- "Paparazzi"- Lady Gaga
- "Close To Me (with Diplo)"- Ellie Goulding feat. Swae Lee

- "Suffer"- Charlie Puth
- "Don't Stop Me Now"- Queen
- "Finesse (Remix)"- Bruno Mars feat. Cardi B
- "Fuck Apologies"- JoJo feat. Wiz Khalifa
- Find Playlist on Spotify

NICKNAMES

Mason Nova: Casanova/Mase
Kayla Dennings: Kay/PF/Smalls/Short Stack
E (Eric) Dennings
CK (Chris) Kent
Em (Emma) Logan
Q (Quinn)
JT (James) Taylor <CTG BFF- Cradle-To-Grave Best Friend
Forever>
T (Tessa) Taylor
Pops (James) Taylor Sr.
G (Grant) Grayson
D (Dante) Grayson
Mama G- Mrs. Grayson
Papa G- Mr. Grayson
B (Ben) Turner

KAYLA

I've just put the key into the lock of the dorm I'll be calling home for my sophomore year at the University of Jersey when my phone rings, blaring "Whip My Hair" by Willow Smith.

I swipe to answer the call. "Hey, Bette."

"Kay! Back at school yet?" It's an innocent enough question, but I can tell my sister-in-law is fishing.

"Yup, just got here," I answer, using my shoulder to hold my phone to my ear so I can wheel my two large suitcases inside.

"How's the dorm?"

"Hold on."

I switch the call over to a video chat and let her come on the tour of my new place.

The setup is nice with its four bedrooms and two full baths. I'll have to share the space with three roommates, but I'll have one of those bedrooms to myself, which is a major perk.

Bette *oohs* and *aahs* as we pass the first set of rooms, continuing down the hall until it opens into the communal living space. There's a living room to the left with a red couch and loveseat bracketing a wooden coffee table, all facing a decent-looking entertainment center.

"Nice TV. Eric would approve," Bette comments, referring to the large flat-screen my brother would undoubtedly appreciate. Boys and their toys, after all.

Off to my right, separated by a gray laminate peninsula island, is the kitchen decked out with a full-sized fridge, stove, microwave, and dishwasher—*score.*

"Better tell G he has to bring his own chair when he comes over for dinner." Bette points to the four barstools at the island.

The mention of one of my closest friends here at school instantly brings a smile to my face. As a person who prefers to stay out of the limelight, the star power forward for the U of J Hawks basketball team is the least likely candidate for a bestie, but Grant Grayson—G to us—is a rare breed of human.

"He's not going to let a little thing like not having somewhere to sit keep him from coming over if food is involved."

The dude is a bottomless pit. He should weigh like four hundred pounds, but with his metabolism and the grueling workout regimen he maintains to play D1 basketball, he's all ripped lean sexy lines. He could pass as Tyrese Gibson's brother and is almost too good-looking for his own good.

"Nice," Bette murmurs as I walk into the only bedroom with its door open—mine.

I nod in agreement, taking in the full-sized bed, desk, and large wardrobe.

"You nervous about meeting the new roomies?"

I shake my head even though, yes, a part of me is. To tell the truth, I was a little apprehensive when we were picking our living arrangements. I liked the idea of the apartment-style dorm but wasn't—and still am not—sure how to feel about having to live with two strangers. My history with cheerleaders is precarious at best, but Em (Emma) wiggled herself into my heart and mended it enough to take a chance on having two of her squadmates as our new roommates. I figured the devil I knew—in this case, Em—would be best.

"You *will* tell us if you have any issues. You hear me, Kayla?" The steel in Bette's tone tells me I flipped her mama bear switch. She spent years of her life raising me through the worst of mine, and I hate when I provoke this side of her.

Hell, the main reason I stay at school instead of at my childhood home less than an hour away is so she'll actually live in the same state as her husband. You would think she'd have eased up after a year without…issues.

Are you really complaining about the fact that she wants what's best for you? my conscience asks.

No, because outside of when Moms Taylor was alive, Bette is the only "real" mom I've ever had.

"I'll be fine." I hope.

The sigh that comes through the phone is heavy enough to be bench-pressed. "Is it really so wrong to wish you lived at home? The commute isn't bad."

"I like living at school. Besides"—I heft my bags onto the bed—"aren't you the one trying to tell me it's good to step outside my comfort zone?"

"I hate when you use my own advice against me," she grumbles.

I roll my eyes. She's ridiculous when she misses me.

"You taught me well."

She makes a face, not at all comforted by my platitude. "Fine. Just don't forget if you need me, I'll be there. Baltimore is an easy drive." This is true—three hours to home, four to the U of J.

"I know. Now, if you're done helicopter-parenting, I'm gonna go unload the rest of my stuff from Pinky so I can unpack."

"You joke, but you love me." She blows me a kiss.

"Very much." I give her the most exaggerated wink possible and hang up.

Outside, I find the aforementioned Pinky—my two-door, hot pink with snow white trim Jeep Rubicon 4x4—and grab the last of my bags.

I can't believe the summer break is already over. As much as I put up a strong independent front for Bette, there is a large part of me that is going to miss spending time with my family.

With all my belongings brought in, I pull out my MacBook and bring up my Spotify playlist. Before the electric beats of Ed Sheeran can fill the room, a video chat notification pops up.

"Is this some kind of check-on-Kay tag team you and Bette are doing today?" I ask as the smiling face of my oldest and dearest friend James Taylor fills the screen.

"Don't act like you don't love us, PF." Whereas everyone who uses the nickname he bestowed upon me when we were younger says the two letters P and F, my smartass cradle-to-grave bestie loves to pronounce it as *pff*.

"Whatever you say, JT," I retort with a grin, angling the screen so we can see each other while I unpack my animal print bedding.

"Anyway…" He gives me the *Lord you test my patience* look I've experienced more than a time or two in our almost twenty years of life. "You good? You settled? You meet the roomies? Do I need to worry about them?"

Blowing out a breath, I take a moment before responding to his rapid-fire questioning. Like Bette, he's only asking because he cares. He—along with E and Bette—has been there for me through all the bad and helped serve as my strength when I broke.

Neither one of us likes being seven hundred miles apart, but again, like I did with Bette, I insisted he put himself first for once.

"I'm good. I'm at school. As you can see"—I wave a hand at the partially made bed—"I'm still getting settled. The roomies are still at cheer practice, and I'll be *fine*."

His brown eyes darken dubiously at the way I draw out the last word to multiple syllables.

How much time has to pass before everyone stops handling me with kid gloves?

I'm almost done unpacking when I hear my roommates return home. I let my eyes fall closed and inhale a calming breath in an effort to rid myself of the bugs-crawling-under-my-skin feeling the sound of the door opening brings with it.

You can do this. Look how good things turned out with letting Em into your life. Think of how different your college experience would be without her. Plus, wouldn't it be nice to have more female friends your own age instead of always hanging out with high schoolers?

There's not much time to reflect on my inner thoughts because Em rushes into the room.

"I'm so happy you're here." Arms wrap around me in a fierce hug.

As both a flyer and a base on the Red Squad, U of J's co-ed

cheerleading squad, Em is your typical gorgeous cheerleader; Britney-Spears-in-her-prime-level muscle tone, shoulder-length chestnut brown hair, cognac-colored eyes framed by Ellen-Pompeo-perfect eyebrows—seriously, so perfect and even—and average height, though at five-five she looks huge standing next to me. What can I say? I'm a shrimp.

"Thanks for letting me move in early." I return her embrace with the same amount of enthusiasm.

"*Gurrlll*...we're here anyway." She hops up onto my bed. "I'm just glad you took me up on the offer. I wasn't sure if you would or not."

Until two days ago, neither was I.

"Quinn, Bailey, get your asses in here and meet Kay," Em shouts.

It doesn't take long for the door to my bedroom to be filled with a Demi Lovato Latina lookalike and a girl so pretty I want to call her Cheerleader Barbie.

I'm a *little* intimidated by our other roommates.

My pulse starts to pound and my hands get clammy as flash-backs from high school hit me.

Don't jump to conclusions, Kay.

The mental pep talk does nothing to talk me off the ledge of panic, but when Quinn—Ms. Lovato's twin—gives me a beaming smile and waves, it starts to ebb. I'm mature enough to know better than to lump all cheerleaders together, but it's hard to fight my instinct for self-preservation.

Out of the corner of my eye, I can see Em give me an encouraging nod, and another layer of reservation falls away.

"Wow!" Quinn walks over to the huge makeup artist kit open on my desk. "This is such an awesome setup."

"Thanks. My sister-in-law is a stylist so she hooks me up big time. If you ever need anything, let me know. She lets me *abuse* her discount."

"Shut. *Up*." Her eyes go round as saucers as she does her best impression of Mia Thermopolis being told she's a princess.

Em giggles like a loon, and even I can't help being charmed by such a genuine reaction.

"Oh yeah. Kay lets me use it all the time with her," Em confirms, joining Quinn at the case and riffling through the contents, trying to scope out all the new additions.

It doesn't escape my notice that the last time I smiled this much when meeting someone new was when I met Em, G, and CK, the fourth member of our tiny crew.

Could this be a sign?

Those warm fuzzies start to cool when I look to where Bailey, the blonde, stands in the doorway, still not entering the room. She must find me lacking in my blue V-neck *I like to party and by party I mean take naps* tee, jean cutoffs, and royal blue Chuck Taylors—at least that's the impression I get from the forced smile on her face.

Quinn breaks me from the awkward stare-down by coming over and flipping the ends of my long hair between her fingers, fanning the strands out so the colorful highlights underneath show more. "Did your sister-in-law do this?"

"Yeah. She's always foiling in new colors. I swear it feels like I've had the whole rainbow in here." I circle a finger around my head. "It's easiest for me to let her do whatever she wants. My only rule is I have to stay predominately blonde."

"I love it." Quinn's perky friendliness catches me off guard, but not gonna lie, I like it.

"We'll have to take a pic later." I move around her to load four more pairs of shoes into the organizer leaning against the wardrobe. "She's going to *die* when she sees your color."

"Thanks." Quinn fluffs her long, straight, perfect-shade-of-red locks with a beaming smile. "It's a bitch to maintain, but I love it."

I bet it is. I've lost count of the number of times I've heard Bette complain about how fast reds fade.

"Well…after I make her jelly, I can almost *guarantee* she'll send you something to help with that before the week is out."

Bette may be fiercely protective of me, but she also has the biggest heart of anyone I know. How the hell E managed to lock her down as his wife, I'll never know.

"Emma, best roomie recco *ever*!"

"I know." Em gives me a wink.

My heart may be lodged in my throat and a sheen of sweat may be coating my skin, but with each interaction with Quinn, the anxiety starts to ease.

I hate how whenever I'm outside my familiar bubble, I feel like retreating.

You didn't always feel that way.

"We were thinking of going to Jonah's for food. Wanna come?" Em asks a few minutes later.

Oh, a burger from Jonah's would *so* hit the spot right now.

My automatic response would normally be to say no, but as I look at the hopeful expression on Em's face and the excitement on Quinn's, I think, *Why not?* Baby steps.

Ignoring a bored-looking Bailey, I offer to drive.

"You have Pinky?" The way Em starts bouncing on her toes tells me everything I need to know about how she became close with Quinn.

"Who's Pinky?" Quinn asks as we make our way into the living room.

"My Jeep."

"You named your car?"

Why am I not surprised that the first time Bailey speaks to me, it's full of judgment?

"She's worthy of a name," I shrug.

"You *have* to see her. She's so cool," Em gushes. "She's all pink, white, and animal print."

"Really?" The deadpan way Bailey voices the question is lost on Em because she loves my Jeep almost as much as I do.

"Oh yeah. Basically, Barbie has nothing on Kay's Jeep."

I couldn't have said it better myself.

CHAPTER
TWO

T he *tink-tink-tink* of water hits my ears, and without even opening my eyes, I know it's pouring outside. I let out a groan; rain is *so* not a friend to my curly hair.

Snuggling under the covers, I long to stay in bed all day. If the roomies and I didn't have plans to buy our textbooks today, I would do just that.

It's been a week and I still can't believe that, except for the two nights I stayed at the Taylors' house with T (Tessa) when Pops was on shift at the firehouse, I've spent my time with my roommates.

Quinn might be the most adorable human I've ever met. She's perky and bubbly and has a way of making you feel like you've been friends for life, and thanks to her abuela's recipe, she makes the best enchiladas I've *ever* tasted.

Bailey is harder to get a read on. I chalk it up to her spending most nights at the end-of-summer parties happening on Greek Row instead of drinking wine and watching chick flicks with us.

With the shit weather, I pull on a pair of black leggings—because leggings are life and hey, they make my butt look good— red knee-high Hunter rain boots, and a red off-the-shoulder *Nap Team Captain* shirt. On most people, the garment would drape attractively, but on my five-foot—yeah, yeah, four-eleven, but who's checking—self, I need to knot the material at my hip so it doesn't fall to my knees.

My bra, which peeks out of the open collar, is also red, and I finish off my need to match head to toe with a red fitted Yankees ball cap.

Knowing I'll be loaded down with a million pounds of textbooks, I slip my phone into one rain boot and slim wallet with school ID and credit card in the other.

"Ugh, I need coffee if you expect me to function," Em says as I step into the living room.

"Um, have you met me?" I tease. "Coffee is life."

"Coffee now, wine later." Quinn, who I've already started to think of as Q, throws her hands in the air like she just don't care. She's a nut.

"God, how could I forget how much of a morning person you are?" Bailey asks Q, joining us.

"You seem to be faring better than Em and me." I accept the umbrella she's holding out.

"I may not be as morning-averse as you two"—she bounces a finger between me and Em—"but Quinn's picture belongs in the dictionary next to the word."

There may not be a bond forming between us, but I still hold out a fist for Bailey. The chick has her moments of being funny.

"Kay, *caffeine*," Em whines.

I can't help but chuckle as I link our arms. She really is my coffee soul sister.

"Would it make you feel better if I text CK and ask him to grab us some?"

"Yessss." The word comes out as a hiss. "Tell him I love him and I'm so happy you forced him to be our friend."

Now I'm full-out laughing at the spot-on description. Em's status as a member of the Red Squad may have made me reluctant to accept her friendship, but CK (Chris Kent) had a similar issue with me. Because, you see…what I haven't told you is I'm also a cheerleader.

Didn't see that coming, did you?

It's not something I make public knowledge. In fact, Em, CK, and G are the only ones at U of J who know. I have my reasons for not broadcasting this information, but that's a story for another time. Let's just say that went a long way toward gaining CK's acceptance. Thank god for it, too, because I would have failed chemistry without him.

"Have you heard from G at all?" Em pants after our mad dash to Pinky.

"Yeah, I talked to him last night before I fell asleep. He's back, moved into the AK house yesterday." I flip my turn signal on and head for the main section of campus.

"You're dating an Alpha?" Shock laces Bailey's tone.

The way I see her perk up in the rearview mirror has my back up. Remember how I said G was the most unlikely of bestie candidates? Well, it stems from not wanting to be used for my famous associations. The brothers of the Alpha Kappa fraternity? They are the kings of campus. G's lucky I love him.

"No. As much as his mama would prefer otherwise"—more like hopes, prays, and constantly asks if we're *sure*—"we're just friends."

"Do you talk to all your guy *friends* before you go to bed?"

Having lived my whole life with a male best friend, I'm used to this kind of blatant disbelief. Hello, people! It *is* possible for two straight people of opposite sexes to be *just* friends.

"No, just two." I hold up two fingers for emphasis.

"Oh, right there." Em's arm brushes my nose as she thrusts it out, pointing to an open spot close to The Hawk Nest. The three-story student center, more commonly known as The Nest, features a large food-court-style cafeteria that serves up an amazing selection of food all day, a coffee shop, and the school's bookstore. We spend a lot of time here.

The four of us clamber out of the Jeep and huddle under our umbrellas—Em and me under one, Bailey and Q the other—hustling inside the building as quickly as possible.

With class not officially starting until tomorrow, I'm surprised by how crowded it is. I scan the tables as we walk, looking past the sorority girls, frat bros, and athletes, searching for the geek-chic, Grant Gustin-looking cutie in the Clark Kent-style glasses.

"CK!" I cry out when I spot him and rush around the table to give him a big hug where he sits behind an open laptop.

"Hey, Kay," he replies, much more subdued.

"Dude, we missed you." Em comes in, and we bookend him

in our embrace. "Why'd you have to go back to Kansas for the summer?"

He looks down when he sees Q and Bailey standing on the other side of the table, still so shy that, even a year later, I feel like we're force-feeding him our friendship. His reaction doesn't shock me. What does is how vivacious, gregarious Q has not said a word. I flick my eyes to Em and we share an *Interesting...* look in response to the blush blooming on Q's cheeks.

Looks like I'm not the only one who should be giving cheerleaders a chance. If only CK saw himself the way we do.

"Please." He waves us off. "You act like any of you were in Jersey."

"Semantics." Em can't hold back a laugh; she lives for teasing him.

"I was here for most of it." I lean forward on my elbows, falling into our typical banter.

"Why do I hang out with you two again?" He closes the lid to his laptop and stows it in his bag. I bet he was working on the video game he's been designing, but it's only a guess. The only person he lets see it is G.

"Because you love us," I smirk.

"And your life would be incomplete without us." Em flashes her dimples.

He looks around the dining room, probably searching for someone to save him from our crazy, but there's no stopping us. Em has pointed out to me—multiple times this week, I might add —how the walls that typically only come down when our small crew hangs haven't been fully up. As I make introductions for Q and Bailey, I can't help but note she's not wrong.

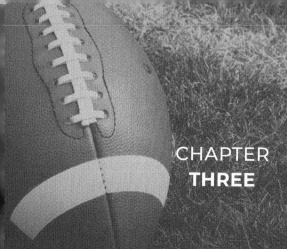

MASON

Lifting the barbell above my chest, my arms shake as I push through the twelfth chest press of this burnout set. Little puffs of air escape my mouth with the effort to make it to the rack.

Burnouts fucking suck.

"Come on, Casanova. Push through it. Don't be a pussy." The devilish smirk of Travis McQueen, my best friend and the Hawks' quarterback, taunts from where he spots me.

If my hands weren't currently wrapped around the stainless-steel bar to keep it from crushing my sternum, I would flip him off.

One…more…inch.

Metal clangs as I rack the bar, Trav's annoying-AF chuckle assaulting my eardrums as I sit up, wiping my face with a towel.

"Nice, man." The fucker holds out a fist to bump. He's lucky I love him like a brother.

"I'm wrecked. I don't know why I let you talk me into burnouts."

I guzzle down an entire bottle of water and leave the towel I used to wipe the rivers of sweat from my face draped over my head.

"Please…you're a total beast. We're gonna kick ass this season." He slaps me on the back.

Damn fucking right we are. We'll be taking it all this year. Classes don't officially start until tomorrow, but already the U of J Hawks have our first official win under our belt. I don't care that the BTU Titans are more known for their hockey program; every win puts us one step closer to the national championship.

Football.

School—because I can't play if my grades suck.

Work out like a beast.

Crush the combine.

Enter the draft.

That's all that matters this year.

Nothing is going to stop us from adding the championship trophy to our case.

Sure, I'll have the occasional hookup—I'm a man, I have needs, and who am I to turn away willing pussy? As both a star football player and an Alpha Kappa brother, there's a lot of it available.

With Trav's torture—er, workout routine—done for the day, we filter into the locker room with the rest of our teammates and hit the showers.

As one of the top collegiate football programs in the country, our boosters have been good to us. Unlike most, our shower area is broken up into individual stalls, half-doors covering us from mid-chest to the knees, the walls low enough to talk over.

"Lunch?" I ask Trav, letting the hot spray work the tension from between my shoulder blades.

"Fuck yeah. The Nest?"

"Works for me." I rinse the soap from my body.

Less than ten minutes later, we are both showered, dressed, and parked in the lot closest to the familiar building. The glass and metal structure is built into the side of a hill, so even though the food court and cafeteria are technically the second floor, it's considered the main level.

Hawk cries ring out and we're surrounded by fans, fellow Greeks, and jersey chasers.

"Hey there, Casanova," a sultry voice calls out before a particularly hot brunette with heavily glossed lips presses the tits spilling out of her skin-tight V-neck against my arm.

"Hey, QB1." Her equally attractive friend does the same to Trav.

Neither of us turn them away—you don't earn the nickname Casanova by ignoring primo talent—and I meet my best friend's *It's good to be king* smile with one of my own.

All thoughts of lunch are put on hold as we bask in the adoration of our awesomeness. It isn't until I see a flash of movement across the room that I even realize how much time has passed.

"Is that Grayson?" Trav asks, spotting our fellow Alpha brother.

Grant Grayson is a hard person to miss. At six-eight, the power forward is one of the only people who can make my six-five stature feel short.

"Yup," I answer then continue to study the person I selected as my "little" brother in the fraternity. With the conflicting schedules of our respective sports plus the fact that we're guys and we don't discuss our *feelings*, I don't know much more about him than that we get along—a fact driven home more by the scene unfolding before us.

With someone wrapped around him, I watch as my friend spins in a circle before placing one of the shortest girls I've ever seen back down. She's tiny, like super tiny, and not just because she stands next to such a giant. If you told me this chick's height broke five feet, I would call bullshit. Her head barely comes to the center of his chest.

"*Damn*," Trav says on an exhalation as shorty stretches up to kiss Grant on the cheek. "I didn't know Grayson had a girl."

Neither did I.

Uncharacteristically ignoring the ladies vying for my attention, I continue to study the couple, marveling at their differences. They are like yin and yang. She's all short stature, milky complexion, and golden hair to his tall, dark looks.

Stop creeping on your bro's girl, Nova. Isn't there enough female talent around you?

Before I can take my own advice, the two of them shift and I get the first glimpse of her smile. Damn if it isn't worthy of a toothpaste commercial.

It's hard to get a read on her thanks to the shade created by the brim of her hat, but I can't recall if I've ever seen her around.

"GRAYSON!" Trav bellows, cupping his hands around his mouth.

Both Grant and his girlfriend look our way, and even without being able to see her eyes, I feel like she's judged me and found me lacking. It's a bit unsettling—more than a bit, if I'm being honest. I can't remember a time a girl felt that way about me, ever.

CHAPTER
FOUR

KAYLA

I *hate* mornings. Like seriously hate them.

Why do early-morning classes have to be what works best with my schedule? Thank god I can braid my hair in pigtails in less than a minute, put mascara on in two, and only need one more to brush my teeth. My red Yankees fitted hides any messiness of my hair, and my tight jeans and red Chuck Taylors make it look like I made an effort when that's actually not the case.

Since I'm allergic to mornings, as my white t-shirt proudly states in red lettering, I snoozed my alarm one too many times to stop for coffee before rushing to class—story of my life.

My phone vibrates in my pocket as I find a seat for my financial management lecture.

> CTG BFF JT: Dude! D is like my favorite person EVER!

> ME: *broken heart emoji* I thought I was your favorite person ever?

Someone pulls out the chair next to mine as I hit send.

Chancing a look, I see the campus playboy himself is my new neighbor.

Mason 'Casanova' Nova, star tight end for the U of J Hawks, is pretty much my wet dream come to life in the looks department, but nowhere else. He represents too much of a time in my life I want to forget to ever imagine going near him.

Of all the classes in all the classrooms in all of campus, he had to walk into mine.

As if they have a mind of their own, my eyes travel over every inch of him I can see. He's wearing a backward Hawks football ball cap, covering what I know are espresso-colored locks. The way the black cap cuts above his eyebrows highlights his seafoam green eyes, the light irises made all the more striking against his olive complexion. His lips are full, with the bottom one slightly bigger, making me want to bite it. And when he smiles his playboy smile, it shows off the most perfect set of dimples guaranteed to make a girl lose a few brain cells.

His matching black Hawks football t-shirt is stretched across his massive shoulders, the red and white logo snug against his equally impressive chest. The black ink from his tribal sleeve tattoo peeks out from the collar of his t-shirt and beneath the sleeve, down to his wrist.

I can feel him studying me back and look away, forcing my attention to my text conversation and not on how attractive he is.

Dammit!

Why is the backward hat look so hot on him?

> CTG BFF JT: You'll always be my #1, you know that. All I'm saying is this kid is cool.

> ME: Kid? He's only a year younger than us. *laughing face emoji* But, yes, I do agree. The younger Grayson is pretty cool. It must run in the family.

"Hi, I'm Mason." His deep voice rumbles through me, making each one of my lady parts stand up and do facial expressions like I'm at the top of a stunt.

"I know who you are, *Casanova*." I give him the brushoff.

"You're Grayson's girl, right?"

Does he not realize I don't want to talk to him?

"His girl?" I scoff and go back to my phone.

CTG BFF JT: I think my flyer might love him.

ME: Well isn't that one of T's perfect storybook romances? The cheerleader and the basketball star—I think I've seen that movie.

I'm spared from having to engage in further conversation with Mason when a cute sorority girl in a skin-tight t-shirt and more makeup than is appropriate for such an early class starts making eyes at him.

"Are you excited for the game this weekend?" Sorority girl leans across the row to stroke Mason's arm, the one with sinew and muscle and gorgeous black ink.

How is his forearm thicker than my upper arm?

Fuck!

Why am I checking him out?

"You know it, darlin'." He shifts into full-blown flirt mode, living up to the Casanova moniker.

"Maybe you and I can celebrate after?" she purrs suggestively.

I can't help letting out a snort when I hear her blatant come-on.

Those gorgeous light eyes shift my way, those tempting lips curling at the corners.

Rah rah sis boom bah! My inner cheerleader shakes her pom-poms. *Shit.* I'm not even that type of cheerleader—I'm an all-star; we don't use poms. What the fuck is this guy doing to me?

The professor enters the room, snapping me out of the spell I've been locked in, and she brings the class to attention.

I concentrate as much as possible on her lecture, but Mason's delectable scent keeps teasing my nostrils. Whatever soap he used after his morning workout with the team is a winner—not that I'll ever tell him that. The less interaction we have, the better.

Even with his aroma tantalizing me, the seventy-five minute class flies by. I gather up my stuff and feel Mason's large presence walking behind me as I exit the business school building.

Not even the sight of G waiting for me by the coffee cart is enough to banish the thoughts of tempting football players. Greek life isn't for me, so I don't stay up to date on all the happenings. It's why, until yesterday, I didn't know my best friend's "big" brother was Casanova.

As I accept the paper to-go cup held out in my direction, I can't help but ruminate on the fact that despite my lack of desire to participate in all things fraternal/sororal, it was helping G claim his Alpha status that led to our close friendship.

"I figured you'd snoozed your alarm too much to get one of these before class," he says, proving once again why he's one of my best friends.

I cradle the cup against me like it's my precious. "This is one of the *many* reasons I love you so much."

My comment earns me a blinding smile before he looks over my head at something—or someone—behind me.

"Hey, man. Whatcha doin' here?" G asks.

"Not much. Just got out of class with your girl." Mason strolls over to join us, his long legs eating up the distance with an easy gait.

God he's too sexy for his own good. Every pair of female eyes in the vicinity is watching him.

I tilt my head back to look at him. "Why do you keep calling me G's girl?"

"Aren't you?"

"No." I keep my response clipped, hoping he'll just move along.

"So you greet all your friends like they're a soldier coming home from deployment?"

One of his dark brows rises and a teasing smirk curves his lips. It only grows when he catches me looking at his mouth.

No! No football players, I remind myself.

My cheeks heat as a realization hits me. *Dammit.* I hang my head and sigh as G starts to laugh, because the answer is no, that isn't my typical greeting—at least not at school.

My friendship with G, such a notable presence on campus, is a delicate balance. He respects my preference to fly under the radar and would never pull me into his spotlight. Yesterday's uncharacteristic greeting can only be explained by the rush of emotions felt from reuniting after our longest separation.

"Don't be embarrassed, Smalls." G drops an arm around my shoulders and pulls me into his side. "It made me feel like I earned official bestie status with you."

I hate how my hang-ups keep me from treating him like that all the time. G likes to joke that I'm like Dr. Jekyll and Mr. Hyde with how I'll act when we're with our crew versus around others. Hell, one of the reasons he and JT have bonded so much is because JT claims I let more of the old Kay shine when I'm with G.

"So you're single?" Mason asks.

"Not for you," I deadpan.

G snorts, and I snap my head up with narrowed eyes. "*Don't you start.*" He lets me go to hold his hands up in surrender. "I talked to JT earlier." I go for a redirection, giving my back to Mason.

"Oh yeah?" I nod. "And is my baby bro driving him crazy yet?"

I shake my head with a snort. "Nope. Sounds like D is settling in just fine down in Kentucky."

"Dante?" Mason asks, butting back into our conversation despite me trying to edge him out.

Why is he still here?

"Yeah." I give G a *Why are you engaging?* look, which he ignores. "He goes to school with my competition."

"UK isn't our rival." Not outside of cheerleading at least.

"I'm not talking about basketball. I mean for your ride or die."

I roll my eyes.

"You're ridiculous—you know that, right?" I blow across the plastic lid and take my first sip of the nectar of the gods. *Ah, that's the stuff.*

"You love me anyway, Smalls."

I twist my lips, neither confirming nor denying. I don't have to; he knows I do. The shit-eating grin stretching across his handsome face confirms it.

Mason has been watching our entire conversation with rapt attention. Honestly, a part of me is surprised he's paying us any mind with the number of girls around blatantly vying for his attention.

"Where's your next class?" G's question pulls my focus off Mason—again. *Gah!* Why? Why can't I stop looking at him?

"Edison Hall." I point toward the stone building with my coffee cup.

"Damn, I'm in the opposite direction."

"No worries. We still on for lunch after?"

Spending time together around campus, like having lunch or studying in the library, took a minute for me to become comfortable with, but with us both having such hectic schedules, I've been able to come to terms with it. The alternative is barely seeing G, and that's not acceptable.

It helps how cognizant he is of the attention he garners, always choosing tables tucked in back corners for us when he can.

"Yup," he says. "I already confirmed with CK. What about Em?"

"I'll text her and see."

In another week we'll have each other's schedules memorized.

"Catch ya later, Kay." G bends to give me a hug, which I return, adding a kiss on his cheek.

"Bye, G."

Mason falls into step beside me as I walk toward Edison Hall, and I tilt my head to the side to look at him.

"Did you need something?"

Why can't he leave me alone?

"So your name is Kay?" he asks instead of answering.

"Yeah. It's short for Kayla."

Are we done here?

"Pretty name."

I let out a snort. "Does that work?"

He looks at me, puzzled. "Does what work?"

"The pretty name line. I would think Mr. Casanova would have better material than that."

He stops walking to stare at me, his gorgeous green eyes flashing. "You don't like me, do you?"

I shrug noncommittally. It's not necessarily that I don't like him; I'm just wary. They may not be the kind you can see with your eyes, but I still have the scars from the last time I let a member of the football set into my life.

"You don't know me, but you don't like me."

His comment brings me up short. "I know your type." I resume walking, and so does he. "Why are you still here?"

Deflection and the cold shoulder are my weapons of choice.

"My next class is in Washington Hall." He points to the building next to mine. "We're practically going to the same place."

Damn, he's right.

I decide to go back to ignoring him and pull out my phone to text Em.

ME: You, me, and the boys for lunch?

EM: The Nest?

ME: Yup.

EM: *thumbs-up emoji* Quinn's in too.

ME: *okay emoji*

Before I can step through the doors to Edison Hall, Mason calls out, "You're gonna like me eventually."

The jerk walks away before I can respond.

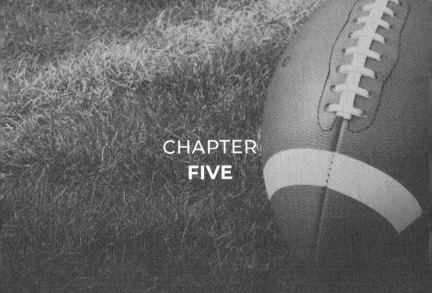

CHAPTER
FIVE

MASON

C lasses may have only begun this week, but the football season is already well underway and practice has turned brutal. I should be dragging ass after the workout Coach put us through in the weight room, but I find myself having a slight pep in my step on the way to my financial management lecture.

Could it have anything to do with a certain blonde with rainbow streaks hidden in her hair?

Yeah, it does. It's been a long time since my thoughts have centered around one woman in particular. I still can't get over how she doesn't react to my charms.

Who doesn't want a piece of all this? I'm grade-A, all-American, athlete-perfection beef.

Kayla acting like I don't exist? Yeah, that stands out.

She gets under my skin in a way no one—not even *her*—has before. I've never looked forward to or wanted to *see* a girl the way I do her. There's just something about Kay that draws me in. The thought should scare me since I have firsthand knowledge of the kind of damage a woman can do to a man if given the chance.

Still…

Is it the challenge? How she doesn't throw herself at me like all the other girls on campus?

When I thought she was Grayson's girl, I had a mild curiosity about her, but now that I know she's single—and yes, I asked Grant her dating status because she refused to give me a straight answer—I need to know more.

If any of the guys on the team or in the frat found out that Casanova, the campus playboy, had to work to get a girl to like him, they would laugh me out of school.

Which brings us to today's icebreaking attempt—coffee.

From my intel-gathering, I've learned Kayla hates mornings but usually doesn't have time to stop for a caffeine fix before her nine AM class.

Unfortunately, when we met up with Grant, he already had a coffee waiting for her. Not wanting to come across as a total stalker, I didn't ask her coffee preferences. I decided to play it safe with the basic girl favorite and grabbed a pumpkin spice latte with my dark roast.

I walk into the lecture hall and there she is, same seat as last time, typing on her MacBook instead of texting. Taking the steps two at a time, I pull out the open seat beside her again and place the paper travel cup next to her computer.

After typing for a few more seconds, she turns to me, pointing at the offending cup. "What's this?"

"It's called coffee. Maybe you've heard of it?"

"No shit, Sherlock." She rolls her eyes. "What I mean is why are you putting it next to my computer?"

God I love her sharp tongue. No girl's ever talked back to me, and not gonna lie, it turns me on. My pants tighten as I imagine what it would feel like dragging up and down my cock.

Down, boy. Flag on the play.

I stare at her, my dick twitching in response to how she looks at me like I'm something she'd find on the bottom of her shoe. *Way to not listen to the play call*, I scold my wayward anatomy.

Her hair is up in one of those messy buns today, and it's the first time I've been able to see her entire face without the brim of a hat obscuring the view. Without the shadows, I can see flecks of blue mixed in with the charcoal hues of her gray eyes, and even her freckles stand out more. This girl is *really* cute.

"It's for you, Skittles."

"Skittles?" She arches a brow at the name.

"Yeah. Your hair is all rainbow-y underneath, so Skittles works."

"Why, because you want to taste my rainbow?"

I can't hold back a laugh. Man, I dig her spunk.

"If you're offering." The suggestion takes me from half-mast to full-on goalpost.

"Don't get any ideas."

Too late.

Inch by inch, our bodies grow closer. My gaze drops and my mouth quirks as I read her *I'm only a morning person on December 25th* shirt. I take note of the matching pair of green Chuck Taylors on her feet.

"You know you want this." Her eyes follow the paper cup moving back and forth under her nose.

"The coffee, yes." Lashes fan as she lifts her gaze to mine. "You…not so much."

"Guess the coffee isn't the only thing that should come with a burn warning."

Another eye roll. *Damn, what does it take to crack her shell?*

I gesture to her shirt with the cup. "Your wardrobe tells me you don't like mornings."

"So you brought me coffee?" Doubt is clear in her voice.

"Yeah."

"Why?" Her head tilts as she eyes me warily.

"Because…" I lean an elbow onto the table. "Contrary to what you think, I *am* a nice guy, and Grayson told me you snooze your alarm too much to allow you time to get coffee."

"Really?"

"Yes really."

"No ulterior motive?"

"No."

"You're not gonna expect me to blow you?"

I have the misfortune of taking a sip of my drink right before she asks this, causing me to choke and sputter a bit. I wipe my chin before responding.

"Baby, I don't have to buy a girl coffee to get her to blow me." Crude but true. "I was just trying to do a nice thing for my bro's friend."

"God you're cocky." Her small hand finally reaches for the cup. "But thank you."

"You're welcome."

"Also, I'm *so* not your baby."

She gets the last word, but there's a small smile playing on her lips.

I take it as a win.

CHAPTER
SIX

KAYLA

I'm not sure what to make of Mason Nova.

I've seen him around campus, living up to his Casanova nickname. One time when I met Em at the practice field the football team and cheerleaders use, I overheard him having sex in the locker room. I'm embarrassed to admit I lingered by the door listening to the sounds of the mystery girl moan, "Oh god," and "Harder, Casanova," and more of the like.

Being handed a cup of coffee and him saying it was because my best friend told him how I don't allow myself time to stop for one before class—it threw me for a loop. Seems like a lot of effort put forth when I've made it blatantly clear he has zero chance of getting in my pants, especially with willing co-eds and jersey chasers abound.

There was a part of me—no matter how small, or how incorrect and irrational—that wondered if he found out who I was and that was why he did it, but I shook that off real quick. For one, it is ridiculous and conceited. Two, Mason Nova may be many things—all of which are why I need to remember to keep my distance—but in need of outside connections to get the NFL interested in him is *not* one of them.

Then there's the most glaringly obvious fact that G would

never betray me by divulging details about me that I painstakingly keep close to the vest.

"You all right?" G asks, pulling me from my musings.

"Hmm?" I blink myself back into the present and watch him steal a fry from my plate. "If you wanted fries, why didn't you get your own?"

"They don't count against my nutrition plan when they come from yours, Smalls."

My nose wrinkles when he boops me on it, and I roll my lips in to hold back a grin. There are days I hate how much the charm from his Southern belle of a mother has rubbed off on him. Combine that with his street-smart swagger from growing up in the Bronx and he is one lethal combination.

"Keep stealing my lunch and I won't give you the leftovers I brought home from the Taylors' house last night."

His dark eyes sparkle—actually sparkle—at the mere mention of the food T and I tend to make when I stay at her place.

"Chili? Please, for the love of all things culinary, tell me you two made chili?"

I confirm the making of Pops Taylor's famous chili recipe with a nod, and G lets out a whoop but quickly calms down when he notices the attention his outburst brings to our table.

"You know I love you, Kay." He clasps his large hands in front of his chest and turns puppy-dog eyes on me. "You're my best friend, my sister. Please, please, *please* share with me? You know you wanna. Don't you love me?"

I hear someone pull out the chair next to me, and even without them saying a word, I know who it is. There's a buzzing under my skin and the hair on the back of my exposed neck stands on end. Still, none of it prepares me for the way my body hums when his deep voice rumbles through me.

"Aww...I'm not the only one you're denying you love, Skittles?"

Love? Love Mason Nova? Yeah right. I won't even admit to lusting him.

I roll my eyes.

Our entire table is struck silent by his presence. CK's brows are practically at his hairline, Em is slack-jawed and her eyes keep bouncing from me to Mason, and poor Q looks both starstruck and confused. G has an air of big brother protection radiating from him, but it doesn't last long before he greets his friend and frat brother with a fist bump over my head. The universe has a twisted sense of humor pairing my best friend with a football player. Don't the Alphas have any other basketball players who would have fit the bill?

Em is the first to recover, asking, "Did you just call her Skittles?" She directs the question to Mason, but to me her eyebrows are all *I know you told me he's been trying to talk to you, but WTF?*

"Yup." When I turn to face our table-crasher, he's wearing that damn smirk and flashing those dimples. *Grrr.* "I told Skit"— a hand lifts to cup the back of my neck and I shiver as he runs a thumb along the base of my skull—"her hair makes me want to taste her rainbow."

Q chokes on her water, CK slams his cup down, and G pauses with another one of my fries halfway to his mouth.

Em just blinks, eyebrows going silent. "And did she introduce you to her right hook when you said that?"

Best friend for life right there.

"You have a mean right hook, I take it?" My chair scrapes as Mason tugs me closer, leaning into my space.

"Yup." I focus on keeping my voice strong, not wanting to give away how my body feels like a live wire from his nearness. "So you better watch out."

It takes everything in me not to show my amusement.

"Can you even reach my face standing up?"

"*Ooo*, a height joke—how original."

"Careful, Nova. She's tiny but mighty," G warns.

Mason ignores the advice, instead pushing in closer until his mouth brushes the shell of my ear as he says, "You can deny it all you want, but we're already on our way to becoming the *best* of friends."

Why does it feel like more of a threat than a promise?

"Never gonna happen." I put a hand on his chest and push him back. It doesn't work; the jerk is too big. No, instead all I get is the feel of the hard muscles flexing underneath my touch.

More than a few heads have turned in our direction since the arrival of Mr. Football, and I dip mine, wishing I were wearing a hat to hide my face. Everywhere Mason goes, people notice him. He tried to walk me to class again today, but I was able to effectively shut him out by calling JT.

People have gotten used to seeing G hanging with us, but Mason? Mason touching me, flirting with me? Not the attention I want or need.

Time to go.

Pushing my tray, which is half-filled with fries, in front of G, I place a quick kiss to his cheek not facing the rest of the cafeteria and press to stand, knocking Mason's hand from me.

"You're leaving?" The concern in G's voice both soothes and cuts deep.

He thinks I'm running, and I hate that part of him is right. I've made major strides in reclaiming the confident I-don't-give-a-fuck side of me in the last four years—my plans with the roomies tonight is proof of how much more I'm opening myself up—but Mason hits too close to the heart of my issues.

KAYLA

My life is a complicated puzzle of those who know all the details about me and those who know only the things I want them to know.

I don't all-out lie—it's one of the reasons I refused to change my last name when E suggested it might give me some anonymity (it helps that Dennings is so common)—but I have a carefully crafted story based on half-truths and omissions.

For example…

Question: Where do you work?

Answer: At a gym. It's technically the truth, but the omission comes from not specifying the type of gym I work for. I let people assume it's your run-of-the-mill gym rat establishment and not the top all-star cheerleading gym in the state.

It's probably a bit much that I keep my cheerleading background a secret, but it can lead directly back to news articles I'd rather not have resurfacing.

He'll never admit it, but I'm pretty sure the main reason JT chose his offer from the University of Kentucky instead of U of J's was because he was worried it would be too obvious who I was if he competed so close to home. All my brothers—both the biological one and those of the heart—are way too overprotective. I'll never fault them for it, though, because when I'm with them it's like all my broken pieces are glued together and I can be me without worrying about anything else.

"Oh man." G groans around a spoonful of chili. "I think I may need to reconsider Mama's stance on us, Kay, because I could *so* get on board with marrying you for this chili."

"You are a bad, bad friend, G," JT complains from the laptop I have open on the coffee table so we can video-chat with him and D.

"Keep teasing us and I'll text Mama you said that, G," D threatens before turning to JT and saying, "Should we start an over/under on how many bridal magazines she shows up with when she comes to our game in a few weeks?"

Even with his dark skin, I see the way G pales at D's threat. I bury my face against his arm so the guys can't see how amused I am, but I'm not fooling anyone. They know me too well.

"Guess that means I'll have to look for a new groom, because T made this batch." I flick my gaze from G to JT on the screen, finding a little too much joy in how the latter's brows pinch at the mention of his high-school-aged sister.

"I love you, G, but don't get any fucking ideas about Tessa."

"Whoa, whoa, whoa." G holds his hands up in surrender, bowl of chili palmed as easily as a basketball in one. "What's with all the hostility?"

"Look, I already have to deal with this Grayson"—JT points at D—"hitting on this sister"—points to me. "I don't need to start worrying about you making moves on my other one."

You would think after all these years my heart wouldn't flutter whenever JT refers to me as his sister, but it does.

"At least wait until she's out of high school, bro." CK wears a Cheshire grin as he keeps his focus on the *Thursday Night Football* game we have playing in the background.

"I think I liked it better when you were too shy around us to give us shit," G grumbles.

"Bullshit," CK counters. "You fools dragged me kicking and screaming into this family. It's not my fault you can't handle the truth."

I pull the collar of my *In my defense, I was left unsupervised* shirt over my mouth, hiding that I'm out-and-out laughing.

It's moments like this that I use to fill the emotional well for when things get shitty and feel like they're too much for me to handle.

"Don't lump me in with numb-nuts over there." G flings an arm out at D. "I tell him all the time to stop putting the moves on Kay, and I've *never* hit on Tessa."

"I think we might be in need of a subject change," CK offers diplomatically.

I hop over G's outstretched legs, leaving the boys to their guy talk, on the hunt for wine. Never in a million years would I have thought I'd be wishing for my roommates to get back from practice, but I feel like I need the backup against all the testosterone filling the apartment.

Guess my walls really are starting to come down.

As if they heard my silent plea, the door to our place opens and Em, Q, and Bailey filter in.

"You're starting without us?" Em asks when she sees the bottle of wine in my hand. I gesture with it to the where the guys are having their pow-wow, and her eyes light with recognition before she sprints off and sits next to G to say hi to JT and D.

"Wine time!" Q dances into the kitchen and accepts the glass I'm holding out.

"Someone please tell me we have Miracle Ice somewhere in this apartment." Bailey drops onto one of the barstools with a groan.

"Em and I do in our bathroom," I confirm before heading off to grab it.

Most people don't realize the beating cheerleaders take on a daily basis. They just see the pretty girls with the big bows who cheer on the sidelines, but they don't see all the bruises, concussions, and broken bones that go into mastering the stunts and tosses performed.

"Thanks," she says when I hand off the salvation in a bottle.

"Kayla Michelle Dennings, you get your tiny butt over here right now." I wince at the admonition I hear in JT's tone.

"Whoa. What's with the full name, James Michael Taylor?" He hisses through his teeth as I drop into G's lap so I can fit on camera.

"You wanna tell me why you've been withholding information from me, young lady?" He looks so much like Pops with his arms folded across his chest, and I can't help but smirk.

"Young lady? I'm a month *older* than you." I roll my eyes.

I don't know why I even bother bringing up the order of our birthdays. Not once in our lives has JT acted as anything other than my big brother.

"Doesn't matter." He waves me off. "Now tell me why you *didn't* say anything about this new friend of yours."

New friend? What is he talking about?

"I told you about the roomies weeks ago."

He hits me with a *Don't play stupid* look, but I honestly have no clue what he means.

"He's talking about a certain football player who's been sniffing around you, KayKay," D clarifies then looks beyond me and hits on the room at large. "Hello there, ladies."

"G!" I whip around, my ponytail hitting him in the face as I stare slack-jawed. There is nothing going on with Mason and me. The last thing I need is for JT to worry about history repeating itself when he's not around to help take care of me.

And, grr...I hate that even without him saying anything, I know he *does* feel like he needs to take care of me.

"It wasn't me." G's eyes shift to the side, and my previously dropped jaw now hits the floor as I realize it was CK who blew up my spot.

"And on that note, I think it's time for you boys to go so our girls night can start." I jump from G's lap and yank on his arm like I have any hope of moving him.

"Don't be like that, Smalls," he says, trying to appease me.

"Nope." Another tug, this time putting my back into it. "Back to the frat house with you, and take Mr. Loose Lips with you."

"KayKay," D whines.

"Nope." I shake my head, still unable to get G to move.

"You can hang up now, but there's no getting out of this conversation. It *will* happen." I give up on trying to move G and bend so I'm the only one the camera is focused on, meeting the concerned eyes of my oldest friend.

He's right. Of course we will talk about this. We tell each other everything—the good, the bad, the ugly.

Mason Nova may be a subject I'd rather *never* discuss, but that will only fly so long with JT.

"Who needs parents when you have the most annoying, overprotective, buttinsky brothers on the planet?" I grumble, but there's no heat in my tone.

"Don't let Pops or Bette hear you say that," JT grins.

"Yeah, yeah, yeah. I'm going now. Goodbye."

"Love you," he singsongs, knowing he'll get me to talk eventually.

"Love you too."

My forehead hits the wood of the coffee table as I drop my head with a sigh. There are days I wish I didn't have enough baggage to fill a 747. Life would be so much simpler.

At not even twenty years old, I should be able to laugh at and even bask in the attention of such a notable person at school. It's cheesy teen movie perfection. Instead, my hang-ups lead me to look for boogeymen that might not even exist.

I feel G place a kiss on the top of my head and lift it in time to see him and CK exit the apartment.

Em's lips are twisted to the side as if she knows G will be on the phone with JT to fill in any blanks before he even hits the elevator. As much as I wish differently, she's probably right.

Q is looking toward the door like someone just took her favorite toy and walked out with it. CK is completely blind to it, but anyone with eyes can see she's crushing on him.

"If you want him, you're gonna have to be the one to make a move," I say, reaching for my wine glass.

"Wh-what?" Q sputters.

"CK." I jerk my chin to the door.

"Give me your phone." Em holds her hand out expectantly.

"Why?"

Em gives her an *Are you serious?* look and wiggles her fingers. "To give you his number. *Duh.*"

"If you're giving out digits, can I have Grant's?" Bailey leans back against the counter on her elbows.

"You'll have to ask G for them yourself," Em answers, knowing G doesn't give out his personal information to just anyone.

"I still can't believe I had no idea you were so close with Grant Grayson." Bailey joins the rest of us on the couches, snuggling up with one of the throw pillows. "Like how are you not all over each other's Instagrams?"

Because I'd have to have an Instagram account to do so, and I'm very careful with the few pictures I let G post of me.

I don't bother telling her how I deleted all my social media accounts in high school. Not a topic I wish to discuss, now or ever.

Just the mention of it has my stomach roiling and a headache pounding behind my eyes.

"What movie should we watch?" I ask, wanting a change of subject.

"Can we go old school and watch *Miss Congeniality*?" Q switches the TV over to our Netflix account.

"Ooo, good choice," Em says, and I agree with a nod.

"I wish we had donuts. It always makes me want donuts when Sandra Bullock tries to smuggle them out in her evening gown."

We all laugh at the dejected frown on Bailey's face.

"We may not have donuts, but we *can* order pizza and get those cinnamon knots they have," I offer, pulling up the number for our favorite pizza place close to campus.

"Oh, good idea. Because while you want donuts, I always want pizza when they go to their paint party," Q adds.

Like it has been so many times in the last few weeks, my night is filled with laughter, wine, and roommates.

CHAPTER
EIGHT

MASON

The Alpha Kappa house is the gem of Greek Row. With a rich alumni base—specifically those who have gone on to play professional sports, which is quite a few of them—it's easy to see why it's the nicest, and not just by frat house standards.

As much as I enjoy having a bedroom to myself—regardless of it including a king-sized bed, a dresser, and a desk—my favorite room is the den. It's tucked in the back left corner of the house, keeping it more private during the parties the Alphas are known for. With a seventy-inch flat-screen, leather couches and recliners, a dart board, and a billiards table adorned in U of J red felt, it's the perfect man cave.

Soon, the guys and I will need to head over to The Huntington, the hotel the team stays in the night before a game not far from campus, but for now Trav, running back Alex Anderson, kicker Noah Mitchell, and defensive end Kevin Sanders are killing time in the den with Grayson and me.

"You guys ready for tomorrow?" Grayson looks up from whatever schoolwork he's doing on his laptop.

"Oh yeah. Kansas is going down," Trav says, confident as always.

"These gimme games are fun, but I can't wait for next week and our first *real* Big Ten matchup," Noah agrees. Yes, BTU was a Big Ten game, but their program is miles below the rest of our conference.

"How's the team looking in your preseason workouts?" Kevin asks, referring to the Hawks' basketball team. Last year they made it to the Final Four but not the championship.

"Pretty good. Some of the freshmen are promising. I wish my brother were one." He shakes a fist in the air. "Damn you, Kentucky."

"You're just gonna have to school him when you guys play." I clink my water bottle to his beer.

Trav and I generally tend to stick with the brothers from the football team, but when Grant decided to rush Alpha Kappa, he was a welcome addition to the fold. With all of us being athletes in Division 1 programs, we don't have a ton of free time, but I've already noticed an increase in the amount of time Grayson is around now that we live in the same house.

Now if only we could get a certain blonde-haired friend of his to join us as well.

Where the hell did that thought come from?

"Hey, turn down the TV," G tells Noah as his Mac rings with an incoming FaceTime call. "Hey, Mama." The woman he greets doesn't look old enough to have a son in college.

"Hey, baby!"

"Dude, that's your mom? How the hell are you so dark?" Kevin asks.

"For real, bro. You're darker than me," Alex adds, coming over to hold his arm next to Grant's, looking from them to the screen.

The rich brown hue of Grant's skin wouldn't hint at coming from a mixed background, but the warm brown eyes blinking at us from the computer are unmistakably the same.

"Because, you idiot, my dad is super dark. Now shut up so I can talk to my mama." Grayson turns his attention back to the screen.

"Where are you, baby?" Mrs. Grayson asks in a deep Southern accent.

"Hanging out at the frat with some of the guys."

"Oh." The smile on her face dims. "It's Friday—you're not with Kay?"

The mention of Skittles grabs my attention. Why can't I get her out of my head? Women have always been for a physical release and that's it. I take my pick of one of the *many* volunteering themselves as tribute to service my dick and then send them on their way.

No emotional connection or messy feelings for this guy. The last thing I need is to let some woman into my life, bringing all kinds of drama with her and messing with my game. Don't even get me started on what Trav and I went through in high school.

"I was with her last night."

He was? The slimy swirl of something I'm not familiar with starts to form in the pit of my stomach.

"That's right." Humor flashes behind Mrs. Grayson's eyes. "Do you have to tease your brother when Kay cooks for you?"

"Does *Dante* have to hit on Kay any time he sees her?" Grant counters.

Excuse me?

Mrs. Grayson lets out a breath and narrows her eyes. *Uh oh.* Looks like she's ready to give her son a piece of her mind. "I don't know why you don't ask her out, Grant."

Say what now?

"Who?" The octave of Grayson's voice rises with his eyebrows. "Kay?"

"Don't play dumb with me, young man. Yes, Kay."

Do they feel that way about each other? Since that first time I noticed them at The Nest, I've spotted them together around campus off and on. There is an easy affection there.

Wait—why do I care?

"You know it's not like that between us, Mama."

"Who's Kay?" Alex asks.

"Grayson's best friend," I explain, hoping he'll shut up so I can listen to what Grant has to say.

"You've met her?" Kevin asks.

"Yeah, we have a class together."

"She cooks?" Of course Trav would pick up on that fact. Dude is ruled by his stomach.

"Is she hot?" I don't know why, but I feel a surge of possessiveness at Noah's question.

Do these jockholes ever shut up?

"She's beautiful and my son is an idiot for not locking it down." Mrs. Grayson crosses her arms.

"Don't use phrases like *locking it down*, Mama." Grayson massages the bridge of his brow.

By now all the guys have crowded behind the couch to see Grant's mom on the screen.

"Back off, assholes." He shoves them back when his laptop gets jostled.

"Grant Samuel, you watch your mouth," Mrs. Grayson scolds.

"*Ooo*, middle-named," Trav teases, pretending to ruffle Grant's fade.

"Bite me." He hits him with an elbow. "Mama...you know she's like a sister to me."

Well that's a relief.

Wait...

What?

Fuck me.

"I know. Lord knows I'd adopt her and make it official if I could."

"E would never allow it."

Who's E?

"I feel like we need to know more about this sister of yours." Noah leans forward on his elbow, putting his face between mine and Grant's only to have it shoved back.

"Do I need to take this to my room so I can finish this call without you as—er, guys interrupting every two seconds?"

Grayson tries to come across tough, but his mama is highly amused if the beauty-pageant-worthy smile she's sporting is any indication.

"Buzzkill," Trav complains, but everyone reclaims their original seats. I do notice that they keep their attention on Grayson and not the game on the TV.

"Mama, why don't you call her? Bette is up this weekend so she's not working."

Who's Bette?

"Heavens to Betsy, I would never intrude on her family time. She gets such a limited amount of it as it is."

Why?

What the fuck, Nova? Why do you care?
Shit!

Wondering about a woman's family situation is not on my checklist for bed partners.

Attractive, ready, willing, not so drunk they can't enthusiastically consent—*that's* what matters.

"Whatever you say." I recognize Grayson's look and tone; I have used it many times with one Grace Nova-Roberts, aka my mom. "I don't think she would mind. I've been getting text updates all night. It's making me kind of jealous."

I'm still struggling to wrap my head around how he can be so close to a person I had no idea existed.

"No. I'll wait for the next time you two are together. I'll get to see two of my three kids that way."

"I'll see her Sunday for the Empire/Crabs game. We can Face-Time then if you want?"

"Oh that would be wonderful, sweetie." Her face lights up at the idea. "Well, I'll let you go. Love you, baby."

"Love you too, Mama."

Well that conversation was both informative and completely lacking in information.

"Dude, you're a total mama's boy." Kevin knocks Grayson in the shoulder after he hangs up.

"And damn proud of it, fucker. Mama is the *best*," he states proudly.

"Forget that. Tell us more about this chick Kay. How hot *is* she?" Alex is always on the prowl for a conquest.

Like Noah's inquiry about Kay, Alex's interest makes me grind my back molars.

Grayson levels Alex with a hard stare. "Kay is *off* limits to you douchebags."

"If she's your best friend, have we met her at an AK party?" Kevin looks like he's mentally flipping through all of the frat's past events.

"No. Frats aren't really her scene."

"You've been holding out on us, man," Alex complains.

"No I haven't. You assholes wouldn't have a chance with her anyway. Just ask Nova how he's struck out." He nudges me in the side with an elbow.

"I've never hit on her, dude." I hold my hands up in surrender. "Please...when I first met her, I thought she was your girlfriend."

"True, but I see you trying to get under her skin. Sorry bro, but it's not gonna work." Yeah, he looks real choked up about it too—not. "She tends to stay away from the football set."

"She doesn't like football?" Noah's tone says *How is that possible?*

"Wait." Trav makes a T with his hands, signaling for a time-out. "Didn't you tell your mom you're going to the Empire/Crabs game with her on Sunday?"

"She likes football. The players...not so much."

Well if that isn't a kick in the jockstrap.

"Is that why she ran away at lunch yesterday?" I ponder.

"Hang on...you've talked to her outside of having class with her?" Trav looks at me like I just broke bro code. I'm not sure why I haven't said anything to him. I guess it's because of how unsettled she makes me feel.

There was also that one time... Even my inner coach knows not to finish *that* thought.

Now Kev cuts in. "Hold up—why'd you think she was Grant's girlfriend?"

"Wait a minute." Alex raises his hands, not letting me answer. "Is she the super-short blonde girl I sometimes see you with around campus?"

"Yeah," Grayson confirms.

"Dude, she looks like you could carry her around in your pocket."

Alex's comment sets off a round of laughter. It's funny because it's true.

"Man." Trav shakes his head, still chuckling under his breath. "I can't wait to meet this chick. If she's not falling for Casanova's charm, she must be special."

He's not wrong.

Again—what the hell?

"Is she on your IG?" Noah pauses in scrolling through his phone.

"Bro, stop stalking." Grayson smacks him upside the head.

Wisely, I keep my mouth shut. No one needs to know how many hours I've spent trying to internet-stalk Kay. It's a good thing I want football to be my day job, because I suck at digging up dirt online. Other than a handful of pictures of her on Grayson's account, I couldn't find a social media footprint.

Strange or intriguing—I can't decide which side of the line that fact falls on. What person our age doesn't have social media?

KAYLA

Pinky isn't even fully shifted into park when Bette comes rushing out the front door of my childhood home.

"Kay! I missed you so much." She pulls me in for the world's hardest hug.

"It's only been a few weeks." My voice is muffled as I'm currently being smothered by her chest, but that doesn't prevent me from returning her embrace with the same ferocity.

How could my love for her be anything less than fierce with how she stepped up for me when our family lawyer told us I would need to go into the foster care system if we couldn't find a suitable guardian to take me?

"What if E and I got married? Could I also be Kayla's legal guardian?" She asked the question to the attorney without any hesitation, unlike my returned, *"Did you guys get engaged and forget to tell me?"*

"Whatever." I get a pinch to the side as she takes my bag from me. "I still miss you like crazy."

"That's because I'm your favorite Dennings."

She barks out a laugh. "Don't tell your brother."

"Puh-lease, I tell him all the time."

Sibling rivalry at its finest.

"I know." She shoots me a satisfied grin. "It's a good thing my husband loves me."

"That he does."

It is impossible for anyone, least of all my brother, not to love Bette. For one, she's *gorgeous*. At five-nine, she's model tall with the body to go with it, long wavy caramel-colored hair with blonde and auburn highlights throughout, and denim blue eyes.

There's also how she changed her entire life to raise her boyfriend's kid sister and committed to keep their romance strong despite the long distance, along with her unwavering support of E's career, all adding up—in my opinion—to the perfect woman.

"Before you start buying and selling real estate, shouldn't we make sure Mr. Dennings agrees with it?" was the next question from our family lawyer.

E, proving he *didn't* take one too many hits to the head on the football field, responded with, *"Are you fucking kidding me? My girl just offered to uproot her entire life to take care of my sister—of course I'm marrying her. As soon as we're done here, we're going to the courthouse and I'm putting a ring on it."*

Needless to say, Bette is hands down my favorite person of all time, with my brother as a close second most days.

We ditch my stuff by the door in time for almost one hundred pounds of blond fur to hurl themselves at my body. The same core muscles I've honed to maintain my position at the top of a stunt keep me from falling to my ass as Herkie, the family yellow Labrador who was aptly named after the cheer jump, puts his large paws on my chest.

"Aww, I missed you too, baby." I give him a good head scratch as he slobbers all over my face.

"Em still coming by?" Bette asks, leaving the two of us to our reunion and heading toward the living room.

"Yup." I check the time on my phone as Herkie follows my every step. My pooch is always glued to my side when we're reunited. "Shouldn't be much longer actually."

"What about Tessa?"

"Nope. She's, ya know, living her own life." I chuckle. More often than not, if I'm in Blackwell, I'm with Tessa Taylor.

"So she's with Savvy." It's a statement, not a question, because if I'm not with T, you can find her with her bestie.

My phone vibrates in my hand.

> EM: On my way! I hope Bette has her scissors!
> *brunette getting a haircut emoji*

I hold it out to show my sister-in-law.
"Oh yeah, I have all my stuff."

> ME: *thumbs-up emoji*

> EM: *GIF of Edward Scissorhands cutting hair*

With Em on the way, we order Chinese and pull up an episode of *Gilmore Girls*, a re-binge favorite of Bette and myself.

By the time I finish setting out what has to be half the items from the menu while Lorelai argues with Luke over coffee, Em arrives. She's just in time for our gluttonous feast.

"I brought *wine*," Em announces, letting herself into the house.

"How did you buy wine?" Bette asks, pausing with the carton of boneless ribs in hand.

"Fake ID." Em's shrug says *Duh*.

Bette cuts a look in my direction. "Yeah, I have one too." No point in lying.

Hear that sigh? Yeah, that's 100% mom sigh right there. When she finally decides to open up a hole in her defensive line and let one of E's swimmers through to make little football player babies with my brother, that kid is screwed.

Dear future niece or nephew,

I promise I'll be the superest (I know, not a word), coolest aunt of all time, the GOAT of all aunts to make up for the fact that your mom honed her mom skills raising me. Oh, and I'll have bail money.

Love,

Auntie Kay

"What?" Uh-oh. Steer away from the mom glare. "We don't go to frat parties. We need to be able to do *something* for fun."

Bette flubbers her lips as she blows out a breath. I'm not sure if it's from the whole fake ID thing or because she's frustrated I'm not having a "normal" college experience. I've lost count of the number of times she's told me college isn't high school, but...

One of the things that made it easy to bond with Em was her aversion to the frat scene. When all our fellow co-eds were off getting drunk on Greek Row, the two of us would explore the local bars and clubs not far from campus.

"As long as you always have a DD, I won't argue." We both nod. Another sigh, then, "Don't tell your brother."

"*Duh.*"

E would shit a brick if he knew I had a fake ID. Overprotective doesn't come close to accurately describing how he is with me. If he could get away with dressing me in a habit and sending me off to the convent, he would.

After everything that went down in high school, I'm sure he wishes he could lock me away in a protective bubble. I also think he wishes he could ban anyone with a penis from coming in contact with me.

"I love this show." Em points at the greatest mother-daughter duo in television with her chopsticks, flinging a lo mien noodle to the floor in the process. Herkie gladly gobbles it up.

Living what at times feels like a double life makes nights like these—vegging out with people I don't have to hide part of myself from—all the more special, though there are times I wish E would just sell this house and be done with it.

Yet, as I glance around the room, at the mantel and shelves displaying our family's timeline and E's and my numerous accomplishments, I can understand why he doesn't. No matter how many bad memories there are, the good far outweigh them. If only the bad were easier to forget.

"So...how are the new roommates?" I'm impressed we made it through half the food and a full bottle of wine before Bette started to fish.

I mull over how to answer. I'm always honest with Bette, but at the same time, it is super easy to trigger her mama bear side when it comes to me.

"Q—with the red hair you covet—is awesome. I don't think I've *ever* met anyone as perky as her."

"Well, seeing as you pretty much grew up at The Barracks surrounded by cheerleaders, that's saying *a lot*." Someone's got jokes tonight.

"Yeah, she's fun." Even now, just remembering her over-the-top antics makes me smile. It is pretty much impossible to be in a bad mood around Q. "Also, I kinda"—I pinch my thumb and forefinger together so there are only millimeters separating them —"think she's crushing on CK."

Em sputters into her wine glass. "You picked up on that too?"

"*Oh* yeah."

"Poor CK." Bette shakes her head, refilling her glass. "He's not going to have any idea how to handle that, is he?"

I shake my head. No, he'll deny, deny, deny and fight it tooth and nail and push Q away the way he tried to do with me. I have faith that she's up for the challenge, though.

"What about the other roommate?"

Why does my stomach feel wobbly like I'm in a stunt about to be dropped?

"Bailey is…" My gaze bounces around the room, looking for the words to describe what I'm not even sure I feel.

"Bailey?" Bette cuts in before I find them.

"Huh?" Herkie lifts his head from my lap at my confusion, and I stroke his silky ear until he resettles.

"You called her Bailey. Why not B?"

Ah, that right there might be the crux of the problem.

"I don't know." Honestly, I don't. "She's funny, comes up with these killer one-liners when you least expect them, but…"

"She has a little bit of jersey chaser hidden behind her cheer uniform," Em finishes for me. "What?" she asks when she sees my wide-eyed stare.

"She's your friend."

"No." Em waves a finger side to side. "She's my *teammate*. Don't get me wrong, she's fine. I have no issues with her as a person, but if she hadn't been Quinn's roommate last year, she wouldn't have been my first choice for our fourth."

Wow. I fall back against the couch, stunned. Here I was thinking I was letting my past prejudice my present, but maybe my instincts were more spot-on than I thought.

"If *you*"—Em grabs my hand in hers—"were anyone else, I don't think there would be an issue. But with you, being…well, you…"

Ugh, it's so frustrating. I'm a nobody. I'm a college student, a cheer coach. Sure, at one point I was one of the top ranked flyers in the world, but the cheer world is such small potatoes compared to the rest. Why do there have to be people out there who look at me and see a stepping stone?

"How careful does Kay have to be about Eric?" Bette cuts to the heart of the matter.

"If you're asking if I think Bailey is going to go internet-stalking Kay, the answer is no."

Shudders rack my body at the thought of what Bailey could find if she did go searching.

Em's lips turn down in a frown before she turns concern-filled eyes my way. "But I wouldn't go broadcasting the information either."

Of all the friends I've made at the U of J—though, yes, there aren't many—Em's friendship has been the one that's touched me the most. Just don't go telling G that, because I would deny it.

What I mean is, Em represents a huge segment of people who made my life miserable. To have her not only be the exact opposite of the school cheerleaders I had experience with but to then become one of my fiercest supporters and most loyal confidants —that's why I consider her my family.

A girl with four boys claiming to be her brothers could always use more sisters, right?

CHAPTER
TEN

MASON

Football is my life. Ever since I put on a uniform at the age of five, I knew it was what I wanted to do. Everything I've done has been undertaken with one goal in mind —the NFL.

I've been blessed to have a family that both supports and helps to facilitate my dream of playing professionally.

If Mom has ever missed one of my games, I couldn't tell you which. I'm pretty sure the main reason she chose to be a stay-at-home mom was so she wouldn't have anything to compete with her three children's rigorous sports schedules.

With another solid win for the Hawks—beating Kansas 21-3 —in the books, Trav, the guys, and I stroll into the AK house to find the victory party well underway.

Hawk cries ring out, fists are held out to bump, and the occasional arm gets thrown around our bodies for a selfie as the crowd parts for us like we're Moses and they're the Red Sea.

Here, we are gods, amid the endless stream of people vying to get close to a campus celebrity and the numerous girls willing to suck my dick just for the chance to say they hooked up with *the* Casanova.

It's a rush, but none of it compares to how it feels to be out on the field.

I spend some time making the rounds, the words from Brantley, my stepdad, ringing in my ears.

"This is your draft year, son."

"We need to make sure teams see you for your full potential."

"Today, players are seen as more than their position on the field. Teams look for the full package. You need to show them you are also a marketing gold mine."

"It's not always the wins that bring in the ticket sales. The fans love a good story."

"Keep an eye on your draft class. You aren't the only tight end entering this year. Remember, Liam Parker from Penn State deferred to this year."

He prattled on and on. I couldn't fault him; he was doing his best to help me appear a cut above the rest while adhering to the strict NCAA regulations.

Still…

There are times—though sparingly—I wish people would see me as more than my status on the gridiron and the potential dollars in my bank account.

You know who doesn't give two shits about your football god status, right?

What?

Why the hell would my subconscious be dragging Kay into my thoughts now? Moreover, why have I caught myself looking for her among the bodies filling the house's makeshift dance floor? Grayson said this wasn't her scene. She wouldn't be here.

I need a beer and a moment to decompress. With a nod of my head, I signal to Trav where I'll be and head in the direction of the den where we keep a keg of the good stuff.

Pushing through the swinging heavy oak door, it's a welcome relief how the noise from the party is muted enough to carry on a conversation without having to shout.

There's a college game playing on the flat-screen, but after the incessant way Brantley hammered on and on about my career, I can't even bring myself to note who is playing.

Spotting Grayson on one of the couches, I drop into the open seat next to him and let my head fall back against the cool leather, my hat getting knocked askew as I close my eyes for a few seconds of peace.

When did all the things I love start to feel so tiring?

I let my mind drift as I listen to the side of Grayson's conversation I can hear.

"Nah, man. You know she won't come to one of these things."

Wonder if he's talking about Kay.

Why are you thinking about some chick during a frat party? my inner coach counters.

"Have you ever been able to convince Kay to do anything she didn't want to?"

He is talking about Skittles, but who is he talking to?

"Good point." He chuckles. I crack an eye open, trying not to make it obvious I'm listening. I still haven't figured out what it is about this woman that makes me want to learn more about her.

It's such a fucking cliché to say I want to know more because she's *different*. You'd think I'd have learned my lesson the last time I believed that. Hell, it almost cost me my best friend. Chicks = drama.

"Fine." Grayson runs a hand over his fade, palming the back of his skull like a basketball. "I'll do my best to convince her. Hold on." He pulls the phone down to his shoulder then shouts to Noah over at the billiards table. "Noah…when's the next invite-only?" he asks, referring to the exclusive parties that have made the AK house the place to be on campus.

"Thursday, bro."

"Thanks." Grayson lifts the phone again. "Okay, I have something that has potential, but if she gets pissed, I'm telling her it was all your idea."

"We're finally going to get to meet this mysterious best friend of yours?" Alex asks, looking up from his game with Noah and proving I'm not the only one eavesdropping.

"Sweet. I've been dying to get a look at her since your mom said she's hot," Noah adds, bending to take a shot.

"Dude, I will seriously kick your ass if you put the moves on her," Grayson warns.

Did you hear that, asshole? Stay the fuck away. Football—focus on football.

"Sure, whatever you say." Another chuckle. "Look, I'll work on Em tomorrow, see if I can get her on board. She's not much for the frat scene either, but honestly, if anyone is going to help me convince Kay to spread her wings, I think it'll have to be someone from the sister camp."

A blast of Post Malone sounds as a group of cheerleaders filter into the den; among them I recognize Kay's roommate Quinn from lunch.

"Yeah, yeah, yeah. Whatever you say, man. Just try to keep my brother out of jail and we'll be good." Grayson ends the call and waves to Quinn. Unfortunately, the move results in another one of the cheerleaders, Bailey, noticing, and she sashays her way over.

I can't fault the guys for watching as her hips sway side to side, drawing attention to her tight skirt. Chick is hot in that bleached blonde, caked on makeup, tries too hard sort of way, but of all the girls I've hooked up with over the years, I've always shied away from cheerleaders. They hit a little too close to home with how involved they are with the team for me to risk inviting that drama.

"Hey, Grant," she purrs, leaning on the arm of the couch and crossing one of her long legs over the other, allowing the already short hem of her skirt to rise another inch or two higher.

"Hey, Bailey." He's not rude, but I still feel the hint of a brushoff. Can't say I blame him. Jersey chasers are a dime a dozen at the big Division 1 schools. Where there are athletes, there are the girls—and guys—looking to hitch their wagon to the next one projected to "make it big," but Bailey has always given off a vibe of being one of those crazy few who would poke holes in the condom to lock you down.

"What are the chances of us running into each other again?" She walks her fingers up his arm, which he removes by wrapping his own around them.

"Seeing as I live here, pretty high."

I can't help but snort, which earns me a grin from Grayson and a hungry once-over from Bailey. "Hey, Casanova."

Why does her gaze make me feel like bugs are crawling all over my skin but Kay's disdain-filled one gets my dick hard?

"I don't know." Another shift, another inch up of her skirt. She's centimeters away from letting the entire den discover if she's wearing panties or not. "First I see you at my place, and now I see you at yours. I think the universe is trying to tell us something."

"Yeah…that you live with my sister," he deadpans.

Grayson has a sister?

Bailey blanches, her jaw working as she tries to think of how to respond. "Kay isn't your sister."

Wait—Bailey lives with Skittles?

"In every way but biologically." Grayson pushes to stand. "As fun as it was catching up…" Sugary-sweet sarcasm drips from his words in a way that would make his Southern mama proud. "Big bro and I have places to be." He jerks his chin, and I take the opportunity to escape.

We exit through the door that leads to the kitchen and head directly for the basement where the beer pong tables are set up. As luxurious as the rest of the house is with its crystal chandeliers, vaulted ceilings, and crown molding, down here is all cinderblock and cement. The scent of sweat and stale beer is heavy in the air.

"Sorry, man." Grayson starts to fill a pitcher for us to join in on the next open game.

"What for?" I start to arrange ten cups in a pyramid shape.

"I didn't mean to cockblock or anything, but there's just something about that chick that rubs me the wrong way."

"I get it." I make sure to keep eye contact so he can see I mean it and that I'm not upset.

"It just gets old only being seen as *Grant Grayson, basketball star*, and it pisses me off that she thinks she can use our mutual connection to…I don't know"—he runs a hand over his head again—"get close."

I give another nod. I understand that too. It doesn't feel good to have someone pretend to care when really they are only using you to get to someone else. I've come a long way from the naive guy I was in high school.

"Fuck." Beer sloshes over the rim of the cup he's filling as he laughs. "Half the reason I love Kay is because she doesn't give two shits about how many three-pointers I can throw."

"How did the two of you become friends?"

They are an odd pairing, and I'm not talking about how opposite they are in the looks department. Grayson may not play into his status the way Trav and I do around campus, but on the rare occasions I have noticed him with Kay, he always seems to keep her shielded from those fawning over him.

"We lived on the same floor last year, and I was in the common room with a few of the guys from the team when she came in on a mission. She ignored Fawkes'"—he points to his teammate and fellow Alpha across the basement—"attempt at hitting on her and was like, 'Yeah, the only stat of yours I care about is if you're tall enough to change the lightbulb in my room.' Then she rolled her eyes in that way she does"—I chuckle, picturing that eye roll perfectly, having been a recipient a time or twenty—"turned to me instead, and that was the start of our beautiful friendship."

We line up across from one of our brothers and his volleyball-playing girlfriend then shoot to see who goes first. The pretty brunette is only an inch or two shorter than me, which brings to mind just how short Kay is.

"Girl is tiny," I comment in response to Grayson's story, lifting the cup from the table and scooping out the yellow smiley ping-pong ball from inside before chugging it down.

"Don't let her size fool you. She's *fiercely* loyal to those she loves. You've already witnessed her less than pleasant side in the mornings."

In the mornings? I don't think the word *pleasant* is in her vocabulary at any time of day when it comes to me. I may have nicknamed her after a candy, but there's zero sugar and spice and everything nice when it comes to Kay in regard to me.

"But she still set an alarm every day during hell week to make sure my ass didn't miss my workouts when I was tired as fuck."

"I'd pay good money to see that." I can't stop the grin that curves my lips, picturing it as I sink a shot down at the other end of the table.

"Trust me"—Grayson places a hand on my shoulder, nostrils flaring along with the corners of his eyes—"you don't want to see it, but in the end, it was worth it. It's how I didn't just become simply Grant Grayson, the person, but G to her."

Would she ever accept me like that?

Better question...do I even want that?

KAYLA

Apart of the reason for the "double life" I lead is an effort to mitigate the guilt my older brother E feels about how his career with the Baltimore Crabs has affected my life. He's so quick to focus on the negative that he forgets all the *great* things him being a professional football player has given us, or how easily he would have given it all up for me.

"Now...there's the issue of guardianship since Kay is under eighteen." Those were the first words I can really remember hearing after Dad was killed by a drunk driver.

Without even blinking, E declared himself my legal guardian, and when our family lawyer told him it would be impossible to do while we resided in separate states because E lived in Pennsylvania during the school year to play football for Penn State, he said, *"You think I'm going to let my sister go into the system just so I can continue to play football? Are you out of your* damn *mind?"*

He loved me enough to give up his dream, to abandon the thing he worked his whole life toward to take care of me. I love him enough to make sure he never comes close to feeling like he needs to do so again.

So, while it might seem like overkill, I keep my history of being an all-star a secret and, except for the small handful of people I've chosen to tell, let the world believe my brother is just a guy named E and not Eric Dennings, #87, star tight end of every football team he ever played on and Super Bowl champion.

It should come as no surprise that E refuses to answer any questions about his personal life that aren't about the wife he loves very much. It's why Bette and I find ourselves entering the grand lobby of The St. James Hotel, where the Crabs stay when they play either New York team. By staying in instead of venturing out, we are less likely to be snapped by the paparazzi.

The soles of my navy blue Chucks squeak across the marble tile as my eyes bounce over the opulence of the indoor fountain and various guests dressed much fancier than my pair of stylishly ripped black jeans and silk top knotted at the waist, showing a sliver of midriff skin.

There, amongst the hotel employees catering to any needs that should arise, is E leaning against one of the marble pillars near the entrance to the hotel's restaurant.

Our gazes meet at the same time, his face breaking out in that smile responsible for landing him numerous endorsement deals as my feet start to rush toward him, not giving a damn about the attention it might bring in my excitement.

I jump into his outstretched arms, similar to how I did with G weeks ago, the brim of my classic Yankees hat knocking against E's forehead and my feet dangling in the air as he swings me around.

"Missed ya, Squirt." He tucks me against his side.

"And I missed you." I crane my neck to see him. Our size difference is almost comical. Where I don't even pass the five-foot marker, he stands solidly between six and seven at six and a half feet tall. We both share Dad's blond hair, but my height and eyes come from Mom.

"Missed you too, wife." When she finally makes it to us, having chosen to walk like a normal person, E pulls Bette into a kiss so passionate I feel like I should offer them a cigarette.

"I bet you did." She goes in for another kiss.

E hooks his free arm around Bette's waist and leads us toward the restaurant. "Come on, time for me to take my girls to dinner."

E and Bette sit together on one side of the booth the hostess shows us to, his arm draped around her. Even after being together for six years, married for four, they still act like newly-weds, and it never fails to make me smile.

"No B tonight?" I ask, referring to Ben Turner, the Crabs' quarterback and E's best friend. It's actually shocking he isn't here with us.

"Nope. I told him I wanted quality time with my girls tonight."

"And he listened?" I quirk a brow. That is so unlike him.

"I may have threatened to ask Jordan for one of her revenge plots if he didn't."

Jordan Donovan is the co-owner of All Things Sports as well as E's publicist. She comes from a hockey dynasty similar to the Mannings in football, and through the years E has been her client, I've heard many a story of the ways she would get back at her brothers and their teammates for their pranks. I can see why B listened.

"How's school been?" E takes a sip of the water the server delivered. No alcohol for him before a game.

"Good so far. Starting to get settled into a routine."

"Still happy with the new dorm?"

Most people would think he was making small talk, but I know he genuinely wants to know the answers. We were always involved in each other's lives growing up, but since Dad's death, E makes a conscious effort to minimize the void left behind.

"Oh yeah. Not that I don't love Em, but it is nice having my own room to sleep in."

"I bet G loves that you have a kitchen."

A smile blooms remembering the other night when he and CK were over for chili. Yes, I can already anticipate many more nights of feeding them.

"And the new roomies?"

I reach for one of the rolls the server dropped off as I debate how best to answer. The crusty shell crinkles as I pull the warm bread apart, the scent of yeast and carby goodness hitting my nostrils as steam rises from the center.

Em and I gave Bette the lowdown last night, but I'm not sure how much she has divulged to E given his insistence that it would be better for me to live at home. There's always the risk something will set him off and he'll throw me over his shoulder and move me out of the dorm, all in the name of protecting me.

"They're...going. I really like one. The other...I'm still feeling out, but so far we've had quite a few nights watching chick flicks."

"And The Barracks?"

Finally, a topic I want to and can talk about for hours.

The biggest reason E didn't pressure me to apply to the University of Maryland only forty minutes from his home was because I wouldn't be able to coach if I went there. I mean, sure, I could have found another all-star gym—the Maryland Twisters are multi-time World Champs—but The Barracks is like my second home.

"They're great. We have a new partner stunt base who's amazing. Reminds me a lot of JT. His sister cheered with us last year, and he tried out for this season. His natural abilities are insane."

"How old?"

"Sixteen. Big for his age, too. He's killing it in partner stunting."

"Wow, that's impressive." E is as well versed in the intricacies of cheerleading as I am in football, so this isn't just a passing comment.

"I'll have to send you some videos. It's crazy how far he's come since May. JT worked with him a lot before heading back to Lexington."

"Well, if he's gonna learn from anyone, JT is the best around."

That's not an opinion; it's fact—at least according to the UCA and the judges at the UCA Partner Stunt Nationals.

Bette draws lazy circles on E's forearm while he plays with the ends of her hair. The two of them are always in contact with each other when they are close. I want that—not with my brother, of course, but with someone special.

Like Mason?

What the what? Is my inner cheerleader drunk or something? It's the only way to explain that not-even-going-to-entertain-it suggestion.

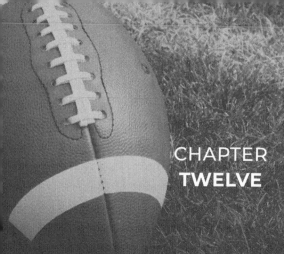

CHAPTER
TWELVE

MASON

Usually the morning after an AK party—especially one after a win—I take advantage of my one day off from practice to sleep in.

Not today. Instead, I'm already downstairs in the kitchen drinking a protein shake.

Last night, I wasn't feeling the whole party scene and called it an early night after two games of beer pong with Grayson.

Don't ask me why. If you do, I'm only going to tell you it's because I was tired after the game and *not* because I had a certain blonde rainbow-haired sass queen on my mind.

"What are you doing up already?" Grayson chooses now to step into the kitchen sporting the red, white, and blue of the New York Empire football team.

"Didn't you say Kay threatened your life if you wore Empire gear?" I shake my head at his ensemble.

"*Pfft.*" He pops a shoulder. "That girl loves me—I'll be fine. Plus, she knows me well enough to know there's no way I'd go see my team play and not represent."

"Whatever you say, man." I finish my shake and toss the cup.

"I'm surprised to see you up so early after last night," he comments as we head toward the front of the house.

It's because my dick was too busy fantasizing about what your best friend would feel like to sink itself into anyone else.

Fuck me. Is that true?

I have no clue.

What I do know is thoughts like that are the quickest way to get my ass kicked.

I also need to figure out how to get Kay out of my head before I end up never getting my dick wet again.

Who locks himself inside his bedroom during a party? What kind of Cinderella bullshit was last night? Asleep by midnight—even I'm embarrassed by my actions.

"Trav and I are going for a run. That is"—I look toward the staircase—"if he ever gets his lazy ass down here."

As if he heard us talking about him, Trav ambles down the stairs, a pretty Latina girl trailing in his wake. At least one of us got laid last night.

"Mornin', sunshine. About time you woke up."

"Whatever." He flips me the bird. "I'm ready, let's go."

Trav opens the door and kisses his hookup goodbye, ever the gentleman, even during the walk of shame. "Oh, what a pretty Jeep," we hear her say as she steps outside.

"Shit." Grayson's body straightens. "Is it pink?" he calls out.

"Yeah."

"Damn." He hustles toward the door. "Gotta go."

I follow behind, joining Trav on the front porch, and sure enough, there's a bright pink Jeep parked at the curb with a familiar-looking blonde standing in the driver's seat.

"Don't you know how to listen?" Kay shouts, hopping down from her vehicle.

"Did you honestly think I would go to an Empire game and not represent, Smalls?" Grayson shakes his head. "You know better than that."

"*That's* Grayson's friend?" Trav steps to my side.

"Yup."

"She's hot," he observes as she hugs Grant.

I agreed wholeheartedly with Trav's assessment even while part of me rebels at the thought of my best friend noticing her.

My long-buried insecurities can't take away from how attractive Kay makes a purple Crabs ball cap, hair hanging out the back in a curly ponytail, big purple hoop earrings all matching the Eric Dennings Crabs jersey knotted at her side.

A tight end jersey. Interesting.

If the top half wasn't hot enough, there's also the way her cutoff jean shorts display her toned legs to perfection before stopping at a pair of purple Chuck Taylors on her tiny feet.

"Do you own Chucks in every color of the rainbow?" I can't help but tease; it's our thing.

You shouldn't have a thing with any girl, Nova. Football and football alone. That's it. If it's not easy pussy, move along.

At the sound of my voice, she spins in my direction. When she gives me a smile, I feel like I've won the lottery. "Pretty much, yeah."

Her gaze tracks to Trav at my side. "Trav, this is Skittles. Skit, this is Trav."

Kay laughs—in my face.

What the hell? I was being a gentleman, making introductions.

"I know who QB1 is." She rolls her eyes at me before turning to him. "Nice to meet you. My real name is Kay."

Trav gives her his lady-killer smile, which gets him a glare from Grayson and has me clenching my fists.

I think I need to meet with the trainers. These urges are not normal.

Kay notices Grant's hard look and pulls him by the arm. "You're riding with Bette."

"What? Why?"

Kay stops dragging him, though I suspect he was moving willingly given their size difference.

"I'm not letting you in my car wearing *that*." She plucks at the offensive jersey.

"Hold up." I run my hands over my backward cap, leaving my hands cupped around the brim. "If you have room, why didn't I get an invite?"

Her smile widens, and my balls tingle at the mischievous gleam in her stormy eyes. "Never gonna happen."

"Why not? We're friends," I counter.

She does this cute little nose scrunch.

Cute? Since when do you think girls are cute, Nova? Don't make me call a flag on the play. You're all out of challenges.

"Not so much."

She tries to sound all confident, but it's a lie. Her eyes keep shifting side to side, to where my biceps are popping like coconuts. She's checked out the way my *Property of U of J Football* shirt stretches across my chest more than once too.

Trav lets out a bark of laughter. "Damn, didn't think I'd *ever* meet a girl who didn't like Casanova."

"Congratulations, now you have." Kay bows.

"You know you like me," I challenge.

"Whatever helps you sleep at night."

Another guffaw from Trav. Asshole.

"If you don't like me, why are you wearing a jersey for a tight end?"

Another one of those eye rolls.

"Just because I like a tight end on an NFL team doesn't mean that extends to every tight end there ever was. Dennings happens to be my last name too. It has *nothing* to do with the position."

I hit her with a *Sure it doesn't* look, and what do I get? You guessed it—another eye roll.

"Just saying that eighty-seven looks good on you."

"It looks even better because it's not yours, Casanova."

Trav is now slapping his knees he's so highly entertained.

"Come on, G." Kay tugs on his jersey again. "We're wasting tailgate time."

Grayson continues to the white Range Rover while Kay heads back to her Jeep.

"Bye boys." She waves and drives off.

Trav turns to watch me as I watch the taillights disappear. I know what he's thinking long before he speaks. "You like her."

"Who? Skittles?"

He nods.

"Yeah, she's cool." I pull my leg into a quad stretch.

"You know what I mean." He mirrors my actions. "It's been a long time since you cared about what a girl thought of you." He would know; he's intimately aware of the last one. "You clearly do with this one."

No point denying it. Trav knows me better than anyone.

"Can we run?"

I need to do something to stop his annoying ass from talking.

Too bad that strategy doesn't work. We haven't even made it out of Greek Row and he's back at it.

"So…you have a nickname for her, huh?"

"*And?*"

"Nothing." I don't like the way he's pausing. "Just proves my point is all."

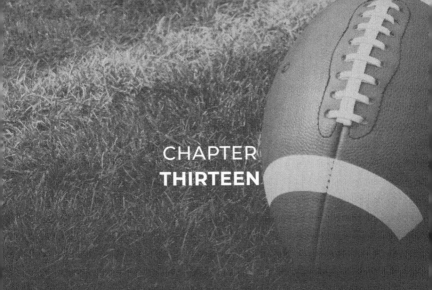

CHAPTER THIRTEEN

MASON

Lockers slam and the occasional towel snaps as two dozen men go through the process of showering then getting ready to head to class after a morning spent in the weight room.

I've never been much of a student. Academia doesn't get my jollies off like football, and I only really do the bare minimum needed to be eligible to play. So, the way I'm rushing through getting dressed to get to class early is unprecedented.

Did I just see a pig fly?

Two days. That's how long it's been since I've seen Kay, and a part of me—dare I say it—misses her. I barely know her and yet the campus playboy, Casanova himself, is missing a girl.

Someone has a thing for Grayson's "sister".

I don't.

To have a *thing* for her would mean I have feelings for her.

I'm Casanova. I don't catch feelings. I'm fully vaccinated.

"Lunch later?" Trav asks as he meets up with me at the coffee cart.

While the barista works on making my coffee and Kay's—something I'm sure Trav will give me shit about—I spin to face my oldest friend.

I love the guy. We have a bromance for the ages, and just like how Grayson thinks of Kay as his sister, I consider Trav my brother.

I loathe the fact that there is a small, tiny, microscopic part of me that harbors a kernel of doubt over the whole Chrissy/Tina debacle. Then again, it's a miracle we were able to salvage our friendship instead of letting it be destroyed by a two-timing bitch.

The two of us may be known for our surface-level hookups, but we're no longer led by our dicks enough to let a girl pretending to be someone else play us for a fool.

"The Nest?"

He arches a brow at the suggestion. Usually we meet at the athletic center where there are special meals meant to meet the nutritional guidelines for the school's athletes. It's not unheard of for us to be found at The Nest, just not typical.

I keep to myself the fact that I want to dine there because Grayson, and therefore Kay, eat there and I'm looking to crash their table—again. A part of me hopes if I show up with reinforcements, she'll be less likely to leave like the other day.

"Sounds like a plan." We bump knuckles as we split up for class.

When I step into the lecture hall, I find Kay in our usual spot. Despite complaining about me sitting next to her, she hasn't found somewhere else to sit.

I take the stairs to our seats and place her coffee next to her laptop like I did last week. Again she looks up at me, surprised, before muttering a soft thank you without questioning it —progress.

Class goes by quickly, and soon we're meeting Grayson before I walk Kay to her next class. Well, that may be stretch. Sure, we walk in the same direction, but Kay keeps to the opposite side of the cobblestone path. I flash her my dimples and she rolls her eyes. This routine of ours we've settled into is nice.

Nice? Is this thing on? *taps microphone* Do you hear yourself? Nice? Some Casanova you are.

My English class drags on endlessly as the coach inside my head berates me for thinking of Kay as anything other than a hot piece of ass.

I need to get laid. Then maybe he'll be less of a cranky son of a bitch.

Trav and I meet up outside The Nest, and after a quick detour for food, I search out the group. I find them at the same table as last week, tucked away in the farthest corner, almost hidden amongst the bustling crowd of co-eds.

Only the top of Kay's ponytail is visible with her head bent over looking at whatever textbook she and CK are conferring about. There's only one seat open at the six-person table—luckily for me, it's next to Skittles—and I snag it while Trav drags a chair over from another, positioning it at the end and straddling it.

A few errant curls smack my cheek, getting stuck in my stubble as her head whips around to see who's crashing lunch.

Storm clouds swirl as she narrows her eyes at me before rolling them.

I'm starting to live for making her roll her eyes.

Especially if I can make them roll back in pleasure.

"So...what?" She points to Trav but keeps her gaze locked on me. "You hoping we'll let you stay because you brought backup?"

"To be fair"—I drop an arm over the back of her chair—"they"—I circle a finger at her friends—"let me stay last time. I think the real question here is are you going to run away again?"

My gaze falls to her mouth as her lips thin. Someone doesn't like being called out for being a coward.

"You're annoyingly persistent."

"And you're just adorable." Her nose twitches after I boop it.

Did I really just boop her nose?

Oh, yeah, real *smooth, Casanova.*

"What ever happened to the more the merrier?"

Another eye roll.

I chuckle and make the formal introductions for those Trav doesn't already know.

"I take it Mase invited himself to join your group?" Trav leans toward Kay like they are the best of friends, and I have to resist the urge to yank him away.

"Yup." Gray eyes dart to me then back to my best friend. "He's like herpes—can't get rid of him."

Trav chokes on his water, spraying the table.

"Gra—" Cough. "Why haven't you brought this chick around

before?" Another cough and a clearing of the throat. "She's hilarious."

I pop Trav in the arm.

"*What?*" He tries to give me an innocent look but fails. "It's not every day I meet a girl who doesn't fall under the Casanova spell. I like it."

He would. Besides, he's one to talk. QB1 drops panties on campus like he completes passes on the gridiron.

"I should have never told you to meet me here for lunch."

Trav lays a smacking kiss on my cheek. Fucker is lucky we can't tackle him at practice.

"I like your shirt." He points to Kay's orange *Because Hogwarts Doesn't Accept FAFSA* tee. "I'm still waiting for my acceptance letter."

"You like *Harry Potter*?" She folds her arms across her open textbook, eyeing him skeptically.

"Yup." There's zero shame in his response.

"The movies?"

"Books too."

Every eye at the table is bouncing between the pair, watching the way they stare each other down like an MMA fight promotion shot. It's intense, silent, and weighted.

"You can stay," Kay declares. Then she points at me with her pen. "Jury's still out on you though."

Oh, you're gonna like me, baby, I promise.

"To be fair." Trav jumps to my defense as any good brother from another mother would. "Mase has read all the books too."

Boom. Mic drop.

"*Really?*" Is there a fishhook in her eyebrow? Damn that thing is arched.

"Gryffindor through and through." I thump my chest twice. "Plus I bring you coffee in the morning—you have to keep me." I lean back, dropping an arm on the back of her chair.

Grayson's eyes slide to her, giving her a look I can't quite read.

"You should take them to Lyle's coffee shop. You know it's a Potterhead's dream," Em suggests, earning herself an open invitation to any AK party should she want it.

"You wanna go on a coffee date with me, Skittles?" I twirl a lock of her hair around my finger, letting the silky smoothness glide over my skin. "Makes sense for our first date. Coffee is our thing, after all."

Shit! I just admitted to us having a thing.

She smacks my hand away and glares daggers at me while an enticing blush works its way up her neck. "*Hard* pass. And you and I will *never* have a *thing*."

That's what you think. Give me ten minutes and I'll show you just how big of a thing we can have.

"How was the game? Grayson didn't sulk too much that his team lost, did he?" Trav asks, trying to break the tension hovering over the table.

"No, he was very gracious." Em pats Grant's arm sympathetically.

"Don't go giving Mr. Bad Taste in Football Teams any more credit than he deserves." It's nice to see Kay give someone who isn't me shit for once. "He was still riding the high from his killer cut."

Grayson only shrugs his shoulders and gives her a wink.

"You got that done at the game?" I point to the back of his head where there's an impressive representation of our Hawk logo shaved into his hair. The detailing of the curled talons and the wings caught mid-flight is exquisite.

"Yeah. Bette did it right there in the parking lot while we were tailgating," Grayson answers.

"Who's Bette?" Trav asks.

"Skittles's family." She looks at me, impressed I remembered.

Another point to me on the scoreboard.

"Bette's the best. She came up a few times during March Madness, keeping me fresh for the tournament."

"Does she only do the designs in your hair?" Trav leans to the side, inspecting the shaving closer.

"Do you mean does she do it for pretty little white boys like you?" Grant taunts him by blowing a kiss.

"Who you calling *little*, asshole?" Trav holds his arms out like *Look at all this.*

"I'll show you mine if you show me yours," Grayson quips back.

"You just want to get a look at my package. I knew you wanted me, Grayson." Trav wiggles his eyebrows at him.

Oh, look at that—Kay is rolling her eyes.

"You guys are such children." There's a hint of a smile playing on her lips. "And to answer your question, she can do shavings for anyone. Her Insta is filled with all the cool shit she's done."

He already has his phone out to show us, and Trav and I lean over to check it out. As we scroll through her page, I catch sight of some seriously epic shavings and wicked cool color jobs, including some very familiar-looking blonde-and-rainbow locks. I make note of the handle to see if I can find Kay's account through this one—anything that can give me an edge.

Constant hawk cries ring out as people pass, and more often than not, fans and groupies stop by to chat. With Trav and me at the same table, not to mention Grayson, it was inevitable that we would attract attention.

As the stream of admirers continues, I can feel Kay move her chair over to distance herself from me. I frown when she adjusts her seat so much my arm is forced from its resting place. When I look over, her back is to me and her body is positioned in a way to make her as invisible as possible.

I've grown used to people trying to be close to me for either my attention or to be able to share a piece of the spotlight I carry with me.

This distance? You could say it's different.

I shouldn't like it, but I do.

Is this what Grayson meant?

She's like a goddamn breath of fresh air.

Stop worrying about the blonde and focus on the jersey chasers. Look at those tits. Just one little tug on that shirt and they could be in your mouth.

Sports are life at the U of J, with football and basketball reigning supreme. Even without it being their season, people are already asking Grayson questions about it. As much as my inner coach wants me to ignore Kay in favor of the willing pussy around me, I don't miss the way Grant shifts away from her, keeping the melee separate from her.

Trav and I are asked about the upcoming game and how we feel about our chances of bringing home the national championship, some people request to take selfies, and we even sign a handful of autographs. With billboards and stories-high posters of many of us up around campus and the surrounding towns, we're used to it.

This is the life. It's fucking good being king.

So why is it my crown feels like it's made of cheap plastic when I notice Kay is gone?

CHAPTER
FOURTEEN

I pull into my spot at The Barracks and shift Pinky into park. The same sense of calm I always feel when I catch sight of the impressive, hundred-thousand-square-foot facility washes over me.

The building is so much more than just the home base of the New Jersey All-Stars; it is *my* home away from home. It has nothing to do with the top-of-the-line equipment, the multiple competition floors, the three tumble tracks, the foam pit for practice flips, or the full CrossFit gym. No, what makes this place special is the people who fill it seven days a week.

When I was faced with the biggest tragedy of my life—losing Dad so suddenly and dramatically—they rallied around me and served as a shield, sometimes literally using their bodies between me and those looking to exploit me.

Whenever life became too much to deal with, I would come here. Nothing resets me when I'm spiraling like the blue mats I grew up on.

If I ever needed a reset, now would be the time. I've had so many feelings boiling inside me since Mason Nova walked into my life with that damn backward hat and those you-can-swim-in-them-they-are-so-deep dimples, forcing coffee on me and crashing my lunch table. My stomach is more twisted up than a tumbling pass.

It's why I'm pulling open the door an hour before I need to be here for tonight's Admirals—our co-ed senior level six and my old squad—practice.

My footsteps are silent as I walk through the lobby, past all the megaphone-topped trophies from national championships and globes from Worlds, giving a small wave to the front desk clerk.

There's no one in the pro shop, but I can hear voices trickling down the stairwell leading to the parents lounge and viewing area on the second floor.

The light is on inside Coach Kris's office as I pass. It's no surprise she is here early too; as the owner and head coach, she's the only one who spends more time here than I do.

A few people call out my name as I follow the blue camouflage path to the locker rooms at the back of the gym.

Slowly, I lift the strap of my duffle over my head and let the bag fall to the floor with a plop, and then I drop onto the wooden bench in front of my designated staff locker.

I let out a breath, resting my elbows on my knees and leaning forward, staring down at my spread fingers and the different jeweled birthstone rings adorning them.

The aquamarine on my left and the orange topaz on the right are especially bright under the florescent lights as my conversation with G from earlier plays back inside my head.

"Come to the AK party tomorrow."

I snort again at how serious he sounded.

"It's an invite-only. It'll be small—you'll have fun."

Not fucking likely.

"Look, Smalls." He takes me by both my shoulders, holding me in front of him, making it so I have to crane my head to a one-hundred-and-eighty-degree angle to be able to see his face. *"I love you and I'm not saying you should go onto the school's Insta page and tell them all your deets, but I think you're hiding."*

He's damn right I'm hiding. I'm a chickenshit. Just considering stepping out of my carefully crafted bubble of my people makes me break out in a cold sweat.

I work my five rings over my knuckles and place them into the small case I use to store them.

"Even JT thinks it will be good for you. Let yourself step outside your comfort zone knowing I'll be there to have your back."

Damn brothers don't know how to mind their own business.

Still, the thought that both G and JT are right churns in my belly as I pull on a black t-shirt with 'Coach PF' written in NJA's blue camouflage and tie my cheer shoes.

"Why would I want to go to a frat party? They have never been my scene, G."

"Because I'll be there."

Dropping to the mat at the end of one of the tumbling tracks, I limber up with my usual stretches.

"But I can see you any time. I don't need to go to the AK house for that."

"I'm not saying we have to spend all our time there, but you know being an Alpha is part of my life. If I'm always hanging at your place, how am I supposed to cultivate the relationships and connections that led me to even joining?"

Each flip and twist down the track does nothing to bring clarity.

"I know you're scared of letting people in. With your history, who wouldn't be?"

"I let people in—you, Em, CK." I tick each of them off on my fingers. *"Q and I have been bonding."*

"She's not the only one."

I end up throwing a double full as I think about the way he evaded answering me when I asked what he meant by *that*.

You know who he means. My inner cheerleader fluffs her bow.

"You wanna tell me what's got you so worked up?" Coach Kris eyes me from the end of the track.

"What are you talking about?" I bounce like Tigger back to her.

"Don't play games, Kay." She checks her watch. "The Admirals will be walking through those doors soon. Let's not waste the little bit of time we have bullshitting."

"Ooo, must be serious if you're calling me Kay." My smartass remark earns me her killer *Do you really wanna test me?* glare that has had many a cheerleader quaking in their bloomers.

"If it were gym business making you flip like a maniac, I'd call you PF, but this is personal."

And this right here is why I wouldn't work at any other gym.

Coach Kris is so much more than just a coach, just a boss. Her athletes and employees are her family. I've been a member of NJA since I was three, and she's been helping raise me since long before I lost my parents.

"What did JT do?" she asks, and I snap my gaze down from the hundreds of banners the NJA teams have won in competition to meet hers. "What?" She shrugs. "When you come here to work out your frustrations, he's usually the culprit."

"It's nothing." I get *the look* again. "Fine." I sigh. "He and G want me to go to one of G's frat's parties."

"And you're afraid it's going to be like high school?" I nod. "Understandable."

My jaw hits the blue mat under my feet. That is *not* what I expected her to say.

"You're not looking for my approval, Kay." She puts a comforting hand on my arm. "You have to make the decision for yourself. But"—she arches a brow—"there is one thing you should consider."

I look at her with pleading eyes.

"Look how well things have turned out so far with you letting in non-NJA cheerleaders. Who's to say this wouldn't be the same?"

I rub a thumb over my now bare right middle finger, still feeling the weight of the diamond band I wear for T and Em. It's true. If I had stuck to my original plan last year, I would have never gained not just a friend, but a sister in Em.

"I'll consider it."

"That's all anyone can ask." She gives my arm a squeeze then claps her hands. "Now how 'bout we whip these Admirals into shape? They have a Worlds title they need to reclaim."

Now that's a plan I can get on board with.

KAYLA

I'm in the shower jamming along with Lizzo in an effort to get myself pumped for tonight when I hear the door open and close. Peeling back the edge of the shower curtain, shampoo-filled curls swinging forward into my eye, I see Em sitting on the closed toilet lid, legs crossed, hands folded daintily at the wrist.

"Em?" I question, intrigued not by what she's doing in here—this isn't our first shower-time convo—but more as a general curiosity.

"So…" She gives me a sheepish smile before I duck back in to wash the shampoo from my hair.

"So…"

"You're not mad at me, are you?" I don't have to see her to know she's picking at her cuticles.

One of the reasons I was able to drop my walls enough to let her in is because she's the most empathetic person I've ever met, quite a feat considering her upbringing.

"Em, what in the world would I be mad at you for?"

I make it through conditioning my hair and washing my face before she answers.

"Because I sided with the guys about going tonight."

This girl. Her heart is almost too big at times.

I may have put up a fight—albeit a small one—when G invited us to tonight's party, but I've seen the writing on the wall. Helping him through pledging was one of the things that bonded us. Burying my head in the sand may be my preferred method of dealing with things I don't want to face, but my academic scholarship is proof I'm not stupid enough to not see this as an eventuality.

You know what I didn't see coming?

Mason Nova.

That his prodding and promise of having tonight's *Thursday Night Football* game on so I could watch E and the Crabs play Pittsburgh in the highly anticipated divisional matchup would be what ultimately had me agreeing—yeah, unexpected.

Sure, I let him believe it was just because I'm a Crabs fan—not a lie—and not because I'll be rooting for my brother. Just because he brings me coffee doesn't mean I'm going to divulge all my secrets.

When are you going to admit the coffee thing is a good move?

My inner cheerleader needs to butt out of my business.

Umm…I'm the mental manifestation of your thoughts. Doesn't that literally make me your business?

Ugh!

It doesn't help that the tempting tight end—the position, not his backside, though that's not bad either—has been the star of my thoughts way more than I would like to admit.

Yes, I've seen his Casanova side, but it's the others, the ones at odds with that reputation that I can't stop thinking about.

There's his funny side and his jokes to go along with my punny shirts.

And that he's a Potterhead.

No. Time to stop all thoughts of Mason, because it's one hell of a slippery slope.

It leads to thinking of that damn backward hat.

And those dimples.

I hate them. Okay, not really. I just hate that they make me want to kiss him.

I. Do. Not. Kiss. Football. Players.

"Kay?"

Shit! I never answered. "No, Em. I'm not mad. I promise."

One of my hot pink towels pushes past the curtain after the water cuts off.

"We're cool. Seriously." I reach for the second towel and wrap it around my head à la Marge Simpson.

When Em still looks unsure, I pull her into a hug, neither one of us caring that I'm in a towel and she's still in her practice gear.

"Now hurry up and shower then come to my room to get ready. I expect Bette will be video-calling to dispense her advice on what we should wear."

"If we're gonna go to our first frat party, might as well do it up."

I agree with a nod, exiting the bathroom and heading for my room.

By the time I've exchanged my terry cloth for a pair of U of J sweats and a t-shirt, dried my hair, and plugged in the straightener, Em is done with her own shower and Bette is ringing through on my laptop.

Except…

My sister-in-law's beautiful face isn't the only one filling the screen. JT in a hat and shit-eating grin is plastered on the other side in a split screen.

"Why do I feel like I'm being ambushed right now?"

"You think I'd miss *this*, PF?" JT and I clearly spend too much time together, because he rolls his eyes.

"Can't blame him. When you told me your plans for tonight, I swore I was being punked." Bette nods emphatically.

"No, sorry, Ashton Kutcher wasn't available," I deadpan.

"Also, he stopped doing the show in 2012 and has since moved on to *Shark Tank*," JT adds knowingly.

"You and G got your way—do you have to be a smartass?" I finish straightening the bottom layer of curls and pull down a new section to work on.

"Hey, Em babes." He greets her, ignoring me completely.

"Don't gloat, bro." Em leans a hip against my desk, dressed in her own pre-party outfit of sweats and a tank top. "We agreed to go, but if you rub it in, I'm pulling out the Ben & Jerry's and calling it a night."

Sisters before misters.

"Oh em gee," Bette squeals. "You're straightening your hair?"

Is she only just noticing? "I *love* when you wear it straight." This is true.

"Do you have to be such a girl?" JT complains.

"It's kind of the whole reason for this call. It's been so long since Kay's been to a party—I need to make sure she isn't going to try to go wearing that." Bette waves a hand at my comfy attire.

"It hasn't been *that* long." Just because frat parties aren't my scene, they act like I'm a hermit.

"Oh yeah?" JT folds his arms over his chest. "When was the last time you went to a party?"

I mentally flip through the calendar. "King's before you had to go back to Lexington." I wince even as I say the words.

"A Royal Ball?" JT barks out a laugh. "Yeah, PF, you *need* to go out tonight."

I roll my eyes at the stupid nickname for the parties Carter King throws. Hanging out around a bonfire is not a *ball*.

"Plus"—JT eyes me from under the brim of his hat—"you spent more than half the night hanging with Tessa and Savvy. Time to spend some time with people your own age and not two high school juniors."

Another eye roll. Whatever.

"Hey girl hey!" Q dances into the room with her typical flare. "What do we have here?" She props herself next to Em.

"Q, this is my sister-in-law, Bette, and my G before I had a G, JT." They both wave from their side of the camera. With the number of times my roomies have been around when I've video chatted with JT, this is the first formal introduction.

"Holy shit!" Q's eyes go wider than I've ever seen on a human being, and she leans over my shoulder, getting closer to the laptop. "You're JT Taylor."

Deer caught in headlights is too tame of a description for how those of us in the room and those on the call freeze.

What the hell?

How does she know that?

It's then I realize JT is wearing a UK hat. But…still…

"And—oh my god!" Q whips around to face me, staring at me like it's the first time she's seeing me. "*You're* his flyer PF." She smacks her forehead. "Oh…my god." Another rapid blink. "You are! You're PF Dennings."

Em rushes over and shuts the door to my room. I wondered

where Bailey was, but now I'm grateful she isn't here to witness this.

"How?" One word. That's all JT—or any of us—manage to get out.

"I cheered for Cheer Athletics." Q's hand splays across her chest. "NJA was always one of our biggest competitors at Worlds, and I *never* missed seeing you two compete in partner stunt. You are *legends*." She whips around to face me again. "Why aren't you in Kentucky cheering with him?" She whirls to point at JT. "Better yet, why aren't you *both* cheering *here*? The Red Squad would *kill* to have you two."

Well…this night has already taken an interesting turn, and we haven't even gotten to the AK house yet.

"I don't really like to broadcast my cheering history."

JT's jaw twitches, and I know he's kicking himself right now. He's going to blame himself for this when it isn't anyone's fault. His instincts are always going to be to protect me, and if he could, he would be crawling through the screen to do so right now.

"Why not?" Q's always-on-the-go movements stop dead and she goes, "Oh." The way her tone drops like it fell off a cliff tells me she made the connection.

Sure, I said I didn't change my name to come to school, and yes I was announced as PF at competitions, but that was only because I've been PF to NJA since I was seven. The secrecy nowadays is because I knew to anyone who got too curious, it's only a hop, skip, and a jump away to connect Kayla Dennings to PF Dennings—just a small step to all the news articles.

I'm not talking about the cheering ones.

"And you don't want people to know Eric Dennings—*the* Eric Dennings is your brother?"

Among other things.

I nod.

"Okay." Q's head bobs like a bobblehead. "Got it." More bobbing. "Damn your hair is *loooong* when it isn't curly." She runs her fingers through the locks now hanging to my waist.

That's it? That's all the reaction she has? She cared more about me cheering than anything else? Okay.

"I have a lot of it, that's for sure," I agree.

"Look at how cool the colors come through." She flips the ends, fanning them out.

"That's why I always straighten it when I see her." Bette beams, rolling with the change of topic. "Okay, ladies." She claps her hands, ignoring JT's protest over being lumped in as a lady. "Now for the important part…what are you wearing?"

The roomies and I step out of the Uber XL, staring up at the large gray four-story mansion with a red door and six white columns supporting a deck on the fourth floor. I can't help but think the place makes me think more of the plantation houses where Mama G grew up and not a frat house.

What the fuck am I doing here?

"I still can't believe you had to be *convinced* to go to an exclusive AK party," Bailey says, not for the first time.

"I'm not really into the whole frat party scene." I shrug.

I have no shame admitting this. I'm a big girl. I don't give in to peer pressure just because all the cool kids are doing it.

Isn't that why you're here tonight?

No. I'm going out of loyalty to G and trying to overcome my fears. Big difference.

My inner cheerleader fluffs her bow and rolls her eyes at me.

"But it's an *Alpha invite-only* party. These invitations are harder to come by than a Willy Wonka golden ticket."

I snort. Another one-liner for the win.

"Well, we're here."

"And looking *dayum* fine too." Q drags out damn to multiple syllables, tilting her head around for effect.

She isn't wrong. She sports a Kelly green crocheted crop top that looks amazing with her red hair, tan skin, white skinny jeans, and black leather knee-high boots. Her hair is barrel-curled, and she finished off her look with a classic cat eye and red lip.

Then there's Em in a 50s-pinup-style white halter, mint-colored skinny jeans, and tan equestrienne-style tall boots. A clip holds her hair up in a messy style, loose pieces falling around her face, which is made up in a light brown smokey eye and hot pink lip.

Bailey went a little more party girl than us, but she is rocking her gray cropped spaghetti-strap tank, super short black skirt, cowboy boots, and full-on smokey eye, coral lipstick, and hair tussled in a just-had-sex do.

I rock back onto the heels of my gray distressed leather biker-style boots, the buckles and chains wrapped around my ankles jingling as I try to gather my nerve.

"You good?" Em asks from my right.

No. I nod anyway. She links her arm with mine, and we walk up the path leading to the mansion.

We're hit with a wave of sound when the door opens, the pounding beat of the base spilling out as if it can't be contained. Two brothers, each sporting a different Alpha Kappa t-shirt, check the invite on my phone then step aside for us to enter.

Bailey splits off as soon as we get inside, and though it is nowhere near as crowded as I've heard their normal ragers get, I still can't find G in the crowd. Why can't I find him? He's stupidly tall. Shouldn't that help?

"You look a little lost." A cute guy in a black polo shirt with the AK crest stitched over the left pec stops in front of the three of us. "I'm Robbie, Alpha president. Can I give you a tour of the house?"

"No thanks." I decline with a small smile. I'll give the guy credit—his offer sounds genuine and not the least bit creepy. "But maybe you can help me." I push up on my toes so he can hear me better over the music. "I'm looking for G."

"G?" His brow scrunches, and it's then I remember they don't know him as G here.

"Do you mean Grayson?" asks the blond AK brother in the *too*-tight, as-if-trying-to-make-his-muscles-look-bigger-than-they-are Alpha t-shirt.

I nod, and blond bro proceeds to check me out, looking me up and down in an obvious manner. I cross my arms over my chest when he leers at my boobs a little too long for comfort. Thank god the shirt Em gave me to wear doesn't actually show off the girls.

"So *you're* the friend we've been hearing so much about," he finally says—to my boobs.

"Excuse me?" Em pushes against my side, Q closing in on the other.

"*Adam*," Robbie warns Mr. Douchebag.

"What?" Adam turns to Robbie, who just shakes his head.

"I'm pretty sure I saw Grant in the den earlier. I can show you where it is." Robbie waves a hand behind him.

Em and Q each give a nod, and I tell Robbie to lead the way.

"Thanks." I face my friends. "You guys wanna come with or do your own thing?"

Em looks to Q, who nods in agreement. "We'll stick with you."

"Okay great." I don't want to be here to begin with, and being alone with Mr. Frat Bro is the last thing that would make the list of what I'd like to experience while here. "Lead the way." I gesture to Robbie.

We—and unfortunately Adam—follow him down a long hallway and step inside a man cave where the noise from the party is muted.

"Grayson!" Adam, aka Douchey McDouche, yells out obnoxiously. "Found something that belongs to you."

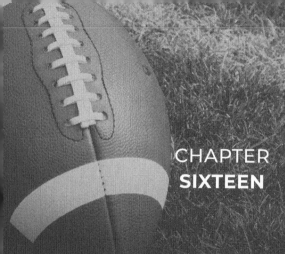

CHAPTER
SIXTEEN

MASON

T he Baltimore/Pittsburgh game is in the second quarter when there's a commotion by the door leading from the front of the house.

"Grayson! Found something that belongs to you." Adam's shout causes all heads in the room to turn in his direction.

Grant, CK, and I pause mid-conversation, and it takes a moment for my brain to register what my eyes are seeing. If it weren't for Em and Quinn standing next to her, I don't know if I would have recognized Kay.

Did I recently only think of her as cute? Because, holy fuck, she's a smoke show.

Gone are her curls, and instead her blonde-and-rainbow hair hangs around her in a straight curtain. She has more makeup on then I've ever seen her wear, and the deep blood red color coating her pouty mouth only makes me imagine what it would look like smeared on my dick.

Her slender neck has a thin black necklace wrapped around it, and all I want to do is sink my teeth into the skin bared by the off-the-shoulder collar.

Fuck me *sideways* was she hiding a tight-as-fuck body underneath those cute shirts she loves.

Her tits are more than a handful pressed against the black material, and the expanse of exposed pale tummy has cuts of abdominals that make me wonder what it is she does to have a body like that.

For someone so tiny, I'm surprised by how long her legs look in her tight black skinny jeans. I'm dying for her to turn around so I can give her ass the appreciation I'm sure it deserves.

Fuck. The guys are going to be all over her.

Not your problem, bro. Football—do I really have to spell it out for you?

I can already see the appreciative looks she's drawing from the room. Granted, the guys are also checking out Em and Quinn, who I'll admit look hot too. The only difference is I don't feel like stalking over and claiming *mine* like I do with Kay.

Fuck. Say it with me: F-O-O-T-B-A-L-L.

Quinn wiggles into the free spot next to CK on the couch while Em and Kay settle onto the wide armrests of Grayson's recliner. I mentally fist-pump when Kay is forced to take the one closest to me.

"You know"—I tap Kay's knee—"I wasn't sure if you were actually going to show."

"Eh." She shrugs one of her bare shoulders, the line of her collarbone popping and drawing my eye. "You *did* promise to have my football game on. Plus…free beer."

An unexpected bark of laughter escapes me. I *highly* doubt free beer was a motivating factor—not that I care. All that matters is she's here.

"Who scored?" She hooks a thumb at the TV.

"Your boy Dennings," I say, remembering she wore the tight end's jersey.

Kay's gray eyes flare and I think I hear both CK and Quinn cough, but that doesn't make sense.

"Sweet. I love when I have a player in the Thursday game. Best way to start off the fantasy week."

"You have a fantasy football team?"

What is she doing to me? She needs to stop revealing attributes that make her *more* attractive to me.

"She cheats," Grayson whines, and a fan of hair flies through the air as Kay whips around to face him. "And she's a bad friend." He folds his lips in as if to suppress a smile.

"*Excuse* me?" Kay holds up a hand as if flipping him off, except it's her ring finger. "You, sir, are lucky this"—she taps the orange band—"is also for Bette, or I'd take it off."

"Don't be salty, Smalls." He takes her hand and kisses the ring. "If you ditched mine, you'd have to ditch JT's too, and then you'd be out half your bling. So sit back, relax, watch your football, and at halftime, you and Em can go off on one of your dance parties."

Kay mutters as she shifts to lean back. It's nice to witness someone else get the less-than-welcoming side I always seem to bring out in her.

We watch the game for another set of downs until it goes to a commercial break.

"Thanks for having the game on," Kay says, giving me my first ever unprompted sign of gratitude from her.

There was very little chance that it wouldn't have been on anyway, but if I'm gonna be given credit for it, you're damn right I'm gonna take it.

"You said you didn't want to miss it, and it was easy enough to make it happen for you. We are friends, after all." I flash her my dimples, and there's no missing how her gaze falls to them.

"We're friends?" That fishhook is back in her eyebrow.

"Albeit reluctantly on your part, but yu*p*." I emphasize the P.

Shit—do you hear yourself? Friends? You're happy about being friends with a girl? It's like I don't even know who you are anymore. I'm done.

Ignoring my inner coach has become a new habit of mine when it comes to Kay. Instead of retreating or all-out hitting on her like he wants but which would only be counterproductive, I take one of her hands in mine. It's so small it almost disappears in my grip.

"There's a story here"—I run a thumb over the two jeweled bands adorning her left hand—"isn't there?"

She brings her other hand around, laying it across the inside of my wrist, and the slide of her fingertips brushing the sensitive skin sends a bolt of lust straight to my dick. Fuck me I'm further gone for this chick than I realized if *that* is revving me up.

"They're the birthstones for all the people I consider family."

"Not me," CK says behind me, and Kay shifts her gaze to him.

"Don't be like that, CK," she cajoles. "G and Em are only on the board already because they are piggybacking off of existing people." She holds up a hand to stop him before he cuts in. "But I'll start looking for an emerald one I like."

"All I'm trying to say is a bright green one would look good with your collection."

It's weird to see that eye roll when I'm not the cause.

Wanna know what else is new?

Kay hasn't pulled away. I give the hand I'm still holding a squeeze, bringing her attention back around.

"This one is for Bette, my sister-in-law, and G." She taps me with her right ring finger. "This is the 'sister' band because it's for T and Em." The diamond band on her middle finger sparkles as she taps it. "E and Pops." The ruby stones shine when she points. "JT." She holds up the finger on her left hand that bears a light blue ring. "And finally"—she flips me off to show the purple amethyst band—"me and Dad."

I've overheard her use all these names in the time I've hung around, but I don't know the significance of all of them. Unfortunately, an AK party is not the time or the place for a conversation like that.

Their little group heads off to explore the rest of the party at halftime, and I wait a few minutes, taking the time to fill my Solo cup with a fresh beer before going to find them.

Grayson and CK are standing against a wall not far from where the girls are dancing when I approach. He may have been here before the ladies, but poor CK does not look the least bit comfortable.

"Not your typical Thursday night?" I tilt my cup at him.

"*Pfft.* Not even close."

"Blame Smalls." Grayson grins knowingly.

"Have you *ever* been able to tell her no?" CK taunts.

"Yeah. Right."

They bicker like an old married couple, and I damn near drown choking on a swallow of beer as I look up. Holy fuck Kay knows how to move her hips.

YESSSS! You're finally speaking my language. That's all you need to know. If she can move her hips on the dance floor, she'll know what she's doing when she rides your dick.

Watching is enough to have me chub up behind my zipper; I

don't need the added visuals my inner coach is trying to shove at me. The situation in my pants only intensifies when thunderous clouds turn my way.

Unlike how Bailey's physical touch made my balls want to crawl up into my body last week, the way Kay's eyes ghost over me has them ready to run for a ninety-yard touchdown.

I can't help myself—I flex. Her eyes flare, and I smirk at the blush she tries to hide by turning away.

She can deny it all day long, but she wants me.

My hips sway and my shoulders roll as Em, Q, and I dance along to "Shape of You" by Ed Sheeran. I try to get lost in the steady rhythm, paying no mind to the taunting of my inner cheerleader.

Look around you, Kay. She strokes the leather armrests on the Barcalounger she's stretched out in. *A girl could be really comfortable watching football here.* Since the moment we arrived, she's been trying to convince me to make this my new place to hang.

I cast a glance in CK's direction, checking in, and my heart wobbles like it's trying to save a stunt from falling at the sight of Mason with him. I know better than to stereotype, but I also know exactly what it means to CK for someone like Mason to not treat him like a social nerd.

Those seafoam green eyes burn as Mason blatantly eye-fucks me from across the room. My hormones take off in a standing full, and my panties? *What panties?* is more like it. They were incinerated under his heated stare.

Shit! If he can affect me with a look, I can't even begin to imagine what he would be able to do if I let him put his Casanova moves on me.

I need to keep my distance.

Like a minimum of a full football field away from him.

Don't be like that. My inner cheerleader pouts. *Look how mouth-watering he looks tonight.* Her bow may be huge, but I still see the tips of her devil horns peeking through.

Still, she's not wrong.

He's all olive skin, sexy black ink, snug black AK t-shirt stretched across his muscular chest, biceps pushing the sleeves up, and—the coup de grâce—that ever-present black baseball cap.

Black, black, black. All of it adds to his bad boy appeal.

Oooo, gurrrrl. You are so screwed.

He really needs to stop being so *damn* good-looking.

"How come we've never seen you ladies around here before?" A voice comes from behind us as two attractive AK brothers move into our circle, finally pulling my attention *off* Mason.

Why is it I have zero reaction to them?

They are harmless flirts; too bad the same can't be said when Adam butts into our little cluster.

"That's 'cause Grayson's been keeping her a secret." He points to me.

I roll my eyes. This guy gives off an entitled, douchey vibe that grates on my nerves.

"I didn't know Grant had a girlfriend," one of them states.

"I'm not his girlfriend. I'm his best friend."

"Yeah." Adam chuckles to himself like he's the funniest man alive, and I curl my hand into a fist in an effort not to punch him. "Grayson probably didn't want anyone to know he wasn't dating a sista."

He did not just say that.

"Oh my god!" Em gasps.

I look down at my empty plastic cup, *wishing* I hadn't finished my beer so I'd have something to throw in this dick's face.

"God you're a racist asshole," Q says, appalled.

"You know his mom is white, right?" I toss the fact out there even though it shouldn't fucking matter.

Adam looks over at G. "No way. He's way too dark to be mixed."

A collective groan sounds through our group. "Oh my god." I

feel a massive headache forming. "You're so ignorant, I can't even."

I never thought I would say this, but *thank god* Mason chooses that moment to make his way over. He must have read the tension amongst the group, because he bends down to say, "Everything all right?"

His lips graze the shell of my ear, and I shiver at the contact. It takes me a moment to regain my bearings, his touch and my anger a volatile combination, and by the time I'm able to formulate a response, he has pulled back and is looking at me with concern in his light eyes.

"Sure...just learning how *some* of your brothers suck at life."

His laughter rumbles through me, easing some of the tension knotting my muscles.

"Do you need me to handle it?"

I give my head a shake. We don't need the drama that would bring.

He studies me a moment longer before saying, "The guys said the third quarter started."

"Oh crap. Thanks."

See? Why does he have to be thoughtful, too?

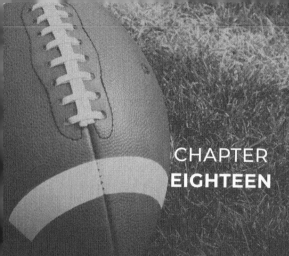

MASON

Seeing two of my fellow fraternity brothers talking to Kay and her friends isn't my favorite way to spend a Thursday night, but if I go over there and interrupt for no reason, I would probably face death by eye roll.

I look away to check the text from Trav saying the third quarter started, and when I look back at the girls, my brow furrows at Kay's unhappy expression. Even when she's giving me a hard time, there's always a hint of a smile on her face; it's absence now is telling.

I stalk over to the group, the angle of my body projecting *Back off, she's mine* vibes, and I lean close, speaking for only her to hear.

With our bodies almost touching, I don't miss how she shivers when my lips graze her ear.

I haven't had many chances to be this close to her, and I catch a whiff of peppermint. Inhaling deeper, I realize it must be from her shampoo or something, and I've never wanted to suck on a candy cane the way I want to suck on her body.

She's slow to answer, her throat working with a swallow. I keep my eyes locked on hers, noting the thick black outer circles. I could stare into them all day.

No, no, no. Her eyes? Really? I thought we were making progress!

The way she doesn't pull any punches, telling me how some of my fraternity brothers suck at life is a major turn-on.

Oh my god! *throws whistle* I give up.

"Do you need me to handle it?" I offer. I want her to know I'll have her back, even with my own fraternity brothers.

When she shakes her head, I tell her about the game being back on.

"You guys coming?" she asks Em and Q.

A look of disgust crosses Em's face as she looks at Adam. "Yeah. It's gotten a little *crowded* here."

When we make it back to the den, the seating in front of the TV is almost entirely filled with my teammates who are members of the fraternity. I'm able to claim my original spot but, much to my disappointment, Kay and her crew hang back by the open pool table.

I bullshit with the guys while the game's on commercial.

"I can see why Grayson's mom wants him to ask her out. She's hot." Kevin nods in Kay's direction.

A murmur of agreement sounds throughout the group.

"She's got a quick wit, too. She doesn't fall for any of Nova's shit." Trav laughs over his beer at my expense, puckering his lips to blow kisses at me when I flip him off.

"Wow." Noah leans forward. "I don't think I've ever heard of a girl not falling for the Nova charm."

Thanks for the reminder.

"Yeah, yeah, yuck it up, assholes."

The game comes back and there's still a grouping of trainers surrounding a player down on the field. The injury must be bad if they haven't cleared it by now.

A hush falls over the group as Kay walks closer, her eyes trained on what's happening on the TV.

"Who's hurt?" Her voice wobbles around the question.

"Dennings," Noah answers.

"Matthews nailed him with a late hit," Alex, one of the team's running backs, explains.

"It was dirty, too. They ejected him from the game," Trav adds.

"Damn," she whispers under her breath. She looks so concerned, and it's cute.

Again with this cute bullshit.

The network replays the hit. Dennings is one of the biggest tight ends in the league, and seeing his large body get crushed beneath players even has me wincing. After they show the hit in real time, they show it in slow motion from a few different angles, and none of them are good.

I suck in a harsh breath at one particular angle. It *was* dirty. If the fact that he's still down wasn't a clue of a potential head injury, the way he impacted the ground would definitely be cause for concern.

Everyone else has their attention focused on what's happening, but my eyes remain locked on Kay. Grayson comes up behind her, and she sags into him.

The punch of jealousy I feel at the easy way he holds her to him is foolish and hits me out of nowhere.

Not wanting to lend fuel to the suspicious fire burning inside me, I drag my gaze away from where the two of them are whispering, Grayson's head bent low so Kay can talk in his ear, and I focus on where the trainers are now helping Dennings up.

The announcers drone on, saying he will be taken back for evaluation and musing on a potential concussion and dislocated shoulder.

When I can no longer resist the urge, I shift to find Kay again, only to see she's gone—again.

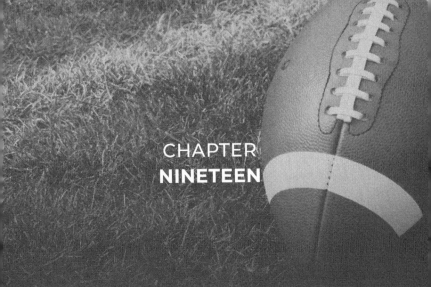

MASON

Twelve hours later and I still haven't been able to get Kay's abrupt departure out of my mind, or rid myself of the overwhelming disappointment I've felt since I noticed.

Where did she go?

Why did she leave?

Is everything okay?

Shit, man. Are you growing a vagina or something? Why are you so hung up on this chick?

None of the mental chastising does anything to curb my thoughts.

Today is a travel day for the team, and I plan on using the two-hour flight to Ohio to internet-stalk the shit out of Skittles. I have so many questions, and I need answers.

Jesus Christ, is it too late to draft a new player? Asking for a friend. Shit, Nova. You're killing me here. A girl? A motherfucking girl? That's what you're going to use your time on? It's not like Ohio State is one of the toughest matches we'll face from the Big Ten or anything. Nah, let's not focus on football. It definitely isn't our whole future or anything. You're right, investing in hard-to-get pussy when the sure-thing variety is thrown at you from everywhere else is a much better use of our time.

I ignore the sarcasm of my inner voice and lean back in my seat on the team's custom Boeing 747. When you have to travel around the country for half your games, what better way than to do it than on a plane with two levels of fully reclining seating pods, individual televisions, and U of J logos everywhere.

Once in the air, we are cleared to turn our electronics back on, and I waste no time pulling out my phone, connecting to the plane's wifi, and getting to work.

Work? Pfft. Work would be pulling out the playbook, talking to the other captains about the best strategy to beat the Buckeyes. Hell, at this point I'd even settle for you looking up the Buckeyes' social media accounts. No—you, sir, are not working. You are internet-stalking pussy. The worst part? You aren't even good at it.

My inner coach is right, and that pisses me off. Except for the rare picture of Kay on Grayson's and Em's Instagrams, she has zero social media footprint. Why can't I find her accounts? Haven't these people heard of tagging?

Anything that has held potential for connecting the dots has only led to dead ends thanks to privacy settings.

Why can't I stop thinking about her?

Is my inner coach right? Is it the fact that she doesn't fall for my Casanova charm that makes me want her?

I'm back to Grayson's Instagram, pulling up one of his more recent posts from when they all went to the Empire/Crabs game last weekend.

TheGreatestGrayson37: Best buds for life even if she doesn't respect my brilliant choice of football team. *football emoji* #GottaRepresent #FootballSunday #BFFL #ThisIsOurEmpire #SomeoneGetThisGirlAnEmpireJersey
picture of Em, CK, and Grayson with Kay caught mid-laugh pulling on Grayson's Empire jersey

If I only want Kay because I actually have to pursue her, why does seeing her smiling face in this picture make me want to make sure she always smiles like that?

It doesn't make any sense. Women are good for one thing and one thing only—release. And before you get your panties in a twist, that release is always mutual. I may not be a gentleman, but I am Casanova. I'm fucking amazing—pun intended.

"You okay, bro?" Trav leans over to not be overheard by the others.

"Yeah, dude."

"You sure?" His eyes flit down to my phone. "You haven't been acting like yourself lately."

I force myself not to react. I'm pretty sure I know where he's going with this, but I feel him out anyway.

"Whatever, bruh. I'm just as much of a stud as I've always been."

"That's what I mean." His blue eyes narrow as he studies me. "I haven't seen you go off with a chick since school started."

Well damn. I guess there is one downside to someone knowing you as well as you know yourself.

He looks down at my phone again, screen still lit from my thumb hovering over Grayson's open Insta.

"Actually…the only chick you've even remotely flirted with is Kay."

I press my lips together in an effort to stay silent. No need to give myself away when denial works.

"I like her, ya know." He nods at my phone.

I whip my head around to face him.

Best friend or not, Skittles is mine, not his.

Er—time out. *Mine?* Did I really just think that? What the fuck is happening to me?

The sparkling gleam in Trav's eyes tells me my mask has slipped.

"Relax. I just meant she's a cool chick. This isn't Tina/Chrissy 2.0."

They say when you lose a limb, you sometimes experience phantom pain, and the mention of the girl who almost blew up our friendship always makes my hasn't-been-let-out-again heart bleed inside my chest.

"How can you—" I start but can't even finish the question, too scared of the answer.

"How can I what?" Trav knows me well enough to know what I was attempting to say, but I voice it anyway.

"How can you tell it's not going to be…a 2.0 situation, as you put it?"

The flight attendants come around offering refreshments, but we decline.

"For one, as much as people would accuse you of being a dumb jock, you aren't."

"Feeling the love, bro." I get a smacking kiss in response. Asshole.

I'm wiping the slobber from my cheek when he continues. "And for two"—he levels me with a look, waiting for me to interrupt again, but I don't—"I think we both learned enough from that disaster to *never* let it happen again."

The engines whir along with my mind as we settle into our cruising altitude. I wait out a pocket of turbulence before voicing my biggest concern.

"Why can't I find her anywhere online? It's like she's a ghost."

Trav tugs at his ear the way he always does when he's thinking hard about something. The sounds of our teammates around us fade into white noise.

"Okay…yeah…that's a *little* weird, but look"—he touches the picture still on the screen—"she's real. *And*…she's connected to *our* friend."

This is true. Plus, another difference is she didn't pursue me. Pretty much every time we've spent time together has been because I went seeking her out. *I* brought her coffee. *I* crashed her lunch table. Me, me, me, not Kay looking to use my social status or my football pedigree to get ahead.

"She doesn't make a big deal about us playing football."

"Nope," Trav agrees, making me realize I said that last part out loud. "Most of the time I think it's actually a negative in her mind."

Correct again.

Don't even ask me how much time I've spent trying to figure out that one with how much she loves the Crabs.

"You might be right." I click the home button, getting rid of the picture. I can't look at it any longer. Besides, I'm no closer to finding Kay online than I was an hour ago.

"You know…" I hit the button to recline my seat into a bed, spinning my hat forward. "I never thought I'd say this, but I think I like that she doesn't see us as stars of the gridiron."

"I feel that." Trav does the same with his seat, getting comfortable. "So…"

I lift the brim from where it shields my eyes.

"You gonna make a move or what?"

Isn't that the million-dollar question.

KAYLA

Getting E to rest is a full-time job. I never thought I'd say this, but he's *damn* lucky he's recovering from a concussion or there is a very real possibility I would have smacked him already. He is the *worst* patient *ever*.

I've already had to banish him to his bedroom because he refused to stay seated while watching college football.

"I can't believe you're making me watch football on this tiny-ass TV." E thrusts an arm out at the sixty-inch flat-screen hanging on the wall when I walk into the master suite.

"Yeah, *sooo* tiny, E." I roll my eyes. Yes, the one downstairs is a massive eighty-inch screen, but it's not like he's being forced to watch it on his phone.

"You're a mean nurse."

"Yeah, well, if you could work on regaining consciousness faster, I wouldn't have to be here." I scoot Herkie over and join E on the bed.

"You act like that's something I can control."

"Still…if you could not scare me like that again, that would be great." I say this in my best *Office Space* impression.

Herkie shifts, resettling himself with his head on my lap. We got him as a puppy the year before Dad died, and I probably miss him more than anyone when I'm away at school.

"You know…" E looks to where I'm scratching Herkie behind the ears. "If you lived at home instead of the dorms, you'd be able to keep him with you."

I sigh. I would love nothing more.

"It wouldn't be fair. I'm barely home as it is between school and the gym."

"If you say so."

I've never understood E's preference for me to live at home. It's not like we can't afford the room and board. Bette suspects it stems from him feeling like he can't protect me when I'm at school. I like to think he's overreacting, but there is that doubt that hovers in the back of my mind.

"Oh." I remember the text I received while getting our snacks downstairs. "I have a message for you."

Pulling up the text thread, I hold my phone out so he can see the last message I received from Naples, aka Mike Napolitano, a tight end for New England. It's a GIF of him in his football jersey, tapping his chest twice then pointing at the camera, the words 'I got you' displayed above his head.

"What a fucker." E laughs, groaning as it jostles his recently reset shoulder.

"Well *someone* has to score my team some points with you on the disabled list." The trash talk that happens from the players I've met through E sometimes gives me the impression they are five-year-olds and not grown men.

"I don't know if I love or *hate* that you have me on your fantasy team." Not the first time he's said this. "I swear you are more demanding than Coach."

I love this comment so much.

"You love me."

"I do."

"Plus, it could be worse."

"How?"

"You could be on your wife's team."

And now I'm deaf. I knuckle my ear, trying to rid it of the ringing his sudden bark of laughter left me with.

Thankfully, before I have to remind him *again* he's supposed to be resting, the U of J/Ohio State game kicks off and the two of us settle in to watch. Even playing professionally hasn't diminished E's love for watching the game, and college football is his favorite. He says he needs to keep an eye on the future competition.

The camera pans to show Mason and Travis laughing on the sidelines, and I can't help but notice how hot he looks in his white and red away jersey, the sleeves tucked underneath the ends of his shoulder pads, highlighting the obsidian ink swirling down his left arm.

"Stupid lunch-crashing football players," I mutter under my breath.

"Umm...*excuse* me." E holds a finger up like a student waiting to be called on. "Did *you* just say something about having lunch with *football* players?" His sarcasm is strong.

"Not by choice."

"Explain." There's a hardening to his tone. Why does my brother have to be one of those rare men who listen?

"Mason Nova and Travis McQueen are brothers in the Alpha Kappa fraternity."

Now E has his uninjured arm wrapped around his middle as he straight-up guffaws at this revelation.

Me? Yeah, I don't find it funny *at all*.

"I don't want to hear it," I warn.

"Hear what? That being friends with G would expose you to more athletes? Or that it's the first time you've hung out with a tight end who isn't me since high school? *No*, I wouldn't dream of mentioning any of that."

Sarcastic asshole.

"Shut it, you." My laughter belies my threat.

"I take it they don't know I'm your brother?"

"That would be a hard no."

"Just checking. You did tell me your one roommate knows."

Two days later and I'm still mildly reeling from Q figuring out my secrets.

Earlier today, we received a huge and unexpected lunch care package from her and Em. It was the included notecard that really touched me, though.

This is so you don't have to worry about cooking.

*Make sure you check underneath, there's a bottle—A
LARGE ONE—to help you and Bette survive.
Love,
Em and Q*

*P.S. You tell that brother of yours no one cares he
won a Super Bowl—he needs to listen to you. And
if he fights you, just remind him YOU hold more
World Champion titles than he does. XOXO, Q*

The NFL and the USASF (the U.S. All Star Federation) are two entirely different things, but Q's postscript solidifies her place in our crew.

"So…" E looks from the where the cameras have panned to another close-up of Mason then back to me. "Hanging out with football players, huh?"

Why is he bringing this up again? I thought we were done with this topic.

"Not willingly," I grumble.

Herkie lifts his head at E's burst of laughter. "Since when do you do something you don't want to?"

"Since my best friend moved into the frat house and told me his big brother is Mason Nova."

"And that equates to you eating lunch with him and the QB… how?" he mumbles around a mouthful of popcorn.

"Long story short, I have a class with Mason and he thought I was G's girlfriend and decided to be all buddy-buddy with me. He then proceeded to invite himself to join us for lunch, and it evolved from there."

"Sounds like this guy likes you."

"Who? Mason?" I give him a *yeah right* look.

"Yup." E bobs his head up and down.

"No way. He's the campus playboy. His freaking nickname is Casanova, for crying out loud." I stuff a handful of popcorn in my mouth.

"Mmmhmm."

Clearly his concussion is affecting him more than I thought, because he is *not* making sense.

"He's a football player."

"So?"

Don't hit him, Kay. He's injured.

"Not only is he a football player, he's a tight end."

"I'm a tight end." E gives me a *Try again* look, which I return with a *You can't be serious* stare.

I blow out a breath and run a hand roughly through my curls. An entire Ohio State possession happens before E speaks again.

"I get why you're hesitant." He waits until I lift my gaze to his. "*Really*, I do, but you can't let what happened with—" I throw up a hand before he can say his name. "*Him* control your life forever."

My inner cheerleader turns her back and tosses a middle finger up over her shoulder. She doesn't like thinking about He-who-shall-not-be-named any more than I do.

"E." His name is a warning, a plea, an *Oh fuck*.

"I'll stop." He holds his hands up in surrender.

"Thank you," I whisper.

"I just worry."

"I know." I really do get it. E is so much more than just my brother; he would lay down his life if he thought it would lead to my happiness, and I would do the same for him.

"What about Pops?" I remember asking him about JT's dad back when we worried about my guardianship.

"No," E says firmly, brooking no room for argument.

"Why not?" I had to try.

"I'm your brother. You are my responsibility, Kay."

We had always been close despite the five years between us. That day only strengthened that bond.

"I don't want you to miss out on something in the future because of something that happened in the past."

I nod, blinking back tears as I turn back to the football game.

I like to think I'm doing exactly what E is saying. My friendships with Em and G are proof enough. And now Q? Yeah, I'm losing the shackles of my past. Doesn't mean I can't play other things close to the vest.

"He's in the public eye, especially around campus. What if…" My words trail off as I push down the flashback of panic surging to the forefront.

"What if what?" Any hint of amusement is gone as E watches me with a critical eye, trying to read between my lines.

"It's like the most conceited thing ever, but what if being around him brings attention onto me?" I shake my hands out when they start to tingle, trying to rid myself of the anxious sensation. "What if it only makes me a target again?"

"The internet breeds assholes—that's a fact of life. Do I think it would get like it did in high school for you?" He shakes his head. "I doubt it. You've found ways to cope with what happened, and look at how successful you've been managing being friends with G. Who's to say that wouldn't work if you wanted to add to your friend group?"

I nod, hoping we can drop the topic for now.

We keep the rest of the conversation light and focus instead on the battle between the Hawks and the Buckeyes.

By the start of the fourth quarter, the game is tied at twenty-eight all. We watch as Travis gets sacked hard, both of us sucking in a breath at the hit.

"I feel ya, man." E rubs his sore shoulder.

Bette walks into the room then, home from work and once again proving their almost psychic connection—I swear I've never met two people more perfect for each other than E and Bette—when she smacks an ice pack to activate it before placing it against his shoulder.

"Thanks, babe," E says with a sigh.

Bette leans down for a kiss before he pulls her in to snuggle against his good side.

"Glad to see your sister is keeping you in line." Bette shoots me a wink.

It's now fourth and one for the Hawks, but instead of punting like you'd expect, they go for it.

Travis takes the snap, dropping back to look for a receiver. Mason gets off a sweet block, allowing Travis time to wait for Alex to get downfield. Travis lets it fly, a deep sixty-yard bomb into Alex's waiting hands, and he runs it in for a touchdown.

"Damn." I whistle in appreciation. "They keep making plays like that and they'll for sure end up in the national championship again."

"Absolutely," E agrees.

"I have a feeling it's all gonna come down to the last game of the season against Penn State."

E's alma mater is the U of J's biggest rival, and this year the teams are slated to play each other for their final game of the season. Last year the Nittany Lions won the bragging rights.

This year...

Tension is already thick, the Hawks hungry for redemption.

I've never looked forward to a game of football more in my life.

My body isn't even completely dry, the cotton of my t-shirt sticking to the droplets of water coating my spine, as I hurry through getting dressed.

I don't give a fuck if my clothes are damp; I need to see Kay. For the first time in...probably *ever*, I've felt anxious, unable to get her off my mind.

Five days.

That's how long it's been since Kay rushed out of the AK house, never to be heard from again.

Man you are dramatic. See what happens when you let a chick tie your balls in a knot instead of emptying them?

I mentally give my inner coach the finger. We've been butting heads more and more lately, but I'm going with my gut on this one.

It doesn't matter that any time we are together, she spends it giving me more shit than my teammates do. When I'm with her, I feel more like myself than I have in a long time. I guess I didn't realize how much of a wall I put up after the whole Chrissy/Tina fiasco, how often I've been wearing a mask.

There's no risk of someone getting close enough to break my heart again if all they ever see is Casanova.

"Where you rushing off to, Nova?" Kev asks.

"Trying to get a quickie in before your first class or something?" Noah nudges me with his elbow and waggles an eyebrow.

"Wouldn't you like to know." I hook the strap of my backpack over my shoulder and turn to Trav. "See you for lunch?"

"You know it."

I call out, "Later, assholes," and make my way to the coffee cart.

My thoughts drift back to Kay while I wait for the barista to make our drinks—though, to be fair, she hasn't been far from my mind all weekend. After the team beat Ohio State, all I wanted to do was call her to see if she watched.

What did it matter? Why did I care?

Those questions went unanswered because I don't have her number.

For days, I debated asking Grayson for it, but I'm not ready for anyone, even her best friend—*especially* her best friend—to know how much she affects me. I'm Casanova. I don't chase girls; they chase me.

You keep telling yourself that because I don't believe you for a second. Maybe you should try catnip instead of coffee—it's known to drive pussy crazy.

My inner coach is still berating me when I step through the doors to our financial management class, my gaze automatically going to where we sit. Like a shanked field goal, my spirits drop. I try telling myself I could have beaten her here. I did get here earlier than normal.

When she still hasn't shown by the time class starts, the worry is real.

First she rushed from the party, and now she's missing class. I may have only known her a few weeks, but it's not hard to see how seriously she takes her academics.

Each minute feels like two, and by the time the seventy-five-minute lecture is over, I'm ready to run through my classmates like they're a defensive line. All I can think of is seeing Grayson and convincing him to give me Kay's number.

Fuck it all. I *need* to know if my girl is alright.

Son of a fucking bitch. Your girl? You called her YOUR GIRL? You have officially lost your motherfucking mind. You are benched. BENCHED. Ride that pine, baby.

I'm fidgeting like a virgin on prom night waiting for Grayson —or at least how I imagine one would.

Grant greets me with our usual complicated handshake and gives the barista his order. Waiting for him to get his coffee instead of automatically asking for what I want is a true test of my patience, especially when he doesn't comment on our missing companion.

"Hey." I clear my throat, going for nonchalance. "Can I have Kay's number?"

He rears back, eyeing me suspiciously.

"She didn't give it to you?" Each word is measured, testing me.

"Never thought to ask." He still doesn't look sure if he wants to give out Kay's information, so I play what I hope is my trump card. "She wasn't in class—didn't know if she would need notes or not."

There's another lengthy silence. Then, "All right. Give me your phone." He takes it from me but pauses in the middle of typing in the number. "I know you're my big brother and all, but I swear to god if you use this to hit on her like one of your jersey chasers, I'll fucking *end* you."

I'm not quite sure how to react. There's an edge to Grayson's voice I've never heard before. He's typically a laid-back guy, but his loyalties seem to bring out the Pitbull in him.

"You feel me?" he asks when I still don't say anything.

"Yeah. We're straight, bro."

He continues to take my measure.

I think I'm going to enjoy watching him kick your ass. Maybe then you'll get your head out of it and back on football where it belongs.

I must pass the test because Grant finishes inputting Kay's number and hands me back my phone.

"Thanks man." I note the time. "See you at The Nest?"

"Yup."

We say goodbye with the same bro-shake as before.

ME: Hey, Skittles, where've you been?

Her answer comes in a few moments later.

SKITTLES (yes this is how I have her saved in my phone): Mason?

And my day just got a whole lot better.

I may have had to miss two days of classes helping take care of E, but it's what family does. He has since been cleared to resume light workouts with the team, so my job here is done. There is a perk of my unexpected trip to Maryland—Bette.

Here, let me explain.

More often than not, when I'm around my sister-in-law for extended periods of time, her hairstylist side gets twitchy and she plays around with the colors she foils throughout my hair.

That is why I am currently serving as a human Troll doll while she revamps the purple, pink, and red, going as far as adding a few black pieces to really make the others pop.

My phone vibrates against my leg, and when I see the preview of the message, I have a good feeling who my texter is.

UNKNOWN: Hey, Skittles, where've you been?

ME: Mason?

MASON: Yup!

> MASON: *GIF of guy dressed as a bag of Skittles dancing*

Three texts in and I'm already rolling my eyes. He's so proud of his oh-so-clever nickname.

Guuuurl! Don't play. You know you're charmed by it.

Nope. I refuse to let him work his Casanova-ness on me.

> ME: How'd you get my number?

> MASON: Grayson.

That gives me pause. I would have thought if anyone gave it to him, it would be Em, the little matchmaker.

What is happening here?

First there was E, though not necessarily advocating for Mason specifically, telling me to at least crack a window when it comes to letting the football set into my life.

Now G is…what? Giving Mason his stamp of approval?

What's going on?

> ME: Why did G give you my number?

> MASON: I decided to take my life in my hands and ask him for it because I was worried about you.

I blink. And blink again.

That answer is so unexpected I'm not really sure what to think.

Are you serious? How are you not aww-ing right now? That was totally sweet.

Sweet? *Sweet?* No. Uh-huh. I cannot think of anything Mason Nova does as sweet.

> ME: Why?

> MASON: You weren't in class, and the last time I saw you, you were upset and doing your best Cinderella impression, except you forgot to leave a shoe behind.

Do not be charmed by him. I repeat, do not *be charmed by him.*

"What's got you all smiley over there?" Lyle, one of Bette's longtime clients, asks from his chair across from me. He's the owner of Espresso Patronum, the same coffee shop Em joked I should take Mason to, and he makes the trek down from Jersey for color touchups to his neon green and hot pink tips and side shavings.

Am I smiley? *Shit!* I am. It's bad enough my inner cheerleader is doing toe touches and herkies over Mason's text messages. *I* need to stay strong.

"Nothing."

"Friends don't lie to each other. Come on, Kay, tell Uncle Lyle why you look so happy staring at your phone."

"Uncle Lyle?" Bette snorts.

"What?" He shrugs. "Between you doing my hair and all of you coming to Espresso Patronum through the years, haven't I earned honorary uncle status?"

Lyle is one of my favorite people on earth. He's ridiculous, flamboyant, and just generally awesome. Add in his epic *Harry Potter*-themed coffee shop and it was destiny for him to be a part of my life.

"Oh wait, let me guess—is it a dick pic?" His turquoise eyes glitter with possibility.

"*Lyle!*" Bette chastises.

"What?" He's the picture of innocence. "If I got sent a dick pic, I'd be smiling."

"You're saying Kyle has been sending you pictures of his dick while you've been here?" Bette's hands go to her hips.

"Ooo, good question. You *have* been smiling a lot," I add.

"No." Lyle's pout is a thing of sympathy-inducing beauty. "The only pictures my husband has sent me are of babies and toddlers while he spends the day playing uncle."

"He's with Holly and the kids?" Bette asks, referring to Kyle's best friend.

"Yup, and he *did* send me some quality DILF porn." He pulls his phone from his pocket. "Here, look."

Bette's hands cover my *virginal* eyes as if I've never seen porn before. "*Lyle!*"

"What?"

I push Bette's hands off me to see the screen, but the image on it is far from X-rated. It's hot AF, but definitely safely in the PG category.

"Shit, I think my ovaries just exploded." Bette sighs.

"Good—I'm dying to become an aunt." My comment earns me a flick on the ear.

I may not be ready for the whole kids thing like my very married, very in love, very needs to get on procreating because I want to spoil some babies sister-in-law, but I can't deny it's a very accurate description.

How else is a woman supposed to react to seeing MMA Champion Vince Steele cradling his baby against his sexy bare chest?

> MASON: *GIF of Chris Pine saying, "I'm Cinderella's prince."*

> MASON: Where'd you go? Don't ghost on me again without telling me if you're okay.

What is he trying to do to me? He's a playboy—he shouldn't care why I disappeared. Honestly, I'm surprised he noticed and wasn't too busy with a jersey chaser to do so.

> ME: I'm fine. Everything is good.

> MASON: Why'd you run out of the party?

That's a little tricky to explain. I don't want to lie to him—for some reason the idea doesn't sit right with me, which is yet another thing for me to worry about when it comes to Mason Nova—but I can be vague on the specifics.

> ME: My brother was in the hospital.

> MASON: Is he okay?

> ME: Yeah he's fine.

> MASON: Really? You've been MIA for days.

He really seems concerned.

So? You've seen he's not a bad person.

That is true. Mason is a good person, but he's still a fuckboy. I need to remember that.

> ME: Yeah really. He's the WORLD'S WORST patient, so I stayed to help Bette take care of him.

> MASON: Got it. When are you coming back? I miss you.

My heart trips when I read that.
Shit!
Not good.
You stay the fuck out of this, heart. We will not be falling for Casanova.

> ME: *rolls eyes*

When in doubt? Use sarcasm.

> MASON: Seriously, class is boring without you.

> ME: You'll see me Thursday. And don't you have a class right now?

> MASON: Yeah, but this one is boring too.

> ME: I'm sensing a trend here...

> MASON: It's your fault.

> ME: How?

> MASON: I had to drink 2—yes, count them, 2— coffees today because you weren't there. So now you need to entertain me.

> ME: Yeah...I wouldn't go that far.

> MASON: What are you doing?

> ME: Being Bette's coloring book.

MASON: ??? *hand up questioning face emoji*

ME: She wanted to try these new colors in my hair so she's adding more flavors to the rainbow.

I laugh at my joke that plays on his corny nickname for me.

MASON: Show me.

I snap a pic of me with the foils in my hair making a funny face and hit send.

MASON: It's a good look for you, Skits. *winky face emoji*

ME: Pay attention to class.

MASON: *thumbs-up emoji*

Why does he have to be so charming?

Playboy.

Football player.

Constantly in the spotlight.

Still, as much as I remind myself of all the reasons why I should stay away from Mason, I can't help but return his texts.

"Oh...I see," Bette singsongs, blatantly reading my screen from over my shoulder.

"What?" I hide my phone under my leg.

She's silent while she sections out another chunk of hair, the foil crinkling in my ear as I wait.

"I was hesitant to believe the guys when they told me, but all *evidence*"—her eyes shift to the leg hiding my phone then back to me—"proves they might be correct."

Say what now?

"Don't give me that face, Kay."

I work to smooth out the wrinkles forming between my brows. "You know I hate when you guys 'discuss' me." I make exaggerated air quotes around the word.

"Eh." There's zero shame in her response. "I'll never apologize for checking in and making sure you're okay."

"And yet…instead of asking *me*, you pow-wow with my brothers. Yeah, makes total sense."

"Don't go getting butthurt." Done with my hair, Bette comes around to sit in the free chair next to me. "You are one of the most obstinate people I know." She holds up a hand when I try to interrupt. "It's not necessarily a bad thing"—that's a bald-faced lie—"but you do this thing…"

"What thing?" I prod when she doesn't continue.

Bette jumps up from her seat, shuffling around, cleaning up. She can never sit still when she's anxious about something. In this case, something = me.

"You…" Sheet by sheet, she lays the loose foils on top of each other, avoiding all eye contact.

"Bette."

She blows out a breath with enough force to ruffle her bangs.

"You do this thing where you put on a brave face to make sure none of us worry about you. It's like all the time you needed us maxed out your capacity to let others take care of you, so you hold back."

"I don't do that."

"Not with us." She retakes her seat and takes my hands in hers, running her thumbs over the rings of my family. "The only time you ever act like the old Kay is when you're at The Barracks or with us, but when others are around…you retreat, hiding the outgoing, confident Kay who dominates the tops of stunts."

I look away, unable to handle the compassion swimming in her eyes. She's right. In the last year, as my circle continues to grow and the opportunities to be the old Kay, as she put it, lessen, I have become more cognizant of the divide in my personality.

"What does this have to do with…Mason?" I choke out his name.

"G says when you're around him, you aren't just Kay, you're PF."

Is that true? Am I my true self with Mason? And if so, what does that mean?

An hour later, with my hair washed and blown out straight and my side bangs freshly trimmed, I'm climbing into Pinky when my phone vibrates in my pocket. Sure enough, it's my new pen pal.

> MASON: We miss you!!!!

> MASON: *picture of the lunch crew with sad faces*

I shake my head and laugh. Damn charming bastard.

> ME: Since when did you all become so codependent?

> MASON: Well I don't know about the girls, but Grayson, Trav, and I don't have anyone to steal fries from. *three French fry emojis*

Of course they want me for my food.

> ME: You could try buying your own for a change *emoji of girl with head tilt and hand out*

> MASON: But I like the way yours taste *rainbow emoji* *tongue emoji*

> ME: *rolls eyes* Stop trying to make it sound dirty.

> MASON: When will you be back???

> ME: I'm trying to leave to drive back now but SOMEONE won't stop texting me.

> MASON: You CAN'T be talking about me. You KNOW you wait with bated breath for my messages to come through.

God, so cocky.

> ME: Whatever helps you sleep at night.

> MASON: I know you love me. *winky face emoji*
> Drive safe.

He sure thinks a lot of himself.
Don't act like you don't like him.
NO!

> ME: I will.

> MASON: So you don't deny you love me?

Damn he's incorrigible.

> ME: *rolls eyes* Puh-lease.

I drop my phone in the cup holder, start Pinky, and put her into gear. As much as I want to, I can't deny that I have a smile on my face as I head back to school. Maybe Bette has a point.

CHAPTER
TWENTY-THREE

I should be drained.

I should go back to the frat, grab some food, call Brantley back, and then pass out on my bed, maybe toss in some studying for good measure.

What I shouldn't do is see Kay.

Hell, I shouldn't even *want* to see her.

Except…

Walking out of the indoor practice field, what do I do?

I pull out my phone and text her.

I have no way of explaining it, and no matter how hard I try to deny it, I want to see her.

No.

I *need* to see her.

> ME: Are you back yet?

> SKITTLES: Got back about an hour ago.

> ME: What are you doing?

> SKITTLES: Studying in my room.

Jackpot!

Now I know where to find her.

Shifting my Shelby into gear, I head for her dorm. I park in the lot closest to Eagle Hall—thanks to my supreme eavesdropping skills, I know the building and room number—only to smother a curse when I see I need keycard access to enter.

Well, there's your sign. Do I need to put it on the jumbotron for you to get the message? FIND. EASIER. PUSSY.

You would think he would know better by now. I don't give up.

Besides, I'm Casanova, one of the kings of campus—who's gonna tell me no?

I spot a cluster of students among the benches in the courtyard, and after the typical round of "Hey, Casanova," "Good game last week," etc., one of them lets me into the building.

Having been delayed enough, I forego the elevator, taking the stairs two at a time until I reach the third floor and head for apartment 311.

Now what? What's the play? You don't have a plan, do you? Oh, that's rich. Way to fumble, Nova.

Sonofabitch. That fucker in my head is right. What the hell is my plan? I can't stand out here all night staring at the door.

Deep breath in. *Hut-hut.*

Knock-knock.

My palms are sweaty, and my heart beats like I've run a forty-yard dash as nerves course through my body while I wait for someone to open the door. I don't even recognize this person whose hair stands on end at the soft pad of footsteps from within the apartment.

All of that fades away when my reason for being here is revealed.

"Mason?"

Fuck me sideways.

I couldn't even count the number of times I'm hit on throughout the course of a day by women in much skimpier clothes than this, but with Kay standing before me with her long colorful blonde hair—straight again, not curly—falling around her shoulders and down her back in a white beater-style tank and a pair of baggy U of J sweats hanging low on her hips, I don't think I've seen a sexier sight.

The top is tight enough that it displays all those mouth-watering curves I only just learned she has, and the sweats emphasize her tiny stature with the way they still end up covering her feet even while rolled at the waist.

My gaze homes in on the strip of pale skin revealed between the hem of her tank and the top of the lounge pants. Nothing else registers as I'm transfixed by the nip of her waist and the swell of her hips. She may be pint-sized, but she's still *all* woman.

Gorgeous, sexy, I-need-to-fuck-her woman.

"Mason?" Questions swirl in the dark storm clouds of her eyes.

This is where you say something, Nova.

The sound of my name falling from those lips that have tempted me from day one breaks me from my stupor.

Two steps and I'm in front of her.

The rest happens like it's the final seconds of the game and we're down by six.

One second and my hands reach out.

One more and I'm cupping her face.

Tick-tock. My fingers are tangled in her hair.

Tick-tock. Her face is tilted up to mine.

3

I'm bending.

2

I close the last inch of space.

1

My mouth crashes to hers.

Touchdown!

The first taste of her lips feels like coming home.

I'm no longer lost, and all is right in the world.

I've never *wanted* a woman before. They always seemed to be available. If I wanted one, all I had to do was look up and there'd be one willing to service my dick. Putting in work to get a female's attention? I don't know what that is.

But this? Kay? It feels like the missing piece of the puzzle falling into place.

Honestly, I'm not even sure if she likes me all that much, but I can't stay away.

Her lips part with the need to breathe, and I slip my tongue inside to explore and tangle with hers.

If I thought the first touch of her mouth was life-altering, nothing, I mean *nothing* could have prepared me for when she kisses me back.

Tentatively her hands skim up the contours of my stomach, and my abdominals contract under the touch. Her fingers continue up my chest, knocking against the brim of my backward Hawks cap as they lock around my neck.

Time has lost all meaning, my play clock down for the count. It could have been seconds, minutes, *hours* that we kiss in the open doorway before I finally manage to pull away.

If I thought she was beautiful before, she's a fucking vision now: lips swollen from our kisses, eyes dazed as they blink up at me, chest heaving trying to catch her breath, pulse pounding on the side of her neck, begging me to bite it.

I squeeze my eyes shut; if I look at her any longer I'm liable to pick her up, find the nearest flat surface, and fuck her so hard she won't know where she ends and I begin.

"What—" Her voice croaks, and she clears it. "What was *that*?"

Making a gameday decision, I drop the Casanova persona I use as a shield and go with the truth.

"Something I've been thinking about doing for a while now."

My honesty pays off as one of those smiles she generally reserves for anyone who *isn't* me spreads across her face.

"And now that you have?" she sasses.

Of course she wouldn't let me completely off the hook.

"I want to do it again." I move an arm to hook around her waist, pulling her in so our bodies are flush against each other.

"Do you now?" One sculpted brow rises toward her hairline.

"Oh yeah. The sooner the better."

I bend down to do just that, but she stops me with a hand on my chest. "I'm not one of your jersey chasers, Mase."

It's the first time she's called me Mase, and I gotta say, I dig it.

"I know that, Skittles. I've never tracked down a jersey chaser before."

"*Mmmhmm.*"

I squeeze her tighter. "You're pretty much all I've thought about since you Cinderella-ed."

Yeah. *snorts* Only since then. *To borrow a move from your precious Skittles, this is me rolling my eyes.*

"I can't believe you're using a Disney princess as a verb."

"You going to invite me in, Skit?"

Her cute little nose scrunches in thought. "I'm thinking about it."

I stroke my thumb along her jaw. "Come on. You know you wanna."

"I'm not going to have sex with you." She drops down from where she rose up on tiptoe and steps out of my hold.

"That's not why I want to come in."

She gives me a *Get real* look, and I laugh.

"I haven't seen you in almost *five* fucking days. You're *all* I've thought about, and it's been driving me crazy. When you weren't in class this morning, I almost walked out to track you down."

Holy shit. Who are you and what have you done with the real Mason Nova?

"I just want to spend time with you." I nudge her backward. "So come on, Skit." Another nudge. "Invite me in."

Why don't you offer her your balls too, you should-be-playing-second-string-you're-acting-like-such-a-pussy impostor.

I get one of her signature eyes rolls, but she gestures for me to enter. Not giving her a chance to change her mind, I shut the door behind me and follow her to the bedroom.

There's an old episode of *Gilmore Girls* playing on the small flat-screen on her desk, and a textbook is spread out on her hot pink comforter.

"*Ooo*, KayKay has a boy in her room." The singsong voice brings my attention to the open laptop also on her bed.

"Says the guy who had a random chick in his bed when I came by to pick you up for class this morning," the guy in the blue University of Kentucky hat says to the first one; I suspect it's Dante Grayson.

"I thought you had a thing for Rei?" Kay asks, walking closer to her laptop.

"She was *not* random—she's on the volleyball team," Dante says to blue hat then turns familiar-looking brown eyes to Kay. "And I *hate* that you two"—he bounces a finger between Kay and her friend—"talk all the time. Besides, KayKay, you know you are the one who owns my heart. When are you going to make Mama's dreams come true and marry me?"

"I'm not even going to dignify that with a response." Kay laughs, looking over her shoulder at me and rolling her eyes.

"Ouch," Dante cries. "What the fuck, JT?"

"Stop hitting on my best friend," blue hat—JT, I guess—warns.

"As riveting as I find old reruns of *Beavis and Butt-Head*, I think I'll skip this particular episode. Don't get arrested. Love you." Kay ends the call as they say their goodbyes then turns to me, pink coloring her cheeks.

"I take it that was the younger Grayson?" I point toward her computer.

She nods. "And my best friend JT."

My eyebrows rise when she walks around me to shut the door.

"If I leave it open, we'll have all my roommates in here in minutes and I'll *never* get back to studying."

I toe off my sneakers, grab one of her zebra print pillows, and settle onto the bed.

"Sure, just make yourself at home." Still, she climbs up next to me, pulling on the legs of her sweats and situating her laptop after crossing them.

"Cute." I tap one of the footballs on the socks peeking out from under her bent knee.

Wrapping my hand around her tiny foot, I run a finger up her instep, unable to resist touching her.

Five days is way too long to go without seeing her. It's like the drought forced me to acknowledge that…I'm starting to…catch…

…

…*feelings*.

That is one scary-as-fuck realization.

"How's your brother doing?" It's the only thing I can think to ask with my mind spinning.

"Better. Thanks for asking." I get another one of those smiles.

"Can I ask you a personal question?"

Her eyes crinkle in the corners, and I can feel her gearing up to give me shit.

"Since when do you *ask* permission?"

I give her foot a warning squeeze.

"What happened to your parents?"

She drops her gaze, her comforter suddenly fascinating. "My dad was killed by a drunk driver when I was in high school."

"Damn, baby." I run my thumb over the ball of her foot, trying to soothe her. I had suspected as much, but it still sucks to hear.

I notice she didn't say anything about her mom, but she looks too crestfallen to push.

"Is that why you two are so close?"

"Yeah." There's a long beat of silence before her gaze finally rises back to mine. "He almost gave up everything to be able to be my guardian." She laughs, but there's no humor in it. "The easiest solution would have been to let Pops, JT's dad"—she points to her laptop, indicating the friend she was talking to when I showed up—"take me, but he refused. It was quite the declaration."

"Wow."

"Yeah." She starts to pick at invisible lint on her sweats. "I admire E so much for his conviction when it came to me, but Bette is still my favorite person of their duo."

"You call her Bette?"

She tilts her head at me as if confused by my question. "It's her name."

"I get that. What I mean is you call everyone else you're close with by a letter, so why don't you call her B?"

She takes a moment, almost as if she didn't notice she did it. "I guess it's because she's more like a mom than my sister-in-law."

"So, it's like a sign of respect?"

"I guess." She shifts the laptop onto the bed. "She married my brother—which was always in the cards for them—to qualify as my guardian too. She put her entire life on hold to make sure mine didn't have to change. I never want her to doubt how grateful I am for everything she's done for me."

Taking a chance, I shift my hand from her foot up her leg, massaging her calf until I reach her knee.

"My dad died when I was younger too."

"He did?"

"It's different than yours. I was only two so I don't even remember it, but...yeah."

She still hasn't shifted away from my touch, and in my boldest move since kissing her, I pull her to rest against my side.

"It doesn't make the loss any easier, though."

"No." I run a hand along her arm, the silky quality of her skin too much to resist. "But like you, I also got lucky."

"How so?" Goose bumps follow in the wake of my touch down to her wrist.

"First there's my mom, who is the best." She stiffens, but I just continue to run my fingertips down toward her hand then up to her elbow and back again. "And Brantley, my stepdad, doesn't treat me any different than my half-siblings."

"You have siblings?" She starts to play with the hem of my t-shirt, the sporadic touches on my stomach making it hard to concentrate.

"Yeah, twins actually. They're in high school now."

"Wow, twins."

My dick twitches at the scrape of a nail under my navel.

"I've met a few sets of twins before. I'm always fascinated when they have that twin connection."

I laugh, nodding. My brother and sister definitely have that.

When her fingers make their way fully underneath my shirt, stroking the cuts of my abs, the last of my control snaps. I bend over and plant my lips on hers.

This time she doesn't hesitate in kissing me back. Her mouth opens to mine and I suck her bottom lip between my own. Her nails rake across the back of my neck, the action causing a shiver to run down my spine and straight to my dick.

I've hooked up with a lot of girls—and I mean *a lot*; I'm not going to apologize for it—but none of those encounters compare to kissing Kay.

It might be because I barely kissed most of them, but I suspect it was the lack of emotion that made them fall flat.

With Kay? I can't stop the feels, and that scares the *shit* out of me.

I. Don't. Date.

So why do I want to date her?

Date? DATE? Why can't you just fuck her and be done with it? Why do you have to date?

Not wanting to ruin the moment by thinking too hard, I trail kisses along her jaw, down her neck, and behind her ear. Inhaling deeply, I'm hit with the same peppermint scent as the night of the Alpha party.

"Why does your hair smell like peppermint?" I can't help but ask.

"It's my conditioner." She moans when I take her earlobe between my teeth and nibble.

"I like it."

"We need to stop." She presses a hand to my chest when I move to lay her under me. "I really do need to study."

With all the blood in my body pooled in my dick, even my inner coach doesn't have an opinion.

I'm all for studying—at least if it's her naked body. I go for another kiss only to be halted again.

"If you keep trying to distract me, I'm going to kick you out."

That is the last thing I want. I pull back, lifting her up in the process.

"I'll be good. I promise." I draw an X over my heart.

"Somehow I doubt that," she says, but she shoots me a grin.

Needing to prove her wrong, I reach into my bag for my English textbook. Might as well get a jump on the chapters I need to read.

Our little make-out sesh caused her purple highlighter to fall off the bed, so Kay hops down to retrieve it. When she bends over, she flips her hair over her shoulder, and I catch a glimpse of black I never noticed by her ear.

"How have I never noticed this before?" I stroke a finger down the four black silhouettes running behind her left ear.

"I guess because you're usually on my right side." She tries for nonchalance, but her nipples are currently doing their best to poke through her top. "Plus, it's small." She starts to trace some of the lines of my tribal sleeve.

I've had many ladies feel up my tattoo before, but none felt as sensual as her casual touch.

She reclaims her spot on the bed, but I tilt her head and continue to admire the ink. I don't know why I'm so shocked she has a tattoo, but I am.

"Why does this look so familiar?" I continue to trace it.

"It's Peter Pan, Wendy, and her brothers flying to Neverland." Her voice comes out breathy.

"Why?"

She shakes her head. "It's personal."

"One day you'll have to tell me about it. Do you have any others?"

She nods and shifts to lean back against the pillows again, my hand finally dropping with the movement.

She pushes on the band of her sweatpants, causing my dick to jerk back to attention, the breath stilling in my lungs at the glimpse of a Calvin Klein band before it's also lowered and a set of angel wings appears on her right hip.

The detailing on the tattoo is exquisite. I try to focus on it, really I do, but the sight of her hip bone and the proximity of the tattoo to the place I only need her to shift the fabric down another few inches to see has my balls jockeying to the line of scrimmage.

I'm painfully hard, the zipper of my jeans doing its best to brand me in a place no man wants branded.

Like I did with the ink behind her ear, I reach out to trace this one as well.

"It's for my dad," she croaks.

"I could have guessed that."

Bullshit. You probably couldn't even tell her your own name if asked right now. The only thing you'd be able to guess is what she tastes like.

"Okay, you *really* need to stop touching me. I have to study."

We shift back to rest side by side against her pillows—me with my book, her with her laptop—and we settle in to work.

Trav: Dude where you at?

I read Trav's message, surprised to see it's almost midnight. Kay and I have been studying for hours.

There may have been a lot more touches and a few kisses thrown in, but you're not gonna hear a complaint from me.

My dick, however? He hasn't stopped bitching about turning into a Smurf my balls are so blue.

ME: Damn, didn't realize it was so late. I'll be back soon.

TRAV: Where'd you go?

ME: Studying with Skittles.

TRAV: Studying? *wink wink*

ME: Yeah, you know, with books and stuff *book emoji*

TRAV: I'm not sure what to address first, the fact that YOU are STUDYING, like ACTUALLY studying, or that it's with a chick.

ME: *middle finger emoji*

TRAV: LOL. You wish you could have a piece of this.

TRAV: *boomerang of Trav's body*

ME: Moron.

TRAV: Love you too, bro.

"Leaving?" Kay looks over when I start to pack up.

"Yeah, I didn't realize how late it is. I have to be at the gym at six."

"Just thinking of being up that early makes me want to throw up."

Her disgusted look is comical.

"I'll walk you out." She hops off the bed.

The apartment is quiet, all the other doors closed; most likely everyone else is asleep.

Kay opens the front door with a quick, "Bye." If she thinks I'm going to leave with only a lame goodbye, she has another thing coming.

I pull her body flush with mine, every inch I can manage in

contact with her. Using my free hand, I tilt her face up and kiss her.

I keep this one sweet instead of letting it heat like its predecessors.

"Sweet dreams, Skittles," I breathe against her lips.

"Bye, Mase." Her voice hitches on my name then squeaks when I give her ass a hard squeeze for the road.

I could get used to her calling me Mase.

My head is still spinning from the kiss—well, I guess kisses—Mason laid on me last night.

Hold up. Don't undersell this. *fans self* That hot piece of man meat laid the fiercest first kiss on your lips. Oh boy, I need a Gatorade just thinking about it.

I can't even deny my inner cheerleader. That kiss damn near melted my brain it was so straight fire—which, if you ask me, is totally unfair. How the hell am I supposed to resist him when he looks the way he does and goes around kissing me like *that*?

Actually…

If I'm being really honest, I had Mason on the brain *before* he came in with his kamikaze lips.

I haven't been able to get Bette's words out of my head since she dropped them like a bomb.

For G, a person who doesn't even get to witness the PF side of me all that often, to be the one to say that's how I am with Mason makes me reevaluate our every encounter. It's not right. That can't be true. Can it?

God! Even to myself I sound like a crazy person.

Still…

Walking across the blue mat, shoulders rolled back, spine

straight, head not hidden by a hat but held high, giant bow firmly in place, I am 100% PF Dennings. She was born here at The Barracks.

This place.

This home.

It's my sanctuary. No bullies. No worries about the press. No one caring who I am outside of one half of a stunting pair that could consistently hit tricks few in the world can.

Put me at the top of the pyramid and my smile and facials will be so big I'll be damned if the judges will be able to look away.

I wouldn't still be here—or a functioning human being—if it weren't for this place. Hell, half the reason coaching is so important to me is to hopefully be for someone what Coach Kris was to me.

But, outside these walls? When I'm off mat at a competition? I avoid attention like it carries Ebola.

So why am I drawn to Mason Nova when he's patient zero?

I'm folded over, my chest to the mat, legs spread in a full straddle when my phone vibrates beside me.

MASON: Hey Skittles! Wanna hang out later?

ME: Shouldn't you be at practice right now?

MASON: Taking a short break.

ME: Do you regularly text girls during practice?

MASON: Girls? No. You? You're worth the risk of having to run suicides.

Damn you, Mason Nova, stop being so damn charming.

MASON: So what do you say? Study together again later?

ME: Can't, I'm working.

I tell myself that's not disappointment I feel. Also, why am I texting him back? Why am I engaging?

Because you liiiiiiiike him, my inner cheerleader singsongs.

I swear if she starts singing about us kissing in a tree, I'm gonna slap a bitch.

> MASON: *GIF of J-Lo folding her arms and pouting*

Shit! I totally like him.
I'm so screwed.

> ME: Go back to practice. Michigan isn't going to beat themselves this weekend, especially on the road.

> MASON: It's hot when you talk football.

> ME: *rolls eyes*

> MASON: Did I ever tell you how I LIVE for making you roll your eyes at me?

I swear he must be incapable of turning off the charm.

> ME: Mase.

> MASON: OMG you called me Mase. *heart eyes emoji*

I hope he does have to run suicides later. With full pads, too.

> ME: Grrr.

> MASON: *GIF of Barbie saying, "Rawr."*

> ME: OMG! I'm gonna stop answering now!!!!

> ME: PRACTICE!!!!!!!!!!!

> MASON: Fine. BE that way! I'll see you in the AM. I'll be the ridiculously attractive guy holding your coffee.

Mason's penchant for bringing me coffee and sitting with me in class has already made the rounds on the UofJ411 Instagram account. Social media is the bane of my existence, and Mason Nova? Well let's just say #CasanovaWatch trends *all* the time around campus.

Yet I don't put a stop to his escalating attention. Deep down, I don't want to.

Shit! I can't think about this stuff anymore. I specifically came to The Barracks over an hour early again to banish the frustrating —and yes, attractive—coffee-bringing football player from my thoughts.

Tonight I need to focus on my plan for rearranging a few partner stunt pairings on the Admirals.

The marriage between base and flyer is a delicate balance. Sure, the flyer is the one getting tossed in the air, doing flips and tricks, but they are only able to accomplish them if they can trust their base is there to catch them—literally.

Coach Kris has taken my skill as a flyer and my history with JT, helping me hone it and develop it into having the best eye in finding these pairings.

Turning up the volume of the Birds of Prey song playing through my AirPods, I warm up on the tumble track to get my head on straight.

Bye-bye thoughts of Mason Nova.

Time to get to work.

CHAPTER
TWENTY-FIVE

My texts with Kay play through my mind while I wait for the barista to make our coffees. To say I was disappointed she was too busy to hang out last night would be an understatement.

I can't believe how much not seeing her is messing with my head.

Females affecting the great Casanova longer than it takes to tie the condom off is rarer than me fumbling the football.

I don't fumble—ever.

I hope you're okay giving up football, asshole, because they don't let women play in the NFL, and you, sir, are growing a vagina.

Kay, Kay, Kay. It's all Kayla this and Skittles that with you. What the fuck happened to football? You know, the thing you've been working toward your whole life?

Fuck me, my inner coach has been entirely too vocal since Kay came into my life. I don't understand the problem. You would think out of any chick on campus, he'd be happy I chose to text one who yells at me to actually focus on football.

Kay is back in her usual seat when I walk in, and when she looks up, for the first time ever, she gives me a smile.

Mine.

I stride across the room and up the stairs with purpose. We may have spent the hours after she got home from work texting before she went to bed, but it's not enough. I need to learn her class schedule. I refuse to go another day without being able to see her. It's unacceptable.

*I'm done, Nova. *tosses clipboard and stalks off the field**

Unlike the other times I've brought her caffeine fix, she doesn't wait for me to push it on her. Our fingers brush as she takes the paper cup from my hand, and I don't miss the way her nostrils flare at the contact.

Deny it all you want, but we both know you want me, baby.

With renewed swagger, I take my seat next to her, lean over to drop a kiss on the crown of her head, and settle back with my arm draped over the back of her chair.

Charcoal and blue swirl like a storm when she snaps her gaze to me. "*What* was *that*?" she whisper-shouts at me.

Giving her the biggest, dimple-showing, Casanova-y smile I have, I answer with, "Just saying hi."

Her eyes go from tropical storm to full-on Category 5 hurricane. "Since when do you say *hi* like *that*?"

I shrug and brush the hair that fell into her face during her huff behind her ear.

I don't answer, just stare. She's so damn beautiful. I hate that she hides under Yankees hats.

Out of the corner of my eye, I see the professor enter the classroom, and I know I'll only have another minute or two before class starts.

I shift again, bringing my face down to hers and simply inhale against her skin.

Strawberries?

A puff of air ghosts over my cheek as she trembles—mother*fucking* trembles—from my nearness.

"What happened to the peppermint?" I ask.

"Wh-what?" she stutters.

Not so unaffected now, are you, baby?

"Your hair." I run my fingers through her still-straight locks and flip them to my nose, breathing in the sweet scent of strawberries again.

"Oh." Her lashes flutter as she blinks out of the daze I put her in. "It's my dry shampoo." The multicolored strands slip from between my fingers as she jerks away from me. "Don't try to change the subject." She narrows her eyes. "Answer my question."

"What question might that be?"

The blush creeping up her neck might just be my favorite thing ever.

"Don't act like a dumb jock, Mason. That"—she bounces a finger between my mouth and her head—"is *not* how we say *hi*."

"I thought we cleared this up the other night."

Before she can lay into me for my non-answer, the lecture begins.

The next hour and fifteen minutes are the most entertaining of my college experience. Every side-eye given to me, every huff of frustration when Kay notices the questioning looks sent in our direction only spurs me on.

I absentmindedly trace patterns on her shoulder, play with the ends of her hair, and lean over to write in her notebook or to point out something on her laptop.

Never have I been known to stake a claim on a person like I'm blatantly doing with Kay, but I get a rush from it all the same.

When class is dismissed, I walk with my arm around Kay's shoulders, keeping her close to my body to avoid the bustle of students around us. She's so tiny I don't know how she doesn't get lost in the flow on the reg.

She tries and fails to push the limb off of her, and any time she does it, I only pull her to me tighter.

"*Seriously*, Mase." Ooo, that glare is colder than Green Bay in the playoffs. "What the *hell* are you doing?"

Instead of exiting the building, I guide us over to the wall and box her in with my body. Elbows braced on either side of her head, I bend down, lips brushing the shell of her ear as I whisper, "Have I told you what it does to me when you call me Mase?"

She shudders, chest heaving, eyes falling closed.

"Like I mentioned earlier..." I drag my nose down the fluttering pulse in her neck. "I thought we cleared this up the other night."

The moan that escapes when I place a kiss on the soft spot behind her ear goes straight to my balls.

"Still—" She clears her throat. "Still not clear."

Another kiss. "I told you." A nip of my teeth. "I don't chase girls."

"Then what—" She's practically vibrating as I trail kisses down her neck. "What do you call this?" She knocks her fist against my chest.

I place my thumbs underneath her chin, lifting her face to mine. "Me staking my claim." I take her lips with mine before she can push me away.

I meant for it to be quick, but like the other night, this kiss takes on a life of its own. Pillowy lips, the hint of coffee, little moans of pleasure, and that sense of…home.

The sound of catcalls is what gives me the presence of mind to pull away.

Fuck!

What this girl does to me…

Resting my forehead on hers, I try to regain my equilibrium.

"Come on, babe." I tuck her back under my arm. "Time to meet Grayson."

A small part of me—the one concerned with self-preservation —takes note of how Grant's eyebrows rise and his head cocks to the side when he spots us.

"No idea," Kay says to answer his silent question. "For some reason, this fool"—she jerks a thumb at me—"thinks he can go around kissing me and calling me babe like I'm his girlfriend or something."

Shit!

Am I acting like she's my girlfriend?

Do I even want a girlfriend?

Umm…

Spotting one of those famous eye rolls, I think if Kay is the one to fill the position, I can get on board with the girlfriend thing.

"You still walking me, *Cas-a-no-va*?" The sarcasm practically drips off my nickname.

"You know it, babe."

I wink.

She rolls her eyes—again.

She may have been the one to bring up me walking her, but she still avoids me by staying on the other side of the path. It's annoying.

It doesn't help that I spend the entire journey waffling between asking her out and cutting all ties.

Football has been my focus for so long, and it's hard to contemplate letting anything else matter as much.

It isn't until she tries to duck inside without saying a word that I jump into action, wrapping a hand around her wrist, stopping her and pinning her to a wall for the second time today. "Skittles." She tries to hide it, but I see the way her lips twitch. *Progress.* "Would you *please* do me the honor of going on a date with me?"

She blinks, not saying a word.

Finally, she rises up on her toes and presses a kiss to the underside of my jaw.

"I'll think about it."

Then she slips under my arm and disappears into the building before I can demand a real answer.

I rub a thumb over the spot she kissed, wondering what the hell just happened.

#THEGRAM

UofJ411

10,328 views

UofJ411 Who's the coffee for @CasaNova87 ?
#CoffeeDate #CasanovaWatch

@Bestiesandbooks: Are you taking orders @CasaNova87 ?
#IllTakeAPSL
@_The_art_of_reading_: Why does @CasaNova87 have TWO cups of coffee? #IsThatForMe #CasanovaWatch

UofJ411

12,8961 views

UofJ411 Study Buddies
#KillerGPA #CasanovaWatch

@68blackburnc: Need a tutor @CasaNova87?
@Acolon1729: What class is this? Is it human sexuality by any chance? #IllBringTheFlashCards #CasanovaWatch
@Annielaurel: Does he always cozy up like this in class? How do I get this assigned seating? #SaveMeASeat #CasanovaWatch

UofJ411

Mason caging Kay against the wall

15,683 views

UofJ411 Who's the girl @CasaNova87 ?
#KeepingSecrets #CasanovaWatch

@Ash_lovesbooks: Are you seeing this? #CasanovaWatch
@AshWonderWoman: Who are you kissing @CasaNova87
#SpinTheBottleMyWay
@Beccalynn1010: Pucker up baby! #KissKiss #CasanovaWatch

I love Fridays.

Who doesn't? TGIF and all that jazz.

We've already established how much I hate the AM, so any day I don't have to set an alarm automatically gets bumped to the top of the list.

Without any classes, the day is my own.

I sleep in.

Study.

Binge-watch some more *Gilmore Girls*.

All in all, a nice lazy day.

Typically I don't work on Fridays as there are no team practices, but I offered to run a stunting clinic since the roomies are traveling for an away game and I need a way to channel my energy into anything that isn't Mason Nova.

He wants to go on a date?

Can I do that? I mean, sure, I'm *capable* of doing it, but dating Mason Nova comes with all kinds of risks.

I'm pulling my hair into my classic high pony when my phone dings with a text.

Mase.

Oh my god. Why does the sight of his name on the screen make me smile? And when did I start thinking of him as Mase?

> MASE (Shit I'm screwed—I totally changed his contact name): You still owe me an answer.

> ME: New phone, who dis?

> MASE: Haha very funny, Skittles.

> ME: You know me. I'm a regular comedienne.

> ME: *GIF of man saying, "From what I hear, I'm very funny."*

> MASE: I miss you.

Damn! When he says stuff like that, it makes it hard to keep him at arm's length.

This sweet side is the one that has me wanting to ignore the drama, the speculation that surrounds him, and let him in.

Not now.

Time for a redirect.

> ME: How was the flight to Michigan?

> MASE: The usual, nothing special. What are you doing?

> ME: Heading to work then going out with G.

I chose my words purposely, and when his next text comes in, I know I hit my mark.

> MASE: So you can go out with him but not me???

> ME: ...

I know I'm evil.

G, CK, and I had plans to watch the U of J play Michigan at Jonah's, but I busted my knee falling from a stunt during the clinic last night.

Pizza in the dorm it is.

"Damn, Kay." CK hisses through his teeth when he catches sight of my swollen knee propped on a pillow.

"Yeah, not so fun." I shift, trying to find a more comfortable position.

"Do you need an ice pack?" He points toward the fridge.

I nod. "I'm so lucky to have you as a friend."

Even after a year, a blush still stains his cheeks at the compliment. There isn't a day that goes by that I regret forcing my friendship on CK. He is one of the most genuine, kindhearted people I know.

"Damn, Smalls." G walks in carrying the four pizzas I ordered. "Did you invite the Ninja Turtles over and forget to tell us?"

"Don't act like you and CK won't each polish off a pie. If you guys stay late enough, I might not even have leftovers."

"You know us so well," G states proudly, setting the pies out in the kitchen. He makes us each a plate then plops down next to me on the couch. "How'd you manage this anyway?" He lifts my legs to stretch them across his lap, readjusting the ice pack once I'm properly elevated.

"Stunting," I mumble around a bite of pizza as I watch our boys kick off to the Wolverines.

"JT isn't going to be happy when he hears about this." G taps the ice pack. "You know he hates when you have to stunt without him around."

When you're a female and your best friends in life are males, you get used to their overprotective tendencies, even when they're irrational. Also, a banged-up knee doesn't even come close to the worst injury I've sustained cheering. Plus it will be healed in under a week.

My gaze goes from where the Hawks hold the Wolverines to a fourth and three and shifts to G. I narrow my eyes and level him with a *You don't want to mess with me* look.

"And that is why we *don't* have to say anything to him about it."

"Mum's the word, Smalls." He mimes zipping his lips and throwing away the key. "Can I ask you a serious question now?"

I straighten at his tone, my knee twinging with the movement. No topic is off limits for us, but for him to ask permission lends weight.

"Of course, G." I reach for his hand, linking my fingers with his.

"Have you been holding up okay?"

"With?" I make a rolling motion with my hand.

"I know you avoid social media like the plague, but I also know T keeps you informed on anything she deems necessary for you to see."

Ah, okay, he means how I've been popping up in the CasanovaWatch hashtag.

"It's not my favorite thing." I choose my words carefully. If I show how stressed I've been, all my brothers will activate their overprotective mode. "But I got used to it with you." It's a lesser scale with G because he's not the campus playboy. "People grew bored with us, and I gotta hope the same will eventually happen here."

He watches me, his brown eyes boring into me as if looking for anything I might not be saying. Thank god he can't read me as accurately as JT can.

"Fine." He gives my hand a squeeze. "Just remember I got your back."

"Always."

The game continues and the Hawks look good. At some point, the camera pans over the cheerleaders, and we get a clear shot of Q.

"You know she likes you, right?" I casually say to CK.

The startled look on his face makes me laugh.

"I don't get why you're so surprised."

"It doesn't make sense," CK mutters.

"Why not?"

"Have you *seen* the way she looks?"

Yes, Q is gorgeous, but what CK fails to realize is he's no longer the same guy who arrived on the U of J campus as a freshman.

He's ditched the unfortunate glasses that did nothing for his face and replaced them with sleek Clark Kent-style frames that show off his beautiful baby blues. His crazy mop of hair is always—albeit reluctantly—cut and stylish thanks to Bette. Once G jumped on the make-CK-our-friend train, he started dragging CK along with him to the gym and now he fills out his t-shirts like never before.

"What's that got to do with anything, man?" G asks, echoing my thoughts.

"Girls like that don't go for guys like me."

"That's a load of crap," I argue.

I hate that he sees himself as an ugly duckling and not the adorkable swan he truly is. Damn high school bullies.

"Besides, she's a *cheerleader*."

Living in a small town in Kansas, he had to deal with every stereotypical jock/nerd scenario.

"So? I'm a cheerleader."

"That's different."

I know what he means. Being an all-star didn't prevent me from being bullied by my high school's cheerleaders. I at least had JT and a few others to help protect me from the worst of it, but not CK. He had to travel more than 1,200 miles to find his tribe—us.

"I think you should give her a chance." I wait for him to make eye contact before continuing. "I have a good feeling about her."

"You're just saying that."

"Pfft." I wave away the ludicrous statement. "I did tell her about E."

"She figured out your identity."

"Semantics."

I hold his gaze, letting what I'm saying really sink in. People are so focused on having that Instagram-perfect existence that they only see what looks good on paper instead of what really matters. Even after being friends for a year, it's a constant struggle for CK to see past how little sense our friendship makes held to those standards.

It's going to be exponentially harder for Q to get him to take her interest seriously.

"I'll think about it," he finally concedes.

Satisfied by his response, I let him off the hook—for now—and go back to watching the game.

Hours later, after the game is over, the Hawks having beat the Wolverines by two touchdowns, G and CK are gone and I've showered, and I do something I *never* thought I would. I initiate a conversation with Mason.

> ME: Only 2 TDs? Slacker *crazy-faced emoji with tongue out*

> MASE: I can't be a ball hog, baby. Gotta spread the love.

> ME: Didn't take you for a gentleman.

> MASE: I'll show you my chivalry.

> ME: Only YOU could make that a sexual innuendo.

> MASE: *GIF of Chris Tucker in The Fifth Element dancing and saying, "All night long."*

> ME: *rolls eyes*

> MASE: I love it when you roll your eyes at me, baby.

> ME: *big sigh* Stop calling me baby.

To be honest, I love it when he calls me pet names, which is the issue. Then again, that's the problem with kryptonite—it's your weakness.

> MASE: Why???

> ME: Because I'm not your baby.

> MASE: We'll see about that.

God he's so cocky.

And so, *so* bad for my self-control.

> ME: I'm surprised you're texting me.

> MASE: No one else I'd rather talk to. I'd call you if I wasn't at the hotel bar with the guys.

This is the Mason I'm having trouble wrapping my head around.

The charming, attentive, not-at-all-the-Casanova-he's-known-as guy.

> ME: Tell Trav that was one of the most BEAUTIFUL spirals I've EVER seen to Alex in the third, and tell Alex the breakaway it resulted in was its own type of beautiful as he crossed the goal line.

> ME: Also tell Noah what a bomb! *bomb emoji* *football emoji* 55 yarder! HOLY SHIT!!!

> ME: And tell Kevin I swear I felt the force of his sack in the fourth through the TV.

While I wait for him to respond, I pull up another episode of *Gilmore Girls*. I'm laughing at Kirk doing one of his many odd jobs when the episode is cut off by a FaceTime call.

Mase.

I run my hand through my damp curls, trying to tame my hair, and accept the call.

Mason, Trav, Noah, Alex, and Kevin are all jockeying for position in front of the camera.

"Hi?" I answer, confused.

"Skittles!" Mason shouts to be heard over the noise in the bar.

I see Trav shove him in the shoulder before taking the phone. "Kay, what are you doing wasting your time talking to this fool when you clearly like me so much more?"

More jockeying and Noah takes over. "No way, you two suck. She knows I can go the distance."

"Please. Who wants to sleep with the kicker?" Alex jokes from somewhere off to the side.

Again another change of hands. "Ladies...she obviously

needs a *real* man, and that's me." Kevin flashes me a flirtatious grin.

My belly hurts from laughing at all their posturing. "Boys, boys, boys. Who says I want *any* of you?"

"*Ooo*, you're a feisty one, aren't ya?" Alex asks.

Mason shoves his friends out of the way and reclaims his phone. "Will you assholes back off? I don't even know why I let you jerks take my phone."

Mason looks hot as always. His ever-present backward ball cap is on his head, and his eyes sparkle with excitement even with exhaustion behind them.

"I thought you said you weren't able to call?" I tease.

His dimples come out to play. "It is a little hard to hear you, but when I showed the guys your *compliments*, they kinda commandeered my phone."

"Aww, they love me."

His lips turn down in a frown. "Don't encourage them."

"Who me?" I place a hand on my chest.

"You still owe me an answer."

"I know." I give him a wink. "I'm gonna let you go so you can celebrate with the team."

His eyes narrow, the light green color made more prominent by the thick black lashes surrounding them.

Ooo, he's all smolder-y.

Time to go before my inner cheerleader has me agreeing to things I shouldn't.

"Bye Mase."

I hang up without waiting for a response. Almost as soon as I do, my phone pings with a text.

> MASE: You can't avoid me forever. Sooner or later you're gonna have to give me an answer.

CHAPTER
TWENTY-EIGHT

T he adrenaline from our win against Michigan yesterday hasn't eased as the plane rolls to a stop on the tarmac.

Last year we were good, but the way we're gelling now, there's no way we won't win it all this year.

Brantley hasn't stopped blowing up my phone since the game. Even now, a steady stream of texts and plans are coming through, the most recent a request for me to swing by the house to discuss what's next.

I love him and I appreciate all he does to help make this dream of mine come true, but *man*, it can be exhausting.

I'll admit, football is my life. Everything I've ever done can be traced back to trying to make it to the NFL one day.

So why is it I'm pulling up Kay's contact instead of my stepdad's?

> ME: Honey I'm home!!

> SKITTLES: Honey?? *rolls eyes* First babe, now honey?

> ME: What, you don't like pet names?

SKITTLES: Normally I would say you use them because you can't remember my name, but as much as I wish you WOULD forget my name, you haven't.

ME: So what's the problem with them?

ME: And I could NEVER forget your name, Skittles.

Trav claims the open seat next to mine on the team bus and laughs when he sees me texting. He doesn't need to ask to know who it is. The bastard takes great pleasure in how immune Kay is to my charms.

"Kay still giving you shit?" He doesn't even attempt to keep the laughter out of his voice.

"When isn't she?" I return my best friend's grin with one of my own.

SKITTLES: Thankfully for the Hawks, you have more follow-through on the gridiron than you do in your "dating" life.

Trav whistles through his teeth when I show him the screen. "Damn, bro. I take it you haven't tried asking her on a date again?"

"Haven't had a chance with us flying out to Michigan."

"So ask her out for this Friday. It's the last home game before we have to start reporting to the hotel early." He jerks his chin toward my phone. "I just wouldn't do it in a text."

Trav speaks with all the authority of the world's best boyfriend. One—disastrous—relationship does not make him an expert, especially when he's really as much, if not more of a manwhore as I am now—or at least was prior to meeting Kay.

Well if that isn't a sign, I don't know what is.

"You're probably right."

"So whatcha doin?" he asks when he sees me typing out a new message.

I may wait to ask her out until I see her in person, but there's no way in hell I'm waiting to do that any longer than I already have to. Brantley can wait.

> ME: I'll show you follow-through, babe.

> ME: Whatcha doin?

Trav rests his chin on my shoulder, blatantly reading the conversation.

"Dude, you are so clueless when it comes to this chick."

"Shut it."

> SKITTLES: Why should I tell YOU, "babe"?

"Have I mentioned how much I like her?"

"Back off." I growl at my friend.

> ME: Skit...

> SKITTLES: *rolls eyes* It's football Sunday—what do you THINK I'm doing?

> ME: I've told you you're perfect, right?

"Dude, your charm has never worked on her before." Another annoying chuckle. "What makes you think it will now?"

"Not helping." I hold up a hand with my thumb and forefinger less than an inch apart. "And you're this close to losing your best friend card."

> SKITTLES: When will you learn I'm immune to your charm?

Trav's bark of laughter when he reads that particular message almost makes me go deaf. "*Seriously* love her."

> ME: Want to watch the games together?

> SKITTLES: It wouldn't count as a date.

> ME: Wouldn't DREAM of it. I just want to see you.

> SKITTLES: FINE. The guys are coming over too so I GUESS you can join.

> ME: Trav says he's coming too.

> SKITTLES: Hi Trav!!! *smiley face emoji*

Trav nudges me with his elbow. "See? She *likes* me."
Hopefully not too much.
"Fuck off, bro, or I won't bring you."

> ME: Why does Trav get a smiley and not me??

> SKITTLES: *rolls eyes* Bring beer.

"I think she may have just replaced *you* as my best friend, bro."

I don't have anything to say to Trav's statement, because a part of me kind of feels the same way.

After a quick stop at the liquor store for the requested beer, Trav and I arrive at Kay's. We're hit with the delicious aroma of chili as soon as we step inside, and on cue, both our stomachs let out an audible rumble.

Spread out around the living room are all the people who make up our new crew of friends. My eyes track over each of their faces until they land on the one I'm searching for.

Mine.

Something—I'm not sure what—settles inside me when I spot her on the loveseat, loose *GIRLS WHO LOVE FOOTBALL ARE NOT WEIRD THEY'RE A RARE GIFT FROM GOD* shirt hanging down her arm and exposing her slender shoulder, legs sporting football-printed leggings thrown across Grayson's lap. I frown when I spot an ice pack resting over one of her knees.

"Beer here!" Trav calls out like a vendor at a baseball game.

"Hey, T," Kay calls back with a smile.

"What, no hello for me?" I tease.

"Well I'm happy to see Trav." Her gaze does a pass over my body. "Still not sure how I feel about you."

She's such a pretty little liar.

"What happened to the knee, Short Stack?" Trav passes out a round of beers before putting the rest in the fridge.

"Ooo, a crack about my size—how original."

I roll my eyes at them, Kay's signature move rubbing off on me.

"So what happened to the knee, Skittles?"

"Nothing really." She shrugs like it's no big deal. "Fell at work yesterday."

"Bad?" I don't like the idea of her being hurt.

"Nah, should be fine in a few days."

Grayson scoffs.

"Shut it, you." She pops him in the chest. "I swear all the men in my life are such babies."

"*All* the men in your life?" I arch a brow, projecting aloofness while I'm a riot of possessive jealousy on the inside. She is mine even if she doesn't realize it yet, and I don't share.

She rolls her eyes—of course. "You know that's not what I meant."

Agree to disagree, but we can revisit this later.

"Yeah, yeah, Skit. Let me see the knee." I tap the ice pack.

"It really is only a bruise."

"Then it won't take long for me to check it out."

"*Seriously?*" Another eye roll.

"Seriously, babe."

"Uck." She complains but rolls up the leg of her pants, revealing her swollen kneecap and one hell of an ugly bruise.

"Damn, babe." I circle my thumb across her battered knee. "That can't be fun to walk on."

"It does make things interesting." She pushes me on the shoulder. "Now move, I have to pee." She favors her leg as she gets up. "Grant Samuel Grayson, don't even think about it," she warns when he tries to pick her up.

He puts his hands up and slowly sits back down.

"Damn, full-named," CK murmurs around his beer, causing the others to laugh.

Each limping step she takes makes me want to scoop her up into my own arms. I do *not* like seeing her hurt.

"There's chili and brown rice in the crockpots on the counter. Help yourselves," she calls out before stepping into the bathroom.

Trav doesn't waste any time loading up bowls for us, moaning around the first spoonful.

"Who made the chili?" he mumbles between bites.

"Kay," Quinn answers.

"Oh man, Mase." He claims an open seat by Em. "You better lock this chick down." He shovels in another spoonful.

Trav may be ruled by his stomach, but I don't need it telling me what I already know. Kay is mine. Time she recognizes it.

She pulls up short when she sees me leaning against the wall outside the bathroom, and I don't miss the way she checks out the muscles in my arms where they're folded over my chest.

I push off the wall and stalk in her direction. As much as she tries to put up a hard front and act like I don't affect her, it all goes away the instant my lips touch hers.

I pull back before I completely lose my head, and dazed gray eyes blink at me.

"Mase?"

I swear my dick twitches any time she says my name.

"So what do you say, Skittles? Wanna go to dinner with me Friday night?"

The smile I'm not used to seeing aimed in my direction spreads across her face, and fuck if it's not the most gorgeous thing I've ever seen.

"Took you long enough."

Of course she couldn't answer with a simple yes.

"Yeah, yeah, yeah." I brush a curl behind her ear. "Shut up and kiss me again, smartass."

And she does.

I scoop her into my arms when we finally break apart. She may not have let Grayson help her, but I'll be damned if I'm going to watch her struggle again.

"Mase! What the hell are you doing? Put me down."

"My job."

"What does football have to do with carrying me?"

See this? How she refers to football as my job? This is what makes her different. Her inherent understanding of what I'm meant to do is why I could never consider her a jersey chaser.

"Nothing, but it's my job to help take care of my girlfriend." I'm shocked by how easy it was to say that. The word girlfriend hasn't been in my vocabulary for a long time. I became practically allergic to it, but it's like Kay is my EpiPen.

"Now I'm your *girlfriend*?" she taunts from the cradle of my arms.

"I *thought* we settled this."

"And I *thought* we cleared up the fact that you never actually asked."

"Isn't that what I just did?"

"No, you asked me on a date."

I rest my forehead on hers. "You're killing me."

"So put me down."

I shake my head. "I'm not talking about holding your weight."

I spin on my heel, taking us to her bedroom instead of the living room. Clearly, we have a few things to straighten out, and I'd prefer to do it without an audience.

Kicking the door shut, I stride over to the bed, settling her in my lap when I sit.

"I told you, babe—I don't date." I stop her before she can butt in. "So all this"—I circle a finger in the air—"the texting, the late-night hangouts where we *only* study, the walking you to class even from a distance, the kissing in public...those are all ways for me to say to you, and everyone else, that you are *mine*."

She drops her head and bangs it lightly on my chest. "Why is it that even when you say the most boneheaded things, you still manage to make me melt a little?"

I'm pretty sure she didn't mean it in a sexual way, but come on, I'm a guy—of course my mind goes there.

"You're melting? Can I feel?"

"*Mase.*" The way she groans my name goes straight to my dick.

I skim a hand over her legs and squeeze her body tighter against me. "Yeah, baby. Moan my name."

"You know what I *mean*." She pinches my side.

"I know." I palm her ass. "You're just so fun to tease. I think the better question is, do *you* know what *I* mean?"

"Yeah, even if you are a moron."

"You always say the nicest things to me." I feel her laugh as I kiss her forehead.

"Whatever. Can we please go back to watching football now?"

"Sure, babe."

With her still in my arms, I claim her original seat next to Grayson, settling with her in my lap and letting her stretch her leg out over him again.

"Do you want the ice pack back?" I point to it on the coffee table.

"She's already at her limit. She can ice again later."

It's nice to see I'm not the only one who induces an eye roll from Kay when Grayson answers for her.

"No, sorry, Dant—I was talking to Mase about Kay," he says, continuing his phone call.

"You're talking to D?" Kay asks.

"Yup."

"Tell him I said hi."

"Kay says hi." There's a pause as he listens to the end of the conversation we can't hear. "No, I'm not gonna tell her that. Fuck, Dant."

Kay giggles, and I can only assume the younger Grayson was making a pass at her—even if only by proxy.

"No, she banged up her knee, and the stubborn girl hasn't rested it the way she should."

"Drama queens," Kay complains.

A strand of her long blonde hair gets caught in the stubble I never bother to shave when we travel for away games, and I breathe in the familiar peppermint scent. Distantly, I hear Grayson talking to his brother. "Sure man, put him on."

He holds the phone out to Kay. "JT wants to talk to you."

Kay's head, which is resting against my chest, drops down a little as she sighs. "I swear I need new friends." She takes the phone and, as her greeting, says, "Don't even start with me."

All my focus is on her side of the conversation.

"It's *just* a bruise." Pause to listen. "I'm not lying." Big sigh. "I've been hurt worse." Longer pause. "Well I don't really have a choice now do I since you went to school seven hundred miles away." Pause. "James Michael Taylor, don't make me call Pops." Pause. "You know I would." Pause. "Well next time you're home you can be the one to help me instead." Pause. "Why don't you stop worrying about me and go worry about whether D is going to break your flyer's heart?" Pause. "Yeah, yeah, love you too."

My inner coach is up pacing the sidelines, and it takes everything in me to curb the jealousy I feel hearing her tell another man she loves him. Intellectually, I know this is her childhood best friend and I witnessed their easy affection earlier this week, but it doesn't mean I have to like it.

Kay hangs up and hands the phone back to Grayson. "I can't believe you ratted me out to JT."

"I didn't rat you out. He's watching the game with Dante. When he heard you were hurt, he demanded the phone."

"Damn overprotective bastard," she grumbles.

"You would think you'd be used to us by now," he muses.

The beast inside me settles as Kay snuggles back into my hold.

"I thought your brother's name was E?" Trav asks.

"It is."

"Who's JT?"

"He's my OG G. My un-biological brother."

"If you guys are so close, what made him pick Kentucky?" I ask.

I couldn't imagine going to school without Trav. The only way we both managed being at the U of J is because he redshirted freshman year.

"They gave him a full ride," Kay explains.

"He's a ballplayer?"

"Cheerleader."

"For real?" Trav chuckles.

"Yeah." Kay cuts a hard look at him. "He's the best *damn* partner stunt base in the country—hell, technically the world at one point."

"Yeah he is," Quinn agrees.

"You know him?" Trav asks.

"Not personally. I knew *of* him from all-stars. He and—" Her words cut off and she flicks her gaze to Kay, but it happens so fast I'm not sure. "He and his partner are *legends* in the all-star cheerleading circles."

"Oh no." Em snickers.

"I feel like we should make a drinking game out of this." Kay's tiny body bounces against me as she laughs.

"We'd be drunk every day."

"Could be fun."

"You guys suck." Quinn whacks Em with a pillow.

"It's not our fault you fangirl over him any time he video-chats with Kay."

Kay giggles then ducks as the pillow comes flying in her direction. She places a soft kiss to my jaw when I catch it easily, keeping her safe.

The ladies school Trav in all things collegiate cheerleading, but I lose track of the conversation when Kay starts to trace the lines of my tattoo. I don't even think she's aware she's doing it, but I sure as hell am.

It's not a grope or even an invitation into her panties like how the jersey chasers touch me, but the unconscious way she's doing it has me so hard I need to adjust her position in my lap.

"Selfishly I wish he had accepted the U of J's offer, but I can't fault him for taking Kentucky's," I hear Kay say when I focus back on the conversation.

Quinn whistles through her teeth. "Don't let Bailey know. She has a major lady boner for him. She practically tried to stalk him at StuntFest."

"Not that I'm complaining or anything, but where *is* your other roommate?" I ask.

"Oh shit—I forgot Bailey lives here too," Trav says around yet another spoonful of chili. He's on his second or maybe third bowl.

"My guess is she's still sleeping off her hangover," Quinn states.

"Oh yeah, she was partying it up big time at the hotel bar last night," Em adds.

My first two years, I took advantage of every opportunity my position on the football team and in the fraternity afforded me. I used to hate missing out on the celebration parties the AKs would throw whenever the football team won.

Now though? I couldn't care less.

What the hell is Kay doing to me?

The next hour or so is spent bullshitting, eating chili, and drinking beer while we watch the end of the one o'clock game.

Dallas is driving toward the end zone, completing a beautiful touchdown pass to their running back Miles Dennings. The play causes Kay to let out a whoop of glee, and Grayson groans as he hangs his head in shame.

Kay does a little victory dance in my lap, the movements going straight to my dick, and I need to reposition her again.

"Don't hate. It's not my fault you can't handle the Dennings Family Reunion."

"Clever play on your name, babe." I curl a hand over her hip, my thumb slipping beneath the hem of her shirt and tracing a figure eight on her soft skin.

She shifts to look at me, another one of those smiles in place. "It's also because I have *all* the Dennings in the league on my team too."

"Damn your team is stacked."

"I know."

Her confidence in her football knowledge is sexy as fuck.

"Can you get me another ice pack?" She nudges G with a foot.

"I'll get it for you," I offer.

"No. I'm comfy." She snuggles deeper into my embrace.

Progress, baby.

CHAPTER
TWENTY-NINE

KAYLA

The week passes by surprisingly quickly, and now it is the night of my big date with Mason. I'm still not sure how I feel about it. He represents everything I've shied away from for the last few years, but even I have to admit there is something that draws me to him.

Mason told me we weren't going anywhere too fancy, so I try to keep that in mind as I get dressed. I pull on a pair of light blue skinny jeans that have big rips throughout, but instead of showing skin, the holes reveal silk fabric in leopard print. They are stylish and make my butt look good.

With my jeans being a little edgier, I choose a simple tight black V-neck tee, and I finish off my outfit with a pair of kickass, black leather, over-the-knee high-heeled boots.

I leave my curls to tumble around me and keep my makeup in a simple pinup style. Before I know it, he's knocking on the door.

I open it and swallow hard at the sight in front of me.

Mason in a U of J football shirt and backward hat is hot.

But Mason in a black polo shirt, dark wash jeans, and hair styled in spiky disarray? That's next level.

"Damn, babe," he says as he does his own scan of me.

"Right back at ya."

He gives me one of his killer smiles, dimples and all, before pulling me into his body and claiming my mouth in a bone-melting kiss.

Any time he puts his mouth on me, my brain shuts off. I get lost in the press of his lips, in the stroke of his tongue, and the way he cradles my body makes me feel protected instead of tiny.

"Isn't the kiss supposed to be at the end of the night?" I ask when we finally break apart.

"Yeah, but if I didn't do that *now*, it would be *all* I thought about the whole time." He runs a thumb along my bottom lip. "Damn, not even smudged a little," he observes, referencing my red lips.

"It's a color stain. It's not meant to come off."

"I can think of a few ways we could put it to the test."

He keeps staring at my mouth, that finger still in place, the green of his eyes darkening more the longer he stares, acting like he didn't just throw down the naughty gauntlet.

"Should we go?" I put a hand on his chest and gently push him back out the door, closing it behind me.

"Nope." He drops an arm around my shoulders, not letting me put space between us as we walk toward the elevator. "This is a date, and I intend to get the full experience."

Holding hands and general touching happens in relation-ships, and I knew going into tonight I wouldn't be able to keep maintaining my distance. I tried to talk myself into ending things before they really start, but I couldn't.

"Holy shit." My steps halt as a steel gray 1967 Ford Mustang Shelby GT500 comes into view. "You have an *Eleanor?*" My feet carry me across the distance and I run a hand along the sleek line of the roof.

Mason reaches around me to open the door, caging me in between him and the car. "You just earned some major points knowing *Gone in 60 Seconds.*"

I want to tell him you don't grow up in Blackwell without developing an appreciation for sports cars, but I'm too distracted by his nose skimming up the side of my neck. Plus, it would require me telling him *where* I grew up, and I don't want him connecting the dots back to E.

"She's a beaut." I climb in the car and shut the door.

"Even if it's not pink?"

I eye him, watching the way his left hand is almost casually draped over the steering wheel and how he seamlessly shifts with the right as he drives.

Why is that so sexy?

"You couldn't pull off the pink," I finally say.

About ten minutes later, we pull into the lot of Mama Italia, a cute mom-and-pop restaurant. It's a casual and cozy place with amazing food.

I take in our surroundings as the hostess shows us to a small two-top in a back corner. The walls are all dark paneling and modern sconces, leaving the space dimly lit. The white fabric tablecloth gives an elegant feel, but without any candles or flowers, it isn't too fancy.

"You know…" I lean my elbows on the table and rest my chin in my hands after the server leaves with our drink order. "This is the perfect place for a first date."

He mirrors my position, those light eyes studying me. "Why do you sound so surprised?"

"Don't know." I shrug. "I guess maybe I expected you to pick—"

The sound of his phone ringing interrupts before I can finish, and a sheepish expression crosses his face. "Sorry, I thought I put it on silent." He pulls his phone out, Trav's name flashing on the screen as he silences it.

"It's a little early for the 'something bad happened' phone call." I use air quotes around the phrase.

Almost as soon as the first call ends, I can tell it goes off again, followed by a third time.

"Do you mind if I answer? Trav knows I'm out with you and it's not like him to call so many times in a row. Something must be up."

"No, go ahead."

With my okay, he answers Trav's fourth call. "Hey man, what's going on?"

Mason's brow furrows in concern as he listens to whatever Trav tells him.

"What? Is he okay?" Pause. "Did he say *why* he's there?" Another pause and he looks at me. "Tell him I'll be there in fifteen." His head falls forward. "Thanks."

After ending the call, he looks back at me guiltily.

"Everything okay?" I place a hand on his forearm.

"You have *no* idea how much I don't want to say this, but we have to go. Apparently my younger brother got into a fight with my stepdad and is at the AK house looking for me."

"Let's go." I unhook my purse from my chair and stand, ready to leave. If anyone understands how important it is to be there for family in their time of need, it's me. The brief smile he gives me tell me he's able to read my understanding in my expression.

On the short drive back to Alpha, gone is the playful, fun-loving Mason I've come to know, and in his place is someone I almost don't recognize. He's super quiet, his strong jaw clenched, and he has a white-knuckle grip on the steering wheel. Whatever is going on with his brother is obviously weighing on his mind.

It bothers me more than I thought it would to see him upset. I reach over the center console, place my hand on his thigh, and give it a squeeze, the action breaking through the fog of stress he's feeling. He turns to give me a smile and threads his fingers through mine. We stay like that the rest of the drive, no words needed.

When we get to the AK house, Mason doesn't bother going around to the lot in the back, instead opting to park right in front. As soon as the car is off, he's out, only slowing down long enough to take my hand when I join him. I'm practically running to keep up with his long-legged stride up the path.

Opening the front door, he leads us through the house and back to the den, where he finally lets go of my hand. He moves to kneel in front of a slightly smaller figure sitting on the couch.

"Olly, what's wrong? What happened? Are you okay?" The urgency in his voice grows with each question.

Though he hasn't said much about his siblings, I can tell he loves them very much. Witnessing the deep concern he has for them stirs something deep inside me.

"Umm...so..."

"Olly." Mason repositions himself to sit on the coffee table instead of squatting and reaches a hand out to his brother. "Hold on." He holds up a palm. "Does Mom know you're here? And *how* did you get here?"

"Uber," Olly answers at the same time Trav says, "I made him text Livi," from behind me.

Mason and Olly both move to look in Trav's direction, Olly's eyes going wide at the same time as mine.

Holy shit! Mason's brother Olly is my Olly?

"Coach?"

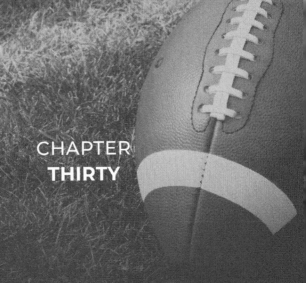

CHAPTER
THIRTY

MASON

Coach? Did Olly just call Kay Coach? Why would he call her that? I have so many questions and only add more to the list when Kay gives him a small wave and says, "Hey, Olly."

"You're dating my coach?" My brother turns back to me, his brown eyes wide with curiosity.

"You coach football, Skittles?" I ask Kay.

She shakes her head, eyes bouncing around the room like she doesn't want to answer, before finally saying, "Cheerleading."

"Huh?" Now I'm even more confused. Kay cheers? *Olly* cheers?

"You're a pom, Short Stack? Why aren't you on the Red Squad?" Trav pulls her against his side.

"I was an all-star, not a pom, but that's not the point right now." She gestures to Olly sitting in front of me.

She's right.

"Okay." I grip the back of my neck, digging into the tight muscles. "How about this—let's start with a few easy questions."

"Okay."

"You're not playing football?"

He shakes his head no.

"You're cheering?"

He nods.

"You said you were an all-star?" When I point to Kay, it's her turn to nod as my mind works to put the things I do know together. "So I take it you joined NJA with Livi?"

Another nod.

"And you didn't tell Dad."

This time Olly looks to the ground as he shakes his head. I don't know why, but I brace myself for his answer when I ask why not.

"Because there's not a future in cheerleading like there is in football."

I frown, not liking the implication. Parents can pressure their children to follow all sorts of career paths, but playing a sport—any sport—professionally requires the athlete himself to have a certain inherent internal drive to succeed. I love Brantley. He's a good guy and an excellent father, but he can have tunnel vision when it comes to what he thinks is best.

I blow out a breath and rub my temples. This is *so* not how I expected this night to go. Nothing puts a damper on a first date like family drama.

"Okay, here's what we're going to do." I flick my gaze first to Kay then over to Trav, who pulls his keys from his pocket in answer to my silent question. "Trav will drive Kay to her apartment so I can go home and talk to Dad with you."

I have no clue what I will say, but Olly is my brother, so I have to try. If I don't, Brantley will steamroll right over him.

Because what Brantley Roberts wants, Brantley Roberts gets.

I've imagined countless scenarios where I told Mason I used to be a cheerleader, but none of them included being outed by coming face to face with one of my athletes, least of all one who is a member of his family.

Unlike with Q, the name PF Dennings would have no significant meaning to Mase, but where E paid people to scrub Kayla Dennings from most of the internet, PF Dennings lives on. NJA team videos and ones of my own partner stunting are easily searched on YouTube. It's the lingering connections there that lead to the secrecy.

The struggle between being there for his brother and continuing on with the date I made him work so hard to get is a palpable thing. Honestly, it's the only reason I can think of that compels the next words out of my mouth.

"Would it be easier if I went with you?"

Both brothers stare at me in shock, and if I'm not mistaken, Trav looks mildly proud.

"I get that there's no professional cheerleading like football." I put a hand on Olly's shoulder, offering support. "But you know there is collegiate potential"—he's JT's prodigy—"and Livi cheers, so your dad can't be *completely* against the sport."

"Are you sure, Skittles?" The hope shining in Mason's eyes has me swallowing down the ball of anxiety rising in my throat.

"Why not? You do owe me a date, after all."

His dimples come out in full force, and the last of my reservations fall away.

"Who needs flowers and candy when you can enjoy a nice serving of family drama?" He pushes to stand, my eyes falling to watch the way his muscles move under the cotton clinging to them as he rounds the couch to wrap an arm around my middle. "You sure?"

No, but the PF is out of the bag, so I nod yes anyway.

"Holy shit." The curse slips past my lips of its own accord.

"Yup." Mason pops his P with a chuckle. "That's *exactly* the reaction Brantley was going for," he says as the Shelby pulls through two ornate lion statues bookending the entrance to the long driveway.

E's home in Baltimore cost a chunk of his signing bonus when he purchased it, but this? Oh boy, this is a whole other level of wealth. The massive gray stone mansion with its large white columns is gorgeous, but it screams "MONEY" in a way E's never will.

Before we can make it to the front door, it opens to reveal a worried-looking Grace Roberts. As she rushes out to pull Olly into a hug, I still can't believe her kids are Mason's siblings.

"I understand why you left, but why didn't you tell me where you were going?" she scolds her son.

"Sorry, Mom. I texted Livi."

"That's the *only* reason I'm not grounding you." She releases Olly and stretches up to kiss Mason on the cheek. "Hi, sweetheart. Thanks for bringing him home."

"Of course," he says with a small smile.

"Come on into the house, boys. Your father is in his office. We'll figure this all out. You're not quitting NJA if you don't want to, Olly."

"Thanks." Olly's shoulders sag in relief.

During the exchange, I've gone unnoticed, one of the side

effects of being under five feet, but once Mason turns to take my hand, Grace's eyes land on me for the first time.

"PF, honey, is that you?"

"Hi, Mrs. Roberts."

"Oh, dear, I thought I told you to call me Grace."

"Yes, sorry." I can't help but grin. This may only be Olly's first year with NJA, but his sister transferred to our gym over a year ago. In one season, Grace Roberts has managed to become one of my favorite NJA parents.

"Not that this isn't a pleasant surprise, but what are you doing here?"

My heels click-clack across the marble title of a foyer so large I think my entire dorm could fit inside. Mason guides me through it and down a long hallway filled with what I can only assume are priceless works of art, heading toward the kitchen in the back. I'm too distracted by the grandeur around me to concentrate on Grace's question.

"She was with Mase when he came to bring me home," Olly answers for me.

"Really?" She arches a brow.

Seeing Grace and Mason side by side, I notice the similarities in them. Whereas the twins have black hair and deep brown eyes, she shares the same espresso-colored locks—hers perfectly styled in a sleek bob—and those seafoam green irises that hold me in their spell. It's so obvious they are related. Did I try so hard to ignore the things Mason makes me feel I never made the connection?

"They were on a *date*."

Grace's jaw falls open, clearly not expecting *that* as the answer, but before anyone else can say anything, a dark-haired figure I recognize as Livi rushes into the room and launches herself at her twin.

"Coach?" She blinks at me with her arms still wrapped around Olly.

"Hey, Livi."

"Why are you in my house?"

"She's Mase's *girlfriend*," Olly says gleefully.

"WHAT!" Livi and Grace exclaim together.

Livi pulls back, and her shocked gaze snaps to her older

brother while her mother pauses from pulling drinking glasses down, a similar look on her face.

A blush heats my cheeks at their scrutiny.

"I didn't realize that word was part of your vocabulary," Grace jokes.

"Nice, Mom," Mason groans.

"Shut up! *Really*? This is so awesome." Livi jumps up and down in excitement.

"So..." Grace circles a finger at where Mason has pulled me down to snuggle into his side on one of the built-in bench seats surrounding the kitchen table. "Small world, you two dating."

The smallest. As if dating Mason didn't carry a dangerous weight with respect to how I choose to live my life now, being connected to *both* sides of me could prove catastrophic.

Before either of us get a chance to answer, the twins start to lob more questions at us, each one tripping over the other in their hunt for information.

"What's going on in here?" a voice booms, bringing the buzz in the kitchen crashing down like a dropped stunt.

"Sweetheart." Grace rises from her chair, going to her husband.

"Mason? What are you doing home? You have a game tomorrow."

I take a moment to study Brantley Roberts while his attention is elsewhere. He still has a full head of black hair, even if it's sprinkled with salt, and despite it being a Friday evening, he is wearing dress slacks and a white Oxford shirt.

"Just bringing Olly back."

If I thought Brantley Roberts looked unhappy when he made his appearance, he now takes a turn toward displeased when he spots me under Mason's arm.

Ooo, somebody has a stick up their butt, my inner cheerleader whispers behind her hand.

"And who's this?"

"Mase's girlfriend," Livi says with a hint of bragging in her tone. She and Olly crack me up.

"Girlfriend?" Brantley's dark brows hit the hairline of his carefully combed locks.

"Sweetheart." Grace directs him to the open chair next to hers. "This is PF. She coaches the twins."

"Coaches? Is this about the cheerleading bullshit you have in your head?"

Did I say he looks displeased? Now he's downright sour. If the way I feel Mason's delicious muscles tighten against me is any indication, I'm not the only one picking up on the hostility pulsing off his stepfather. Talk about making a good impression on the family, huh?

"Dad," Olly says.

"Don't *Dad* me, young man. You are quitting this cheer-leading thing and joining the football team like originally planned."

"I like NJA."

"There's no future in cheerleading."

"Yes there is, Dad."

"Not professionally."

"I don't want to play professional ball. I don't love it like Mase does."

"What about college?"

"Like paying for college was ever going to be an issue," Olly scoffs sarcastically. "Besides, if I get good enough, I can go for cheerleading."

"Dad." Livi tries to ease the tension. Thank god, because this is starting to get awkward. "You support me cheering."

There's a stretch of silence. The whole reason I came is because I offered to help. Time to do that.

"Sir, your son is good—*really* good. He's a natural, one of the best talents I've seen since my old partner, who is on a full ride at Kentucky." Olly's jaw hits the table as if he can't believe I've compared him to JT. It's not a lie though.

Brantley looks to Olly, a hint of pride bleeding into his eyes before he folds his arms on top of the table and turns all his attention on me.

Uh-oh.

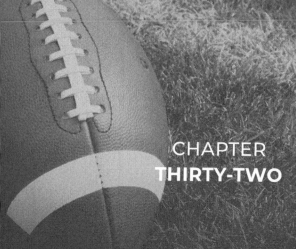

CHAPTER
THIRTY-TWO

MASON

I recognize Brantley's shark side the instant he switches it on. It's always been impressive to witness, but I don't like seeing it turned on my girl.

"Dad." It doesn't surprise me that Livi is trying to play mediator. No one has Olly's back the way she does. "The main reason I tried out for the Admirals was to work with Coach."

I'm still reeling over the fact that Kay is even a cheerleader. She lives with three members of the Red Squad—how has this never come up?

"Okay then. What makes *you* qualified?"

I run a hand down Kay's arm, linking our fingers together and giving them a squeeze. When she offered to come to support Olly, I was floored, but now I'm regretting accepting the offer. Getting the third degree from my stepdad is far from the first date I had planned.

Then, shocking me, Kay squares her shoulders. The way her features transform and confidence pours off of her is new. It's also hot as hell, and I need to not focus on that or I'll be popping an erection in front of my entire family. Talk about awkward.

"I've been cheering at NJA since I was three years old, competing since I was five, and I became a member of the Admirals as soon as I was old enough to meet the age requirement at twelve. Not counting the titles with prior teams, I've won dozens of national championships and five Worlds titles as a member of the Admirals. Outside of being a member of one of the top large senior six co-ed teams of the last decade, I also have four Worlds titles in partner stunting."

Kay ticks off each of her accolades with her fingers, and with how long Livi has been cheering, I know these aren't small achievements. Why does she keep them a secret?

The twins are both bouncing in their seats, and I can tell they are itching to add their two cents. If we are going to have any hope of salvaging any semblance of this date before I have to report to the hotel, we need to leave before they start.

"Come on, Skittles." Holding her hand, I pull her from the bench. "Like you said...I still owe you a date."

We say our goodbyes, and as we head for the front door, I tuck her against my side, relishing these moments of her allowing me this close.

"How do you feel about pizza?" I ask when we get to the Shelby.

"It's only one of the major food groups."

"Damn, babe." I hug her close then open the passenger side door. "Once again proving you're perfect for me."

Those seductive red lips part, and I reach out and run a thumb over the bottom one. I want to see them wrapped around my cock more than my next breath. That's not surprising, but what is unexpected is how much I meant it when I said she's perfect for me.

Adjusting boner number who-knows-I've-lost-count of the night, I climb inside the Shelby and shift it into drive.

Villa Pizza is about five minutes from campus and is a tiny hole-in-the-wall type of place. Ninety percent of their business is takeout deliveries to U of J students, but they do have a few tables for any lunch or late-night stranglers who wander in.

Kay and I each order a soda and two slices before settling at one of the high-tops next to the front window.

"Okay." I rub my hands together. "I have *so* many questions, but first, why don't you tell people you're a cheerleader?"

Her eyes drop to the left, the condensation running down her glass her sole focus.

"Can't be questioned about why you don't cheer for a school with a top team if they don't know you have the background."

"You get asked that?"

She nods, not adding anything else on the subject, so I let it drop.

"Okay, next one. How the hell do you get PF as a nickname from Kayla?"

She gives a cute little chuckle and swallows. "How do you know about that?"

"That's how everyone referred to you tonight. Plus, Livi's talked about you…*a lot*."

"I still can't believe my twins are *your* twins."

Spicy pepperoni and tangy tomato sauce explode across my tongue. I do like how she considers my family hers.

"It's short for PF Flyer."

"Like the sneakers from *The Sandlot*?"

"Yup."

"Okay, one"—I hold up a finger—"makes no sense for your nickname to be longer than your real name so I get why they use just PF. And two"—I add a second finger—"not quite sure I get the reference. Explain."

She fiddles with the straw in her cup. "So, JT"—she waits for my nod of recognition—"and I have cheered together our whole lives and have been stunt partners since the beginning."

A pause for more pizza.

"We used to love *The Sandlot*, watched it all the time, and seven-year-old JT thinks he's *sooo* clever when he goes, 'Hey Kay, you're awesome like those sneakers and a flyer too. From now on, you'll be known as PF,' and ever since, I've been PF at the gym."

"You know, it's funny." I drop a hand to her knee where it touches mine under the table.

"What is?" She does this cute head tilt, her long hair falling around her shoulders.

"That I feel like I have to compete with my siblings for who likes you more."

It's totally cheesy, but when one of her pretty blushes stains her cheeks, it's worth the shit my inner coach will be slinging my way later.

"I still can't believe I didn't know they were related to you."

"To be fair, we have different last names."

"True. But now, seeing you with your mom"—she reaches across the table and caresses my brow with her thumb—"you have the same eyes."

I wiggle my eyebrows, making her laugh.

"They're beautiful, you know." Her unexpected compliment catches me off guard.

"My eyes?"

"Yeah. They're such a striking contrast against your darker features."

"Wow." I fall back against my chair.

"What?"

"You just paid me a compliment."

Her face breaks out into a grin. "Don't get used to it."

I let out a bark of laughter. This girl. She's just what I need.

We talk a little longer as we finish our pizza before leaving to head back to campus.

I pull my car up in front of her building, parking in the fire zone instead of finding a spot.

I grab what I left in the back seat and get out of the car, going around to her side to open the door. Once she's out, I close it and press her up against it. I wrap my arms around her waist, resting my hands on the top swell of her delectable ass, and pull her tighter against me. I love the feel of her tiny but curvy body pressed against my much larger frame. She fills a void I wasn't aware existed.

"I'm going to say goodbye to you here."

Her beautiful gray eyes look up at me, unsure, a little V forming between her brows. "Why?"

"Because." I tighten my arms, pressing us closer. "I need to be at the hotel soon. If I walk you to your door, I'm gonna stay…" I brush my nose against hers. "Coach would have my ass." I drag my nose along her cheek and behind her ear, placing a gentle kiss in the soft spot there. "Besides…" I nudge her hair out of the way and continue my kisses down her neck. "You need to be up early to coach"—I lean in and whisper—"*cheerleading*."

And there it is, one of those eye rolls I adore so much.

"You're coming to the game tomorrow, right?"

I don't know why, but her answer, to this, feels really important.

"Yeah, I usually go with G and CK."

"You guys sit in the student section?"

"Yeah." Her look says *Duh.*

"How about an upgrade?"

"What do you mean?"

"My family has a box, so the tickets I get are always available. How about you use them? Fourth row on the fifty-yard line, behind the team bench."

Her eyes widen in surprise. "For real?"

I nod. I want her there, where I can see her.

After a moment, her happy expression falls. "Don't you only get two tickets?"

"Yeah."

"Then I can't use them. I'm not going to choose between G and CK."

"You don't have to, babe." I palm her ass and she squirms in my hold. "Trav's family sits with mine, so you can have his tickets too."

"Oh my god!"

She throws her arms around my neck, hugging me. When she pulls back, I move one of my hands behind her head and angle it for my kiss.

I feel her rise up onto her toes as her arms tighten while our lips meet. I can't help but smile as we do. The more often I kiss her, the less hesitant she becomes.

I force myself to break away before I go back on everything I said earlier.

"I'll see you tomorrow after the game."

"Okay." Her voice comes out all breathy.

She pushes off the car and moves toward the door of the building.

"Hey, babe." I stop her before she gets too far.

I reach for the hoodie I tossed on the roof of the Shelby and hold it out to her.

"Wear this to the game tomorrow."

She takes my red team hoodie and raises one of her sculpted brows.

"I know what this is."

Of course she does.

"Good. Then you know why I want you to wear it."

She holds it out in front of her, the back facing her, my name and number looking back. She's bucked almost every attempt I've made to stake my claim publicly. It's time for that to end.

"I hate you." The smile she gives me takes all the sting out of her words.

"Sure you do, babe."

CHAPTER
THIRTY-THREE

Memories of last night have been playing on a loop in my brain since I collapsed on my bed when I got home. I still can't believe any of it was real.

I went on a date with a football player, and not just any ol' football player. No, I decided to break my self-imposed rule with none other than Mason 'Casanova' Nova himself.

Except…

The more I get to know him, the less I see him as Casanova.

Family drama aside, our first official date was fun.

And that goodnight kiss?

Oh. My. God. Spec*tac*ular.

I need to stick my head in the freezer just thinking about it.

Dating Mason Nova is one thing. His attempts at PDA—though I've fended off most—have not gone unnoticed.

Now he wants me to wear his team hoodie? With his name and number in big fucking black lettering on the back?

I don't know if I can handle that.

Okay, that's a lie. It's a hoodie, a super-soft, well-worn, still-smells-like-him piece of cotton. I *can* wear it. I'd be really comfortable in it too. It's all the…attention that *will* come with it that I'm not sure if I can handle. Letting him mark me will take the casual interest and send it into the stratosphere.

Choosing to date Mason can open all kinds of cans of worms. I'm not sure if I'm ready for that.

But then I think about how he was with Olly and it makes me go all mushy inside. His concern and support for his brother above all else showed me another side of him I didn't expect.

Honestly, I shouldn't be surprised anymore; every time I'm with him, he does something unexpected.

"When you offered to bring me today, I thought it would be fun to have some sister time, but *damn*, PF, you have been lost in your head the *whole* time," Tessa complains as I shift Pinky into park at The Barracks.

I thunk my head against my steering wheel, hiding my face against the leather.

"Shit, T, I'm sorry."

"Why are you being weird? I haven't told you that anything new popped up on Instagram, so it's not that."

Sonofabitch. See this? This is one of the worms I was talking about. How pathetic am I that I need someone still in high school to vet social media for me?

How am I supposed to be the girlfriend of a guy who is constantly trending?

"Mason knows I'm a cheerleader." I keep my voice low as we walk through the gym, heading for the locker rooms.

"You told him?" Her midnight blue eyes widen to where I can see a full ring of white around them.

"Not exactly." She makes a rolling motion with her hand for me to continue. "You know the twins?"

"Livi and Olly?"

I nod. We have a few sets of twins amongst the hundreds of athletes that make up our teams, but the Roberts twins are the only set on my main team.

"Mason is their brother."

"Shut the front door!"

I snort then tell her about all about the CW-show-worthy drama that went down last night while I tie my cheer shoes.

"Oh my god, I *love* this." She would—*Gossip Girl* is her favorite show. I can't even get mad at her for how she's clapping her hands in glee. It is so rare for her to act her age; most of the time I swear she's the older one in our relationship.

We make our way out to the main gym, and the other twenty-one ladies who make up the Marshals—NJA's small senior six all-girl team—start to trickle in. The Admirals are the main team I coach, but I help with the stunting for any team that needs it. With my mind all swirly, I'm grateful to have the double practice before the football game.

"I think you should wear the hoodie." My head snaps up, my ponytail whipping my back as I blink at T like she's lost her mind.

"Why?" I ask cautiously.

"You and JT are always trying to teach me to own who I am and not let others put me down." T may only be a junior, but she's already the favorite to be class valedictorian. Her bullies may be different than mine, but they are still bullies. "Don't you think *maybe* you should start taking your own advice?"

Oh, look at that. Is my shoe untied? I'm supposed to be demonstrating stunting today, can't have that. It's not safe.

"Kay," she prods.

I hate when the Taylors call me Kay.

"Don't call me Kay. It's weird."

A divot forms in her cheek. The brat is biting back a smile.

"Then woman up and start setting a proper example for us impressionable young minds."

Tessa may be a smartass, but she's not wrong.

"I'm scared," I whisper.

Petrified is more like it. High school may be over, but the internet lives forever.

I didn't just retreat behind those who love me. With each omission and selective piece of information told, I've dug a moat and raised the drawbridge.

Choosing to be with Mason has the potential to serve as a Trojan horse that will change…*everything*.

"I'm not saying you should make Mason your profile picture" —I'd have to have a profile to do that—"or to tell him about E right now, but…"

But maybe it's time to stop hiding.

"I don't know if I should be pumped for the game or upset Nova didn't offer me these seats sooner," G says as we settle into the red plastic chairs.

Nothing beats field-level seats. The smell of the turf and the closeness to the action are where it's at for me.

"Don't be jealous he likes me more." I pat his chest.

"Still can't believe that either."

You and me both, G.

Around us, the stadium is quickly filling with the sold-out crowd that came to watch tonight's Big Ten matchup against the Northwestern Wildcats. They are a strong team this season, and a win is important for the Hawks' rankings toward the national championship.

I haven't decided what I'm going to do about the hoodie. For now, the offending garment is draped over my purse. It's too hot to wear it anyway.

Because my brothers are all a bunch of gossiping girls, I fill G and CK in on everything that went down last night. All conversation cuts off as the intro video for the Hawks starts playing on the jumbotron, and a flash of heat hits me when I see Mase on the screen. "Thunderstruck" by AC/DC starts to play as the team comes running out of the tunnel, and my gaze automatically finds number eighty-seven in the sea of large bodies.

Hands held, the captains head out for the coin toss, which the Wildcats win, opting to receive the ball first. The guys make their way back to the bench as the defense gets ready to take the field.

Our fancy new seats are directly behind the Hawks bench, giving me a great vantage point to watch Mase.

Shit! I'm thinking of him as Mase again. I'm totally going to end up wearing his hoodie.

I track him as he talks to his teammates, slapping helmets and shoulder pads along the way. He makes his way behind the bench, moving closer to the stands, looking at the crowd instead of the field.

What the hell is he doing?

I don't think I can recall him *ever* not being 100% focused on the game. Then he finds what he's searching for—me.

Holy shit. Ohmygodohmygodohmygod. He's looking at us. Do you see that? Do you? DO YOU?

Mase's face breaks out in a smile but falls a moment later.

He points to me then himself, pulling at his jersey and lifting his hands in question. *Ah, he wants to know why I'm not wearing his hoodie.*

I pantomime my response back, shaking my head while pretending to be cold. He nods his understanding, and then in the *biggest* shock of all, he blows me a kiss before turning around.

Oh. Em. Gee. *spirit fingers*

Our exchange hasn't gone unnoticed. G and CK look at me with knowing smirks while I hear others around us trying to figure out who Casanova was blowing kisses to.

That familiar surge starts to bubble up inside me, but I try not to think too much about it and focus my attention on the game. Our defense holds the Wildcats, forcing them to punt. Mase, Trav, and the rest of the offense take the field.

On first down, Mase performs a beautiful block, creating a hole for Alex to run through for a thirty-yard run. The first play sets the tone for the rest of the drive, and several plays later, Alex runs the ball in for a touchdown. The crowd goes wild.

7-0 Hawks.

The remainder of the first and almost all of the second are a battle of defense, neither team able to get into scoring position.

The Wildcats finally manage to punch through and we end the half tied 7-7.

During halftime, we all take a bathroom break, and by the time I return to my seat, the temperature has dropped enough for me to need *the hoodie*.

I worry the cotton between my fingers, getting lost in thoughts of the past. I'm no longer sure if the goose bumps coating my arms are from the chilly breeze blowing through the stadium or an almost PTSD-like side effect.

Dating is supposed to be fun. Boy likes girl, girl likes boy. Why do other people have to get involved and make it more complicated than that?

Why does it feel like I'm about to put a target on my back? Why can't it *just* be a hoodie?

Deep breath.

Here goes nothing.

I pull it over my head and straighten the material down. Mase is so much larger than me the hem of it covers my knees.

I can feel the moment G and CK notice the large NOVA and #87.

"Damn. I guess he wasn't kidding about being serious," G says.

I don't acknowledge G's comment or how much of a Neil-Armstrong-type step this is for my relationship with Mase.

Behind us, people talk, and based on the few words I'm able to pick up on, I know my brothers aren't the only ones who've noticed the stamp on my back.

The teams make their way back onto the field, and like earlier, Mase goes behind the bench to find me in the stands. He looks so good down there with his helmet lifted on his head, the ear pads resting on his temples to keep it up, and his mouth guard hanging out to the side. The sleeves of his jersey are tucked up under his pads, displaying his bulging biceps in all their glory.

When he sees me in his hoodie, he smiles so wide his dimples appear. Damn those dimples. He blows me another kiss before heading out for the first play of the second half.

The Hawks come out guns blazing, and the punt return gives them good field position on their own forty-five. Trav runs the ball for a first down, and Mase gets another nice block for Alex to run for the next first, finally ending in a beautiful twenty-yard spiral from Trav that connects with Mase, who runs it in for a touchdown.

14-7 Hawks.

Our defense comes out swinging as hard as the offense. Kevin sacks the quarterback hard, causing a fumble that the Hawks run in for another TD.

21-7 Hawks.

The hundred-thousand-plus capacity crowd roars with the momentum generated on the field below. The action doesn't let up for the rest of the game, but the score remains the same, with the U of J Hawks defeating the Northwestern Wildcats 21-7.

#THEGRAM

UofJ411

"Mason looking up at the stands"

13,482 views

UofJ411 Looking for me @CasaNova87 ?
#ISeeYouBaby #CasanovaWatch

@Behawks87: Who is @CasaNova87 looking at?
#YouLookingAtMe
@Bellebookblog: @CasaNova87 can look at me like that any
day of the week #HolySmolder
@Bestiesandbooks: Pick me, pick me @CasaNova87

UofJ411

"Recollecting of Mason blowing a kiss"

13,482 views

UofJ411 *kissy face emoji*
#PuckerUp #CasanovaWatch

@Braun.lauren: I'm fully stocked on ChapStick @CasaNova87
#PillowySoft
@_Bsdmbutch: I'll show you 7 minutes in heaven
@CasaNova87 #MwahMwah
@Caysmama: Give me some sugar #KissTheGirl
#CasanovaWatch

UofJ411

picture of Kay from the back wearing Mason's hoodie

♡ ○ ▽   🔖

UofJ411 OMG! Is that one of the player's team hoodies? #DoYouHaveAGirlfriend #CasanovaWatch

@Cheril2412: SHUT THE FRONT DOOR!! Who is this? #CasanovaWatch
@Christyheartsbooks: Holy shit! That's @CasaNova87 team hoodie #Fashion
@Cmd427: Does @CasaNova87 have a girlfriend? #AskingForAFriend
@Cr8zysockbookblock: Say it ain't so @CasaNova87 #Heart1Broken
@Dalner81: How did we not know @CasaNova87 was accepting applications for GIRLFRIEND? I would have applied #IVolunteerAsTribute
@Doterragirl2020: Please tell me this is his sister or something? #ItCantBeTrue #CasanovaWatch

---

UofJ411

picture of a side profile shot of Kay wearing the hoodie

♡ ○ ▽   🔖

UofJ411 Who has the deets? #CasanovaWatch #CasanovasMysteryGirl

@Filthylittlereader: Is this the chick he's been spotted kissing around campus? #DetectiveWork #CasanovaWatch #CasanovasMysteryGirl
@Fununderthecovers: Who is she? #NeedTheDeets #CasanovaWatch #CasanovasMysteryGirl
@Hbletsch: Who has the 411? #INeedToKnow #CasanovaWatch #CasanovasMysteryGirl

MASON

The locker room after a win is one of my favorite places to be. "Say Amen (Saturday Night)" by Panic! At The Disco blasts, and the controlled chaos of two dozen players in various states of undress and celebration is a spectacle in and of itself.

The reporters allowed access make their rounds, not fazed by the naked skin on display. I give my sound bites when they make their way to me, keeping to canned responses on what I think about our chances of making it to the national championship again and if I'm prepared for the draft. The former is easy—*Hell fucking yes we are taking it all this year*; the latter is lacking some of my typical conviction.

What is that about?

Press gone, I sit on my bench and reach inside my locker for my phone to text Kay.

Having her in the stands tonight was like a jolt of adrenaline to my system. Seeing her in my hoodie during the second half? Fuck me if that wasn't a better feeling than our win.

Unlocking my phone, I see I have a bunch of messages waiting for me.

LIVI: Shower quick! I'm hungry! Nomnomnomnomnom!!

OLLY: We're meeting you in the tunnel. We're going to Fusion.

MOM: Great game, honey. Nice TD. The twins are gonna meet you in the tunnel. We're going out to dinner to celebrate. Tell Travis his Nana is here and will be joining us as well.

BRANTLEY: Good game, son. Nice to see you having a girlfriend isn't affecting your game. I was worried you were going to be too distracted to focus when I saw you looking to the stands, but the way you are trending right now is marketing gold.

SKITTLES: Since you won does that mean I HAVE to go to the AK house tonight??

I'm not even going to answer Brantley's text. I picked up on his less-than-pleased response to learning I have a girlfriend during all the drama last night. The fact that he now approves because he sees a way to use it as an advantage…yeah, that's not happening.

Checking the time stamp on the twins' texts, I realize I have just enough time to shower without worrying about them loitering in the tunnels too long.

Kay is the only one I bother responding to. If I'm going to dinner, so is she.

ME: Today's your lucky day, babe. No AK tonight, dinner with the fam instead. Meet me and the twins outside the locker room.

SKITTLES: Wasn't I subjected to enough family time last night?

ME: Suck it up, buttercup! You're coming.

SKITTLES: Do I have to??? Can't you just come over after?

> ME: Nope! I don't want to wait any longer to see you.

> SKITTLES: Why do you have to go and say things like that? How am I supposed to say no now?

> ME: OMG! *gasp* Did you just admit to being charmed by me?

> SKITTLES: Don't let it go to your head, hotshot.

> ME: *GIF of Han Solo saying, "Who? Me? Never!"*

> SKITTLES: *eye roll emoji*

> ME: See you soon, babe.

I don't bother waiting for her confirmation. I know she'll be there.

"Dinner with Nana," I say to Trav, removing the rest of my pads and uniform and wrapping a towel around my waist.

"Livi texted." He mirrors my actions and we head for the showers.

Unlike away games where the dress code is suit and tie, home games only require us to wear red polos with the Hawks logo, dark jeans, and black sneakers.

With a grin on my face because Kay has admitted it's a sexy look on me, I pull my Hawks cap on backward.

Shouldering my bag, I turn to Trav. "Meet you outside. I'm gonna go find the twins."

Pushing through the doors, I scan the hallway for my people. The place is crawling with boosters, press, fans, and jersey chasers.

"Mase!" My siblings spot me first and rush me with hugs.

"Hey, kids." I return their embrace.

"Where's Trav? I'm hungry." Livi looks behind me. It's no wonder the two get along so well—they are both ruled by their stomachs.

"He'll be out in a minute." I search for Kay.

The crowd parts and I finally spot her. She's so beautiful it makes my breath hitch. Her tiny body is practically swallowed up by my hoodie, and her long blonde-and-rainbow curls are held back from her face by a red bandana tied like a headband.

Without realizing it, I break away from Livi and Olly and stalk in her direction. I put my hands underneath her delectable ass, squeezing the cheeks as I lift her against me and press her to the wall behind her. Her beautiful gray eyes widen in surprise before closing in pleasure at the feel of my kiss.

The adrenaline from our win flows through my body and into our connection. I widen my stance, supporting her weight with my legs, freeing my hands to run under her hair, cupping her face to change the angle of our kiss.

Everything around me goes fuzzy as I lose myself in the feel of her in my arms. Nothing exists but Kay.

Our tongues battle it out. Her moans make my dick so hard I swear it's going to bear an imprint of my zipper for a week.

It isn't until I hear Trav's booming voice that we finally come up for air. "Mase, how about you get your tongue out of your girlfriend so we can get some grub?"

"Oh my god," Kay whispers, burying her face into my chest like she's trying to disappear.

I can't help but chuckle at how embarrassed she sounds. I lower her from the wall, enjoying the feel of her body sliding down mine.

Behind me, snippets of conversations find their way to my ears.

"Casanova has a girlfriend?"

"No way—he doesn't date…"

"That's what QB1 said."

"He's kissing her…"

"How many times have we seen him doing that or more?"

"But she's wearing his hoodie…"

"Who is she?"

I ignore the jersey chasers and focus on those who are important.

"Come on, babe. Let's eat." I pull her to my side when she tries to step away after tugging the hood of the sweatshirt over her head.

We split up so Kay can drop G and CK off at their respective dorms/houses as I drive Trav, the twins, and myself to the restaurant.

I send the others inside as I wait for Kay to arrive. A few minutes later, her candy-colored Jeep pulls into the lot.

My eyes eat her up as she climbs out and walks in my direction. As much as I like seeing my name and number on her, I do miss watching the sway of her body since it's dwarfed by my hoodie.

"Do you have any idea how hot you look standing like that?" Her gaze rakes over me.

"It's the hat, isn't it?" I don't move from where I'm leaning against the hood of the Shelby, arms and ankles crossed.

"That and the way your tats stand out with your arms crossed."

I release said arms to cradle her against me. "Did that hurt?"

"Did what hurt?" She gets a cute little crinkle between her brows.

"Giving me a compliment?"

"I compliment you. I just try not to do it too often to keep your ego in check."

"Babe"—I drop a kiss to her forehead—"you say the sweetest things." Pushing back, I say, "Let's go. I'm hungry."

"Should I be nervous?" She threads her fingers with mine, her small hand disappearing in my big paw, but the easy acceptance of such a simple move after earlier is everything. I don't know if it's because we're away from campus or because we're official status after our first date, but I'm not going to complain.

"About dinner?"

Her hand flexes in mine, readjusting her hold over and over. I pull us to a stop when I see the worry swimming in her eyes.

"Babe." I stroke the line of her jaw, pleased when she leans into the touch.

"It'll be fun." She scoffs—can't say I blame her after her first experience with my family. "I promise." We start walking again. "Wait until you meet Trav's Nana. She's the *best*."

Nana McQueen is a force to be reckoned with. She's always reminded me of Helen Mirren with her sleek sophistication and almost royal-like air. No one, not even Brantley, dares challenge her.

As much as I love my family, I don't know if we would have

come if Nana wasn't going to be here. There won't even be a veiled dig over the whole Olly-is-a-cheerleader situation in her presence.

The private dining room is set up with a large round table big enough for all of us, and my muscles relax when I see the two seats that are open are between Trav and the twins. I'm hoping being closest to those she's most familiar with will help ease some of Kay's nerves.

"Hey, Short Stack."

"Hey, T. Hell of a game." Kay bumps her knuckles with him.

"Of course it was." He tugs at the shoulders of his polo, vamping it up like *You know me.* "Sure you don't want to ditch this loser and date the real star of the team?" He gives her a wink.

If I wasn't sure he was joking, I would drive my fist into his face—I don't care that he's my best friend. I do put an arm around Kay and pull her in against my side.

Are you sure she wouldn't do something like that? You've seen it happen before.

I shut those thoughts down faster than a center snaps the ball.

"Who is this lovely creature?"

The crown of Nana's white hair peeks out from behind Trav as she peers around him to get a better look at Kay and me.

"Nan, this is Mase's girlfriend, Kay. Short Stack, this is my Nana."

"Mason Nova, you have a girlfriend? I never thought I'd see the day." Nana play gasps.

"I said the same thing, Nan," Mom adds from across the table.

Everyone's got jokes. I can even feel Kay's body shake with repressed laughter.

"Yeah, yeah, yeah, yuck it up," I grumble.

Kay's hand gives my knee a squeeze under the table, and my body settles. Conversation about the game goes on around the group, but I mostly tune it out, focusing more on the press of Kay's body and the scent of her peppermint hair.

"JT texted me earlier," Olly tells Kay.

"I figured he would after I sent him some video from practice."

"You took video?"

"Technically Coach Kris did."

"Can I see?"

"Sure." Kay leans farther into me as she tilts to the side to pull her phone out of her back pocket.

After cueing up the video, she hands the phone to Olly, and I shift so I can also see what is happening on the screen.

Kay looks hot as hell in her practice gear, her toned stomach on display between her sports bra and capris. I can read the word COACH down one leg, and when she turns around, sure enough, PF is written on the back of her top.

I chub up at the sight of her boobs pressed together and her ass in those tight pants. Same as last night, my dick doesn't care that it's totally inappropriate given our current company.

In the video, Olly looks nervous as Kay gestures with her hands. She stands in front of Olly, whose hands are on her hips. They bounce slightly together before Olly lifts her over his head, a foot in each hand. With a small bend of his elbows down, Olly pushes Kay back up where she does a back tuck before Olly catches both her feet in one hand.

The video pans over to show Livi with a college-aged man, and they repeat the same stunt.

"Damn," I say under my breath.

"Yeah, that stunt is actually harder for the flyer, so I wanted to make sure Livi felt solid before having her do it with Olly." Kay's coach side makes an appearance.

As the focus goes back to her and my brother, both Trav and Nana move over to watch.

Olly and Kay are holding hands, each facing the camera. With the same start bounce, her legs curl in and stretch out as he lifts her over his head in a handstand. They hold the pose for a few seconds then repeat the prep bend, and Kay flips up to be held over Olly's head with one leg in his hand while she stretches a foot in front of her by her heel.

You can hear others in the gym cheering them on, and then, like before, we watch Livi and her partner repeat the stunt.

"Your heel stretch is so good. Definitely one of our most flexible flyers," Kay tells Livi. "This is the last stunt Coach Kris taped."

This time, Kay stands a little farther in front of Olly. She does a back handspring into Olly's hands and he pushes her up by the hips to hold her over his head once again.

Before the video can show Livi doing the same, a text notification comes through on Kay's screen.

"Sorry." Kay pulls the phone closer to her, and I can read the text over her shoulder.

> CTG BFF JT: You okay?

A part of me feels like I should look away and not eavesdrop on her conversation, but seeing as how Kay knows I can see her phone from over her shoulder and she hasn't made a move to hide the screen, I assume she doesn't care either way. Plus, someone asking if she's okay when she seems perfectly fine to me tugs at my concern.

> KAY: I'm fine.

> CTG BFF JT: Are you sure? You're ALL over the UofJ411 IG.

> KAY: #LifeGoals

> CTG BFF JT: Don't be a smartass. You know I worry about you.

> KAY: I know you do and I love you for it.

> CTG BFF JT: Love you too. I'm here if you need me.

> KAY: I know that too. *kissy face emoji*

The text exchange happens in such rapid succession, the whole conversation taking place in less than a minute.

Seeing her and another man tell each other they love one another has something ugly bubbling up inside me. Kay's weighted sigh and the way she starts to massage her forehead has concern overtaking it—for now.

"Babe?" There's a heaviness to her that wasn't there before. Her shoulders are slumped, and it's almost like she's trying to disappear inside herself.

"Later?" Her gaze sweeps the table, reminding me we're not alone.

"Okay." This time her sigh is one of relief, and I tell the niggling voice in the back of my mind whispering this is a Chrissy/Tina situation all over again to shut up. If Kay were hiding something, she wouldn't have let me read her texts.

"Damn, Short Stack," Trav says.

"That was nothing, Trav. Check this out." Livi opens up YouTube.

She pulls up a video of a big guy and a tiny girl in blue, white, and black cheer uniforms. I knew Livi was pulling up something that involved Kay, but I was not prepared for how she would look all done up. I usually tend to stay away from the cheerleaders—too much drama with how much they are around the team—but cheerleader Kay? I'll make an exception, because...*hot*.

I watch as JT tosses and flips Kay in the air and over his head. I was impressed with what she was teaching the twins, but the tricks in this video are next level.

"Holy shit, Kay. Why aren't you cheering for the Hawks?" I don't think I've ever seen Trav look so awed. Livi has to reach over and lift his jaw up from where it's hanging out in the bread bowl.

"I wouldn't have time to coach if I cheered for the U of J. As much as I love cheering, coaching is what I was born to do."

"Well, based on that first video the kids showed us, you are very good at that too, my dear," Nana says.

"Thanks Mrs. McQueen." Kay listed off all her accomplishments to Brantley—who was as silent throughout the videos as I expected—yesterday like a boss, but Nana's simple compliment has her blushing.

"Please call me Nana."

I catch Trav's knowing smile out of the corner of my eye. Looks like Nana approves.

Conversation halts as the waiters deliver everyone's food. I cut into my porterhouse, and it's perfect. Kay's fork comes over and steals some of my mac and cheese, so I return the favor by helping myself to her fries. I catch my mother giving me a knowing smirk.

"How did you get into coaching?" The question comes from Mom.

"It was actually an injury that led to me discovering my love for it."

"Do you get hurt a lot?" Nana furrows her brow.

"Cheerleading as a sport is in the top five for injuries. I'm slightly more at risk being a flyer, and my dislocated elbow at that time was one of my most severe. It had me sidelined the longest. I didn't officially become a coach to a team until I graduated, but that was the start of running the stunt clinics like the ones these two take." She hooks a thumb at the twins.

We all tuck into our food as Nana and Mom continue to pepper her with questions, which she answers with such passion.

Eventually Trav reaches across me to sneak a fry off Kay's plate. Just as his hand lifts his prize, she smacks it.

"I swear, you need to learn to get your own food."

"Come on, Short Stack." Trav bats his eyelashes at her. "I'm a growing boy."

I pop my best friend in the chest. "Stop flirting with my girl."

"What? Afraid she'll ditch you?"

Yes.

I flip him the bird and the table laughs around us.

"Don't be an ass, T." Kay snuggles against me and takes the last bite of my lobster mac.

The press of her body against mine calms me instantly. She's done nothing to make me think she would stray, but...I get the impression there's something she isn't telling me.

I drop my arms and pull her in tighter.

"This is why she knows *I'm* the better choice—I let her eat *my* food." I lean down and place a kiss on the top of her head.

Kay shakes her head and rolls her eyes at us. She chooses to ignore us and turns back to talk to the twins.

Dinner winds down and we all make our way back outside. My parents and Trav's family head out first, leaving only the kids behind.

"Mase, are you staying at home tonight?" Livi asks hopefully.

Pulling my phone out of my pocket, I check the time. It's shortly after ten; might as well head home and avoid the chaos at the frat house to sleep in my peaceful bed.

"Sure."

Livi claps her hands in glee and turns her puppy dog eyes on Trav. "You too?" Trav, never able to deny my little sister anything, agrees.

"Movie night?"

"Anything for my favorite girl." Trav scoops Livi up and places her on his shoulders as we make our way to where the cars are parked.

"What about you, babe?"

"Sure," Kay replies, mimicking my response and placing a kiss on the underside of my jaw. "But just so you know"—she steps onto the running board of Pinky to look over her shoulder at me—"I'm not sharing my popcorn with you."

KAYLA

My mind has been plagued with thoughts of what could be posted by that damn UofJ411 to have caused JT's concerned texts. Tessa is the Taylor sibling more trigger-happy about telling me if I show up on social media, but JT? It has to be significant if he's bringing it up.

I can't focus on the potential fallout wearing Mason's hoodie might mean for my anonymity until I have hours of alone time.

I knew the risk when I said yes to Mase asking me out, but knowing and being faced with it are two entirely different things.

Not the time or the place, Kay.

The twins practically bounce into the house, and I let their excitement banish the negativity and old insecurities from my brain.

"We'll get the snacks and popcorn and meet you in the theater room," Olly shouts as they run down the hall to the kitchen.

"Theater room?" I turn to Mase with a raised brow.

A chuckle rumbles through his chest. "Are you really that surprised to learn this monstrosity has its own theater room?"

I shake my head, following him down a different hallway deeper into the house and coming to a stop at a set of impressive mahogany doors with a lighted black and white CINEMA sign.

Inside is a movie buff's dream. A hundred-inch screen dominates a wall in front of two rows of four black leather recliners and a third row made up of a large black leather couch and matching ottomans, practically creating a bed.

Classic movie posters hang on the side walls, and the back has a mini concession stand with a beer and wine fridge.

Trav starts tossing pillows and blankets onto a few of the seats as Mase goes to the bar and uncaps beers for the three of us.

The twins walk in, each carrying a gigantic bowl of popcorn, and Olly hands one to Mase.

"Guess you *are* sharing your popcorn, babe." The waggle of his eyebrows turns my teasing statement from earlier into a double entendre.

After snack distribution is taken care of and the twins select the latest Marvel film, we all settle into our seats.

Mase and I claim the back couches and I snuggle deeper into his side, breathing in the fresh scent of his soap, which I can't get enough of.

Throughout the movie, he runs his hand through my hair, twirling the ends around his fingers. I swear the way he's always touching me—and not in the pervy way, though he does a lot of that too—sets my heart aflutter. It reminds me so much of how Bette and E are with each other, and *they* are #CoupleGoals.

The action is so soothing, and at some point I must fall asleep because next thing I know I'm waking while he carries me up a set of stairs.

"Mase?"

"Hey there, Sleeping Beauty."

"What's going on?" I ask stupidly, my brain still half-asleep.

His smile widens, causing both dimples to now be on display. "I'm taking us to bed. As comfortable as the couch in the theater is, I much rather sleep on the king-sized memory foam mattress in my room."

"I can't just sleep in your bed with you at your parents' house. I should go home." I move to get out of his arms, but they tighten around me.

"Not a chance, Skittles. It's late and both my mom and I don't want you driving. Besides..." His mouth hitches up on one side. "Mom loves you."

He refuses to put me down, even when he needs to open the

door to his room. He carries me like my weight doesn't even register. It's hot.

The large corner room is roughly half the size of my dorm. Off to the left there's a door open to an ensuite bathroom and another I assume leads to a walk-in closet. There is also a set of French doors that open out to a balcony, flanked by large chairs in navy material and metal stud edging.

In the middle of the room is a large California king mattress covered in a matching navy bedspread with nautical accents. A flat-screen takes up one wall while numerous shelves of football awards and accolades decorate the others.

I want to explore, but I'm too tired.

He sets me down next to his bed before moving to the dresser under the TV. Opening a drawer, he pulls something out and tosses it at me. With my sluggish reflexes, it bounces off me and onto the bed. I send a frown in his direction.

"Sorry, babe," he says sheepishly.

"Not your fault—I'm still half-asleep—but what's this for?" I point to the t-shirt on the bed.

"Something comfy to sleep in."

"I have a bag in my car. I was planning on sleeping at home since I have to be at The Barracks tomorrow."

"Get it in the morning. Wear that tonight."

I pick up the gray t-shirt, the material worn and soft to the touch. I'm not surprised it's one of his U of J football shirts; the front reads *Property of U of J Football* with a football emblem sporting #87 in it and NOVA #87 on the back. I roll my eyes. This guy is always trying to mark me.

"What?" He shrugs his shoulders when I look at him. "I like having my name on you."

"Caveman."

"You know it, babe. Now"—he holds his arm out in the direction of his bathroom—"you are more than welcome to use my toothbrush if you want."

"That won't be weird?"

"Not for me. I mean my tongue spends almost as much time in your mouth as it does in mine, so what's the difference?"

My cheeks heat at the mention of how much we've been making out, but he's not wrong.

Dead on my feet, I pick it up to get ready for bed. I brush my teeth and can't help but smile as I think of how grossly cutesy it is to be sharing my boyfriend's toothbrush. How the hell did I even get here, let alone this fast?

Replacing my outfit with his shirt, I fold my jeans, bra, and shirt into a neat pile, open the door to the bedroom, and stop short.

Holy shit.

Mase is standing at the foot of the bed, shirtless and barefoot, the snap of his jeans undone, causing them to sag enough for the band of his red boxer briefs to show, every muscle on display for my eyes to devour.

Each bump and ridge of his glorious eight-pack—yes, eight-pack, and *swoon* because I guess a regular old six-pack isn't good enough for *the* Mason Nova—is nicely framed by the sexy V at his hips. His solid chest—the one that stretches his shirts in the most mouthwatering way—is topped by brown nipples beaded by the cold.

I've seen flashes of other ink when we've made out, but this is the first time I get to see all of it on display. The swirls and lines extend from his shoulder and halfway onto his pec, outlining it before continuing down the side of his ribs and into that V.

When he notices me, his hands flex and clench, making his giant arms bulge and his tribal sleeve dance. Every. *Single*. Detail about him is a girl's wet dream come to life.

I'm hyperaware of the fact that I'm standing in front of him in nothing but a t-shirt and a pair of lacy booty shorts, my braless nipples poking against the fabric in a visceral response to all the hotness in front of me.

"So…" I watch his throat as he swallows. "I usually sleep in my underwear, but if that makes you uncomfortable, I can pull on a pair of sweats."

His consideration for my feelings catches me off guard in the best way possible.

"No, it's fine." I shake my head. "But I can't promise not to have *Roman* hands."

"That was bad. Really bad." He finishes taking off his jeans and tosses them onto one of the chairs. "And I thought I was the Italian one in this relationship."

"Don't hate on my quirky humor." I climb into bed next to him.

"Wouldn't *dream* of it." He hooks an arm around my middle, pulling me in, the little spoon to his much larger big spoon. "I'm quite fond of it in the form of the witty shirts you always wear."

The press of his muscular chest against my back makes me sigh as his body heat envelops mine. I try not to think too much about the fact that this is the first time I'm having a sleepover with a boyfriend.

Mase presses a kiss to the back of my neck, sending a fresh wave of tingles down my spine.

"Sleep, baby," he whispers in my ear as I drift away again.

CHAPTER
THIRTY-EIGHT

Waking up with Kay in my arms is officially my new favorite thing of all time. I've never spent the night with a girl before, and clearly I've been missing out.

One of my arms is serving as a pillow under Kay's head, and the other has found its way under her shirt to cup one of her generous boobs. She's braless, her nipple pushing against my palm, and it takes every ounce of my self-control to not flick it to further attention.

If the way my morning wood is responding to the press of her heart-shaped ass against me is any indication, this is now my *preferred* method of waking up.

Rolling my hips back to ease the pressure on said morning wood, I carefully extract myself from Kay's tempting body to avoid waking her up.

Last night she mentioned having to work at The Barracks today, so after I get dressed in a pair of basketball shorts and a Hawks football cutoff, I take a peek at her phone to make sure the alarm is set.

The tiny clock icon is there, and so are a flood of text notifications. She doesn't have her preview option turned on—and anyway, as much as I'm curious to see what they say, I wouldn't invade her privacy like that—so all I can make out are the names of the senders.

CTG BFF JT.

E.

B.

T.

Bette.

G.

CK.

Savvy.

King.

D.

Em.

Q.

Holy shit!

I recognize most of the names, but not all. Based on the number of notifications, her phone must have been buzzing throughout the night. It's a shock we both managed to sleep through it.

I'd be concerned something was wrong, but if that were the case, Grayson would have reached out to me when Kay didn't answer. Seeing as my phone lacks any missed calls or texts, presumably things are fine.

It doesn't stop my thoughts from running circles around themselves.

Who are all these people? How many of them are guys? What was with the cryptic text from JT about Kay being on the UofJ411 Instagram?

I may have failed at finding Kay's IG handle, but when you have a hashtag dedicated to tracking your movements, it's easy enough to see what people are saying about me.

I've just gotten done grabbing Kay's bag from the car and stealthily dropping it off in my room, and now I am scrolling through posts from the game, shots of me winking at Kay and ones of her wearing my hoodie, when Trav emerges from the guest room he uses whenever he stays over.

"Hey, man." Dressed similarly to me, he greets me with a fist out to bump. "Aw, aren't you the little media darling," he says, looking over my shoulder. "Brantley will love that."

I make a noncommittal sound as we continue our journey down the stairs and into the kitchen to find the rest of my family.

"Where's Coach?" Olly asks as I steal a piece of bacon from his plate.

"Sleeping. She's not much of a morning person."

"Would you boys like eggs for breakfast?" Mom asks from the stove.

"Sure, Moms," Trav answers for us.

"What are your plans for the day?"

"Trav and I are gonna go for a run and then I think we're gonna hang with some of the team to watch football at the AK house."

"So the usual."

"Yup."

Kay makes her way into the kitchen then, looking so damn cute with her hair in a high pony and a purple bow that of course matches her purple marbled leggings and funny black tank with purple writing: *cheerleader: [cheer-lee-der] - noun 1. An attitude with a bow.*

I think I need to make you a punch card for how many times you refer to her as cute. Instead of you getting a free coffee when it's full, you just have to turn in your man card.

"Hey, Coach," the twins say in unison.

"Hey, guys." She greets them with a sleepy smile.

I get up to snag a cup of coffee for her, because let's be honest, we all know how badly she functions without caffeine in the morning.

I'm back in my seat in a flash and Kay settles in besides me, my arm finding its home around her shoulder as I slide the mug in front of her.

Look at us, totally nailing this boyfriend thing.

Her beautiful stormy eyes flit down to it then up to me, tipping up at the corners before she snuggles against me deeper. If you would have told me weeks ago that I, Mason Nova, the Casanova of the U of J, would be cuddling with a girl in my parents' kitchen on a Sunday morning *and* that the girl would be my girlfriend, I would have told you you'd gotten your hands on a bad batch of drugs.

But if you were to tell me I would like it and the feeling of her body against mine would feel like *home*, well, I would ask you to go on because *that* is the *last* thing I would have thought I wanted.

Yet, here we are. And I wouldn't change it for the world.

CHAPTER
THIRTY-NINE

With all the uncertainty and second-guessing I was doing after JT's texts last night, I can't believe how well I slept. Then again, if the way I passed out on Mase during the movie was any indication, I was meant to sleep in his arms.

Waking up alone is a little disorienting. How am I supposed to handle actually leaving the bedroom? Is it weird me being here? He said his mom—no mention of Brantley—wanted me to stay, but what do his parents really think of me sleeping over this early in our relationship?

Sitting up in his large cloudlike bed, I spot my duffle on top of the dresser, and a spark of warmth forms in my stomach at yet another example of his thoughtfulness. For someone who's new to the whole boyfriend / girlfriend thing, he's killing it—not that I would ever *tell* him that.

Buzz! Buzz!

My phone dances across the bedside table, and when I pick it up, I have a staggering number of text messages waiting for me. Luckily the world hasn't exploded the way the notifications would suggest; it's simply those who love me and were there for me at my lowest checking in.

Don't you think it's time to come clean about E and...everything? My inner cheerleader taps her foot at me. She's right. If this relationship is going to be real, Mase deserves to know all the parts of me—eventually.

I find the whole Nova-Roberts clan, plus Trav, in the kitchen. Mason's dimples flash when he sees me, and I watch them deepen as he reads my shirt.

With the speed and grace only a finely trained athlete can accomplish, he's out of his seat and back in it before I can even manage making it to the table. When he pushes a cup of coffee in front of me as I sit, I lean into him and kiss his cheek to show my appreciation.

It's the little things like this—supplying me with coffee in the morning, commenting on my comical shirts—that all add up to show how much he gets me. I try to focus on these things to keep my mind off panicking, because dating Mason Nova is the biggest risk that doesn't include people tossing me in the air that I've allowed myself to take in years.

I need to check Instagram later. I don't want to—it is literally the *last* thing I want to do—but I need to know what I'm up against.

"What percentage of your wardrobe would you say is made up of your funny shirts?" Trav points at me from across the table.

"Shirt-wise?" I consider it for a moment. "At least half."

"Kayla, honey, would you like anything to eat for breakfast?" Grace asks.

"No thank you. We always have food at these coach meetings."

I don't typically work on Sundays unless it's right before a competition, but Coach Kris will take advantage of any NJA alumni in the area when we are trying to work out specific areas giving us trouble.

Buzz! Buzz!

"Look who's little miss popular this morning," Trav teases as he plucks some bacon off Livi's plate. Nice to see I'm not the only one he pirates food from.

"We can blame your best friend for that development."

"Blame?" Mason splays his hand over his made-to-stretch-cotton-against-it chest. "Thank is more like it."

I roll my eyes at his arrogant Casanova side peeking out. I let him have it, though, because he is able to understand what I mean by blame without me telling him the whys.

"I live for your eye rolls, babe." Mase gives me a smacking kiss on my temple.

"There is something seriously wrong with you."

"Agreed," comes from Trav, the twins, and Grace. Nothing from Brantley.

Around the table, everybody laughs, the family dynamics reminding me of all the Dennings/Taylor gatherings I experienced in my life. Again, Bette's comment about being my true self with Mason hits me. The real question is...will he want me when he learns about all the broken pieces? And if he does, will he stay with me because of me, or because I'm Eric Dennings' younger sister?

"So what has your phone doing an Irish jig, Short Stack?"

I bite back a groan at the reminder of how my drive to The Barracks will have to be spent making phone calls instead of rocking out to the radio.

"The CasanovaWatch hashtag." Mase winks when I cant my head to the side.

"Oh-ho-ho." Trav doubles over, clutching his stomach before holding his own phone out to us. "I'm pretty sure *everyone* on the team has sent me this post." On the screen is a boomerang of Mason winking.

"Don't worry, bro." Mase takes the phone, admiring the looping video clip. "I'll teach you how to wink like a pro."

"May I see?" Brantley holds a hand out to Trav, participating in the conversation for the first time since I stepped into the kitchen.

I swallow down the last of my coffee as Mase and Trav battle it out, using the twins as judges to determine who the best winker is.

"As much fun as it is to witness you guys basking in your bromance"—I scoot to the end of the bench—"I need to go."

"I'll walk you out," Mase offers, and I say my goodbyes.

Even for the short walk out to Pinky, he puts his arm around my shoulders to keep me close to his side. I like the way it feels, but I don't know if I can allow this to be our new normal.

"I miss your heels from the other night."

"Is this your way of telling me you're into cross-dressing?" My snark earns me a pinch in the side.

"Don't even try to act like I wouldn't look *stunning* in a sequined dress."

I roll my eyes. He's so ridiculous.

"What I meant was, when you wear heels, it's easier to walk like this because your shoulders aren't down by my hips."

"Hardy-har-har." This time it's his side being pinched.

"Couldn't help myself." He hits me with another one of those winks he most definitely *is* the master of then backs me into the side of my Jeep, the cold metal of the door seeping through the thin material of my shirt.

His hands come up to cradle the back of my head, gently tilting it up.

"Come watch football at the AK house when you get off?"

My heart elevators up to my throat at the suggestion, but I still find myself nodding.

His fingers fan out along my skull and I know I'm going to have to fix my ponytail, but as his lips touch mine, prickly stubble hitting my lips as they part to grant his tongue access, I just don't care about my hair.

I taste the fresh mint of his toothpaste, the salty grease from the bacon, and the addictive flavor of his coffee.

"Fuck, Skittles." His voice is thick with lust as he breathes into the kiss.

"Mase," I whisper back, unable to pull away.

"It makes me hard when you call me Mase." He grinds his hips into me to illustrate just how true that is.

If I don't leave now, I'm going to be late, but with each kiss, nip of his teeth, stroke of his tongue, and squeeze of his fingers, I find it harder to care about that either.

"Should I have the guys start an over/under on whose mouth your tongue spends more time in, Nova?" Trav's amused voice bellows from the house.

Mase, not giving a damn, kisses me for another solid minute before pulling away.

On shaky legs, I climb into Pinky. As I start down the driveway, watching Mase and Trav shove each other playfully in my rearview, the stutter behind my breastbone tells me all I need to know.

I may not have seen any of them coming, but I think I may have to keep them after all.

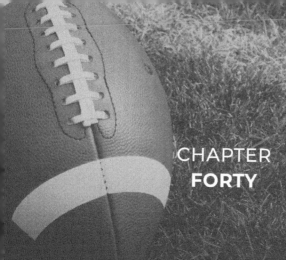

MASON

The squat bar is loaded in the rack with a few hundred pounds as I take my position under it for my set. The first workout of the week helps shake off the cobwebs of the weekend, and Coach always makes it the most brutal. It makes me extremely grateful Trav and I at least run on Sundays.

Alex ambles over after finishing his set on the bench press. "So your chick is pretty cool."

I can't stop my smile at the mention of Kay. "Thanks, man."

"If you mess this up, it's cool if I ask her out, right?"

"Nah, man—I called dibs." Noah sits up on the weight bench.

I clench my jaw to bite back my instant response. They may just be trying to get a rise out of me, but even the thought of her with someone else causes a haze of red to fill my vision.

Kay is mine and no one else's.

What if she doesn't feel the same way? You know, I've been meaning to talk to you about that. Homegirl's been hesitant each step of the way. Made you work for a date. Didn't want to wear the hoodie. Hell, you don't even know her IG handle. It's not official official *until it's on social media.*

Each thought hits my system like poison. My inner coach isn't wrong per se, but I remind myself that even G, her best friend, doesn't tag her in his posts—the rare times she's even in them. And, again, I like how she doesn't want to be in the spotlight.

It's different.

It's refreshing.

Right?

"What we talking 'bout?" Trav makes his way over.

"Which one of us gets to ask Kay out when she finally wises up and gets rid of this dead weight over here." Alex hooks a thumb in my direction.

"Well if she wants a *real* man, you know it's gonna be me, unlike you losers." Kev flexes.

"Guys, give him a break," Trav cuts in.

"Thanks, man." I resume my position in the rack again.

"Besides, it'll be more fun watching him squirm." Trav winks.

"Asshole."

"Love you too." He blows kisses at me. "But, seriously, bro... she's a unicorn. Don't fuck this up."

Noah snorts as he finishes his next bench set. "A unicorn, Trav? Very poetic, bro."

"She's a chick who not only loves football but understands it. Hell, she was calling the damn plays and penalties yesterday. So, yeah, she's a fucking unicorn." Everyone laughs at his explanation. "Plus, we all know she'd pick me."

Trash talk is normal and something I'm used to at practice and in the locker room, but on a day I don't usually see Kay, it only makes the voice in my head louder.

Coach Knight enters the weight room and catches us talking. "Oh, I'm *sorry*. Is my workout interfering with your girl talk?" he shouts.

We scatter back to our respective stations, knowing it's better to stay silent than to respond.

After a punishing two hours of lifting followed by the hottest shower on record, I'm walking across campus for my first class. I pull out my phone to see Kay's answer to my good morning text from earlier.

> SKITTLES: You are so lucky I sleep with my phone on silent, mister. Otherwise you'd be dead right now. *knife emoji* *angry eyed emoji*

Man this chick is the best.

> ME: Whatcha doin, baby?

SKITTLES: In class. What about you, slacker?

> ME: Tell me where you are and I'll show you a slacker.

SKITTLES: Why do you make everything I say sound dirty?

> ME: One of my many special talents.

SKITTLES: *GIF of Michelle Tanner rolling her eyes*

> ME: You know how I feel about you rolling your eyes.

SKITTLES: There is something SERIOUSLY wrong with you.

> ME: And yet YOU still agreed to be my girlfriend. Now tell me where your class is.

SKITTLES: I'm in Jefferson Hall.

Perfect—not too far from where my first class is located. I change direction and head for Jefferson.

> ME: Room #?

SKITTLES: Why?

> ME: Room #?

SKITTLES: Fine.

SKITTLES: 521.

I can tell she's getting all huffy with me even over text. She never falls for my shit, and I can't believe how much of a turn-on it is for me.

I stride through the doors of Jefferson Hall and take the elevator up to the fifth floor. Once I'm outside Kay's classroom, I send her another text.

> ME: Go to the bathroom.

> SKITTLES: What? Why?

This girl is cutely clueless.

> ME: Excuse yourself to go to the bathroom so I can kiss you hello.

> SKITTLES: ????

> SKITTLES: Don't you have class?

Oh, she still has so much to learn about me.

> ME: Get your sexy ass out here.

I watch the three little dots appear and disappear on the screen for a minute, but no new text comes. Then the door to the classroom opens, and out steps my Skittles. I smile when I catch sight of her shirt, another from her funny collection, this one reading *I Speak French* in big letters, and smaller, underneath: *Fries*.

"You should have saved that shirt for lunch with Trav and G."

"True." She agrees with a grin. "What the hell are you doing here?"

"I missed you."

It's true; I missed her more than I probably should as a new couple. With the guys making all those comments, I needed eyes on her to calm the uncertainty and insecurity that periodically creeps in.

"You're gonna be late to class," she cautions, maintaining her distance, standing across the hall. Her head swivels left then right, checking that we are alone.

Our relationship took a number of strides forward this weekend, but right now I feel like we're taking a few steps back.

"That's fine. This is totally worth it." I shift, eliminating the space between us, and pull her into my arms where she belongs.

"What is?" With the way she has to tilt her head all the way back to make eye contact, I can see that V between her brows is back.

"This." I spin her Yankees hat backward, moving the brim out of my way, and drop a kiss on her lips.

I savor it, tunneling my fingers in her hair under her hat, cradling the back of her head as my tongue strokes hers. She tastes like sugar and coffee, and I can't get enough.

Her nails scratch the back of my neck and my own hat goes askew from the way her hands fist.

Her eyes are dazed when they meet mine.

"Now I can get to class. Bye, baby."

#THEGRAM

UofJ411

picture of Kay with Trav at The Nest

52,183 views

UofJ411 Guess best friends share everything?
#SharingIsCaring #CasanovaWatch #CasanovasMysteryGirl

@Heymom05: I don't know @CasaNova87 she looks pretty cozy with @QB1McQueen? #CasanovasMysteryGirl

---

UofJ411

Alex and Kevin walking with Kay around campus

48,537 views

UofJ411 Does the football team have a mascot?
#WhatAboutTheHawk #CasanovaWatch
#CasanovasMysteryGirl

@Hippychick782000: I'd like to be the filling in that sandwich
@CantCatchAnderson22 @SackMasterSanders91
#OreosAreLife #CreamFilling #CasanovaWatch
#CasanovasMysteryGirl
@It.sgottabethebooks: So wait? Is she dating @CasaNova87
or the whole football team? #CasanovasMysteryGirl

UofJ411   ⋮

Noah and Kay at a coffee cart on campus

56,821 views

UofJ411 Musical coffee date? #HoldMyLatte #CasanovaWatch #CasanovaMysteryGirl

@JJennifermarie119: Is @CasaNova87 being *kicked* to the curb by @LacesOutMitchell5
#WhatHappenedToBrosBeforeHoes #CasanovasMysteryGirl
@JJUllom: I'll warm your bed @CasaNova87
#ShoulderToCryOn #CasanovasMysteryGirl

Though I'm still avoiding the Gram—both checking the notifications and being the subject of posts—like it's my job, this week has been unlike any other I've had as a student at the U of J.

My life has officially become invaded by footballers with Mase's teammates—at least the core group he hangs out with—all making it a point to find me around campus. It's hard enough to avoid letting Mase walk with his arm around me; adding in the rest of them has become quite a feat.

Hats are now an everyday staple of my wardrobe, and most days I have my hair gathered in a messy bun out the back to make the colors in it sort of hidden. I've been doing my best to enjoy my budding relationship, but the fear of my identity being revealed hangs like a dark cloud in the form of a hashtag. I thought #CasanovaWatch was bad, but it has nothing on #CasanovasMysteryGirl.

I know I need to woman up and tell Mason about the things I went through, but every time I've tried, I've chickened out. He's so self-assured and doesn't give a fuck what others have to say, and I'm embarrassed to admit that I've been hiding.

I may not know what's being posted, but the annoyed texts

I've received from Mase whenever something does go up have been highly entertaining.

For example:

> BOYFRIEND (and yes this is how he is saved in my phone now. We settled on this after he tried to name himself Ruler of Kay's Universe): You tell those jockholes I'll kick their asses if they try anything.

I find it hysterical he's calling his fellow teammates this.

> BOYFRIEND: I'm the only one who's supposed to bring you coffee.

Yeah, like I'd *ever* agree to that.

> BOYFRIEND: I hate Wednesdays. Why do my friends get to see you and I don't? Grrr not fair.

This point I agree with wholeheartedly.

> BOYFRIEND: Trav and I WILL NOT be replaced by Alex as your favorite.

Stupid children, all of them.

And so on and so on.

What I appreciate about them the most is how they entertain me enough to keep my thoughts off of the actual posts and help keep the panic attacks over them at bay.

My favorite texts, though, are the ones Mase sends every morning when he wakes up for his early workouts and I'm sleeping, just to make sure he's the first person I hear from. I wish we could stay in that bubble.

Being on campus on a Friday is weird, but since I don't have any classes, it was the easiest day for me to schedule a meeting with Charlie, the U of J's drumline captain.

The Nest isn't as empty as I thought it would be, and I catch more than a few people glancing and pointing in my direction. I ignore them all, tugging the brim of my hat a few millimeters lower, and grab a large latte from the coffee shop before looking around for Charlie. I spot someone I think is him on the lounge chairs in one of the corners by the door.

"Are you Charlie?" I ask when I approach.

"Yeah. Are you Dani's friend?" He looks up.

Dani is one of the NJA Marshals alumni who lend their expertise to help when crafting the senior squads' routines. We usually try to have them choreographed and the music selection complete before the end of summer, only tweaking and making upgrades for the larger Nationals and Worlds competitions. This year, however, we've all agreed there was something missing from what we had. That's where Charlie comes in.

"Yeah, Kay." I grin and reach out a hand to shake. "Thanks for agreeing to meet with me."

"No problem." He returns my handshake and gestures for me to take the open seat cushion next to him. "I like Dani a lot, though I gotta say, I am intrigued her request wasn't for the White Squad."

"Dani may rock the hell out of red and white, but she'll always bleed blue camouflage for the New Jersey All-Stars."

"With the exception of the U of J part, that's pretty much how she described you," Charlie chuckles.

I'm in total agreement as I pull my iPad from my bag. "I figured it might be easier if I show you what we're thinking rather than just telling you." I hold up the iPad.

"Sounds good to me. She said what you need is different than what we do for the football games."

"Yes. What we need, and are hoping you can help us with, is to have the drumline create and record a cadence for our two senior squads to use." I flip open the cover and pull up the videos I saved specifically for this meeting. "It wouldn't be for the entire routine, but woven in throughout certain sections."

Charlie nods and pulls out a notepad. We spend the next few minutes bent over the iPad, watching routines from both the Marshals and the Admirals. Periodically, he has me pause or rewind sections to ask questions.

"If it helps, the cadences you guys have for U of J are the style we like." My dream would be to have them, but they are for school use only.

"No that's great. I already have a few ideas, but having that as a baseline will help us create something faster."

He walks me through some of what he's thinking, and we discuss the best ways to incorporate them into the routines. I haven't even heard a note, but already I'm pumped for the possibilities forming in my head.

I'm riding the high only creating NJA routines can give me when the *last* voice I want to hear cuts in.

"*Yet* another guy, huh, *Kayla*?" Adam interrupts.

I turn to face my least favorite Alpha Kappa brother.

"Did you need something, Adam?"

The jerk places his hands on the armrest, invading my personal space so much I catch the scent of coffee on his breath. "No, but if I'd known you were accepting applications, I would have turned in mine instead of you having to slum it with a band geek."

Charlie stiffens beside me. Taking in his appearance, I can see he's anything but a band geek. His black hair has hints of blue and is styled in a faux hawk, and his forearms are corded with muscles from all the drumming and decorated with colorful tattoos.

He's got a badass black spike through his left eyebrow and small gauged earrings in both ears. He may not be a Mason, but he's still built and cute.

"*God*, you are such a jockhole. Please go away." I shoo him and turn my attention back to Charlie.

"Come on, princess, don't be like that. Why don't you stop wasting your time with this guy and spend it with me instead?"

Jeez this guy is such an ass.

I blow out a breath. "Go. Away."

He presses in closer, his nose skimming my cheek. Unlike the tingles Mase gives me when he's this close, Adam's touch has me feeling slimy.

"What do you think Nova would say about this?" I turn my head away as his hot breath blows into my ear with each word.

I'm trapped, caged in between him and the couch. I put my hands on his chest in an effort to free myself and he gives me a triumphant smile, thinking he has some upper hand on me.

"About what?" I push. "Talking to someone? Having coffee with someone?" He goes to cut in, but I continue on undeterred, refusing to be intimidated. "The only thing I can see him having an issue with is *you* harassing me while I'm working on something with Charlie here. Now *seriously* leave."

"You sound awfully sure of yourself, Kayla." He cranes his neck, looking back over his shoulder. "What do you think he's going to say when people start posting the pictures they're snapping of us right now?"

Fucking Instagram. Stupid fucking hashtags. I want to curl up and hide but refuse to give Adam the satisfaction of me doing that or checking to see if he's right.

"What do you want, Adam? What's your endgame?"

There's nothing humorous about the dark chuckle he expels. "Wouldn't you like to know."

With a kiss to my cheek that feels reminiscent of the kiss of death, he finally leaves.

#THEGRAM

UofJ411

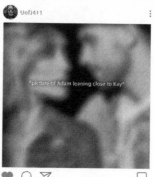
picture of Adam leaning close to Kay

56,821 views

UofJ411 interesting...
#AlphaForEveryDayOfTheWeek #CasanovasMysteryGirl

@Juliedreamsofbooks: Is *cozying* up to @ThirdBaseAdam16
how you get an invite to the AK parties?
#AlphaKappaPartyCentral #CasanovasMysteryGirl
@Kmford2317: Alpha Kappa party favor?
#CasanovasMysteryGirl
@Ladyjanegray75: Yet another guy? #AddingToHerHarem
#CasanovasMysteryGirl

UofJ411

picture of Adam's face next to Kay's

53,592 views

UofJ411 Anything you want to share with the class?
#SecretsSecrets #CasanovasMysteryGirl

@Lagerlefsebookblog: I guess she isn't exclusive with
@CasaNova87 #CanIStillApply #CasanovasMysteryGirl
@Lala_powergirl: Whispering sweet nothings? #FlyOnTheWall
#CasanovasMysteryGirl
@Lonniegallahan: Anyone else wondering what they are
saying? #AskingForAFriend #CasanovasMysteryGirl

UofJ411

picture of Kay's hands on Adam's chest while they look at each other

♥ ◯ ◁

UofJ411 Touchy Touchy #GettingClose #CasanovasMysteryGirl

@Lynnstifle: So much for personal space #IdTouchHimToo #CasanovasMysteryGirl
@Madameizzy: Rounding the bases with @ThirdBaseAdam16 #BatterUp #CasanovasMysteryGirl
@Mimi_reads: Is she playing Alpha sports bingo? First @TheGreatestGrayson37 Then @CasaNova87 Now @ThirdBaseAdam16 Two more sports and she has it #BINGO CasanovasMysteryGirl

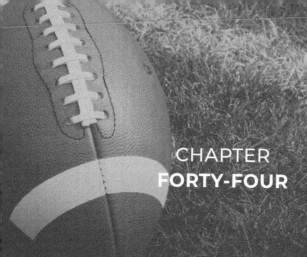

CHAPTER
FORTY-FOUR

MASON

What most people don't realize is a college athlete's life is scheduled as much, if not more so, outside of their games and practices.

Free time is typically a foreign concept, so this whole *me getting a girlfriend* thing has been interesting, to say the least.

Now that we are a third of the way into the season, the window of free time we get on non-travel days before a game is even smaller. No more dinner dates on Friday nights until the season is over.

So what am I doing for those few precious hours between the team's walkthrough practice and when I have to report to dinner at the hotel? Well, I'm going to see my girlfriend, of course.

World's best boyfriend right here. My inner coach waves a foam finger in the air.

Kay answers the door in what I consider her studying uniform: tight beater-style tank in white and a baggy pair of rolled-over U of J sweats, these in red with black writing. Beneath her tank the straps of a red bra show, to match her sweats, of course. As usual, I can't see her feet because they are covered by her pants.

My hands find the bared skin between her tank and her

sweats like a moth to a flame. I stroke my thumbs across the bumps of her hipbones, living for that hitch in her breath. After a moment, I finally give her what we both want and press my lips against hers.

"Hi." She looks up with a dreamy smile on her lovely face.

"Hi, baby."

"What are you doing here?" She moves so I can enter the dorm, shutting the door behind us.

"Is it so wrong I want to see my girlfriend?"

She tosses me a look over her shoulder, rolling her eyes when she catches me checking out her ass, but the tilt of her lips gives away how happy she is to see me.

I wish I were able to read her better. When we're alone or surrounded by our friends, she's open with her affection and lets me pull her into my lap and keep my arm around her. Why is it she won't do the same around campus? Unless it's during class or when I join her for lunch, she keeps me at as much of a distance as she does my boys.

Kay worries so much about eyes on us. Well you know what? There are no other eyes here except us.

She lets out a squeak when I lift her in my arms and press her to the wall right here in the hallway. Her pint-sized-ness makes it easy to cradle her to me like a football, but a pigskin never squeezed its legs around my waist or rubbed itself against the growing bulge in my joggers like my girl is.

"Kay," I warn, sinking my teeth into the curve of her neck.

"Mase," she moans, her head falling to the side, allowing me better access.

Using my lower body to support her, I snake my hands underneath the hem of her tank, skimming them up her back.

She arches, her breasts thrusting against me, the hard points of her nipples pressing into my chest. I want them in my mouth.

She cups my face, lifting it so she can kiss me.

Our mouths meet, our tongues mimicking the movements of our lower bodies, little whimpers escaping each time the ridge of my cock presses on her center.

She moans my name again, and I curl my hands over her shoulders from behind, hook my thumbs in the straps bisecting them, and ease them down her arms.

Pink nipples stare at me, *begging* for my mouth as the material lowers enough to free them.

Who am I to deny what the nipples want?

I barely register the dull thud of my hat hitting the floor when she clutches my head, holding me to her body like I might stop if she doesn't. *Fat chance.* I suckle at her like she's a Gatorade bottle after summer two-a-days.

"Oh god, Mase."

Fuck me if the way she looks, head thrown back, hitting the wall with a bang, eyes closed in pleasure isn't the most erotic sight I've ever seen.

I've had jersey chasers put on a full-on porn star performance while they deep-throat my dick, but none of that can compare to the pure passion my girl is radiating as she rides me through our clothes.

"Mase." Her fingertips ghost over my eight-pack as she tugs my shirt up. "Mase."

Another grind from her. Another roll of the hips from me.

"Mase."

Somewhere in a distant part of my brain, it registers that she's calling me Mase and not Casanova.

"Mase."

Her nipple falls from my mouth as I rise enough for her to peel the cotton over my head, and as soon as my shirt goes the same way as my hat, I'm feasting on the other breast.

She's fire in my arms as my hands palm her ass. I'm about to take this to the bedroom when rapid knocking starts on the door.

Her eyes are almost completely black as she gets that adorable furrow between her brows.

Guess I'm not the only one who showed up unexpectedly.

Granted, I didn't plan on dry-humping Kay in the hallway, but this is the most unwelcome interruption.

"Were you expecting anyone else?" I ask as I help adjust her clothes.

"I wasn't even expecting you." She taps my arm to let her down.

She fiddles with her shirt, trying to get rid of the evidence—even if we didn't get to the good stuff. Anyone looking at her will know what she's been up to.

"Funny," Kay says after opening the door, "I don't remember joining the football team."

Forgetting my shirt on the floor, I close the distance, wrap an arm around Kay's middle, and pull her against my bare chest. She leans into my embrace as I stare at my cockblocking teammates.

Trav, Noah, Alex, and Kev take in my naked torso and Kay's sex hair, smirking like they know *exactly* what they interrupted.

Assholes.

"What makes you say that, Short Stack?" Trav leans against the doorjamb.

"Well, Q-B-1…" Kay enunciates each syllable. "What other reason would there be for so many of the Hawks captains to be at my door the day before a game?"

"We have a few hours to kill," Noah explains.

"Oh-kay…" There's an implied *That doesn't explain anything* in the way Kay lets the sentence trail off.

"Are you not happy to see us, Smalls?" Kev pouts like he's not one of the most feared defensive ends in D1 football.

"Yeah, come on, Smalls," Alex cajoles, also adopting Grayson's nickname for my girl. "We just wanna be where the cool kids are."

"Mase is the only one here." She finally steps aside to let them in.

"We're not here for Casanova." Noah pops me in the arm.

"Yeah, he's lame," Kev adds.

"We're here for you, Short Stack." Trav drops his arm around her shoulders, pulling her away from me with a wink.

Asshole may be my best friend, but he better sleep with one eye open tonight.

"I blame you for this." Kay peers over Trav's arm to level me with a *Look what you did* expression.

"What's that, Skittles?" I pop my head through the opening of my shirt, slipping it back on.

"My life being invaded by football players."

"Don't act like you don't love it."

She's silent, but the quirk of those still-swollen-from-my-kisses lips gives her away.

"So what are we going to do?" Trav walks them into the living room area, the rest of us following behind.

"I *was* studying."

"I bet you were." Trav waggles his eyebrows dramatically and gets himself a backhand to the stomach from Kay.

The guys make themselves at home around her apartment like we hang here on the reg. Much to my pleasure, Kay settles herself in my lap after retrieving her MacBook. She quickly gets back to work, allowing the guys to change the channel on the television without complaint.

Her curls tickle my nose and I smooth them to the side, placing a handful of kisses on her now exposed neck.

From over her shoulder, I get another eye roll, and when she wiggles in my lap, I'm reminded of how blue my balls still are from our earlier interruption. Every now and then, I reach around her and help her by typing on her keyboard, but she smacks my hand away any time I do.

This is the stuff she doesn't allow in public, and to be honest, it's a little bit annoying.

"Damn, Kay." Alex whistles through his teeth, bringing everyone's attention to him. "I think your hashtag might have more hits than Nova's now." He holds his phone out toward us.

Kay's entire body goes rigid. Slowly, as if using great caution to brace herself for what she is about to see, she slides her gaze to the lit screen.

In the post—which already has hundreds of comments—Adam is way too close for my comfort, not to mention Kay's if her stiff shoulders and clenched jaw are any indication.

Based on the way she reacted to Adam at the AK house last weekend when she joined us to watch football, I get the impression she's not his biggest fan.

"Asshole." Kay curses the image and refocuses on her computer.

"You know." I wind my arms around her middle, hugging her tighter until her back rests completely flush against my chest, my thumbs slipping beneath the hem of her tank and stroking across the soft skin of her belly. "There's an easy way to fix all this."

"Hmm?" Kay responds but sounds a million miles away.

"You wore my hoodie, but other than that, we haven't declared anything." *Plus you barely let me act like your boyfriend in public.* I keep that particular thought to myself. "Let's selfie it up.

With one post from each of us, we can clear the air. It'll shut the haters up and the speculators down."

Her laptop slams shut and she whips around, losing her balance until I steady her with a hand curled around her hip.

Her eyes dart around the room, searching for what, I'm not sure.

"No. No posts." She slashes a hand through the air.

It may not be rational, but anger boils up inside me from the tips of my toes to the top of my head.

"Why not?" It takes great effort, but I manage to keep the bite out of my tone.

Again her gaze shifts to the side, to check to see if the guys are paying attention. I'm sure they're listening, but luckily they all have their eyes averted away from us.

"I don't do the whole social media thing." That feels like a half-answer. "I try to keep my picture from being actively posted."

I frown and sit up from my reclined position. "Bullshit."

I've seen pictures of her on Grayson's and Em's Instagrams, and I call her out on it.

The sigh she releases is heavier than a lineman.

"Have you looked, *really* looked at them?"

Yes. I don't admit that, though, not wanting to give away just how much I attempted to internet-stalk her before we started dating.

"Alex, can I have your phone again?" He obliges when she holds out a hand.

All eyes turn her way, no longer pretending they aren't hanging on every touch and swipe of Kay's finger across the screen. When she finds what she's looking for, she flips the phone around, displaying the most recent picture on Grayson's IG with her in it—the one from the Crabs/Empire game.

"See this?" All I see is her beaming smile, the same one that is completely absent in her currently paler-than-normal face. "Every. Single. Shot is like this." I look at it again, not really catching on to what she means.

"Exactly." I point at the post. "That's all I want."

"Mason." Her head falls forward, her hair falling with it and obscuring her face. "Look again."

It's difficult to look away from where she's massaging the

ridge of her brow. The only time I've ever seen her this stressed was when she ran out of the AK house because her brother was in the hospital.

"I get that you want the whole world to see me as your girlfriend."

"*See* you as my girlfriend? What the fuck do you mean by that?" She finches at my curse, and when I glance away to calm myself down, even Trav gives me a look that says *Breathe.*

"Mason—"

"Kayla. Answer the question."

Fuck privacy—I need to know now. Plus, it'll be helpful to have Trav witness her responses. He lived through the lies and was played the same way by *her.* I refuse to live through another Chrissy/Tina debacle.

"On the rare occasion G and Em include me in their posts, it's never of my full face. Either I'm turned away, only showing part of my profile, or it's from behind, from a distance, or like this one"—her nail audibly taps the screen—"a hat covers most of my face."

She's right. I reach out, cradling her hand in mine as I pull the phone in for a closer inspection. I recognized her right away because she was who I was focusing on, but she's right—not many people would.

"You wore my hoodie though."

There's the barest lift of her lips. "I almost didn't."

I don't like that answer.

"So why did you?" I anchor a hand around the back of her neck, keeping her eyes on mine when she tries to look away again.

"Because you asked and I knew it would make you happy. But"—she's quick to cup my cheek, her thumb running along the arch of my cheekbone before I can cut in—"*please* don't ask *this* of me. I'll have to say no, and as much as I wish it were otherwise, I've discovered I don't like saying no to you."

A growl forms in the back of my throat, this one more lust than anger. She claims I'm the charming one in our relationship, but I think she might be underestimating herself in that regard.

Her whole body sags when I nod, the subject dropped.

I get the impression there is more to this than she's letting on, but now is not the time to push.

CHAPTER
FORTY-FIVE

KAYLA

I bite back another yawn as the attendant scans my ticket for today's game.

After Mase and the guys left yesterday, I couldn't shake the blanket of disappointment I felt from not being able to give him what he wanted. From the moment I gave in and texted him back, I've been on borrowed time. I knew before saying yes to our first date if we were going to make it as a couple, I would have to change how I've been living—or more accurately, hiding—my life.

Mase has this way of seeing me how very few people, if any, do. When he looks at me, he doesn't see Eric Dennings' little sister, the girl used by a boy because of who her sibling is, the girl teased and bullied to get a laugh. I'm not the girl who was so broken by her father's death and the events thereafter it became clickbait.

He doesn't see me that way because I haven't told him any of it.

Is it so wrong to bask in it for as long as I can?

Between a night of tossing and turning and today's double practice, I'm completely wiped and need a sugar-free Red Bull in my life stat.

The weather has taken a turn for the craptastic, and if guilt wasn't driving me to show I'm a supportive girlfriend in the few ways I'm comfortable with, I'd be watching the game from home.

By the time I'm making my way down the steps to our seats, the game is already in the second quarter, and the rain is coming down in a steady downpour.

Cinching the strings of "the hoodie" to tighten it over my red Hawks ball cap, I ignore all the pointed looks and whispers cast in my direction as I pass.

With Pops on shift, I spent the night at the Taylors' only to have T finally force me into scrolling through the UofJ411 posts. When she uses logic to make me pull my head out of the sand I try to hide in, she makes me feel like I'm the one in high school and not her.

The number of posts dedicated to Mase and figuring out the identity of his *mystery girl* is insane. I don't understand why the hell it matters who he dates.

It got to the point where I had enough and I left T and Savvy to continue to scroll while I focused on the old episode of *Gossip Girl* they had playing in the background.

"Hard practice?" G eyes the extra-large can in my hand when I plop down in my seat, my legs too tired to hold me up any longer.

I shrug. It's more my restless night than the productive practices that has me mainlining the energy drink instead of coffee.

I look out over the field in search of number eighty-seven and find him with the rest of the offense at the line of scrimmage. I take a moment to admire the way his butt looks in his tight football pants. Because, *hello!* football pants.

A quick glance at the scoreboard shows the Hawks are already up by a touchdown and are driving for a second. The center snaps the ball to Trav, who drops back and pump-fakes before launching the ball downfield into Mason's hands for a touchdown.

The stadium erupts in cheers as the band plays the school's fight song. I'm still on my feet clapping when Mase runs behind the team bench to check out the stands.

His fingers are hooked through the face mask of his helmet, holding it by his side, and his mouthguard is pinched between his molars, hooking around his cheek. His free hand runs through his hair, causing it to stick up in disarray, while he scans the crowd—for me.

The moment his beautiful eyes lock onto me, he smiles, dimples flashing, and tingles shoot down my spine.

This guy.

He is sex on legs and I could look at him for hours.

He points at me with his helmet, winks, blows me a kiss, and heads back to join the rest of the team.

Don't mind me, just over here swooning.

I never stood a chance when it came to Mason Nova.

Hopefully it doesn't end up blowing up in my face.

I let the squishy feeling in my belly warm me, focusing on it and not the countless cellphones I see pointed in my direction.

During halftime, my phone vibrates in my pocket with a text from Charlie telling me they already have something for me to hear. After making sure Mason sees me at the start of the third, I tell G and CK where I'm going and follow Charlie's directions toward the end zone where the drumline sits near the field.

"I can't believe how fast you came up with something," I say to Charlie when he joins me.

With all my personal drama, it's almost hard to believe we met up only yesterday.

"Once we started playing around, it was easy. It's still rough, but do you wanna hear it?"

"Absolutely." I bounce on the balls of my feet, unable to contain my excitement. I tend to geek out when it comes to putting things together for routines.

He may have been concerned—and sure they aren't the beloved cadences they have for the school—but they are amazing.

"What do you think?" he asks when he rejoins me from playing.

"They're great, totally fit our style."

"Cool. If you need us to tweak anything, let me know and we'll take care of it."

The stadium's announcer catches my attention, calling out Kev's sack for a turnover. The special teams is heading out to receive the punt by the time I turn around to face the field.

"Oh shit! Now it makes sense." Charlie's voice holds a note of surprise.

"What does?" I ask, keeping my eyes on the game.

"I was wondering what was up at The Nest yesterday." He leans a hip against the railing next to me. "I didn't realize I was with the famous girl dating Casanova."

"Famous?" This time I do turn around, giving Charlie an incredulous look.

"I mean famous might not be the right word, but the school is buzzing about the girl who got Casanova to settle down."

Unlike the posts from the internet trolls, I don't feel any malicious intentions behind his statement, just a general curiosity.

"It's only been a few weeks, so *settled down* might not be the right description."

"Well he sure seems settled enough to claim you." He points to my back, the skin of which is burning like the black lettering is a brand.

Unfortunately, Charlie isn't the only one who's noticing. I ignore the stares and watch a beautiful handoff to Alex for a first down.

"Well looky-looky who's all cozy again with her new boyfriend."

My shoulders hit my ears at the sound of Adam's voice. I *loathe* this guy so much.

"Go away, Adam. No one invited you." I refuse to turn and give him a chance at getting close enough for another photo op.

"I'm surprised, though. Thought you were more into dark meat."

I whip around so fast my hood flies off, jaw practically on the ground, completely at a loss for words. How the *hell* G stands being around this guy, I have *no* idea.

"You. Are. A. *Despicable*. Human. Being." I spit the words out, venom on my tongue.

I don't have the mental capacity to deal with this right now. I fix my hood and turn my attention to Charlie.

"I'm gonna head back, but thank you so much for what you did."

"You're welcome, Kay. I'll let you know once we have it recorded."

"Sounds good. Bye, Charlie."

"Bye, Kay."

Without sparing a glance at Adam, I head back to the guys.

I try to shake off my frustration, but the pit in my gut tells me I won't be able to ignore Adam forever.

#THEGRAM

UofJ411   ⋮

"picture of Kay wearing the hoodie again"

♡ ◯ ◁   ⊓

UofJ411 Is this our answer?
#CasanovaIsTaken #CasanovaWatch #CasanovasMysteryGirl

@Miss_rae_mcnally: See?? It's true. She's wearing it again.
#CasanovaWatch #CasanovasMysteryGirl
@MomOf2Sk8ters: Nooo!! Say it ain't so @CasaNova87
#HeartBroken #CasanovasMysteryGirl
@Msteresaap: We NEED the deets. Come on @CasaNova87
fill us in. #IGotsToKnow #CasanovasMysteryGirl

UofJ411   ⋮

"boomerang of Mason pointing with his helmet
and winking"

♡ ◯ ◁   ⊓

UofJ411 I'm not ashamed to admit I'm swooning.
#HeartPalpatations #CasanovaWatch #CasanovasMysteryGirl

@Mylifethroughfiction: Holy shit! That wink @CasaNova87
#SomethingInMyEye
@Notnow.imreading: I see you, baby! #CallMe #CasanovaWatch
@Oamberwhereartthou: 😍 😍 #FansSelf
#CasanovaWatch
@Ofbooksandportkeys: I think my ovaries just exploded.
#IWillHaveYourBabies #CasanovaWatch

The days I don't have class with Kay are my least favorite because there's no guarantee I'll see her. I thought my football schedule was nuts, but it has nothing on everything she has going on. Between the nights she coaches at The Barracks, the two nights a week she sleeps over at her little sister's house, and all the studying she does to maintain her academic scholarship, I sometimes feel like I barely see her.

Now I try to make it a point to study at her place to get in as much Skittles time as I can. Plus, spending as much time as possible with her is the only way I can think of for us to overcome the strain I've felt since the whole *Let me post a picture of us* rejection.

Practice tonight was more brutal than usual, and all I want is to feel the softness of my girlfriend's body against mine.

I strip off my practice jersey and pads, sitting down on the bench in front of my locker before heading for the showers.

"Man, Coach kicked our asses tonight." Trav drops down next to me.

"At least you get to redshirt during practice and don't have to get pounded into the ground. Right now I'm not even sure I can make it to the shower, let alone all the way to Kay's."

"You'll feel better after we eat. Come on, man." He thumps me on the back.

I step into one of the individual shower stalls and turn the water on as hot as it goes. My arms go up and brace against the wall, and my head drops forward as I let the water beat against the tense muscles in my neck and shoulders. After this I'm gonna have to swing by the trainers to have them work out some of my kinks before dinner.

I towel off, stopping by the trainers' office on the way to my locker, and unfortunately there are no openings until tomorrow.

I'm not the only one moving a little slower tonight based on how many of my teammates are still hanging around.

Interlacing my fingers, I stretch my arms overhead then roll my shoulders back, letting out a groan.

"Short Stack's not gonna like you skipping out on meeting with the trainers," Trav comments.

One of my favorite things about Kay is that she not only respects the work put in for D1 football, she understands it. The first time I skipped seeing the trainers to get to her faster, she laid into me in a way that would make Coach Knight proud.

"Hey, I tried. They're full up tonight."

"Aww, Nova, does the new girlfriend call the shots?" one of our right tackles calls out.

"Never thought I'd see the day Casanova tied himself to a girl," adds one of our wide receivers.

I don't get defensive; they aren't saying anything I haven't thought myself a million times. Hell, my own inner coach is still on the fence half the time, and not letting my own hang-ups get in the way is an ongoing battle.

Even back in my Casanova days, I was never one for locker room bragging when it came to my hookups, so my girlfriend? Yeah, that's a no-go. Plus, if Grayson heard anything along those lines about Kay, he would *kill* me.

By the time I get done with dinner and head over to her place, it shouldn't be much longer until she's back from The Barracks. Me beating her home happens sometimes, and when it does, I either hang out with Em and Quinn or study in her room.

I knock on the dorm's door and wait for one of her room-mates to answer. Unfortunately, it's Bailey.

"Casanova." She greets me with a sugary-sweet smile.

"Hi Bailey." I may not like the chick, but I can be civil since she's roommates with my girl and they seem to get along.

"Do you want anything to eat?" Bailey reaches out to stroke my forearm.

I pull my arm from under her hand and move toward Kay's room, putting some much needed distance between us.

"No thanks, I ate with the team. I'm just gonna get a jump on studying." I hook a thumb toward Kay's room. "Bye, Bailey." Without waiting for a response, I make my retreat.

The smell of Kay's vanilla and peppermint scent fills my nose as I step inside the bedroom.

I slip off my sneakers, turn on the TV to a channel playing an old episode of *The Fresh Prince of Bel-Air*, climb onto her hot pink bed, and unpack my MacBook Pro and marketing textbook.

Maybe if I get a head start on studying, I can cash in on it with extra make-out time.

My eyes start to cross and my vision gets blurry from reading. The rest of my day combined with the reading must catch up to me, because the next thing I know I'm being woken up by Kay wrapping her arms and legs around me.

CHAPTER
FORTY-EIGHT

I drag myself through the front door of my dorm hours later than normal. Practice was hard tonight. One of our stunt groups had a nasty fall, and I had a base end up with a concussion. The important thing is she's going to be okay, but spending a big chunk of my night getting her checked over in the ER was not fun.

When I open the door to my room, I'm surprised to find a light on; I'm usually good about turning them off before I leave. Then when I see Mase stretched out asleep on my bed, textbook open next to him, I can't help the thump of my heart at the sight.

My phone died back at the hospital and I had no way of letting him know what was going on. Seeing him here makes my night instantly better.

I plug my phone into the charger and take care of my nightly routine. The plus side of spending most of my night in the ER—look at me finding silver linings like a pro—is I don't have to wash my hair. Showered, teeth brushed, one of Mase's football t-shirts and a pair of cotton boy shorts on, I make my way back to my room.

Phone finally charged enough to turn on, I note how late it is and can't bring myself to wake Mase up. I set my alarm for the *ungodly* hour of 5AM in case he didn't set one. If that's not proof of how much I like this guy, I don't know what is. I move his textbook from the bed, grab a blanket, and climb in next to him.

He is so big he practically takes up the entire full-sized mattress. I've never been so grateful for being tiny as I am when I fit my body alongside his and snuggle into his chest. I take a deep breath, inhaling the fresh scent of him and the soap he uses after practice.

I hook a leg between his and curl my arm across his stomach, settling in to sleep.

He shifts, squeezing me tighter, and places a kiss on the top of my head.

"Hey, baby." He voice is all rumbly-sexy from sleep.

"Hey, Mase."

"What time is it?"

"Late."

His muscles bunch and flex as he stretches. "I should go."

"No, stay." I place a hand to his chest. "I set an alarm for you."

"Wow," he says around a yawn. "You must really like me if you're willing to be woken up *sooo* early." He chuckles deep in his throat, and the sound goes straight to my girlie bits.

"I won't be staying up with you. I'll kiss you goodbye and go back to sleep."

"Now *that* sounds like my girl."

I pinch his side, making him jump. "Go back to sleep, babe."

"Do you mind if I get more comfortable?"

In answer, I slip off the bed and refold the extra blanket. Mase sits up and pulls his shirt over his head in that make-a-girl-drool one-handed way before shifting to remove his sweatpants—his gray sweatpants.

If that visual isn't hot enough, I need to bite back a groan, teeth sinking into my bottom lip at the sight of him laid out on my bed in nothing but a pair of tight black boxer briefs. His olive skin highlights every bump and dip of his muscles, the black ink adding to his bad boy appeal.

Pulling back the covers, he retakes his spot next to the wall and gestures for me to join him.

I do without any hesitation, adjusting the covers around us.

"You have no idea how hot you are in my football shirt, my name and number on you." He snuggles into me.

"So caveman of you."

"Only for you." I feel him smell my hair. "*Mmm*, peppermint —my fave."

I roll my eyes.

"Don't roll your eyes at me."

"How the hell did you know? You can't see me."

"I know you, babe."

I can't help but laugh at that. "I guess you do."

"Everything all right? You're back pretty late."

I struggle to focus on what he's saying because I'm distracted by his hand running up and down my back, leaving tingles in its wake.

"One of my bases had a flyer land on her head and I had to get her checked out for a concussion. I'm sorry I didn't call or text, my phone died."

"No worries, babe. Now give me a kiss so I can go to sleep, otherwise I'll be dragging ass tomorrow."

I lift my chin and meet his lips for a chaste kiss. He must really be tired since he doesn't try to turn up the heat.

After contact that's much too brief for my satisfaction, I wrap myself around him like ivy and settle in for sleep. This is the first time we are having a sleepover since the night I stayed over at his parents' house, and I want to enjoy every second of it.

I feel like a squirrel; instead of gathering nuts, I collect little pockets of time I'm able to carve out when it's just the two of us.

He puts one arm under my head, hooking it around to pull me closer, while his other goes around my waist. You would think with him being twice my size it would be awkward, but instead we fit together like puzzle pieces. He also has this uncanny ability to make me feel cherished and protected.

I tip my head back, burying my nose in his neck, breathing in his delicious scent and generally making me want to eat him up.

Almost involuntarily, my lips follow the same path, placing kisses along the way. He groans. I know I should stop—he does need sleep—but I can't help myself.

My fingers follow the groove along his hip, dipping into the V cut there—oh how I love that cut—stroking back and forth across it.

"*Babe*," he groans into the top of my head.

"I know." I hook a foot around his ankle, pressing closer. "I'm sorry," I say. I have every intention of stopping, but I can't.

"Fuck it." He claims my mouth with his and rolls so I'm underneath him.

There's something different about this kiss than all the others we've shared. Over the past few weeks, we've made out to the point of our lips going numb and dry-humped like a couple of high schoolers, not to mention the incident in the hallway, but this? Like I said—*different*.

I lift a leg, wrapping it around his hip and pressing us together until my aching center is riding the hard ridge in his boxers.

Oh god that feels good.

I'm burning up.

I want him.

I *need* him.

I've fought him, fought us, every step of the way, but no more. I'm done running, done letting my past dictate my future.

I'm not saying it's going to be easy—lord knows I've barely acknowledged the attention—but Mase will help me. It's not a question, just fact.

It also means I need to take the biggest risks of our relationship so far, but I'll worry about them later.

For now, I'm going to revel in the feel of Mason's callused palm gliding across my skin as it finds its way under my shirt.

Our tongues tangle, teeth nipping, fire burning in my veins.

It's my turn to reach for the hem of my shirt, dragging it the rest of the way up my body and tossing it on the floor after it clears my head.

"Kay…" He struggles to speak.

"I want you." I scratch the back of his head, my fingers curling over the buzzed hair.

"Are… Are you sure? I don't want to rush you."

Another press of the hips. Another mutual groan.

"I'm sure. Please don't make me wait."

I may not be ready to give him my past, but I am *more than* ready to give him this.

My fingers edge their way under the band of his boxer briefs, struggling to push them out of my way.

"I..." His Adam's apple bobs with a swallow. "I don't want you to feel pressured. We can take this at your speed."

I suck his earlobe into my mouth.

"If that were true, you'd be helping me with these instead of talking." I snap the band of his underwear where it sits on the curve of his glorious ass.

"Babe..." Another swallow. "I'm serious..." Swallow. "This should be special for you."

I pull back, holding his face in both hands to look him in the eyes.

He wants me; it's clear to see in how the irises have darkened to a deep pine color.

Everything we've done has been special, and it's not the act—it's the person. Why is he hesitating now? Does he think...

No.

Except...

"Do you think..." My brow furrows as I try to get my thoughts in order. "I'm not a virgin, and I want you. I want you now."

Even in the dim lighting coming through the spaces in the blinds, I can still make out how his eyes reveal the way my admission affects him. First shock—he really did think I was a virgin! I mean sure, I'm not as experienced as him, but I have some, and by some I mean I've been with one guy, but we don't talk about Voldemort—and second humility, like me choosing to give this part of me is a gift to him.

"What's it gonna be?" I pull him down for another scorching kiss.

"Fuck it," he says against my lips. "Sleep's overrated."

Like a dam breaking, he's all over me. Hands everywhere—in my hair, down my sides, cupping my boobs, pinching my nipples, and finally, *finally* removing my underwear then his own.

After my legs are free of the soft cotton, he cups his hands behind my knees and brings them back to rest around his hips. I squeeze my legs around him, scratch the back of his scalp, and pull his hair.

His groan vibrates through me.

His hard dick bumps along my swollen clit, and I'm dying for him to be inside me.

"Mase…" I sigh. "Stop teasing me." My hips roll and I gasp as the ridge around the head skims my clit. "I need you inside me." A squeeze of my legs. "*Now*," I groan.

"I need…" He slides through my wetness. "Condom." His voice breaks.

Moving as fast as he does on the field, he's retrieved the protection and is suited up and back between my legs.

I wrap my arms and legs around his large frame as he lines himself up with my entrance.

He tilts my hips up with a hand while the other holds his erection, circling my opening with the head, pushing in the barest inch then retreating.

Another inch.

Another retreat.

"*Fuck*, Kay. You're so tight."

Push forward.

Pull back.

"Mase." My breath catches. I'm stretching, already over-whelmingly full, and he's not even really inside me.

His size extends to all of him, and I see the effort it takes for him to hold back, afraid to hurt me.

"Mase." Using the strength I've honed through years of flip-ping across the blue mat, I tilt and press onto him another few inches.

"Kay." My name is a plea.

I clutch him, needing the rest of him in me before I lose my mind.

One more pump of his hips and he's finally filling me completely, wholly, pushing me to the brink of release embarrass-ingly soon.

"*Mase*." My lips press into his chest to stifle my moan.

Emotion surges through me with such intensity it rivals the pleasure he's causing me to experience. It can't be stopped. I meet him thrust for thrust, putting everything I'm feeling but can't say into my movements.

"I wanted this to last longer babe, *much* longer, but I'm not sure if I can hold back." His teeth are clenched in his effort to do just that.

"I'm there." One more push is all it takes then my orgasm consumes me. "Mase." I bite his shoulder to curb the sound.

I tighten around him, my body milking his. One more hard push and I feel him join me.

"*Babe.*" His head drops alongside mine on my pillow.

We continue to rock together as the final waves of pleasure wash over us. I'm not sure how long we lie wrapped in each other's arms while our heartbeats return to normal.

Eventually he withdraws from my body and we both get dressed before each of us takes care of our business in the bathroom.

When I climb back into bed, Mase removes my shirt again, his arms around me, my legs intertwined with his and my head on his chest.

"Now *that's* a hell of a way to say good night," he says into my hair.

"Yeah it is." I kiss his muscular chest.

"Careful now—I might want to sleep over all the time."

*Yes please. Slumber party! *spirit fingers* Correction—NAKED slumber party.* My inner cheerleader is fully on board.

"You're not gonna get any complaints from me."

His chest rumbles under my ear.

"Night, baby." He places a gentle kiss on my head. Always kissing me.

"Night."

I don't even recognize myself in this moment.

CHAPTER
FORTY-NINE

It's not even noon and this day is already shaping up to be one of the best of my life. First I woke up to a mostly naked Kay in my arms. Then, true to her word, she woke up only long enough to kiss me goodbye—with a kiss so hot it was a challenge to not crawl right back into bed with her—before snuggling back under the covers. If I could start every day like that, I would.

One time between her legs and you're already pussy-whipped.

Hold up, I argue with my inner coach. *Are you complaining? Are you telling me last night wasn't the best sex of our lives and having sleep marks from Kay's nipples on our chest isn't your preferred method of waking up?*

The fucker stays silent, not able to argue with that logic.

There are a few things about our epic sexcapades that surprised me, though.

1. Kay wasn't a virgin. If you asked me why I thought she was, I wouldn't be able to tell you, but I did.

2. It wasn't just sex; it was making love. Hot as fuck, yes, but still so much more than *just sex*.

3. I'm pretty sure I'm in love with her, like head over heels, flattened by a linebacker in love with this girl.

Walking into The Nest, the sound of hawk cries greeting me, I head for our table to find Alex, Noah, and Kevin have decided to join our group as well. I can *feel* the eye roll Kay will give when she gets here.

Bailey looks like she's in jersey chaser heaven surrounded by most of the captains from the football team, and I make sure to choose a seat as far away from her as possible.

The guys all cheer when Kay arrives. She laughs at their over-the-top greeting but tugs the brim of her hat another inch lower.

"You guys are *stooopid*," she says to them, coming to stand next to me.

"You love us," Alex says confidently.

"You're okay," she counters.

As I look at her, I hope with everything in me that she does love me, because dammit, against all odds, Casanova has fallen in love with her.

All right. *blows whistle* You know what? I don't want to hear it if she ends up being another Chrissy/Tina thing, but if we're gonna do this, like really *do this, we are going to love the fuck out of this girl.*

"Oh my god! Marry me!" Noah shouts when he sees Kay's *Oh my God, Becky! Look at that PUNT* shirt.

"I take it you like it?" She plucks at the material.

"For reals, marry me."

"She's mine, asshole." I pull Kay tighter against me. "Get your own."

"Relax, Caveman." She smooths a hand down my stomach, and my dick twitches remembering what that hand felt like on him and clamoring for a repeat performance. "Double lunch?" She points to the two trays in front of me.

"One of them is for you."

"*Aww*, you do love me," she jokes, the statement a throwaway like she's used with Grayson countless times.

Little does she know, I'm thinking, *More than you know.*

Grabbing lunch for her may not seem like a big deal to most people, but anything to help her feel comfortable around me and my boys in public the way she does when we're alone, I'll do. The one thing going in our favor is when we are all together in a group, it's like our numbers serve as a shield and she doesn't hide as much.

We haven't discussed the whole Instagram thing for almost a

week, but I do notice the phones trained in our table's direction. While one of my favorite things about Kay is how she doesn't care about my "status," I also wonder if being pulled into this part of my life will be something she can handle.

Fuck that. I'm already working on the playbook for it.

I adjust Kay's seat closer to mine, and shockingly enough, she doesn't push away. She does, however, slouch a little lower and angles herself so my body is blocking most of hers from view. Baby steps.

"Any big plans besides missing me this weekend, babe?" I may joke, but I'll be the one missing her with the team traveling to Pittsburgh for an away game.

"Laundry. *So* much laundry," she says dramatically.

"Ugh, I hate laundry," Em agrees.

"Me too. It doesn't help that the machines are *always* full too," Quinn adds.

"You guys don't travel this weekend, right?" Kay asks them while tracing a part of my tattoo with her finger in a way that makes me think she's not even aware she's doing it. I am, painfully so, as evidenced by the tightness in my pants.

"Yeah, only the White Squad travels for non-conference games," Em confirms.

"I have to go home for T—why don't you guys come with and do it at my house? We'll do it up. Order takeout, watch movies, and all that jazz."

The girls are quick to agree, and they instantly start planning out their weekend.

"Damn. I move into the Alpha house and you just leave me in the dust," Grayson pouts.

"Don't be a baby." Kay rolls her eyes as he steals a fry from her plate. "You know you and CK are invited too."

Usually I like traveling with the team—seeing new places, pranks against teammates, new options for tail—but now it means an extended absence from Kay, which is not my favorite thing.

KAYLA

L aundry, so much laundry.

Sort. Wash. Dry. Fold. Repeat.

It's like a flipping laundromat with how consistently the washer and dryer have been running.

As much as I'm for freeing the house elves, matching socks is the *worst*. At least the tedious task helps distract me from how much I miss Mase. Like I *really* miss him.

I also think I might love him.

Might? No, no. How about…give me an L. Give me an O. Give me a V. Give me an E. What's that spell? Yeah, that's more like it.

I want to argue with my inner cheerleader that we are *not* and that all-stars don't actually cheer, but I'm already on the verge of seeming crazy with how much she talks to me; I don't need to add engaging to the equation.

It's bad enough I've been zoning out all day, and it has not gone unnoticed. Distraction is the name of the game I'm playing.

Currently, Em, Q, CK, G, and I are spread out around the living room of my family home amongst piles of folded laundry, textbooks, laptops, and Thai takeout containers.

"Kay. *Kay.* Earth to Kayla." G waves his large hand in front of my face.

"Sorry." I blink, coming out of yet another Mase stupor. "What was that?"

Around me, they all chortle.

"Damn, Kay. Where have you been all day?" Q can't curb her laughter, and all I can do is blush.

Em's eyes narrow as she studies me closely. "Holy shit! I know what it is." She claps her hands together. "You and Mason totally did it." Her voice sounds so excited you would think she was the one who got laid.

Another blush gives me away so there's no denying it.

"Was it good?" Em asks.

"Of course it was good," Q adds.

"True. He is Casanova."

"But we still need details."

"When did this happen?"

"Where did it happen?"

"I can't believe you didn't tell us."

"Can we not talk about Kay's sex life?" G cuts into Em and Q's barrage of questions. "She's like my sister—it's gross."

"I second that," CK adds with a grimace.

"Guys, guys, guys…timeout." I hold my hands up in a T. "Can we please stop calling him Casanova?"

"Fine." Em nods. "But don't try to change the subject."

"Yeah, give us the deets." Q leans into Em, both of them watching me expectantly.

I take a peek at G, and he's looking a little bit green under his dark skin. Being the *amazing* best friend that I am, I decide to take pity on him.

"I'll spare you the specifics."

"Appreciated." G bows his head forward.

"But I'll tell you this." I lean toward the girls like I'm about to share a secret but don't lower the volume of my voice at all. "It was spectacular."

G falls back on the couch dramatically, clutching a pillow to his stomach.

What? I said I was an amazing best friend—never said anything about not messing with him.

My inner cheerleader winks and salutes from the top of the pyramid.

We're still laughing at G's expense when a FaceTime notification from Mase pops up on my MacBook Pro.

"Hey, Skittles." He gives me a full-dimpled smile when he sees me.

I don't know if it's because I'm missing him or my recent epiphany regarding the extent of my feelings for him, but he looks *so* hot. The things he does for a simple cotton t-shirt and a backward hat should be illegal.

I swear it's half the reason he stole my heart.

"Hey, Caveman." He grins harder at the nickname.

"Whatcha' doin'?"

"Oh, you know"—I shrug—"it's all takeout Thai food, studying, and copious amounts of laundry. Real party over here."

"Is it bad I'm jealous?"

"Not bad. A little sad maybe." I pinch my fingers together. "Where are the guys?" I ask when I notice Mase is the only one in the room. That's not normal.

"Trav and Alex went to prank Noah and Kev's room."

I roll my eyes, earning me a chuckle.

"You guys are *such* children."

He gives me a smirk but doesn't deny it.

"Are you wearing one today?" He brings the phone closer to his face as if it will allow him to see better.

"I wasn't earlier but now I am." I match his smirk with one of my own.

"You gonna show me or what?"

"Dude! Didn't we just cover this? I don't want to hear about your sex life, let alone be witness to your phone sex," G practically wails.

Mason barks out a laugh. "What the hell is Grayson going on about?"

"G is somehow under the impression you and I are about to have phone sex."

"As intriguing as that idea is"—Mase waggles his eyebrows—"I'm not really into sharing."

Of course not. He's too damn alpha to allow that.

"You and I"—he bounces a finger between us—"will be revisiting this topic." The blaze in his green gaze burns me as I read every wicked promise he's not saying out loud.

I shrug, quirking my lips and feigning innocence, causing his eyes to narrow.

"But can you explain why he would think that to begin with?"

"Bro," G yells from his spot on the couch across the room. "You asked her what she's wearing."

"Grayson, get your ass on camera so I don't feel like I'm shouting into thin air."

G gets up and sits down next to me on the floor. I adjust the laptop so both of us can be on screen together.

G jumps right in. "Bro, how many times do I have to say she's like my sister? I'm all for you guys getting it on, but I don't need details, and I *sure* as hell don't need to bear witness to it. So, please, for the *love* of god, don't ask about her underwear in front of me."

One of the most beautiful sights in the world is the way Mason's eyes sparkle with laughter like they are now.

"Grant, listen to me."

Ooo, he's getting all serious calling him Grant.

"Kay is not some hookup to me. She is my girlfriend."

Is it wrong to swoon over such a simple statement?

"But even if she weren't, you should know I am not one to… how do I put this in a way where you won't kick my ass?"

His face scrunches as he thinks, and my inner cheerleader pulls out some popcorn, *living* for the potential drama.

"I'm not one to kiss and tell. I can *assure* you I'm not gonna risk having phone sex with her when there's a chance of the rest of these idiots barging in in the middle of it."

This is so true. This may only be the second away game the team has had since Mase really started to pursue me, but more often than not, if he's calling me, we have an audience.

"Now can you chill so my girlfriend can show me her shirt? I *live* for her comedic wardrobe."

This boy. I can't even begin to describe what he makes me feel when he says stuff like this. He gets me, like really gets me down to the core.

*Duh! *hair flip and eye roll* Why else do you think we fell in love with him?*

I scoot back, tilting the camera to a better angle, and pull the fabric of my shirt taut so it's easier to read. Since I'm home, I'm wearing one of my cheerleading shirts, this one pink with *Forget glass slippers—this princess wears cheer shoes* written in gray.

"I think I'm gonna have to get one of those for Livi for Christmas," Mase declares as I readjust the screen back up.

"Already got it."

"Can't leave Olly out."

Oh the way he loves his siblings.

"You know this is only the second time I've seen one from your cheer collection," he notes.

"I can't very well go around wearing them if I don't want people to know. I usually change into my coaching ones at The Barracks."

"I might have to add that you send me pics of those too, and not just the ones I miss when I'm away."

And now my heart is flipping across the blue mat with my inner cheerleader.

"I might be able to arrange that."

I watch his chest expand and contract as he takes a deep breath.

What is he going to ask? Is he going to bring up our still unresolved conversation about my...aversion to social media?

"I miss you."

Swoon. Yes, we are definitely *swooning now.*

I get all mushy inside while our friends all say, "*Aww.*"

"I miss you too."

I also love you, but I'm sure as hell not saying it first.

I already own the t-shirt from the last time I tried that.

Before either of us can say more, the door to his room bangs open. Shortly after the video on the screen goes wonky as the phone is passed between Trav, Alex, Noah, and Kev, each vying for attention. Em, Q, and CK join G and me, and we all bullshit.

As I laugh at another ridiculous comment from one of the guys, I'm amazed once again by what has developed into my crew. Being guarded about my private life, trying to stay out of the spotlight to hide my past and avoid being used for my connection to my brother, I never realized how much it stifled me.

Even G, one of my best friends—only second to JT in closeness—was a hard-won battle for me to accept with him being a star player for the U of J basketball team. Giving in to that friendship is one of the best decisions I've ever made. Could letting these football players in fall into the same category?

"God I swear I feel like you guys are my brother-husbands the way you always butt into *my* phone calls with *my* girlfriend."

"If we're brother-husbands, does that mean I can kiss her too?" Trav puckers at me.

"If you weren't my best friend, I'd kick your ass right now." Mase rips the phone out of his hand. "I better go before I do something to make these guys too injured to play tomorrow."

There's my Caveman.

"Stay out of trouble." I blow him a kiss and hang up.

I sit and stare blankly at the screen of my laptop after I disconnect the call. As much as I miss him, it's probably good that he's away. I need the time and space to work up the nerve to tell him…well, everything he has a right to know.

"What's with the goofy-ass grin on your face?" G asks.

I tilt my head to face him. "Huh?"

"You have this almost dreamlike expression on your face, but at the same time you look kind of…"

"Scared," CK supplies when G trails off.

My cheeks puff as I blow out a breath. "I'm so screwed."

"Why?" Em asks.

"Because I'm totally in love with a football player," I admit after a long silence.

"I sure hope it's Mason, otherwise things will get *awkward*," Q jokingly singsongs to lighten the mood.

"Thanks, Q."

Shit! Why don't we use pom-poms? I could totally be plucking the ribbons out like, "He loves me. He loves me not." Cheer fail.

"Hey." G places a hand on my arm, bringing me back to the present—again. "If it's any consolation, I've never seen him this way with anyone before."

But is it enough? Will it help me keep him?

I open my mouth to speak but nothing comes out.

"Spit it out, Smalls," G says after my third failed attempt at speech.

"I…" I drop my head to the couch behind me and look to the ceiling. "I stayed away from Mason's type for so long, even fighting him when it came to us in the beginning, and I almost don't know how to admit what I'm really struggling with."

"Tell us, Kay."

I take in my surroundings, the shelves displaying some of my greatest accomplishments and snapshots of all those who've made an impact in my life. Then I look at four sets of eyes, at the people who only ever knew me after and still accept me. I'm hit with the startling realization that this, them—they are my safe space.

Maybe if I give voice to my greatest fear in front of them, it will help give me a boost to admit it *all* to Mason.

CHAPTER
FIFTY-ONE

KAYLA

I take in the beautiful painted Hawk mural and photographs of past U of J players on the walls as I make my way through the tunnels underneath the football stadium to the locker rooms.

The lanyard around my neck keeps me from being stopped by the security guards and officials I pass, and for the millionth time I question how Mase talked me into meeting him down here before the game.

From the beginning, I've said he was the epitome of my personal kryptonite, but tonight sure as hell proves it. Between this and my plans for later, I know I've fallen for him in a serious way.

I have butterflies in my stomach and I might get sick from nerves, but I'm doing this. No turning back.

As I approach the doors I've been looking for, I pull out my phone to text that I'm here. He must have been waiting for me because less than a minute goes by before his massive frame is pushing through the doorway.

I thought I was used to how much bigger he is than me—a foot and a half and well over a hundred pounds—but him being all decked out in his football gear only exaggerates our size difference. His shoulder pads magnify his already impossibly broad shoulders and strong chest, and combined with his tight football pants, it only emphasizes the inverted triangle down to his narrow waist. All that's missing from his uniform is his helmet.

A part of me can't wait for him to turn around so I can catch a glimpse of his butt in those tight pants, because I know *that* is a delicious sight. Thank you god for the invention of football pants.

"Like what you see, babe?" There's laughter in his voice when he speaks.

I have to force my eyes off his body, but when I get to his magazine-cover-worthy face, it doesn't do much to help break me out of my stupor as I get lost in his light green eyes.

His kissable lips are tipped up at the edges as he waits for me to respond.

It's his hands wrapping around my waist that ultimately pierces the haze of lust I'm wrapped in.

"You could say that." With no one around, I rise onto my tiptoes to hook my hands around his neck, bringing our bodies flush against each other.

"If you think I look good in my uniform, you should see what I look like out of it."

"Oh, I have." Our heads draw closer together.

"Annnnddd?" He draws the word out.

"And…it's one of my favorite sights to behold." My lips brush his as I speak.

"Right back at ya, babe," he says before pressing his lips to mine.

My brain, still slow from taking in all the gorgeousness of my man dressed up for a game, completely shuts off when he kisses me. I forget everything else, and it's a struggle to remember what I wanted to talk to him about.

Our tongues dance together before I suck his bottom lip into my mouth and nibble on it, eliciting a groan from him. I'd be afraid of how much he affects me if it wasn't so obvious the feeling is mutual—at least sexually.

It's the need for air that finally breaks us apart. As if unable to fully end our connection, Mase stays bent over with his forehead touching mine. Now able to breathe, I remember what I wanted to ask him.

"Do you have to go to the AK afterparty tonight?" I bite my lip, nervous as I wait for his response.

"Did you have something else in mind?" He rocks his hips against my body.

I'm so twitchy not even his innuendo is enough to calm me.

Here goes nothing.

"I was thinking we could go to my house tonight for some alone time."

His eyebrows rise. Guess I piqued his interest.

"Where are the roomies going to be?"

"Not my dorm. I mean my house, like where I grew up."

His previously raised eyebrows now do their best to disappear into his hairline.

"What's the occasion?"

Oh, only that I need to bare my soul and spill my secrets because that's apparently what mature adults do in relationships.

"I just thought it would be nice to not have to worry about anyone else being around and stuff."

"You *can* be quite loud." He rocks his hips into me again.

I pop him in the chest as I feel a blush spread across my cheeks.

"Pervert." I can't help but smile at him. "Actually, there's some stuff I wanted to talk to you about."

Crinkles fan out from his eyes and his jaw pops from clenching. I can't tell if he's nervous or pissed.

"So...you're telling me 'we need to talk'?"

"Not like *that*." *Shit!* The last thing he needs on his mind during a game is a misunderstanding about our relationship. "It's nothing bad." Relatively speaking. "It's just with our friends' propensity for showing up or dragging us out with them, it might be nice for you and me to go off the grid, so to speak."

Far, far away from those who follow our hashtags.

In need of a distraction, I press my lips to his, but one kiss leads to another, and before I know it we're making out in the tunnel under the stadium. I'm not sure how much time passes before we're interrupted by the clearing of a throat and a gruff, "Nova."

Mason springs back from me like he was electrocuted before cursing softly. "Shit." He turns. "Coach."

Coach Knight is scowling at Mason as I peek around his large frame, but his lips quirk up slightly when he catches sight of me. Not exactly the reaction I thought I would get. "And who is this?"

Mase turns, putting an arm around me, pulling me forward and into his side. "This is my girlfriend, Kay. Skit, this is Coach Knight."

"It's nice to meet you, Coach."

"You too." Coach Knight studies me the way he does his players on the field. Not gonna lie, it's a little intimidating. "Is she the reason I haven't had to hound you about your grades for the first time ever?" He directs the question to Mason.

"Yes, sir."

"Well then…I guess I can forgive this little indiscretion. But, son, do you really think the best thing to do before a game is make out with your girlfriend?"

"Absolutely, sir." Cocky jerk. "She's the best motivation there is."

Aww, don't make me blush. My inner cheerleader preens.

Coach Knight is still studying me closely—then suddenly my worst nightmare rears its ugly head. "We've met before."

Whoop there it is.

I'm not sure I can stop this thread from unraveling now. Damn Coach Knight and his steel trap of a memory.

"Yes, sir."

"We met when I was trying to recruit your older brother."

I feel Mason whip his head down in my direction, but I don't look. I can't.

"I'm surprised you remember me."

"You had grit. I remember thinking to myself I'd recruit you too if you played." Coach chuckles to himself. "You were arguing with a young man about some cheerleading trick you wanted to try."

I can't help but smile at the memory.

"I remember that," I say, thinking of how JT always had to be talked into attempting our craziest stunts.

"The way your brother shifted his focus to your conversation when the topic of you potentially getting hurt came up had the same intensity I've seen him use on the field."

"He always did blame JT if I came home with an injury, even if it was just the nature of the sport."

"It was a real shame he chose Penn State instead." Coach Knight takes off his Hawks Football ball cap and runs a hand over his hair. "I breathed a sigh of relief when he declared for the draft early."

Mason's gaze bounces back and forth between me and his coach. I can tell he's trying to piece together the information.

"Yeah, but Penn is where he met his wife, so I *know* he doesn't regret not choosing the U of J."

"I bet you were happy he was drafted by Baltimore, though. You two seemed pretty close."

I know the moment Mason puts all the pieces together. His body radiates his shock.

"Makes it a lot easier to go to games."

"Okay then." Coach claps his hands in front of him. "Nice to see you again, Kay." He turns his attention to his tight end. "One more minute, Nova. Then get your ass back in my locker room."

As the doors close behind Coach Knight, the tension between Mason and me becomes suffocating. When I look into the seafoam green eyes I love so much, for the first time ever, I can't read what he's thinking in them.

I'm not sure how to handle this. Mase has to go out and play in a few minutes, and this drama is nothing compared to how I thought he was feeling when he thought I meant we need to *talk*.

"Soooo…spoiler alert."

My joke falls flat.

"Eric Dennings is your brother?"

I look down as I nod.

"The pro football player?"

Another nod.

"Why didn't you tell me?" The betrayal I hear in his voice cuts deep.

"I was going to tonight."

"I don't understand why you didn't tell me sooner."

Because if I told you I would have to tell you about all the reasons why I keep it a secret, and I didn't want you to think less of me—or worse, have you only stay with me because of E.

I reach out for one of his large hands, and even with both of mine wrapped around it, it dwarfs them. I force myself to meet his hurt gaze. "I'll explain it all later. I *promise*. Right now you need to focus on kicking Indiana's ass and not this."

"You're right." His voice is cold, his tone sterile. He sounds nothing like the guy who annoyed his way into my heart.

Spinning on his heel, he disappears into the locker room. No kiss. No goodbye. Just...gone.

Those butterflies from earlier now feel like a ball of lead in my stomach.

I was going to tell him.

About E.

About He-who-shall-not-be-named.

About why I'm not on social media—all of it.

I had a plan.

I vaguely knew what I was going to say, even practiced it on my friends. I was prepared to apologize and already had my fingers crossed that he wouldn't be mad.

Why do I feel like none of that matters now?

MASON

For four quarters, I was able to push down any frustration I felt about the situation and concentrate on football.

When the game is over, the adrenaline from both it and the win pumps through my body. I have to force myself to keep from pacing the locker room like a caged lion.

I can barely remember the game. My mind has been spinning over the revelation.

See? I told you girls were a distraction. You're lucky you still played well tonight; otherwise you'd be running suicides.

I try to make heads or tails of the information, going over everything Kay has ever mentioned about her brother, looking for the lie.

Eric Dennings is Kay's brother.

Holy shit.

Eric Dennings is my girlfriend's brother.

He's one of the top tight ends in the league, right up there with Naples, Travis Kelce, and Delanie Walker.

Secrets, secrets, secrets. I feel like everything I've learned about Kay has been born from a secret.

But…

Then again, it was a secret, not a lie. I feel like this is an important distinction I need to make for myself to keep from falling down the rabbit hole left by Chrissy / Tina.

How many more can one person have? Is E being…well…*who* he is why she doesn't want her face on social media? If it is, it's kind of a weak argument.

There's a text with an address waiting for me on my phone. A part of me wants to ignore it and head to the AK house, but the other part, the one that recognizes Kay as my other half knows I won't get any answers by running away.

Decision time.

If it weren't for my GPS, I would have ended up in Narnia instead of Blackwell I'm so lost in my thoughts. I've run through everything I've learned about Kay since we've been together, and almost every single piece of information has come reluctantly.

Looking at the white-sided, black-shuttered colonial, I'm not even sure how much time has passed since I parked the Shelby next to Kay's Jeep.

The leather of my steering wheel creaks under my white-knuckled grip around it.

Buzz!

My phone rattles around on the dash, the screen lighting up with a text.

GRAYSON: Give her a chance to explain.

It doesn't come as any surprise that he is championing for Kay, and his message has almost fortuitous timing. I needed something to knock me from my stupor, and it accomplished just that.

Grayson is right. I have to find a way to push past the hurt so I can listen. When it comes down to it, Kay has become too important to me not to.

With a deep breath, I climb out of the Shelby and head for the front door. My hands clench and unclench as I try to shake the tension from them. Going in hot, prepared for a fight isn't going to do either of us any favors.

Ding-dong!

My heart thunders in my ears as I wait for Kay to answer the door. When she does, it's obvious she has taken the time to shower as well. Her long curls are still damp, hanging around her, leaving droplets of water on her tight blue tank and the swells of her chest. A loose pair of black NJA sweats hang from her hips, completing her comfy vibe.

With the exception of her wearing my clothes or being straight-up naked, this has always been one of my favorite looks on her.

"Mase." There's hesitation in the way she says my name.

"Skittles." I try to reassure her with a grin, but it falls flat.

"Come in." She holds the door open for me to enter.

I focus on every minute detail of where she was raised in an effort to stay out of my head.

She leads me through a large foyer, pale gray walls accenting the dark gray tile. I can see doors open to my left for a bathroom and a laundry room, and off to my right looks like an office. We walk past a staircase and into a spacious eat-in kitchen, the long rectangular table separated from the cooking area by a large peninsula countertop.

She turns left through an archway that opens up to a huge den. The room boasts two-story ceilings, a stone fireplace in the corner, a massive sectional couch, a glass and chrome coffee table, and a separate seating area by a large bay window.

There's a sizeable flat-screen in the space above the fireplace, and along the walls are glass and chrome shelves lined with pictures, awards, trophies, and medals.

Kay sits in a corner of the large couch, curling her feet underneath her, knees up, one arm resting on the back and the other hooked over her knees protectively.

She seems unsure of herself. I don't like it.

I spot a half-full wine glass on the coffee table and quirk a brow.

"Liquid courage," she says when she notices my interest.

"Why?"

The idea of her not being comfortable enough to talk to me without the aid of alcohol does not sit right with me. Since the moment we met, she's given me shit. This reticence has me worried.

"This wasn't really a conversation I was looking forward to having to begin with, but now that I've been outed by someone else..."

"Babe." I wait until her eyes meet mine and I have her full attention. "You can tell me *anything*."

She reaches for her glass and takes a big gulp, and I wander over to the shelving to give her a moment to get her thoughts in order. There are pictures of Kay and her brother at various ages, dressed in their respective football and cheerleading uniforms.

I spot a few photos with an older gentleman who has to be their father. The smiles on their faces are so infectious I can't stop returning them with my own.

There are a few pictures of Kay with a red-haired boy in a matching NJA uniform. I lift one up: Kay on top of his shoulders, medals around their necks, each holding their fingers up in the universal sign of number one.

"That's JT," Kay says from her spot on the couch.

Placing the frame back down, I nod. I remember seeing the red hair in the videos the twins showed.

I continue my perusal of the awards. There are a few hand mannequins with rings adorning the fingers. Some I recognize as football rings awarded for winning the state championships—I have two of them myself—and the ones I don't recognize must be Kay's from cheerleading. The number of accolades in this room is staggering.

"Wow," I say when I finally come to the last display.

"Yeah." She turns her head my way, but it feels like she's looking past me and not at me. "Dad was super proud. We were forbidden from keeping any of them in our rooms."

Sick of the distance, I move to join her on the couch, pulling her feet out from under her and into my lap. Pushing up the bottom of her sweats, I can't stop the small chuckle that escapes at the sight of the blue socks on her feet. "Always matching, babe."

"I can't help it."

Silence falls heavy, thick, and awkward.

Time for answers. It's now or never.

"Tell me."

Air whistles through her teeth as she sucks in a breath, and I try my damnedest not to stare at how the action makes her tits strain against the thin material of her top. Now is not the time to get boned up. I refuse to let my dick distract me from the truth again.

KAYLA

"**T**ell me."

Two words, spoken softly without any hint of command, and still they manage to strike fear deep in my heart.

Why can't I find the words to start? Hell, it should be easy; he already knows the first part.

Except…

As I focus on where the black edge of his backward hat bisects his forehead instead of those eyes I swear can penetrate me down to my soul, I can't help but want to run away.

"Umm…so Eric Dennings on the Baltimore Crabs is my brother."

"So we've established." He squeezes one of my feet. "What I'm not clear on is why you didn't tell me, and—more importantly—why it still seems like you're afraid of talking about it."

The melodic sound of a glass harp echoes in the room as I circle the rim of my wine glass. Round and round my thumb continues to trace the delicate crystal.

"Would you believe me if I said it was complicated?"

Complicated? All the parts of my story are more complex than the Admirals' pyramid sequence.

Rough calluses skim across my leg when he snakes a hand up the inside of my sweats. "I can imagine, but Kay"—he starts to massage my calf—"I need you to try to break it down for me. Help me understand."

I don't deserve his kindness. He's given me so much while getting so little in return. He's entitled to the truth, or at least as much as I can stomach giving him.

"When I was a sophomore, I started dating one of the seniors on our football team." I lift my gaze from my wine and swallow down the giant cheer bow stuck in my throat. "He was a tight end."

"Ah..." The slightest bit of kind humor I most certainly do not deserve creeps into his light eyes. "So you have a type."

My lips twitch at the joke, but I force them down.

"It was one of the reasons I tried to keep my distance from you." Among a million others.

"I take it you didn't have a good breakup?"

"You could say that," I deadpan.

"You know I'm not mad you didn't tell me about your brother, right?"

The crushing weight constricting my chest lifts fractionally.

"I *really was* planning on telling you tonight." I wave a hand around the room. "It's not like I could keep it a secret with pictures of him hanging all over the place."

"What happened with your ex?"

So, *so* much.

"Essentially he used my connection to E—and subsequently Coach Daniels—to garner attention from Penn State, which he didn't already have." I loath to admit he *is* a good football player, even if he needed help getting on such a top program's radar.

Mason's eyes narrow, but I'm not sure what I said that is causing his nostrils to flare. I haven't even gotten to the bad stuff.

"He would be a senior now, right?"

Oh.

I nod.

"Who?" Direct, to the point.

This time I shake my head. I don't want to tell him. The rivalry between the Penn State Nittany Lions and the U of J Hawks is one of the most revered in college football. If it wasn't a crucial detail to the tale, I wouldn't have even told him at all.

The tension is always high during their game. The last thing Mason needs is anything adding to the animosity between the teams and him going off half-cocked because of his feelings for me. The quickest way for a player to lose their place as a draft pick is to be seen as a PR nightmare.

"Kay." The patterns being traced on my skin still. "Who?"

"There's more to the story."

Why am I offering this up?

"We'll circle back. Tell me who your ex is, Kayla."

Full-naming me.

Jaw clenched.

Hardened eyes.

He must mean business.

Fine.

With my voice barely above a whisper, I utter the one name I refused to speak for years. "Liam Parker."

CHAPTER
FIFTY-FOUR

There is no love lost between the Hawks and the Nittany Lions, but hearing that Kay's ex plays for them after using her to help get a spot on the team has me wishing away the days until our two teams play. I need to remember to ask Kev to lay Liam Parker's ass out when we do. Never have I wished to play defense like I do in this moment.

She said there was more to the story, but I shuffle around what I know already to try to start to make sense of it.

Hmm…

It clicks into place. She was afraid to be used again. The stakes are higher, too. Eric can bring attention from the league now.

Grabbing Kay around the knees, I settle her on my lap.

"Baby." I cup the side of her face, making sure I'm her sole focus. "As cool as it is that your brother is who he is, I'm with you because of who *you* are. I'm going to be a first-round draft pick because *I'm* the best tight end entering the draft." *Fuck you, Liam Parker.* "*Not* because of some connection to my girlfriend."

"Always so cocky."

"No, confident." I lean in and steal a kiss from her plump lips, tasting the sweetness from the wine on her tongue. I love how her body melts against mine, always surrendering to the pleasure we generate. Forcing myself to end the kiss, I ask her to tell me the rest.

She works to swallow, and my gut tightens when I see the sheen of unshed tears coating her eyes.

Fuck this is going to be bad.

"Right around bowl time was when my dad died." One of her tears breaks free, and I use the pad of my thumb to wipe it away. It physically pains me to see her so sad. "His death—" She chokes on a sob. "His death set off a chain of events that altered my entire life." Her hands curl into the collar of my polo and watery eyes meet mine. "It's part of why I avoid social media."

A hot poker of guilt hits me at the memory of our argument about her not wanting me to post a selfie of us. My reasonings for wanting to claim her seem so shallow knowing hers stem from the wake of her dad's death.

"Can I…" She stops to take another deep inhalation, following it up with a *long* exhalation. "Can I just tell you the rest bullet-style?"

"Of course." Whatever she needs. I tuck a wayward curl behind her ear.

"E declared for the draft. Liam signed his National Letter of Intent for Penn State. It came out that Liam had been cheating on me the whole time."

"The fucker."

My sudden outburst gets me the briefest hint of a smile. I'll take it.

"That he is. To add insult to injury, he chose to do it with one of our school's cheerleaders. That group already didn't like *anyone* who cheered for NJA, so they took great pleasure in making sure I knew *every* detail of Liam's betrayal."

The final pieces of the puzzle click into place.

"Social media?" I ask.

"Yup. In school, I had people like JT and a few others who protected me, but they couldn't do anything about the straight-up cyberbullying that *flooded* my accounts." She looks away again, and this time I let her.

"Baby, I'm so sorry." I hug her to me.

Her reluctance to let me love up on her around campus, her aversion to our hashtags—it all makes sense now.

"It's not your fault." Her embrace is more of a cling, her hot breath hitting my neck as she buries her face against it.

"I still feel like an ass."

She giggles, the happier side of her breaking through. "Why?"

"Because I got all pissed off you wouldn't let me post us."

Her grip on me tightens, but she doesn't lift her head. "I don't know if I'll ever be comfortable with that, Mase."

"It's fine, baby."

She sits up abruptly and moves to straddle my lap. Luckily she settles herself away from the danger zone, with her ass on top of my knees, blessedly leaving a few much needed—at least if I want to be able to think—inches between her heat and myself.

Her head drops down, chin to chest, fingers kneading my shoulders while she takes deep, almost calming breaths. It seems like she's working up the courage to tell me something, but for the life of me I can't figure out what could be weighing on her mind. We already cleared up the whole issue of her brother and her past.

The best course of action is to wait her out. After two solid minutes of this, she finally breaks the silence.

"*God*, Mase. I'm so sorry. I wanted to tell you. I *planned* to tell you. Then Coach Knight comes out and blows up my spot before I ever get the chance, and all I could think was this is the *last* thing you needed before your game. I sat up in the stands and stressed every play, every down."

She's talking so fast all her words are blending together. She amazes me; she really does. I know she was worried how I would react to the news and what it could mean for our relationship, but that this girl could be concerned about a football game amid all of it blows my mind.

Every day she does something else that makes me fall deeper and deeper in love with her. I've been waiting for the right moment to finally tell her how I feel, wanting it to be perfect, but listening to her take on guilt she doesn't need to carry snaps something in me.

"I squeezed G's hand, praying hearing about E from someone who wasn't me wouldn't mess with your concentration and cause you to make a mistake that could either cost you guys the game, or worse, get you hurt. And it would have been al—"

"I love you," I blurt out, cutting off her tirade.

She sputters mid-sentence, and it takes time for her to recover. "You do?"

Her reaction is so damn cute I can't handle it. I push myself up, my back straight, no longer resting against the couch. I take her face between both my large hands, fingers threading through her curls, and pull her forward to rest my forehead against hers.

"Hell yeah I do," I say confidently, my eyes locking with hers.

Her hands shift on my neck, bumping against the bill of my backward hat. "Lord help me, I love you too, Mase."

My heart bursts in my chest, and the same euphoria I'm used to experiencing when we win a game consumes me. There's absolutely zero possibility of holding back now. I tilt her head up and claim her.

Lips, tongues, and teeth clash as we attack each other with our mouths. This is hands down the hottest kiss we've ever shared, and that's saying a lot. I skim a palm down the length of her spine and pull her against me, a pained groan escaping when her heat surrounds my hardness. Like a dam breaking, the action kicks things into a whole other gear.

Her hands snake under my polo, dragging it up my body before tossing it aside. My hat gets knocked off and her fingers tug at my hair. Her tank—one of those kinds with the built-in bra thing—quickly joins the pile we are creating on the floor, and her glorious tits are exposed for the taking. My mouth leaves hers to feast on the hardened pink nipples begging for my attention.

My tongue traces her areola then my teeth nip at the end of her nipple.

"Oh my god," she says breathlessly, wiggling more in my lap.

"Just Mase is fine."

"Ass." Her chuckle quickly transforms into a moan when I lift my hips, pressing our centers closer together again.

Never one to be passive, Kay gives as good as she gets. Her teeth scrape my collarbone, and oh god the tingles. I didn't think I could get any harder, but it sure as shit happens as her kisses continue to travel all over.

Her hands explore and squeeze my shoulders, my pecs, then over each pack of my abdominals, and when her fingers dip under the waist of my jeans and start to work on my belt and zipper, I'm done—stick a fork in me.

As if reading my mind, she jumps off my lap, hooks her thumbs in her sweats, and pushes them off her hips to the floor. Once she's completely bared to me, she wastes no time removing mine. I give her a little help by lifting my hips off the couch, my dick standing proudly at attention.

She's back on my lap, grinding against me before I have a chance to do anything else. She's wet, *so* wet. The way her bare lips open around my hardness is pure heaven. The heat, the wetness—perfection.

Up and down she bounces in the hottest lap dance in history, her lips coating my dick, and when her hips tilt in a particular way, my tip breaches her opening and I grind my molars to keep myself from sliding the rest of the way home.

"Kayla," I growl.

Instead of heeding my warning, she pushes down harder, causing me to slide in another few inches.

"Kay...baby...I need you to...get off my lap before I can't stop."

That cute V forms between her brows at my words. "Why the *hell* would you stop?" She pushes down another few inches.

"I need to get a condom."

She shakes her head. "I'm on the pill."

I'm blown away. For her to offer herself in this way is completely unexpected.

"I've never—"

"Me either," she says, reading my mind.

"I'm clean. I *swear*. I had a physical at the beginning of the season and haven't been with anyone since."

This seems to shock her. She sits up, causing me to slip out of her slightly.

"*Seriously?*" I nod, and that V grows larger. "How is that even possible? I've seen how the jersey chasers hang off you."

"Very true, but I've found they've completely lost their appeal to me."

"Why?"

"You *really* want to have this discussion *now* when you're sitting in my lap naked?"

"You're right. Later." She rises back up, so wet I'm able to push right in until I'm buried to the hilt in one long thrust.

I have to run through the Hawks' playbook to keep from shooting my load the second I'm inside. I've never been in a woman without the barrier of latex before. I'm religious about wrapping it up, have never even played just the tip before. This feeling is beyond words, the immense sensation of heat, and my brain shuts off as my primal instinct takes over.

Up.

Down.

Push.

Pull.

We move together. I grip her hips, afraid I'll leave bruises from the way I'm squeezing her.

Back and forth we continue to rock. No words are exchanged, only breaths and moans. Her eyes are raging storm clouds consuming me in their wake.

Just as I think I can't take any more, I feel her walls flutter around me and she comes all over my dick, soaking my balls. It's exquisite and I *never* want to have to wrap it up again. Her head falls forward, burying itself in the space where my neck meets my shoulder as she moans through her release.

Her orgasm grants me the permission to follow her over the edge, and I'm not sure if I'll ever be able to recover. Pretty sure she's ruined me for life.

"I love you." I feel more than hear her murmur the words against my neck.

"I love you too." I wrap my arms around her, holding her close, never wanting to let go.

CHAPTER
FIFTY-FIVE

KAYLA

Sunlight filters into my bedroom and I curse myself for not pulling the shades all the way, burying my face deeper into Mase's side, trying to block it out.

"That tickles, babe." His sexy, rough-from-sleep voice rings out.

"Sorry." My own is muffled by his side, head bobbing with his laughter.

"It's okay, I know you hate mornings."

He does. He knows so much more about me than I ever expected him to, and it scares the shit out of me. Hell, there's *so much* that terrifies me about being in a relationship with Mason Nova, but the way he makes my heart feel whole makes it possible—kinda—to deal with.

I love him.

And holy basket toss Batman, he loves me back. Even after learning about the majority of what happened, he *still* told me he loves me.

I can't believe this is real life.

"Can we please go back to sleep?"

Mornings suck giant pom-poms, but waking up wrapped in

Mase's strong arms goes a long way toward making them better. The fact that his delicious body is naked—even better.

His fingers dance along my spine, and I start to drift back to sleep. Naked Mason might be my favorite Mason.

The loud rumble of his stomach interrupts the lineup of all my favorite Masons dancing in my head, the sound so loud it practically echoes off the walls of my bedroom.

"I guess I should feed you, huh?"

I make no attempt to move—too comfy.

"You did say you love me." He places a kiss on top of my head.

Yes I did.

"I'm also a growing boy."

He's no *boy*. He's 100% pure, delicious, sex-in-a-backward-hat man.

"Don't roll your eyes at me." His finger hooks under my chin, lifting my face to his.

"How do you do that?"

"I know you, babe." He smooths his thumb along my bottom lip. "Plus it's one of the quirks I love about you."

Swoon.

"Well, when you put it like that, how am I supposed to say no to you?"

"That's the point—you're not."

I push up to kiss him, getting lost in the soft press of his mouth and the scratch of his stubble.

"I have some bad news for you, though."

"What's that, babe?" A hand squeezes my ass.

"I don't really have any food here."

"I know something I can eat."

My body goes liquid at the naughty implication. He's as skilled with his tongue as he is on the field, but he's right—he needs food.

With one last kiss and grope, I roll away to get ready. If I don't get out of this bed now, I don't think I ever will.

Mason's appeal is so potent that even from across the room, the sight of him bedhead-ed, sleepy-eyed, naked chest on display with the sheets bunched around his trim hips has me wanting to toss the leggings I just grabbed away.

"Can you *stop* looking at my ass and get dressed? You're not the only one who's hungry here."

Plus, I need sustenance if I'm going to gather the nerve to invite him to meet my family when the Hawks travel to play the University of Maryland next weekend.

Lost in my musing, I don't notice that Mason has gotten out of bed until he's taking the purple *Football: What boys do during cheer season* shirt from my hands, casting it aside with a quirk to his lips.

"You know I live for your funny shirts, babe, but no need to trash-talk." Warmth envelops me as those same strong arms I struggled to leave circle my middle until we're flush against one another. My body melts, eyes falling closed.

Lips follow the vein in my neck, beating a staccato only Mase can set. "*Mmm*," he hums, the sound radiating through me. "I love the way I smell on you."

My nose brushes the curve of his biceps when I tilt my head to give him better access. I have to agree. The fresh scent of his soap has easily become my favorite, but inhaling the musk we've created wrapped up in each other is hedonistic.

A startled squeak escapes, my feet leaving the ground as Mason scoops me into his arms. My back meets soft down as my front is covered by his hard body after he drops me back onto the bed.

Lips are on mine, my tongue automatically joining in on the fun. Rough hands skim along the backs of my thighs to hook my legs over his hips, and the thin material of my leggings does nothing to disguise how gloriously hard he is as he grinds against me.

So much for breakfast.

As if reading my mind, Mase starts to work the stretchy elastic down my legs.

Ring! Ring!

My head falls back as the tell-tale ringtone of Tessa Taylor sounds from my bedside table. It's the sense of sibling obligation that has me reaching out to accept the call, hitting the speaker-phone button to make sure everything is all right.

"*Kaaaaaayyyyy*," the twin voices of Tessa and her bestie Savvy cry the moment the call connects. The mischief I can hear in their tone already has me regretting answering.

"What's up, T?"

The buzzed sides of Mason's head prickle along my skin as he groans into my shoulder.

Savvy is quick to cut in. "No, no, no. Before you distract her with cheerleading," she says to T before speaking to me. "Can you explain to me why you have an Eleanor in your driveway? Carter is legit drooling over here." She's referring to her gearhead brother.

Mase chuckles the same way he did when I had a similar reaction the night of our first date. He rolls to the side, bringing me with him as he does.

"What? I like having you close," he explains when I give him a look.

I fall for him a little deeper at those words. For years I've watched how Bette and E interact, the way they move like they gravitate toward each other, always in constant contact. Mase's actions remind me of them, and my heart swells again.

"Oh my god!" T's shout makes me jump. "Mason is at your house? Oh my god, you told him about E? Oh my god, how could JT not tell me? Oh. My. God. How could *you* not tell me?" T has this way of talking a mile a minute when she gets really happy. It's also very amusing how someone who has a vocabulary extensive enough to rival the SATs can fall into valley girl *oh my god* mode when she struggles to process unforeseen information.

"Is this the part where I should say hi?" Mason's eyes are dancing with laughter when I prop my chin on his chest to see him better.

"Oh my god!"

I knuckle my ear at the octave T just hit.

"Was there an actual reason for your call, T?" I love the girl, but she's interrupting sexy time with my man.

"Oh…uh…yeah." With each pause, it's like I can hear her brain shifting gears, and I pass the time waiting by following the lines of black ink curving down Mason's side. "I listened to those files you sent. The drumline killed it. I like them."

"Me too. They may not be my beloved U of J cadences, but Charlie came through in a big way. It will give the routines the edge we've been looking for."

Unlike all those who chose to speculate about if I was

cheating on Mason with Charlie then Adam when the photos from that day started circulating (thanks for that, UofJ411—fun times), Mase knows all about the real reason for the meeting.

"So..." T drawls out, and I know she's winding up to launch into a whole onslaught of questions.

"T." I cut her off before she can pick up steam. "We can talk about everything on Wednesday when I stay over. Love you, bye."

With a reluctant goodbye on her part, we hang up, and I'm free to turn my full attention back to Mase.

"Sorry." I push onto my elbow, closing the distance between our mouths, our lips brushing as I say, "My family is crazy."

He licks across my bottom lip, eliciting a groan from me. "Do you not remember the halftime-performance-worthy drama that happened during our first date?"

I giggle at the reminder only to have it shift into a moan when he rolls me beneath him again.

Elbows braced on either side of my face on the pillow, he cradles my head and stares down at me intently.

"I knew you would be the one to wife me up when we met."

I shake my head. He's so cocky sometimes I almost can't stand it.

"I didn't give you the time of day in the beginning."

"And *that* only made you hotter. You're the first girl I ever needed to put any effort in with."

Give me a swoon! Give me a nee! What's that spell? Swoony! my damn inner cheerleader chants in my head.

"You know what happens next, right?" I stretch up to place kisses along his jawline.

"What?" His Adam's apple bobs under my lips.

"It's time for you to meet my family in person."

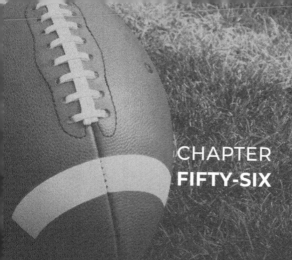

MASON

Our win against Maryland was an absolute slaughter. The team fired on all cylinders in a way that would mean we'd be hoisting the trophy over our heads if today were the national championship.

The best part—

You mean outside of your two touchdowns?

Yeah, yeah, what he said. Anyway… *side-eyes inner coach* The best part was my girl being in the stands to see them. Sure, I didn't *actually* see her like I do when we play at home, but knowing she was somewhere in the stadium lit a fire in me. It makes me wish she was able to come to every away game.

Done with my shower and post-game locker room interviews, I gather up my belongings, making sure I have everything I need since I won't be returning to Jersey on the bus with the team.

The guys have been giving me shit all week, trying to psyche me out of meeting Kay's family. They would be jealous as fuck if they found out one of those family members is a top player in the NFL, not that I would tell them. I wouldn't betray Kay's trust like that.

In all honesty, it's the big brother and not the professional footballer aspect of who E is that has me nervous. He's more than just a brother to Kay; he helped raise her.

Then there's the whole part where I'm afraid he'll lump me into the same camp as Liam Parker when the *last* reason I'm dating Kay would be to use her.

I'm hoping the fact that I think of him as E instead of Eric like Kay does will help keep the fanboying down when we meet.

After meeting up with Kay, the forty-minute drive from College Park where UMD plays to E's house in Baltimore passes in a blur. She's so easy to talk to it's like hanging with the guys—but better because I get to sleep with her. It feels like no time at all before we're driving through a neighborhood filled with waterfront properties, each house larger than the last.

We come to a stop in front of a set of black iron gates. With a push of a button, they open, and Kay pulls her Jeep through.

A long circular drive leads to a gorgeous, sprawling, two-story tan stucco and glass house with a terra cotta roof. Another push of a button has one of the bays on the four-car garage opening for Kay to pull into. The other three spots are filled with a familiar white Range Rover, a black and chrome Escalade, and a badass cerulean blue McLaren 570S.

Kay catches me drooling over the sports car and nudges me along. "That's E's favorite toy."

"I bet." Kay and her friends have a thing for my Shelby, but this car is in a whole other category of automobile.

"Come on." She reaches for my hand and threads her fingers through mine, leading me into the house.

The door opens into a hallway with a mudroom/laundry room combo to the right and a powder room to the left. We walk the length of the hall until it eventually leads into an open concept living space. There's a dining room with a twelve-person table off to the right, a chef's dream kitchen to the left, and a sunken living room beyond that.

The entire back wall is made up of floor-to-ceiling windows and French glass doors that lead to a gray stone patio, outdoor kitchen, and infinity pool.

Having grown up in Brantley's McMansion, I'm used to excessive wealth, but her brother's house has a homey elegance to it.

"We're home!" Kay yells into the empty space.

"Coming!" a feminine voice calls back followed by giggling before E and Bette appear at the top of the stairs, the former with his arm around the latter.

"*Eww*. You guys were *totally* doing it." Kay's nose scrunches at her brother nuzzling his wife's neck while she adjusts her shirt. "Gross." She mimes gagging. "I *so* don't like knowing about your sex life."

"The feeling is mutual, Squirt." E ambles over and lifts Kay off the ground in a bear hug.

With Kay still by his side tucked in his protective embrace, I have to choke down the overwhelming urge to fidget under his scrutinizing glare. The ability to breathe doesn't return until he reaches out a hand for me to shake.

"Heard a lot about you." E's words feel more like a threat than a statement. It's not much of a shock, though. With his insistence on being Kay's guardian when he could have easily passed it off on someone else, I know they are closer than your typical brother and sister.

"Play nice, Eric," Bette says, pulling Kay from him and into a hug.

"Same here." I try to convey that I respect both Kay and what he did for her.

Kay's eyes bounce between us, watching our exchange. Once my hand is free, she takes it. "Come on, Mase. I'll show you where you can put your stuff and get changed."

I let her guide me up the stairs—because I really want to get out of this suit and into some sweats and a t-shirt like E—passing a few doors before turning into a room on the right. Instantly I know it's Kay's.

The bedspread is a mashup of pink, white, and black blocks of leopard, cheetah, tiger, giraffe, and zebra print with hot pink sheets. The furniture—headboard, end tables, desk, and dresser —are all black, and the walls are adorned with black and white photos in various sizes and groupings.

There's a large window seat decorated in fabric that matches her bed set, and it takes up most of the wall overlooking the back yard. There's also an open door that reveals an ensuite bathroom and another I assume is a closet.

My suspicions are confirmed when Kay opens the door, turns on the light, and pushes some clothes down one of the racks.

"You can hang your suit in here." She reaches up to grab the bar before walking back to me and tugging on my tie. "Although, I must say...I do like this look on you. It's very..."

Her voice trails off as she tries to find the right word. I lift a brow to goad her along.

"Dapper." She gives me a bashful smile.

I loop my arms around her hips and cup her ass while holding her against me. "Does this mean you want me to ditch my hat?"

"Not a chance in hell." Her hands move around my neck as she rises up on tiptoes to give me a lingering kiss. "Now hustle up, Caveman. You don't want my brother to think you're having your wicked way with me up here, do you?"

God the way this girl can make me laugh while making my dick twitch is amazing.

I watch in appreciation as she bends over to unzip her boots, shooting me a wink over her shoulder when she catches me in the act.

She sits cross-legged in the center of the bed, returning the favor as I change out of my suit and into a pair of gray joggers and black U of J football t-shirt. She laughs every time I toss a piece of my suit at her before arranging each article of clothing on the appropriate hangers.

We're still laughing as we head back downstairs. I've always been a pretty happy guy, and aside from Dad dying when I was too young to really remember, I've had a blessed life, but I didn't fully understand the meaning of *true* happiness until Kay. She has a way of making even the mundane things feel fuller and more vibrant than before.

We're met with barking as we clear the last step, a large yellow lab bounding toward us. Kay drops to her knees, throws her arms around the wiggling beast, and runs her hands up and down his back while placing kisses on his head.

"Hi, Herkie, baby." She laughs as he licks her face. "I was wondering where you were."

"He was outside trying to kill squirrels." Bette walks into the living room, sitting down next to E, his arm automatically going around her.

Kay pushes me onto the couch, her back leaning against my side, my arm draped over her shoulder, down her chest, around her waist, and her head resting in the groove where my chest meets my shoulder.

Herkie claims the space by her feet and stretches out alongside her body, basking in the attention she's giving him. *Lucky dog.*

"Beer?" E holds out two bottles.

The TV comes back from commercial to the Penn State/Ohio State game, not surprising with E a Nittany Lion alum. I am happy to note they are down by seven at the start of the second half. I don't dare voice that though, enemy territory and all.

We haven't been watching long when we hear the front door open and Herkie takes off barking before someone bellows, "DENNINGS!"

"Damn, I really need to get the codes to the house changed," E jokes before calling out, "Living room, asshole."

"Love you too, bro. Now where's my girl?" The voice is distinctly male.

Kay starts chuckling as E responds with, "Stop trying to cradle-rob, asshole."

There's no time to form an opinion on that because a figure leans over the back of the couch and pulls Kay from my arms.

"Ahh!" she screeches. "B, put me down."

Kay hangs upside down by her ankles, punching at the legs of her captor. My eyes travel up to see who her "attacker" is, and I feel a bolt of shock when I lock eyes on Ben Turner, the quarterback for the Baltimore Crabs.

"What? I thought you like being upside down?" he asks Kay.

"When it's someone I trust not to drop me, yes. You, sir, are not JT," she retorts.

"*What*? I'm good with my hands. I handle a football with precision."

"I'm small, but not *that* small. Now put me down before I nut-punch you."

As surreal as the whole thing is, I can't help but laugh at Kay's feistiness.

Ben lowers her gently to the ground then lifts her into a hug.

"What are you doing here, B?" Kay climbs over the back of the couch to me.

"It's a bye week."

"Bette's lasagna."

"Bette's lasagna," Ben echoes, proving there's a relationship closer than merely a passing friendship because Kay's his teammate's sister.

"Don't feed the strays, Squirt," E advises. "You'll *never* get them to leave if you do."

"Don't I know it." Kay begins tracing the lines of my tattoos. "How else do you think I ended up stuck with the captains of the football team hanging around?"

"Live and learn, little sis. Live and learn." E points his beer bottle in my direction. "B, this is Kay's boyfriend Mason. Mason, this idiot here is Ben—or B, if you're so inclined—our quarterback and, unfortunately, my best friend."

I hold my hand out to shake while trying to keep myself in check and come to terms with professional athletes being a normal part of everyday life for my girlfriend. The last thing I need is Kay razzing me for fanboying.

B—yup, thinking of him as B too—bends to kiss Bette on the cheek before sitting between her and Kay. "A boyfriend, Little D? *Really*? Way to break my heart." He slaps a hand on his chest.

Kay nudges his leg with her foot. "Please, B. You know quarterbacks aren't my type." She presses a kiss to my bicep, making the muscle jump.

At the end of the game—Ohio State luckily holding their lead for the win—we start getting ready for dinner. While Kay and Bette set the dining room table, I brace myself for the interrogation I know is coming my way.

"Mase, T's calling," Kay says when my phone rings from the living room.

"Answer if you want. He's probably calling because he's mad we didn't hang around after long enough for him to see you too."

"She calls you Mase?" E asks me speculatively.

"Yeah...?" It comes out as more of a question as I'm unsure what the big deal is.

Across from me, E and B share a look I can't read.

"Bette's the only person—at least that she's super close to—I've ever heard her call by their name and not letters."

"You know I asked her once why she calls Bette, Bette and not B."

"What did she say?"

"That Bette was special."

A knowing smile spreads across E's face. I take this as a good sign. "Ahh…now it makes sense."

"Short Stack!" Trav's voice rings out—must have been a Face-Time call.

"What's up, brother-husband?" Kay says, and I can't help but laugh.

"Brother-husband?" Ben questions.

I explain how the guys always invade my calls with Kay when we're away, as well as a few of our funnier antics. I can't quite get a read on E's expression, but it seems positive, so I'll take it.

"Nah, we don't need your worse half. Just let him know we called," Trav says as I place the salad bowl on the table. Kay sees me and winks.

E and B aren't far behind, each carrying a large pan of delicious-smelling lasagna. My stomach growls at the aroma, and I can't wait to dig in.

E claps his hands. "Let's eat!"

This has been one of the best yet strangest meals on record.

I don't think any of us—outside of Mase—were surprised B showed up. He and E have been best buds since E's first training camp, and honestly, I think part of the reason I like Trav so much is because his relationship with Mase reminds me so much of the famous B-and-E duo.

"How excited are you to see JT this week?" Bette asks.

"So, so excited." We talk every day and video-chat more often than we don't, but it's not the same as being in the same space together.

"Can't wait to see if he passes." E jerks a chin at Mase.

"Huh?" Mason asks around a mouthful of lasagna.

"The meet-the-family test, bruh." B sounds a tad too gleeful.

Under the table, I squeeze Mason's thigh when he chokes.

"If it makes you feel any better, you're passing this one with flying colors." Bette tips her beer at Mase.

"Hell yeah, dude. You didn't deck me for everything when I showed up, and I'd say that more than passes. Besides"—B points his fork at E—"you handled me way more calmly than this fool does most of the time."

For as long as we've known B, he's joked about us running off and getting married, doing it for the sole purpose of getting under E's skin.

"You're begging for me to kick your ass out," E warns, but it's not a real threat.

"You got jokes, Dennings, but we all know you love me."

"So it's a genetic thing, huh?" Mase whispers against my ear when E rolls his eyes at B. I shiver at his lips brushing the sensitive skin.

Gurl, I'm all for you climbing him like the tree he is and having ALL the wild monkey sex you like, but maybe *you shouldn't be thinking about it with E sitting across the table from us. Just saying.*

"Anyway…" E turns to me, choosing to ignore B. "I told JT I got his ticket all set for his flight back to school next Sunday night."

"You didn't have to do that."

E gives me a *Don't be dumb, it's what family does* look, so I let it go. E doesn't throw his money around, but he always takes care of his own, which in this case includes the Taylors.

"So…" E pushes his plate to the side, resting his elbows on the table and looking every bit super-big-brother as he stares at me. The hairs on the back of my neck stand on end at the shift in his demeanor.

"So…"

"I spoke with Jordan the other day."

Those hairs that were raised are now Riverdancing at the mention of his publicist. I like the hockey queen PR dynamo—we're even loosely connected to her through Lyle—but if E is bringing her up right now, it means *I* was the topic of conversation.

"And?" I ask, needing to know.

"Before you start, I want to preface it by saying I was the one who called her."

Yeah, that doesn't surprise me in the least.

"Oh-kay…"

"Don't look at me like that, Squirt." His voice hardens. "I've noticed all the attention on you since the two of you"—he bounces a finger between Mase and me—"started dating."

Beside me, every one of Mason's muscles lock up.

"Your plan has worked so far, but I wanted to have something in place for if it fails."

I've avoided the issue as much as humanly possible. For the last year, I've lived with that exact fear. We've worked so hard—with Jordan and other professionals—to bury the posts and articles so they don't show up on the first pages of search results, but E is right. It only takes one person and all the things I wish I could forget could be splashed all over the internet—again.

"Can we please talk about *anything* else?" Before I crawl under the table to hide from reality.

"Kay." I know he's serious when he doesn't call me Squirt.

I know he worries, and what's worse is a part of him blames himself for what happened to me. It's not true. The only ones to blame are *them*. He's always done *everything* possible to protect me. I can't fight with him on trying to do exactly that.

They're all joking about Mase passing "the test", but what he doesn't realize and can't without me giving him all the gritty details I withheld is they already approve. If they didn't, my family would be trying to talk me *out* of being with him to keep the threat of my exposure to a minimum, not discussing ways to make it work.

"I know, E." I stretch an arm across the table for his hand. "Make all the contingency plans you want. I promise I won't fight you. But, *please*...for now can we forget about trolls on the internet and just enjoy the next twenty-four hours?"

"Fine." The look he gives me tells me this conversation is far from over. "What do you want to talk about?"

"I have something." Mase speaks up, and if I didn't already love him, I might have fallen right there.

"*Ooo.*" Now B is the one resting his elbows on the table. Miss Manners would so not approve of us. "Go ahead. We're listening."

"Is getting my own funny shirt a sign that I've been fully accepted into the tribe?" Mase points to E's *My sister is flyer than yours* shirt.

"Mase has a thing for my t-shirt collection," I clarify with a shrug.

"Careful." E plucks at his shirt. "That's a can of worms you might not want to open."

"Especially if she's the one picking," B adds.

"I'll remember that when I do my Christmas shopping this year," I threaten.

B toasts me with his beer bottle.

"Don't worry, babe." I snuggle into Mason's side. "I already have some ideas for you."

He gives me a kiss and starts to twirl the ends of my hair. "More colors again?"

"Bette added them last night."

"Well I like it, Skittles. Gotta keep the rainbow fresh."

Bette plays with her fingers the way she does whenever she really wants to cut someone's hair. I decide to give her the opening she craves.

"It's nice not having to worry about where to get my next haircut. Bette gets twitchy if I don't let her do something to it whenever I see her."

"Like cutting hair at a tailgate?" He mentions G's parking-lot barbershop from when we went to the Crabs game a few weeks ago.

"Yup." I reach up and lift his hat off his head. "You know…" I finger his shaggy espresso locks. "You're kinda due for a cut. She could always hook you up with something cool, you know? Make G jealous."

Bette is practically bouncing in her seat at the possibility.

"Sure. I'm down for something shaved into the sides."

"And that right there just solidified your place in this family, at least according to my wife." E leans back, finishing off his beer.

I couldn't have scripted a better introduction to my family myself.

CHAPTER
FIFTY-EIGHT

I reach out a hand for Kay and am met with cool sheets. Lifting my head, I squint my eyes against the sunlight breaking through around the edges of the shades, but I still don't see any evidence of her in the room. A quick glance toward the open door of the ensuite bathroom confirms she's not there either.

Tossing the covers aside, I climb out of the bed to pull some clothes on, ready to find my missing girl.

Herkie is also absent from the room and is the *only* reason I can fathom Kay being awake before me. That dog has been glued to her side since we arrived, even crashed in bed with us. Kay had to move him when he tried to get in between us, and he eventually settled by our feet.

Aww, look who's turning into Mr. Family Man. All you need now is the white picket fence, two point five kids, and a Volvo. My inner coach is a dick.

I walk down the hall, passing various pictures of Kay and her family, still having a hard time believing Kay's brother is Eric Dennings and I'm in his house. I can't help but chuckle at some of the shots E and Bette chose to decorate their walls with.

There are just as many candid shots as posed pictures on the walls, and the theme in all of them is happiness.

I head down the stairs leading directly into the living room, but still no sight of Skittles.

The scent of coffee draws my attention to the kitchen, the open concept floor plan making it easy for the smell to travel. I may not be as adverse to mornings as Kay, but coffee is never something I'll turn down.

Wearing only a pair of blue plaid sleep pants, E is still an imposing presence as he leans against the counter with his ankles crossed while drinking his coffee.

"Coffee?" He points to the Keurig.

"Yeesss." I drag the word out.

"Pick your poison." He gestures to the carousel next to the machine.

I peruse the selection, spotting some of Kay's favorites along the way, and settle for a French roast. Popping the pod into the machine, I wait for my coffee to brew, pulling out the cup when it's done to drink it black and mirroring E's stance against the island.

"You really did play a hell of a game yesterday. The way you and McQueen connect is something else," E comments over the rim of his cup.

Eric Dennings is complimenting the way we play. *fist pump* Fuck yeah.

"We've been teammates since our Pop Warner days. Playing together is almost as easy as breathing."

"It shows."

Epic fist-pumping session about to happen. Shit, move over Jersey Shore *GIFs—I'm about to set the new standard.*

Trav would lose his shit if he heard about E complimenting his game, but it isn't my place to tell him about Kay's brother.

But will it stay a secret for much longer?

I didn't say anything yesterday when they discussed the posts on the UofJ411 Instagram, but there was no way to miss the genuine concern about it.

"Any time you want to talk football or the game, I'm here," E says, shocking me.

"I appreciate the offer. *Really*...more than you could know, but for now I think we should shy away from anything football-related. I don't want Kay to be reminded of that douchemonkey she used to date."

E's brows rise in surprise, and I can see the respect for me grow in his eyes at my words.

"Besides, I'm coming for all your records when I go pro," I add cockily.

"Bring it on, pretty boy."

"Pretty boy, huh? Sorry, E, you're not really my type."

He scoffs in response.

I take a moment to drink my coffee, but still no Kay in sight. "Any idea where your sister is?"

"Yeah. She and Bette are down in the gym." E rinses out his coffee mug and loads it into the dishwasher before tapping me on the shoulder. "Come on, I'll show you where it is. With B crashing the party last night, you never got the full tour."

I fall into step and follow him out of the kitchen, through the living room, down a few steps and a long hallway. The sounds of Queen and laughter float down it as we walk toward a set of open double doors.

E leans against the doorjamb to the right so I take up the left with my shoulder as my anchor, arms and ankles crossed, taking in the room in front of me.

E's home gym is a thing of beauty. The two-thousand-square-foot rectangular space is equipped like a gym rat's dream. The entire outside wall is made up of floor-to-ceiling windows overlooking the lush back yard and water, and floor-length mirrors line the opposite wall.

In the middle of the room on brightly colored yoga mats are Kay and Bette. I can't make out what they are saying over the music, but their laughter is unmistakable.

"You two have *got* to be the worst yogis ever," E calls out to the girls.

They both look up from their bent-over positions and laugh harder.

In downward dog, wearing a black sports bra with criss-crossing straps playing peekaboo with her cleavage and black leggings that open below the knee and wrap around her calves like a ribbon, Kay becomes my focus, my vision going blurry along the edges.

The stretchy material hugs her body, displaying the strong

muscles of her legs and the firm bubble of her ass in all their glory. I could look at her all day and never get bored.

"Babe, you know you can't do yoga in front of me. That's how you end up pregnant," E says to his wife.

Kay whips her head around so fast she falls to the mat. "I'm gonna be an aunt?" she screeches.

"Shit." E's curse is only loud enough for me to hear. "No, Squirt. That didn't come out how I meant it."

"Damn." The smile on Kay's face falls. "Well can you get on that already please? I personally think it's time to pull the goalie."

"A hockey metaphor? I would think the queen of funny shirts would have a football one at the ready," E teases.

"I'll work on it, and you work on knocking up your wife."

"Geez, I thought you didn't like talking about my sex life."

"I don't. I am, however, *all* about being an aunt. Just saying." She pops a shoulder before standing up and bouncing over in my direction to give me a kiss.

I pull her into me, looping my arms around her hips, resting my hands on the top curve of her delectable ass.

"Hey, Caveman," she says against my lips.

"Morning, Skittles." I force myself to keep our kiss brief. I don't need E wanting to kick my ass or anything. "Never thought I'd see the day you woke up before me."

"Yeah, I wouldn't get used to it, though."

"Wouldn't dream of it." I return her playful smirk.

"Come on, lovebirds." E walks out of the gym. "Let's eat before you have to get on the road."

"I fully approve of your workout apparel." I reach down and palm her ass. I might have a slight obsession with it. "I think you should dress like this all the time."

"Perv."

"You know you love me."

"That I do."

After spending almost twenty-one years actively avoiding anything having to do with feelings, I'm still trying to get used to the warmth I feel in my chest whenever she tells me she loves me.

When breakfast is over, Kay and I bring our bags down and drop them next to the couch. We each pull on our U of J football hoodies, preparing to leave, and I place my ball cap on my head, adjusting the bill behind me.

"No, no, no, no, no." Bette walks over to me.

"What?" I ask, having no idea what I did wrong.

She reaches up and removes my hat from my head. "You are not covering up my new masterpiece with this thing." She tosses my hat to Kay.

"Sorry?"

"As you should be. Now sit your ass down and let me style it then you can be on your way."

I do as I'm told. After teasing and tugging the short strands how she wants them, she pats me on the shoulder, declaring me good to go.

Deciding she did enough driving this weekend, Kay hands me her keys and hops into the passenger seat of Pinky after we say our goodbyes. I can't say I mind this arrangement when she spends most of the drive tracing her fingers along the new carvings shaved into the side of my head.

I don't care what my inner coach has to say—I sure as hell could get used to this.

KAYLA

"**S**on of a bitch." Mason's voice booms over Pinky's Bluetooth. "This is all your fault, you know."

I laugh at the accusation. "How's that, Caveman?"

Sounds of male voices issuing more curses and trash talk come through the speakers.

"If you were going to be home tonight, I wouldn't be here getting my ass kicked in Madden," he complains.

It's true, most nights—especially on days when we don't have class together—Mase and I hang out and sometimes study, but tonight I'm headed to The Huntington near campus where the University of Kentucky's basketball and cheerleading teams are staying. It's been over two months since I've seen JT in person, and I know Mase understands; he just doesn't necessarily like it.

"I'm sure you'll be fine. Plus, I made sure to come find you before you had to watch film."

"Yeah, yeah, yeah, but you're much more fun to hang out with than these assholes."

I can hear Trav, Alex, Noah, and Kev slinging barbs at him in the background.

"Fuck you, Nova."

"You're lucky we still let *you* hang out with *us*."

"Yeah, spending all your time with your girlfriend."

"Totally pussy-whipped."

I roll my eyes. I swear I doubt they'll ever grow up.

"You're just jealous you're not getting laid on the reg. You jockholes have seen my girl—*of course* I'd rather hang out with her. She's much better to look at than you douchebags," Mase throws right back, not bothered at all by being called pussy-whipped.

"I smell better too, I'm sure," I toss out.

"Hell yeah you do, babe."

I turn into the parking lot of The Huntington and find a space close to the front doors. Time to wrap up my call.

"All right, I'm here."

"Okay, have fun, baby. See you in class." There's another murmur of voices before Mase comes back on the line. "G says if you see his brother, give him a smack upside the head for him."

I chuckle at that. "Will do. Now rally and kick some Madden ass."

"You got it, babe."

"Bye, Mase."

"Bye, Skittles."

I hit the button on my steering wheel to disconnect the call and grab my bag. JT sent me a text earlier saying he and a bunch of his squadmates would be hanging out in the front lounge by the bar. Sure enough, I find him and a few others donning UK gear spread out among the couches, the low tables in front of them playing host to plates of food in various stages of consumption.

JT's size and dark red hair make him super easy to spot, and as I walk in his direction, he looks up, catching sight of me.

"PF!" He jumps up, really dragging out *Pfffff*. His long legs eat up the space between us and he lifts me in his arms, my legs wrapping around him as he spins us, hugging the stuffing out of me. "Damn I've missed you."

I return the sentiment, squeezing him equally as hard.

"I know some of you have met her already," he says when we rejoin the others, "but for those of you who haven't, this is the infamous PF you've heard so much about."

While I keep my cheerleading identity a secret at the U of J, it's almost an impossibility with the UK Blue Squad. JT is too well known in the cheer community for them to not know the name of his partner—me. Thankfully none of them have seemed to care about me other than the tricks JT and I pull off when we stunt.

From the faces I see, most of his squad is downstairs, including Rei, his flyer. I give her a hug, having grown closest with her because of our mutual connection with JT.

He retakes his spot on the couch and I settle in like always, with my legs across his lap.

"I'm surprised you guys don't have curfew," I observe.

"Coach is pretty lenient when it's not a competition. We just can't leave the hotel," Rei says.

"Besides grilling the new boyfriend, what's the plan for the weekend?" JT says with a smirk.

I roll my eyes.

"Mama and Papa G are gonna meet me at my dorm. We have the game, and afterward they're taking us all out to dinner. I figure we stay on campus for the night and head home in the morning. Then your next three days will be spent helping me run partner stunt clinics, with a majority of our focus on the twins."

"I take it Olly is excited?" JT asks, referring to his protégé.

"When he heard I was seeing you tonight, he *begged* me to bring him."

"Probably for the best he's not here. I'm sure you have a whole crazy checklist of stunts you want me to help him master by the end of the weekend, don't you?" He arches a brow at me.

"You know it." I pop him in the arm playfully. "So prepare to work."

"My pint-sized cheer Nazi."

I give him an eye roll.

"I just *love* being compared to Hitler and his followers." My sarcasm is thick.

JT flashes me a shit-eating grin, which I ignore.

"We should probably head to The Barracks early on Friday, work out any kinks. It's been a few months since we've stunted together—who knows if we still have it?"

JT pulls me into a one-armed headlock. "Them be fighting words."

"Let go." I bat at his arm. "Seriously, get off or I'll have my football player boyfriend beat you up."

JT lets out a bark of laughter. "If I'm not afraid of E, I'm not gonna be afraid of this guy."

"Asshole."

"Love you too, babe." JT blows me a kiss. Always the smartass. "Anyway…if you think I'm gonna let you get away with that trash talk tonight, we *must* have been apart for too long."

JT and I, much to our parents' dismay, would work on our stunts anywhere we could. Back yards, gyms, living rooms, conference rooms—pretty much any place with a high enough ceiling was fair game, and I've just unintentionally thrown down the gauntlet for us to be up to our old tricks.

"I'm sure there's an empty ballroom around here somewhere," he muses, confirming my thoughts.

Time to have some fun.

#THEGRAM

 CheerQueen   ⋮

"video of JT and Kay stunting at The Huntington"

♥ ◯ ◁   ⊓

34,297 views

CheerQueen Getting the band back together LOL. Honored
to watch cheer royalty in person!!!!
#KingAndQueenOfStunting #MyHeroes
#IWantToBeLikePFWhenIGrowUp #BowDown #PFandJT
#TransferToUK

MASON

A whole new level of anti-morning sentiment greets me when I walk into class to find Kay flopped over the desk, ponytail hanging down the side out the back of her hat.

Stopping at the row below ours, I wave her coffee as close to her nose as possible, the scent of java rousing her.

"Oh, *god*, I love you," she moans, my dick jumping at the sensual sound. Blindly she reaches out a small hand, wrapping it around the paper cup.

"Of course you do, Skittles." I drop a kiss to the back of her head and go around to my seat.

Moving with all the speed and grace of a geriatric, she finally sits up, cradling the cup under her chin, breathing in the aroma like it is the essence of life. To be fair, for her, it just might be.

"You're so cocky," she mumbles sleepily before taking her first sip.

"You know it, babe." I thrust my hips in her direction before sitting down.

"*Ugh.*" Eye roll. "You are *so* lucky you bring me caffeine." She rubs the back of her neck and groans, another sound that goes straight to my dick.

I replace her hand with my own and dig into the knots there. When she moans again, it takes everything in me not to carry her out of this lecture hall and take her in the stairwell.

"Did you have fun last night?"

"Yeah." Her head drops with a slump. "I didn't realize I was so out of shape, though."

I barely hold back a snort. Kay is far from "out of shape". Given her young age and years of experience, she is a unique hybrid coach for NJA, often demonstrating stunts and tumbling herself. Still, even I can tell this is a different degree of exhaustion for her.

"Feeling a little beat up today, are we?"

"There's a good chance I'll be dead by the end of this weekend from all the clinics we're running."

I can't help chuckling at how serious she sounds. "I'm sure you'll be fine. By the end of tomorrow, your body will have adjusted." She shifts back to rest her head on my shoulder in a rare display of not-quite-PDA. She really is tired. "But if it makes you feel any better, I got my ass kicked in Madden last night."

"It's okay, babe." She pats my chest limply. "I'll teach you how to win."

Is it wrong that I'm enjoying her being too sleepy to worry about keeping her distance?

I'm about to shoot back a retort to her claim of being a Madden expert when my phone vibrates in my pocket.

> GRAYSON: Please tell me Kay is with you?

> ME: Of course she is.

> GRAYSON: Can you ask her WHY THE HELL SHE ISN'T ANSWERING HER PHONE?

The shift to shouty capitals has a prickle of unease forming between my shoulder blades that only intensifies at the way Kay stiffens when she reads the message on the screen.

"It's back at my dorm. I didn't even realize I forgot it until I was on the bus over to campus."

I relay the info to Grayson.

> GRAYSON: Show her this.

I click on the Instagram link he sent, which pulls up a video of Kay in the blue camouflage striped leggings and electric blue racerback *Cheer Coach, because Freakin Awesome is NOT an official job title* tank she sent me a picture of her in last night.

Kay's hand flies to cover her mouth as she watches the video, her gray eyes bugging out of her face.

I recognize JT behind her as the two share a smile—one I'm not quite comfortable seeing her exchange with another man—clasp hands, and bounce before Kay is lifted over his head in a handstand. They hold the position for a few seconds before Kay is flipped around and stands with both her feet in one of his hands.

There's no hat blocking her face, and her hair is pulled back in a high ponytail complete with giant blue camouflage bow. She even goes as far as to smile and wink as she gets tossed from one of JT's hands to the other.

The minute-long clip ends with the two of them hugging.

My mind spins as class is called to order, though not with thoughts of how ghostly the pallor of Kay's skin is or how her hand shakes when she reaches up to tug the brim of her hat lower.

Nope.

That honor goes to wondering how the same woman who wouldn't even let me post a simple selfie of us on my Instagram can have an entire video of her on someone else's.

#THEGRAM

USASF_cheer

video of JT and Kay stunting at The Huntington

68,497 views

USASF_cheer Check out these former World Champs
#TheyStillGotIt #PFandJT
REPOSTED

KentuckyCheer: Our very own @CheerGodJT proving why he's
the best #NationalChamp #AllTheRings #OGStuntPartner
#PFandJT ***REPOSTED***
VarsityAllstar: #TBT with these two former World Champs
@CheerGodJT #PFandJT ***REPOSTED***
NCAcheer: No one does it better. Learn how to stunt like JT
and PF from @TheBarracksAtNJA @NJA_Admirals at camp. Be
on the lookout for signups #NCAcamp #PFandJT ***REPOSTED***
UCAupdates: Is this a preview of what @CheerGodJT will be
bringing to Nationals with @CheerNinja #RoadToNationals
#PFandJT ***REPOSTED***
CheerUpdates: Behind the scenes with how these two former
World Champs out of @TheBarracksAtNJA @NJA_Admirals train
#GodparentsOfStunting #DidYouSeeThat #PFandJT
REPOSTED

Of all the days to forget my phone, it had to be today.

Mason's phone may have timed out, the screen gone dark, but the video of JT and me is still playing on repeat in my mind.

How did this happen?

It's one thing for JT's squadmates to know about my PF alter ego; it's another entirely for them to share posts of me, especially without my knowledge or consent.

Bile rises in my throat and a buzz fills my ears, making me feel like I'm trapped underwater.

I have no idea what today's session was about when class ends, trapped in my own head, lost to every worst-case scenario I can imagine.

Autopilot has me following Mase to meet G.

My cheek presses against damp cotton when he pulls me into a tight hug, his normally warm body now sweaty from running to me.

"JT said he's already gotten the post taken down." G's hand covers the entire side of my face as he continues to hold me in his embrace. "But Kay…"

I push away when his words trail off into nothingness.

He grabs at the back of his neck.

Time slows down. He's nervous.

I look back at Mase. He's been unnaturally quiet, instead scrolling through something on his own phone.

It might make me a bad girlfriend, but right now I don't have the mental capacity to figure out what's going on with him. I'll ask when I'm not in the middle of freaking the fuck out.

"G," I prompt.

"Em sent me these." He holds his phone out for me to take, his message thread with her open on a picture.

With great trepidation, I accept the offering and start flipping through the photos at G's instruction.

There are about a dozen screenshots of different Instagram accounts—most for major cheerleading outlets—and with each one, the weight of my dread continues to grow.

I freeze. I don't breathe. I'm pretty sure if it were possible, my heart would stop beating.

I don't have a profile to tag, but both The Barracks and the Admirals' accounts have been tagged. It's only a small hop to connect the PF from NJA to Kayla Dennings.

I was so worried being with Mason would out me. Who would have guessed it could potentially be caused by me doing the one thing that helped save my sanity during the worst of things?

The only thing keeping be from being completely hysterical is that so far the #CasanovasMysteryGirl posts haven't connected the me from the hashtag with the me in the now viral video.

Still…

This is bad. So, so bad.

My phone. Why did I forget my phone?

I need to regroup.

Talk to E to see what contingencies he and Jordan came up with.

An old panic runs through my veins and makes my hair stand on end.

What am I going to do?

#THEGRAM

UofJ411

video of JT and Kay stunting at The Huntington

UofJ411 #CasanovasMysteryGirl
REPOSTED: video of JT and Kay stunting at The Huntington

@Raineydaybookreviewslorraine: Wait? Hold on a second? Is this @CasaNova87 girlfriend? #CasanovasMysteryGirl #CantQuitePutMyFingerOnIt
@Redhatterbookblog: Those rainbow highlights do look familiar. #ISeeYou #CasanovasMysteryGirl
@Reynereadsalot: She's a cheerleader?? #ThisIsBrandNewInformation #CasanovasMysteryGirl
@Rock_n_read719: Really? The football player and the cheerleader? #CanYouBeMoreCliche #CasanovasMysteryGirl
@shenanigator: Anyone else wondering why she's with @KentuckyCheer and not @UofJCheerleading #AskingForAFriend #CasanovasMysteryGirl

UofJ411

Side-by-side picture of a screen grab of Kay and JT in the video and JT in his UK uniform.

UofJ411 I need a second opinion .. is this who I think it is? AmISeeingThings #CasanovaWatch #CasanovasMysteryGirl

@Sjenkins31: Okay, so the guy in the video is @CheerGodJT. How can we use this to find out who #CasanovasMysteryGirl is? #DetectiveWork

UofJ411   ⋮

"Side-by-side picture of a screen grab of Kay and JT in the video and JT in his NJA uniform."

♡ ◯ ▷   🔖
51,876 views
UofJ411 Any all-star cheerleaders follow us? #PhoneAFriend #CasanovasMysteryGirl

@Slomo9311: #CheerGodJT used to cheer for @TheBarracksAtNJA for the @NJA_Admirals #FoundNemo #CasanovasMysteryGirl

---

UofJ411   ⋮

"Side-by-side picture of a screen grab of Kay and JT in the video and them in their Admirals uniforms"

♡ ◯ ▷   🔖
41,795 views
UofJ411 She cheered for @NJA_Admirals too. #NoMoreHiding #CasanovasMysteryGirl

@Smalltown_booklover: OMG! You found her!! #WinnerWinnerChickenDinner

*picture from JT's IG of him and Kay in their
Admirals uniforms after winning Worlds*

79,216 views

UofJ411 More info #SpillingTheTea #CasanovasMysteryGirl
***REPOSTED—CheerGodJT: Me and @FlyerQueenPF kicking
assand taking names!! Love this chick!! #WorldChamps
#CheerWorlds #CantTouchUs #WeSetTheStandard
#CTGBFF***

@Sparksandmoonlight: @FlyerQueenPF isn't an active
account anymore. Anyone find her info?
#CasanovasMysteryGirl
@Summerlynn83: Nothing on IG but @TheBarracksAtNJA has
a PF Dennings listed on their website as a member of their
coaching staff #CallMeSherlock #CasanovasMysteryGirl
@Suntan_malone: That's her. 100% she is PF Dennings. All the
other posts use #PFandJT #CasanovasMysteryGirl

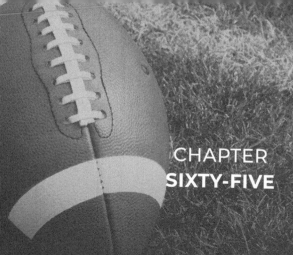

MASON

Not even the toughest practice day of the week is sufficiently distracting to bring my head around.

The aches and the pains aren't enough to get Kay off the brain.

Except I can't shake the feeling that I wasn't told the whole truth when Kay was coming clean.

My gut reaction to the video was to be pissed that Kay let someone else post stuff on their Instagram without her hiding most of her face, but her unfiltered reaction of almost abject terror was clue enough that she had no idea.

In the wake of my fading anger, guilt set in and has been my constant companion ever since. It certainly doesn't help that she ended up skipping out on lunch to deal with the fallout of the video going viral. Grayson told me E was freaking out about it too.

Stripping out of my practice jersey and shoulder pads, I sit on the padded seat in front of my locker and reach inside for my phone to text Kay.

Tapping to wake up the screen, I watch it fill with more Instagram notifications from the CasanovaWatch and CasanovasMysteryGirl hashtags than I can count. Ignoring them for the moment, I instead click on the message from Kay I see waiting for me.

> SKITTLES: I'm skipping out on the game and staying at the dorm *kissy face emoji*

On board with this change of plans, I'm going to put my phone away to shower when my fat finger ends up opening one of the notification banners.

A prickly sensation starts at the base of my skull when I see Kay's beaming smile on the screen. She's in her NJA cheer uniform with a blue camouflage and rhinestone bow topping off her unobscured face.

My skin feels hot and agitation bubbles under its surface as I take in the account information the picture was reposted from.

JT.

What the fuck?

She lets him post pictures with her?

She is adamant about staying off mine. Never mind that with one selfie of us on my page, we could bring a stop to the CasanovasMysteryGirl hashtag, the same one she worries will lead people to discovering she's related to Eric Dennings.

But JT gets to post? How is that fair?

Then it happens.

I read what he wrote in his post, and you know what I find?

Kay has an Instagram handle.

Would you look at that.

Clearly a glutton for punishment, I start to read through some of the comments.

PF Dennings.

JT Taylor and PF Dennings won multiple Worlds titles.

PF Dennings.

NJA has a PF Dennings listed as one of their coaches.

It's the last one that gets me. I understood when she told me PF was her cheering nickname, but would the gym really list an employee by a nickname?

Shit! This is the Chrissy / Tina thing all over again, isn't it?

"Motherfucker!"

I shut the screen off and chuck my phone into my locker so aggressively it bounces back out.

"Mase?" Trav approaches tentatively, scooping up my phone and plugging in my passcode to see what set me off.

"She *fucking* played me," I mutter through clenched teeth before stalking off for the shower.

"P. F. P *motherfucking* F." I slap the wall with each syllable.

"I need you to break it down for me, bro, because you aren't making much sense right now." Trav keeps his voice calm and steady as he steps into the stall beside mine.

"She had this whole story about how she got the name PF at the gym. And I mean, what kind of name is PF anyway?" I rake both hands through my hair, pushing the wet strands around and tugging on them. "It made sense that it was a nickname and Kay is her name."

"Mason." Trav rests his elbows on the half-wall separating us. "What's got you so worked up? You've known Kay cheers for weeks."

I let out a humorless laugh. Yeah…if only that were it.

"She has Instagram."

"Oh-kay?" Trav eyes me like I'm a crazy person, and maybe I am. We are two grown men having a heart-to-heart naked in the shower.

"Her profile is listed as PF."

"And yours is Casanova. People use nicknames on their profiles all the time, so I'm gonna need you to take a breath and explain why that has you wanting to Hulk out."

"She's PF on an Instagram I didn't know she had. She's listed as PF Dennings on the NJA website. The kicker is she has full-faced, smiling selfies posted on her *friend* JT's profile. *Fuck!*" I throw my shampoo bottle, sending it skidding across the floor. "This is Chrissy all over again."

My hands ball into fists and I brace them against the wall, letting the water beat between my shoulder blades.

The exhaustion from minutes ago is gone, replaced by the need to get back on the field and run tackle drills. Instead I'll settle for going to Kay's dorm to get some answers.

KAYLA

Worry prickles at me like I'm at the top of a stunt and it's about to come crashing down.

I don't think I've sat down since I got back to my dorm.

I hated having to cancel my plans with the Graysons, but being in an arena filled with U of J students did not seem like the best idea given the still evolving circumstances.

E is losing his mind, and it took the combined efforts of Bette, JT, and me to keep him from driving up here and incurring all kinds of fines for skipping out on practices.

I put on a brave face for my brothers and sister-in-law but internally was freaking the fuck out. I even gave in and used the Admirals' Instagram account to check to see what's circulating from the UofJ411.

It finally happened. They figured out who I am.

Well…not completely. So far the only connection that's been made is that I'm PF Dennings, but I sense the Kayla Dennings revelation isn't far behind.

Bang! Bang! Bang!

The booming knocks bring my pacing to a halt, causing me to

look at the door like I'm Supergirl and I can see through it to whoever's on the other side.

An overwhelming sense of trepidation washes over me. The soles of my shoes drag across the carpet, my feet unable to rise enough to take clean steps as I make my way to the door.

Bang! Bang! Bang!

A second round of knocks hits it, each pound hitting me like a blow to the gut.

My fingers curl around the cool metal of the doorknob, and with a squaring off of my shoulders, I twist my hand and open it.

Like a deflated balloon, my entire body sags in relief at the sight of my boyfriend on the other side.

"Mase." I move to wrap my arms around him, seeking the comfort. I know the feel of his strong embrace will quiet the noise of this clusterfuck of a day and give me the last bit of nerves to share all the details I withheld.

I love this man so much. I never expected to, tried to fight it because I was afraid he would use me. It wasn't right, and it wasn't fair to him, but with every day I wake up to a good-morning kiss or a text after the nights we don't spend together, my gratitude for how he relentlessly pursued me grows.

It wasn't until I was in the thick of what my family considered damage control that the true depth of my feelings hit me.

I'm not saying I'm over here all zen-like and okay with the possibility of my past coming out and people discussing the worst year of my life like it's the latest episode of the Kardashians, because I sure as hell am not.

But I feel like it deserves to be mentioned that my concern over my shit being used in a way that could negatively impact Mase was a startling realization.

Except…

Before I can make contact with the cotton of his football shirt I know is so well worn it feels like the softest silk whenever I snuggle against it, Mase shifts, avoiding my touch, and steps around me to enter my dorm.

What is that about?

I shake it off.

The snick of the door latching sounds like a gunshot. The earlier anxiety returns full force, and when I turn and catch the angry glint in Mason's eyes, I instinctively take a step back. It's

not that I think he would hurt me, but I've never seen him look...
so...volatile.

"Mason? What's wrong?"

"I don't know. Why don't you tell me, P. F."

Huh?

He never calls me PF, and why the hell did he say it like *that*?
Like each letter of my nickname offends him?

"Since when do you use my gym name?"

He scoffs. "*Gym* name."

What the what?

"Mason, what the hell is going on?"

"I feel like I should applaud you." He starts to slow clap, each
smack of his hands causing me to flinch. "You really had me
fooled."

Fooled? What?

"Again...what are you talking about?"

"Were you even bullied? Or is that just some lie you used to
get me to stop pushing the issue of posting about us on my social
media?"

That. Hurts.

Still, I can't fault him; he doesn't know the full extent of what
I went through, doesn't know how I was and the details leading
to the worst of it because I didn't tell him. I didn't want him to
look at me and see the same broken girl everyone else did.

"Why would I lie about something like that?" I fold my arms
over my chest.

"You tell me." He mirrors my action, and I have to force my
eyes back up to his face in an effort to not be distracted by the
way the muscles of his arms bulge. I have no idea what is
going on so I'm going to need all my brain cells to figure it
out.

Gone is the love I usually see shining in his green gaze, deep
disdain in its place.

"Outside of you wearing my hoodie and when we're sitting
next to each other in class or at lunch, you keep as much space
between us as you do between you and our friends."

I don't let any of our friends kiss me against walls. I keep that
thought to myself, though. He has enough attitude for the both of
us; we don't need to add mine to the mix.

"You would stress when told there were posts of you with

Trav. With Alex and Kev. Of Noah bringing you coffee and people accusing you of cheating on me with Adam."

My back molars snap together at the mention of that creep.

"I gave you an easy solution to shut the haters up. You wouldn't have to do a thing except smile for the camera, and yet you refused."

Are we back to this again? I thought we squashed it.

"You told me you don't like having your full face show in pictures." He pulls out his phone and thrusts his arm out until it is inches below my nose. There's a picture of JT and me after winning Worlds reposted from JT's page onto UofJ411's.

"That picture is like five years old." Wow. They've really been digging if that's the picture they used to learn my name.

Mason ignores that comment and re-pockets his phone. "So what I really want to know, Kayla—*if* that's even your real name—"

What's that supposed to mean?

"—is if you didn't want things posted of us because you were worried about your other boyfriend finding out."

"What are you talking about?" I can't keep the confusion out of my voice.

His eyes still have that blank stare, and with each second it remains, my heart cracks a little more.

"JT is just a friend. He's as much a brother to me as E." I throw my arms out in frustration. Why are we even fighting about this?

"Yeah, and in Biz Markie's song, that's exactly what the bitch says when she's actually hooking up with the other guy."

I let out a growl.

So many emotions swirl within me.

Frustration.

Anger.

Betrayal.

Confusion.

But the most prevalent is hurt. I'm hurt because he doesn't trust me. It's ironic that the campus playboy is the one accusing *me* of cheating.

"This was a mistake," he says, his voice defeated.

"That's what I'm trying to tell you," I implore, reaching out to him, but he steps back before I can make contact—again.

"No. I mean this." He bounces a finger between us. "This is the reason I don't do relationships."

I stop breathing. He can't be saying what I think he's saying, right?

"Are you breaking up with me?" I croak.

He doesn't look at me when he answers. "Yes." Then he steps around me, careful to make sure our bodies don't even so much as brush against each other, opens the door, and leaves.

I can't move.

I can't breathe.

My heart is breaking.

Mason, the first guy I've taken a chance on in years, just dumped me.

Mason, the campus playboy, thinks *I* was unfaithful. The concept would be funny if it didn't hurt so much.

Instead I feel like I'm dying on the inside.

Once again, social media takes from me.

Tears leak down my face as I fall to the floor, my legs no longer able to support me under the crushing weight of my despair.

What the hell just happened?

Okay, okay I totally hear your shouty capitals before you even type them. I'm sure you're like WTF ALLEY!!! I need to know what happens.

Good news! Book 2 is available now! *Game Changer (# UofJ2)* Read free in KU HERE!

Jordan Donovan (E's mentioned PR person) is the matriarch of the BTU Alumni world and you can meet her in *Power Play* if you were curious about her story.

Are you one of the cool people who writes reviews? *Looking To Score can be found on* Goodreads, BookBub, and Amazon.

Remember Tessa's bestie Savvy? Well good news. Savvy King has forcefully shoved her way out of my brain and is out now. This Royalty Crew U of J Spin-Off Duet starts with *Savage Queen* is available to Read FREE in KU HERE! Keep scrolling for a peek at chapter 1.

RANDOMNESS FOR MY READERS

Whoop!

Now I know I left you on a cliffy with Kay and Mase…but don't worry book 2 is out and you can get *Game Changer* here.

For those of you who have read my words before you may have noticed a few cameos from my BTU Alumni Squad. If you are new to my crazy and haven't run screaming from the room you can be sure to check out the BTU Alumni while you wait for #UofJ2. Don't worry these are stand-alones.

So I like to give you my fun facts in bullet style but I'll leave this one out on it's own because it's **special.**

I actually wrote the U of J books before I ever published my first book *Power Play*. I had been invited—no idea how, so don't ask me—to join a NaNo writing group on Facebook with so many of my favorite authors and thus this brain child was born.

So now for a little bullet style fun facts:

- It's because of these books that I got the idea to make *Tap Out* part of the BTU Alumni world. Plus TO is where Lyle our Espresso Patronum barista makes his first appearance there.
- Jordan Donovan (E's mentioned PR person) is the matriarch of the BTU Alumni world and you can meet her in *Power Play* if you were curious about her story.
- The majority of the funny t-shirts on my Pinterest started because of Kay.

- Kay and Em are my anti-morning fictional soul sisters. Then again, this is probably why I do most of my writing in the middle of the night #NightOwl
- I didn't actual cheer because my high school didn't have a good program but my sister-in-law cheered for the Central Jersey All-Stars (who NJA was loosely based on)
- I love the look of a backward hat. Mr. Alley rocks one like no other. Probably why I ended up married to him and procreating with him 3 times lol.
- My high school varsity jacket for lending the inspiration for the title design lol.
- Most of the IG handles you see in the comments are from my reader Covenettes. So many are great bookstagrammers I would check them out.

If you don't want to miss out on anything new coming or when my crazy characters pop in with extra goodies make sure to sign up for my newsletter! If my rambling hasn't turned you off and you are like "This chick is my kind of crazy," feel free to reach out!

Lots of Love,

Alley

ACKNOWLEDGMENTS

This is where I get to say thank you, hopefully I don't miss anyone. If I do I'm sorry and I still love you, just you know, mommy brain.

I'll start with the Hubs—who I can already hear giving me crap **again** that *this* book also isn't dedicated to him he's still the real MVP—he has to deal with my lack of sleep, putting off laundry *because… laundry* and helping to hold the fort down with our three crazy mini royals. You truly are my best friend. Also, I'm sure he would want me to make sure I say thanks for all the hero inspiration, but it is true (even if he has no ink *winking emoji*)

To Jenny my PA, the other half of my brain, the bestest best friend a girl could ask for. Why the hell do you live across the pond? Mase is yours and **yes** he is the *ONE* hero I will confirm you can claim. I live for every shouty capital message you send me while you read my words 97398479 times.

To Meg for being my first ever beta reader who wasn't related to me. I'm so grateful this book brought you into my life.

To my group chats that give me life and help keep me sane: The OG Coven, The MINS, The Tacos, The Book Coven.

To all my author besties that were okay with me forcing my friendship on them and now are some of my favorite people to talk to on the inter webs. Laura, Maria, Kelsey, Lindsey, Kristy, Stefanie, Becca, Samantha (both of you), Renee, Dana, Lianne, and Anna.

To Sarah and Julie the most amazing graphics people ever in existence. Yeah I said it lol.

To Jules my cover designer, for going above and then again with designing this cover. I can't even handle the epicness of it.

To Jess my editor, who is always pushing me to make the story better, stronger…giving such evil inspiration that leads to shouty capitals from readers that even led to a complete overhaul of these first 3 U of J books.

To Caitlin my other editor who helps clean up the mess I send her while at the same time totally getting my crazy.

To Gemma for going from my proofreader to fangirl and being so invested in my characters stories to threaten my life *lovingly of course*.

To Dawn for giving my books their final spit shine.

To my street team for being the best pimps ever. Seriously, you guys rock my socks.

To my ARC team for giving my books some early love and getting the word out there.

To Christine and Wildfire PR for taking on my crazy and helping me spread the word of my books.

To Wander and his team for being beyond amazing to work with and this custom shoot for all of the Mase and Kay books. And Wayne and Megan for being the perfect models! Seriously i think the world can hear my fangirl squee whenever I get to message with you both on IG.

To every blogger and bookstagrammer that takes a chance and reads my words and writes about them.

To my fellow Covenettes for making my reader group one of my happy places. Whenever you guys post things that you know belong there I squeal a little. And for letting me use your IG handles.

And, of course, to you my fabulous reader, for picking up my book and giving me a chance. Without you I wouldn't be able to live my dream of bringing to life the stories the voices in my head tell me.

Lots of Love,
Alley

FOR A GOOD TIME CALL

Do you want to stay up-to-date on releases, be the first to see cover reveals, excerpts from upcoming books, deleted scenes, sales, freebies, and all sorts of insider information you can't get anywhere else?

If you're like "Duh! Come on Alley." Make sure you sign up for my newsletter.

Ask yourself this:
   * Are you a Romance Junkie?
   * Do you like book boyfriends and book besties? (yes this is a thing)
   * Is your GIF game strong?
   * Want to get inside the crazy world of Alley Ciz?

If any of your answers are yes, maybe you should join my Facebook reader group, Romance Junkie's Coven

Join The Coven

Stalk Alley
Master Blogger List
Join The Coven
Get the Newsletter
Like Alley on Facebook
Follow Alley on Instagram
Follow Alley on TikTok
Hang with Alley on Goodreads
Follow Alley on Amazon
Follow Alley on BookBub
Subscribe on YouTube for Book Trailers
Follow Alley's inspiration boards on Pinterest
All the Swag
Book Playlists
All Things Alley

ALSO BY ALLEY CIZ

.

.

.

.

.

Stay Connected With Alley

Amazon

FB Reader Group

Website

ABOUT THE AUTHOR

Alley Ciz is an internationally bestselling indie author of sassy heroines and the alpha men that fall on their knees for them. She is a romance junkie whose love for books turned into her telling the stories of the crazies who live in her head...even if they don't know how to stay in their lane.

This Potterhead can typically be found in the wild wearing a funny T-shirt, connected to an IV drip of coffee, stuffing her face with pizza and tacos, chasing behind her 3 minis, all while her 95lb yellow lab—the best behaved child—watches on in amusement.

facebook.com/AlleyCizAuthor

instagram.com/alley.ciz

pinterest.com/alleyciz

goodreads.com/alleyciz

bookbub.com/profile/alley-ciz

amazon.com/author/alleyciz

Made in the USA
Middletown, DE
26 October 2023

41402491R00210